FALL

FOR ME

BOOK ONE: THE ROCK GODS

by Ann Lister

Music Between The Sheets!

Ann Lister

FALL FOR ME

This book is a product of the SleighFarm Publishing Group.

DEDICATION

I am blessed with an abundance of creative talents that pour
from me in many different formats.
The flow of inspiration comes to me from a variety of sources;
channeled through me from a spirit guide named Sarah, and the
many organic inspirations that surround me on a daily basis –
living on this island and beyond.
Music is the one consistent inspiration in my life, running
through me
like blood through veins; as necessary as my next breath.
With a constant musical soundtrack playing inside my head,
I give you the stories inspired by this music.
~ ~ ~

I dedicate this book to the many muses in my life, musical,
spiritual, and life nurturing.
All of you play a tremendous role in my writing process.
I thank you from the bottom of my heart.

To Bob, my other true consistent inspiration and life-mate.
You inspire me to be a better author and person
and I love you for that.
To my beautiful daughters, watching you grow into intelligent
and gracious adult women fills me with such pride.
I love you both so much.

To Frank, I am blessed to have you as co-pilot alongside me to
experience this great life adventure.
I thank you for your dedicated input, help,
and guidance in these projects.
Without you, this would not happen.

Additional Thanks
Special Technical Adviser: Leo Leoncio
Cover Art Design: Kari Ayasha
Interior Formatting and Editing: Franklyn Sledd

CHAPTER ONE

Dagger Drummond finished the final encore of his show at the Staples Center in Los Angeles. He wiped the sweat from his brow using the back of his hand and looked toward the ceiling at the glaring purple, red, and white lights bathing him from above. His voice was hoarse from singing lead vocals with his band, Black Ice, and he needed a drink. He signaled toward stage right for his guitar tech and handed him the Gibson rhythm guitar hanging around his neck in exchange for a bottle of chilled water the tech was holding.

He stood there at center stage beneath the unbearably hot lights and guzzled half the bottle, listening to the deafening roar of the audience spread out before him like a sea of bodies writhing in ecstasy. Judging from the sound rising from the gathered crowd, it seemed to be just as entertaining for the fans to watch him chug water as it was to listen to his music.

Dagger smiled at the reality of that, then turned slightly and waved for his other three band members to join him at the edge of the stage. They stood in a line and held hands, raising arms over head and then bending forward bowing to the crowd. After one final wave, they exited one by one from the stage.

This concert, like most on their tour schedule, was sold out. Thousands upon thousands of adoring fans screaming his name with every swish and gyration of his hips or chord he played on his guitar. Overwhelming to some, but for Dagger it was simply another day at the office. Thirteen years in the music business made them a little bit like American rock royalty; much like Bruce Springsteen, but certainly not on the level of the U.K.'s Rolling Stones. This was something Dagger tried not to take for granted. He knew firsthand how fleeting fame could be; one minute they loved you, the next you were dog shit.

He accepted a towel from a guy in their road crew and wiped off his face and neck, then made his way down the corridor toward his dressing room. His long dark hair was matted to his head from sweat, crimson-colored silk dress shirt stuck to his chest, black leather pants adhered to his legs like a second skin. No question about it, he needed to clean up and change clothes.

He opened the dressing room door and stepped inside the small square room, finding his manager Tony Marlow waiting for him; expecting to go over his schedule for the next few days. All Dagger wanted to do was shower, maybe get a blow job from some willing groupie, and possibly sleep in his own bed for a change, instead of his tour bus. Was that too much to ask?

He gave a hundred and fifty percent of himself to each and every show Black Ice performed. When the show was over he was spent, and needed time to recharge his batteries. Having a few hours at the end of each night, in his opinion, was not a lot to ask for what he gave, and as far as he was concerned this was not negotiable.

"You've got an interview in an hour," Tony said, "With Ryan Pierce from Music Spin."

"Ah, fuck. Is that tonight?" Dagger complained. "Get him on the phone and cancel it. See if he can do it tomorrow night before the show. I'm not in the mood to answer a bunch of stupid questions right now."

Dagger made it outside to the arena parking lot and climbed the stairs to his tour bus; forty-five feet of pure luxury, made precisely to his specifications. The two-story bus was a hotel penthouse suite on wheels, solid black with plum and silver colored wave patterns painted down both sides that looked like fluttering ribbons. Tinted windows made the bus sleek and very private. A master suite with king-sized bed occupied the rear end, two full baths with showers, a stocked kitchen, bar, and state-of-the-art entertainment center with a sixty inch flat screen television mounted above the bar completed the layout for the bus.

Dagger owned his bus; paid over half a million dollars for the decadent vehicle, and kept it parked at his Los Angeles estate when he wasn't touring. So many memories had been made on this bus: parties with his band, sex with groupies. The closets were filled to the brim with his secrets, and that's how he hoped to keep it. He loved this bus. It suited him and it felt more like home to him than his actual house.

He stepped onto the narrow staircase and punched in the security code, locking the bus door behind him. A slender man with sandy blond hair waited for him in the plush living room; a welcoming smile on his pretty-boy face. Dagger walked to him, slid a hand behind his neck and pulled him in for a rough kiss.

"Hey, Chris," Dagger said, disengaging himself from the lip lock. "Glad you could make it."

"A text message from you is always the highlight of my day," Chris said, running his hands down the front of Dagger's chest and stopping on the buckle of his pants.

"I need a shower," Dagger said. He looked down and watched the young man's fingers unzipping his leather pants.

"Yes, you do," Chris said.

Dagger stepped back and pulled the sweat-dampened shirt over his head and started walking toward the mid section of the bus where the larger of the two showers was located. Keeping the hallway door open, he jerked on the handle of the glass door to the over-sized shower stall and glanced back at Chris still standing in the living room.

"Join me," Dagger said, and turned on the water.

Ryan Pierce pushed his way through the over-crowded backstage area of another sold out performance by Black Ice. It was after midnight and he was on deadline, trying to make it on time to his scheduled interview with Dagger Drummond. Meeting a rock star on his tour bus after a show was never a good idea – unless you had a penchant for illegal activities or a serious taste for debauchery. Ryan didn't necessarily have a need for either. His job required him to interview musicians for Music Spin, the publication for which he was currently working, and that meant he sometimes had to venture into places he didn't really want to be.

Ryan was a few inches over six feet of alpha brawn, with broad shoulders, narrow hips and long legs that looked like he could step over people rather than go around them. He had thick dark hair, loosely combed with his fingers and brushing the collar of his wine-colored shirt. Gray-blue eyes and a thin layer of beard growth – grown more out of laziness than a fashion statement. It all made for an enticing package that no one would dispute was easy on the eyes. Many mistook him for being a male model, which annoyed the hell out of Ryan.

He had no problem navigating his way through the corridors of the Staples Center with Dagger's agent, Tony, doing his best to match each of Ryan's long strides. He flashed the security team his backstage credentials hanging around his neck and slipped out the rear door into the private parking lot. Tony walked him through a maze of eighteen-wheelers and tour buses, then stopped at one and punched in a security code to open the door.

"Dagger," Tony called out, standing on the bottom step. "Ryan Pierce is here for your interview."

No reply could be heard above the loud rock music playing inside the bus. Tony pressed a few buttons on the wall of the stairwell and the music became softer.

"Go on up," Tony said. "He's probably in the shower, but he's expecting you."

Ryan nodded and took the steps of the bus. He heard the door close behind him and the lock engage. He'd done dozens of interviews just like this and never felt one hundred percent relaxed going into them. Once a dialog started between them, he was fine, but those first few minutes were always a little unnerving for him. He rounded the corner by the driver's cab, and made his way back into the living room. He removed a pad of paper from his back pocket and sat down on a black leather couch.

His eyes darted around the large room: matching couch on the opposite side, solid cherry bar with hand-carved corners and a marble top was positioned on one end, a huge flat screen television mounted above it, and recessed lights spotted the ceiling. This was, by far, one of the nicest tour buses Ryan had ever been on.

He looked to the left and noticed the open door leading into the private back section of the bus. A glass shower unit, misty with steam, was positioned just beyond the doorway. Overhead lights illuminated movement inside the large stall – the figures of more than one person, and one of them was kneeling.

Shit. Waiting while Dagger was in the shower was one thing. Being able to *watch* him shower, when it was obvious he wasn't alone, was another. Ryan considered shutting the hallway door to give Dagger some privacy and shifted on the couch. Another option was leaving the bus and rescheduling the interview. His eyes moved around the bus, studying the framed photographs of Dagger hanging on the walls; shots of him taken during previous performances, and a few beautiful oil paintings. He stood up from the couch to step closer to a painting of a mountain range, trying to see if he'd recognize the artists name.

Dagger turned inside the shower stall. His eyes caught shadowed movement in his living room. He wiped the steamed glass wall with his hand for a better look and saw a man crossing the floor. This man was too tall to be Tony and no one else had access to his bus, so who the fuck was standing in his living room? Panic flooded him and a slur of curses rolled from his mouth. He stumbled from the shower, slammed the hallway door behind him, and charged into the living room. The towel loosely clutched at his groin barely concealed his cock and not much more. He watched the man jump at his surprise entrance.

"Who the fuck are you?" Dagger asked. "And how the hell did you get onto my bus?" Dagger watched the man turn around and his breath caught at the gorgeous man standing before him. Thick, dark hair covered his head, curling at the ends against the collar of his dress shirt. Wide, muscled shoulders, narrow hips, and jeans that creased in just the right places to frame an enticing package.

Holy. Shit.

Dagger unconsciously wet his lips. He was having trouble remembering why he was so pissed off. He watched the man run his long fingers through the thick bangs covering his forehead, then deep blue eyes captured Dagger's and his anger was all but forgotten. A strange look washed over Dagger's face; the anger folding into an expression far less threatening. He watched the man raise the small pad of paper and pen he was holding up in the air.

"I'm Ryan Pierce from Music Spin Magazine," the man said. "Your manager let me in. We have an interview scheduled."

Ryan's gaze dropped to Dagger's exposed skin. He couldn't stop his eyes from canvassing every wet inch. Water dripped down his very muscled chest and stomach; the evidence of an erection slightly tented the towel. A large Celtic cross tattoo was inked on his left bicep and a ribbon of barbed wire circled the right bicep. A third tattoo was partially exposed low on his right hip; very close to his trimmed strip of pubic hair. It looked like an animal of some sort. Ryan couldn't be sure, then he cursed himself for paying that much attention to it and the man's body in general. Since when did he check-out men?

Dagger pushed the long, wet hair off his forehead and swore again. The backward swish of his hair revealed several small hoop earrings of different sizes in both ear lobes; another detail about Dagger Ryan didn't miss. What the hell is wrong with me, Ryan thought, and looked away.

"Fucking Tony," Dagger said. "I asked him to reschedule that."

"Want me to leave?" Ryan asked, a little too nervous to make eye contact with Dagger.

Dagger looked at Ryan and wiped the shower water from his face. As mad as he knew he should be for the interruption, this Ryan Pierce guy was positively breathtaking and Dagger wasn't ready for him to leave his bus just yet. Maybe he should drop the towel, he thought, and see what kind of reaction he'd get. The thorough way Ryan had inspected him from the big head down to the other head between his legs, gave Dagger's gaydar reason to believe there might be some interest. Could he possibly be that lucky?

"I'll leave if you want," Ryan said. "Have your manager call the magazine and set up something else." Ryan began moving toward the exit. "No guarantee it will be with me, but you'll get your interview."

"Wait," Dagger said. "Tony will rip me a new one if I don't do this with you." He tied the towel off at his hip and glanced back at the hallway door. "Take a seat. I'll be right back."

Several minutes later, Dagger reappeared; this time wearing black athletic pants and a Metallica t-shirt, his hair was combed from his face but still wet. He padded barefoot across the kitchen to the refrigerator and pulled out two chilled bottles of water. He came back to the living room and flopped down into a leather chair at the end of the couch and set his feet up onto the glass-topped coffee table. He looked toward Ryan and those mesmerizing blue eyes were staring back at him. Heat spiked inside him and he wondered if he was the only one feeling it. The game face Ryan wore revealed nothing, but fuck, he was nice to look at. It made him want to forget about the man waiting for him in his bedroom.

Shit. Pull yourself together!

"Okay," Dagger said, tossing a bottle of water at Ryan. "Let's do this."

Ryan caught the plastic bottle and studied Dagger. His position in the chair was relaxed but every muscle in the man's body seemed tight; as if on alert, his eyes narrowed on Ryan. Talk about a passive aggressive posturing, Ryan thought. And the way Dagger's hazel eyes followed his every move was equally unnerving. If he survived this interview, it'd be a miracle.

"You sure about this?" Ryan asked.

Dagger pulled in a long breath and let it out. "I'm a dead man if I don't," Dagger said.

Ryan forced his eyes away from Dagger and nodded. He opened up his pad of paper and set a tiny recording device onto the coffee table and pressed the record button. "I guess we might as well start with the obvious question then: is Dagger Drummond your birth name?"

"No – but that's the name you'll be using in your article, correct?"

Ryan heard the idle threat in Dagger's tone and paused, contemplating the best method to move forward with the interview. His instincts were keen and honed, when it came to manipulating the line of questions to get the information he wanted, but Dagger seemed just as skilled in dancing around the answers. Ryan smiled faintly to himself at that bit of knowledge. It looked like Ryan might have finally met his match. Reading between the lines with Dagger would reveal nothing more than a blurred, skewed line of truth. It would be up to Ryan to sift through the bullshit Dagger served him and bring the truth into focus.

"Your music has been described as dark and moody; filled with angst," Ryan said. "Where do you get your inspiration?"

"I'm a dark and moody kind of guy," Dagger said.

"That doesn't answer my question," Ryan said, and slid back in his seat; setting his ankle on top of the opposite knee. Dagger was annoying; beginning to inch across that imaginary line of pissing Ryan off. If Dagger's passive-aggression continued, Ryan could see himself walking out of the interview and telling Dagger to shove it up his ass. It might end up being a nice early night after all, Ryan thought, flipping the page in his notepad. And, it didn't help matters with the way Dagger was looking at him; predatory, like he wanted to eat Ryan alive. Ryan couldn't tell if Dagger was being hostile or if this was his idea of being friendly. Either way, he'd had about all he could take.

Dagger's leg began to bounce with nervous energy. Ryan watched the movement for a moment, then pulled his eyes back up to Dagger's face and those hypnotic hazel eyes. Dagger was clearly uncomfortable answering the questions and Ryan couldn't understand why. If need be, he might be able to use Dagger's uncertainty to benefit the interview process, Ryan thought – one of many tactics in his arsenal of interview methods.

"Life," Dagger said after a long, awkward pause.

"What about it?" Ryan asked.

"That's where I get my inspiration," Dagger said. "I'm surrounded on a daily basis with a constant supply of dysfunction, hate, love – you name it. I've either lived it, dreamed it, or watched someone else be consumed by it. Let's just say I don't have to go far to be inspired."

Ryan held Dagger's gaze and saw his eyes darken; the moss green turning chocolate brown. It made him wonder if at that very moment Dagger might be remembering some of the life events that had offered him inspiration. He thought of pushing Dagger on that, but didn't want to alienate the man too soon. He needed to keep Dagger talking, see how far he would let Ryan go before being shut down.

"The lyrics to *Bait Me*," Ryan ventured. "You talk about deception from multiple sources. Care to explain where that song came from?"

"*Bait Me* is a spin on the phrase: bite me," Dagger said. "It's about people lying about who they really are and the bullshit that spins off of that." Dagger leaned back in the leather chair and swung his leg over the arm of it; his bare foot peeked out from the hem of his pants. His thighs spread open revealing a bulge; as he settled into the corner of the chair, his arm draped over his bent knee. "Whether it be from a friend, the media, or a lover, we're all baited into believing half-truths about the people we think we know."

Ryan studied Dagger's movements. His eyes followed the chiseled line of Dagger's jaw, the column of his throat, the broad expanse of chest, and down onto those long, toned legs outlined beneath the athletic pants. His gaze stopped when it reached Dagger's bare foot. The skin was beautifully tanned, slender arch, perfect toes … Jesus! Was it possible for a man's foot to be sexy?

"I would agree," Ryan said. He tore his eyes away from Dagger's foot and cleared his throat, then scribbled a note in his pad. He needed to get a grip if he was going to finish this interview. "Any time line for the next album?"

Dagger ran a hand through his damp hair. "Depends on who you ask."

"I'm asking you," Ryan said.

"My time line is far different than my manager or our record label," Dagger said. "We released our recent album, *Indifferent*, a few months back and we're busy promoting that right now on tour. Our record label wants to see something new as soon as year's end. We're on tour for the next several months, so I'm not sure how the fuck they think that's gonna happen. My time line is more realistic."

"And, what would that be?" Ryan asked.

"When I'm damned good and ready," Dagger said. "I do most of my creating on the road. Odd time to do it, I know, with so many distractions, but that's when the lyrics seem to come to me. Once we get off the road I'll probably go into seclusion and create the music to go along with the lyrics, then we'll record in my studio."

"You have your own studio?" Ryan asked.

"Little known fun fact for you," Dagger said with a hint of a smile. "I have a full-blown recording studio right on my Los Angeles property. It makes the commute to work easy."

"Is that a fact you'd like me to use in this piece?" Ryan asked.

"You're implying I have a choice in what you print," Dagger said.

Ryan looked down at his notes and grinned. "It sounds like you've been burned by the press in the past."

"I've been burned so many fucking times, I've lost count," Dagger said. "I expect it now. It seems to hurt less if I remain ambivalent."

"I have no intention of burning you, Dagger."

"That's what they all say – right before they fuck you," Dagger said. He held Ryan's gaze, allowing his brain a few seconds imagining this beautiful man naked. And if Ryan turned out to be straight – damn! he hoped that wasn't the case, but how much fun would he have trying to pull Ryan over to the dark side? Dagger felt his groin begin to tighten and changed positions in the chair to hide it.

Twenty minutes later, Dagger was just starting to relax a bit and let down his guard, after drawing a very clear line which he expected Ryan not to cross: no questions about his personal life. Even still, Ryan wouldn't be doing his job if he didn't go there – at least once.

"One final question and I'll leave you alone," Ryan said, "Do you have a girlfriend or wife?"

"Nope. Why? You looking for a date?" Dagger asked. He made the comment with anger, but if Ryan had said yes, he would have been all over it.

And, that brought them to the end of the interview. Ryan took Dagger's angry cue and closed his note pad. "I guess that'll do it," he said, and stood up from the leather couch. "I'll let you know when the article goes to print."

Dagger watched Ryan walk toward the door, his eyes glued to Ryan's fluid form. The fucking guy looked just as hot from behind as he did from the front, he thought. Ryan was almost to the stairwell when Dagger's brain connected to his tongue and called his name. "Hey Ryan! Did you see the show tonight?" Dagger asked.

Ryan turned around and nodded. He watched Dagger moving across the room toward him with confident strides.

"And?"

"And, what?" Ryan asked.

"Did you like what you saw?" Dagger asked. He folded his muscled arms across his chest and squared his hips; tipping them forward slightly, as if declaring something.

Ryan observed Dagger's stance and that uncomfortable feeling returned to his gut. He looked down at his feet, confused by Dagger's question. "I've always enjoyed your music," Ryan said. "Tonight was no different."

Dagger smiled, seemingly pleased with Ryan's answer.

"Thanks for the interview," Ryan said. He gave Dagger a final wave and started down the stairs. He pressed on the handle of the bus door and opened it, the cool night air swirled in around him. That had to be one of the most unusual interviews of his career, he thought, then realized he'd left his audio recorder on the coffee table in the living room. He swore under his breath and shut the door, walking back up the stairs of the bus.

"Sorry for the second interruption," Ryan said, rising from the stairwell to the main floor. He looked across the expanse of the living room. The door to the back hallway was open again. A slender man with dirty blond hair stood in the opening; naked and fully aroused. Dagger was already in the process of pulling the t-shirt over his head as he walked toward the man.

Ryan reached for the tape recorder on the table, apologized again, and walked back to the stairs.

"What the fuck is your problem?" Dagger asked.

Ryan quickly realized the heated question was poised at him and turned around to face a very angry Dagger Drummond.

"I forgot this," Ryan said, waving the tiny device in the air.

"Get the hell out and make sure the door locks behind you."

Ryan drove home in silence. His ears were ringing from the concert; his heart still raced from the awkward confrontation with Dagger and the weird vibe coming from the man. Jesus, he couldn't believe what he had seen inside that bus! Nowhere in his research did he see Dagger's sexuality questioned. There were no rumors swirling around the music industry and no record of exes willing to spill their story about Dagger for a tidy price tag. His research had unearthed countless articles and photographs chronicling Dagger's trysts with female groupies, models – basically anything with tits, but not one hint he also pitched for the opposite team.

It was almost two in the morning when Ryan finally made it home to his two bedroom apartment. He tossed his keys on the kitchen table, poured himself a shot of Jack Daniels to calm his nerves and went into the spare bedroom he used as a home office. He turned on his laptop and started reading through his interview notes. After highlighting a few points, he pressed the play button on the tape recorder and began to listen to the rich timbre of Dagger's voice. It was no wonder the man had women falling at his feet. Everything about the man oozed sex, including his voice.

Ryan fast forwarded the tape to the end. He heard the interview conclude and his good-bye. Then after a moment of silence Ryan heard Dagger start talking again, followed by another man's voice.

"Looks like you started without me," Dagger said.

"Just keeping it hard for you," the man said.

Ryan shut off the recorder and rubbed at his face. If he had any doubts of Dagger's sexual orientation before, none remained.

CHAPTER TWO

Ryan had trouble concentrating at work. He couldn't stop thinking about his interview with Dagger the previous night and the visuals he saw while on Dagger's tour bus kept flashing over and over before his eyes, playing like a movie stuck in the same spot. The dialog he heard on the audio tape passing between Dagger and the blond guy kept repeating in his brain, too, making his head ache.

"Looks like you started without me," Dagger's voice flowed through the tiny recording device.

"Just keeping it hard for you," said the other voice on the tape.

Ryan massaged his forehead, trying to get the pounding to stop. Next time Ryan saw Dagger he'd have to thank Dagger for the added stress he unwittingly dumped into his lap. Next time he saw Dagger? Where the hell had that idea come from?

It hadn't taken Ryan long to decide to keep that piece of Dagger's life out of the article he would write. So, why couldn't he get beyond what he'd seen and heard? Catching Dagger with a guy was hardly a life changing event for Ryan, and Lord knew he'd witnessed far worse in his many years of being an entertainment reporter. So, why couldn't he forget about the images and get on with his life?

The phone call that afternoon from Dagger's manager came as a surprise to Ryan. His first thought was he was in trouble for walking in on Dagger or something else equally as stupid. Instead, the man insisted Ryan come back for the second show at the Staples Center and allow Dagger a chance to personally apologize for his behavior after the show the night before. Ryan attempted to turn down the offer but the manager persisted. In the end, Ryan agreed to another meeting.

The scenario played out much like it did the first time; with Ryan meeting the manager in the backstage hall of the arena. They made small talk together before Tony escorted Ryan through the maze of concrete corridors leading to the equipment loading docks at the back of the building. They descended a set of stairs and Ryan saw the row of buses.

"Why do I feel like I've been here before?" Ryan asked with a hint of sarcasm.

"Maybe because you have," Tony said.

They walked along the side of Dagger's tour bus and Tony stopped at the door. He entered the security code to the bus and opened the door; then he motioned Ryan inside in front of him.

Ryan stood in place and shook his head. "You first," he said to Tony. "I'm not looking for a repeat of last night."

Ryan followed Tony to the top of the stairs and turned toward the living room. Dagger was a few feet away sitting on the couch with two silicone Barbie doll women; one straddled his lap, the other had his mouth occupied with pleasuring her nipple. When Dagger saw Ryan and Tony he pulled away from the girls and asked them to leave; swatting one girl on the ass as she hopped off the couch. Ryan and Tony watched the girls wiggle by them and down the stairs of the bus.

"You dragged me down here to see that?" Ryan asked Tony.

When Tony said nothing, Ryan began walking to the exit.

"Where're you going?" Dagger asked, the volume of his voice increased.

"I'm not interested in wasting anymore of my time," Ryan said.

"I asked you back so I could apologize," Dagger said.

"You could have done that over the phone!"

Dagger motioned Tony with his eyes and the manager left the bus, leaving Dagger and Ryan alone.

"Please. Sit," Dagger said.

"No thanks. I'll stand."

"Apologies piss you off?" Dagger asked. He allowed himself a quick scan of Ryan's tight-fitting jeans. Ryan's sapphire blue dress shirt had three buttons undone at the top and allowed a peek of his dark chest hair. Damn, this was one fine piece of man, Dagger thought, and swallowed hard.

"Being *played* pisses me off," Ryan said.

"How am I doing that?" Dagger asked, his eyes settling on Ryan's mouth.

"Do you really want to have this conversation?" Ryan asked.

"Yeah, I do," Dagger said. "I'm a little curious to hear why you're so mad."

Ryan plunked himself down into the leather chair beside the couch. His eyes narrowed on Dagger, annoyed with everything about the man. There certainly was no lack of confidence in Dagger Drummond, although right now it was coming across more like smugness and arrogance. Neither trait impressed Ryan.

Dagger smoothed down his dark jeans and set one ankle on his opposite knee, then he folded his hands behind his head. The vintage t-shirt he wore stretched tight across his broad chest.

"You staged that little show for me to walk in on," Ryan finally said.

Dagger's smile was slow; his deep hazel eyes twinkled with mischief. "Shit like that happens to me every day," Dagger said. "I have no need to fake – or stage, anything."

Ryan rubbed at his face and sighed loudly. "The little show I walked in on last night was very real. Tonight was staged. But what pisses me off, is you thinking I give a shit who you fuck."

Dagger leaned forward; his eyes glaring at Ryan, his forearms resting on his knees. "There was no *show* last night." He said the words slow and methodical, almost as if he needed to say it that way for it to be truth.

"You're unbelievable," Ryan said, and stood up to leave. "Last night you and your *boyfriend* both had boners the size of the Space Needle and tonight with two girls bouncing on your lap you had nothing. You tell me why I'd think tonight was staged."

"I find it interesting you'd focus on *that* particular detail over anything else you saw," Dagger said. "Unless you're into Space Needles?"

"Fuck you," Ryan said, and started to leave.

"Ryan, could you tell me about the article you're writing about me?" Dagger asked.

Ryan faced him, the reason for the staged three-way with the girl's becoming more clear with every passing second. "If you're worried I'm planning on 'outing' you in the magazine, you're dead wrong. I told you, my article will be about your music and that's it. In fact, there will be very little personal information in it at all – partly because you gave me nothing to work with."

Dagger sat back against the couch tipped his head back, letting a loud groan of frustration rattle from his throat. A moment later he looked back at Ryan. "Look, I'm really sorry," he said, his posture softening. "For everything. My intention wasn't to drag you into this, but Tony thought it was worth a shot."

Dagger's last comment made everything fall into place for Ryan. "Holy shit," he said almost on a sigh. "No one knows, do they?" Ryan asked.

Dagger's eyes met Ryan's; emotion was making them shimmer. "My manager knows and a few ... others. Tony is concerned about the general public knowing and what it might mean to my career."

"I don't give a shit who you sleep with, Dagger. It's none of my business and I don't make judgments."

Dagger nodded and clasped his hands between his spread thighs, linking the long fingers, then his eyes locked again with Ryan's. "For the record, he's not my boyfriend," Dagger said with a shrug. "We hook-up every once in a while. That's it."

Ryan sat back down in the chair with a heavy thud. He was somewhat stunned by Dagger's admission. He couldn't understand why Dagger was confessing these things; wasn't sure how to respond, or if he was expected to. Before Ryan's eyes, everything about Dagger seemed to relax. The thick, protective shell surrounding the man started to crack and the rock star cockiness began to fade. In its place was a new vulnerability Ryan found endearing and Dagger seemed almost human; normal, with a fragile easiness about him. The transformation made Ryan's breath catch. The man sitting before him now with uncertainty shadowing the masculine features of his face, was downright likable.

"I'm usually very careful not to get caught," Dagger said. "But last night … I was over-tired and obviously stupid, and then you showed up; distracted the hell out of me, and I panicked."

"My interview distracted you?" Ryan asked.

"No – *you* did."

Ryan digested Dagger's comment and noted the half-smile on Dagger's face. If a woman had said that to him, he'd know what it meant. Dagger saying it was confusing. Dagger had just admitted to being gay, so why would he be saying shit like that to him? Did Dagger think *he* was gay?

Was Dagger interested? Fuck that! He hadn't given any signals to Dagger, had he?

"I'm sorry you feel it's necessary to hide that part of yourself," Ryan said.

"You straight?" Dagger asked.

Ryan tipped his head at the question and wondered why the answer wasn't obvious to Dagger. No one had ever questioned his sexual orientation before. That coupled with Dagger's previous comment about being distracted, had Ryan's forehead starting to sweat.

"Yeah, of course," Ryan said.

"Then, you have no idea what it's like to live with this."

"No, I guess I wouldn't," Ryan said.

Ryan held Dagger's intense gaze for a moment and something odd passed between them. An understanding of sorts? Knowledge? Ryan wasn't sure what the hell it was, but the feeling washing over him had his stomach knotting. He stood up again and this time he pulled a business card from his wallet and handed it to Dagger. "If you have any questions about the article or if you just want to talk, give me a call," he said.

Dagger read the information on the card, then looked up at Ryan and smiled warmly. "I really appreciate this," he said, flicking the card with his index finger. "And, I might actually take you up on the offer."

Ryan nodded, gave Dagger a wave, and left the bus.

Two nights later, Ryan's cell phone was ringing at two forty-five in the morning. He rolled out of a sound sleep toward the bedside table and grabbed his phone. He glanced at the caller I.D. He didn't recognize the phone number displayed, but decided to answer the call.

"Ryan Pierce," he said, in a drowsy slurred voice.

"Hey, Ryan. It's Dagger. Sounds like I woke you?"

"Yeah, you did," he said, pushing himself up against the headboard of the bed. "Is something wrong?" he asked.

"I was wondering when your article will print and if I'd get a chance to see a copy beforehand?"

"Don't tell me you're still worried about the content of my story," Ryan said.

Dagger laughed; a deep, throaty laugh that vibrated inside Ryan's head and every cell in his body started to wake.

"Do you blame me?" Dagger asked.

"I suppose not," Ryan said. "But I gave you my word."

There was a pause on the line and Ryan closed his eyes, fighting the urge to doze.

"Sleeping or screwing?" Dagger asked.

This time Ryan was the one to laugh. "If I were screwing, your call would've gone directly to voice mail."

"I would hope so!" Dagger said, another chuckle rolling from his mouth and then he became quiet. "I'm trying not to be, but I'm nervous about that article."

24

"Don't be," Ryan said. "My deadline is in a couple of weeks and I'll see if I can get a copy to you before it prints – not for your approval, because what I send you will be the final draft. Just so we're clear."

Dagger sighed loudly. "I understand and I'll appreciate anything you can do."

"No problem."

"You're being nice to me and I'm not sure I deserve it," Dagger said. "I was such a dick to you when we met."

"I walked in on you," Ryan said. "You had a right to give me attitude."

"I gave you my full-on, bad ass attitude," Dagger said. "I'm surprised you're talking to me."

"By the time I left, you seemed to have calmed down," Ryan said. "Almost turned into a nice guy."

"Almost?" Dagger chuckled. "I *am* a nice guy – to the people that matter to me."

"Lucky them," Ryan said. "I guess you save your other side for reporters, like me."

"Get to know me better and you could see the good side of me all the time," Dagger said.

"I'm not sure what you mean by that, Dagger."

Dagger let that comment slide and said, "How much did you see?"

"Which time?"

Both of them laughed at that.

"Was your boyfriend pissed I interrupted?" Ryan asked.

"I told you, he's not my boyfriend," Dagger said. "What about you, Ry, you got a girl?"

"No, not since..."

"Since what?"

Ryan turned again in bed, uncomfortable with the new direction the conversation was heading. Nonetheless, he was enjoying this chat with Dagger – even though it was in the middle of the night.

"Too personal?" Dagger asked.

"I suppose not," Ryan said. "I was living with a girl for a while."

"How long?" Dagger asked.

"About four years."

"That's a long time, Ry. What happened?"

"She dumped me," Ryan said. "She said I wasn't emotionally invested in the relationship – whatever the hell that means."

Dagger started laughing. "Man, not that!"

"I was living with her," Ryan said. "How much more invested could I get?"

"Sounds like she was looking for a ring."

Ryan massaged his forehead. "I'm pretty sure that's what she wanted, and she knew I wasn't feeling it, so she walked away. Looking back, she did us a favor."

"How long ago did it happen?"

"Last year."

"And you haven't gotten laid since?" Dagger asked.

Ryan flopped back against the pillows at the headboard. "I didn't say that."

"Damn, you need to come out with me," Dagger said. "I'll get you laid. You can keep the girls busy while I defile their boyfriends."

"Helluva plan, Dagger."

Ryan smiled. Talking to Dagger felt comfortable, relaxed; like they'd known each other for a long time. Ryan was a little surprised at himself for sharing some of the things he was with Dagger. He couldn't explain why, but it felt good to be talking to someone that seemed to understand. There was something else there, too, and it was the other little *something* that was making Ryan uncomfortable.

"I've been too busy with work," Ryan said. "Just haven't had much time to socialize."

"Poor excuse," Dagger said. "Sex and relationships should be a priority in everyone's life."

"When it's meant to happen, it will," Ryan said. "I'm not worried."

"A good looking guy like you should not be sleeping alone. Ever."

Dagger's words gave pause to Ryan. A man had never complimented him the way Dagger did – especially a man he now knew preferred sleeping with men. It was a little weird, but if he were to be totally honest, it also felt good and he wasn't sure why. His face flushed in the darkened room and Ryan was grateful he was alone.

"Hey Ry, I'm sorry about that."

"Sorry for what?" Ryan asked.

"I have a feeling what I just said freaked you out a bit," Dagger said. "I'll admit I'm attracted to you, but I also know you're straight and nothing could ever happen between us, so you're safe."

Christ, suddenly his bedroom seemed so small, Ryan thought, and his chest felt tight. And why was he sweating? He kicked the covers off his legs and sprawled on top of the sheets. Was it regret he was feeling or happiness to hear he was 'safe' where Dagger was concerned? And what the hell did *safe* mean?

The thoughts began to swirl in his head. Clearly he *liked* Dagger or this conversation would have ended long ago, but he didn't like him *that* way. Of course not! That wasn't possible. Or was it? Sure, Dagger was an incredibly sexy man, but acknowledging that didn't mean anything, right? Wasn't it normal for a man to think of another man as sexy? Fuck. He needed to hang up.

"Don't over-think it," Dagger said.

Ryan chucked. "My ex was always saying I over-analyzed every thing I did."

"If you spend too much time thinking about doing something, you won't ever have enough time to experience it – or *feel* it. And feeling is the best part of anything. That's how we know we're alive."

"Words to live by?" Ryan asked.

"Absolutely," Dagger said. "I should have that printed on t-shirts and sell them at our shows."

"Maybe you should give that idea to your merchandisers," Ryan said.

"How long have you been with Music Spin, Ry?" Dagger asked.

"I started as an intern while in college at Stanford," Ryan said. "They hired me on full time right after I graduated."

"Do you like what you do?" Dagger asked.

"I love it," Ryan said. "How about you? Do you love performing?"

Dagger sighed. "Yeah, after all this time I can still say I love the entire process. The buzz I get from being on stage and watching the audience sing my songs along with me … is like nothing else you'll ever experience."

"I can't even imagine what that's like," Ryan said.

"I could do without media exploiting my private life though," Dagger said. "That part of this job sucks, but the perks are over the top."

"Do you still think I'm gonna burn you?" Silence came through the phone and Ryan exhaled loudly. "Dagger, I gave my word. I won't out you."

"Ry, you seem like an upstanding guy, but I'm just getting to know you," Dagger said. "If you'd lived the life I've lived for the past decade, you'd understand my mistrust of everyone around me. Very few get close enough to really know me."

"Trust is earned," Ryan said.

"That, it is," Dagger said. "And, once it's lost, it's near impossible to get back."

Ryan continued to listen while Dagger told him stories of his years on the road. The non-stop parties, a never ending stream of groupies in and out of his bed; it was all entertaining to hear, to say the least.

"You're gay, but you talk about screwing countless women, many at the same time," Ryan said. "Wouldn't that make you bi?"

"I don't like labels, Ry," Dagger said. "Sex is sex. I can get off with women, but I prefer being with a man, and the only emotional connections I've ever felt are with men. I think that makes me very gay."

Before long, Ryan saw slivers of the days first light seeping in through the window shades in his bedroom. He mentioned that fact to Dagger and reluctantly they decided to end the call.

Ryan turned in bed and glanced at his alarm clock. In thirty-five minutes the buzzer would be going off to get him out of bed for work. Had he really been talking to Dagger that long? Did the man ever get tired or need sleep? And yet there hadn't been one lull in their conversation and Ryan had enjoyed each and every minute. They had managed to hit upon every subject imaginable: politics, religion, food, and of course sex. Although, Ryan had done a fine job of dancing around that subject and moving Dagger onto something different - something safe.

Safe. Middle ground. Vanilla.

Hadn't he lived his entire life doing just that? Everything about him suddenly seemed beige. Even the walls in his apartment were beige! Listening to some of the life experiences Dagger had lived made him feel bored with his own existence. When had he become so predictable and dull?

Ryan swung his legs off the bed and stood up. He walked to the bathroom and turned on the shower waiting for the water to heat, and studied his reflection in the mirror. He was barely into his thirty-first year, yet in some ways, he felt as if he might as well be in his eighties. He needed to do something about that. Maybe Dagger could show him how to live, he thought, then laughed. He'd be nervous to make such a suggestion to Dagger, for fear of the other things he may want to show him.

CHAPTER THREE

Ryan arrived for work at the main offices for Music Spin Magazine in downtown Los Angeles. The Music Spin offices were located on the tenth floor of a high-rise downtown. Ryan stepped off the elevator and nodded at the company receptionist, as he made his way down the hall toward his office. He was twenty minutes late; unusual for him, and he felt like the walking dead from lack of sleep. He walked into his office, and shut the door behind him, hoping no one would bother him until it was time to go home.

By the time lunch break came, he was exhausted and desperate for a nap. The notes from his interview with Dagger were slowly taking on the shape of an article as he connected the details together, much like connecting the dots of a puzzle.

Ryan's thoughts then went to Dagger: the man behind the music. He smiled when thinking of their exceptionally long phone conversation in the wee hours of the morning, getting to know each other. He was starting to see the real man hidden beneath layers and years of having to hide who he was and was really beginning to like him.

He wondered if Dagger was also tired this morning. Ryan shook his head in doubt at that. It was unlikely Dagger was suffering any ill effects from talking so late last night. After all, his normal schedule was working the graveyard shift and sleeping until mid-afternoon, only to get up and do it all over again the next night.

His cell phone started to vibrate on his desk, stirring him from this thoughts. Ryan glanced at the caller I.D. and felt his face heat. It was Dagger. Again.

"Did you get to work on time this morning?" Dagger asked.

"I was a few minutes late," Ryan said. "How about you? Were you on time to your radio interview?"

"It just wrapped up," Dagger said. "But I wanted to make sure you were doing okay."

"No worse for the wear," Ryan said.

"I sometimes forget not everyone keeps the late hours I do or are even in the same time zone as me, so I apologize for waking you and keeping you up so late."

"Forget about it," Ryan said.

"Maybe when I'm back in L.A. you'll let me take you out for a beer or something," Dagger said. "You know, to make it up to you."

"That's not necessary," Ryan said. "Besides, I'd be a little concerned where you'd take me."

Dagger laughed. "No gay bars, if that's what you're worried about, my nervous, straight friend," he said. "Hell, I don't even go to them – out of fear of being recognized, so your gay bar virginity is safe with me."

"For some reason your comment doesn't make me feel any safer," Ryan said.

The laugh resonating from Dagger was downright lecherous and Ryan felt his face heat.

"Sorry, Ry. I can't seem to help myself around you."

"Try harder," Ryan said.

Dagger closed his eyes and exhaled. The more he talked to Ryan, the more the smooth, deep texture of Ryan's voice affected him. Ryan was wonderfully calming to him and they were well on their way to becoming good friends. This was something Dagger hadn't risked with a non-musician in many years – especially a straight man, that also happened to work for the entertainment media.

There were so many reasons why Dagger knew it wasn't smart opening himself up to Ryan; as trusting someone didn't come easy for Dagger. But, with Ryan it seemed impossible *not* to trust. Dagger could feel himself blurring the lines of friendship and wanting a whole lot more from Ryan than friendship or the physical mating one night could offer; which was something else he hadn't risked doing in years.

"I'm off to New Jersey tomorrow and then down to Maryland day after that," Dagger said.

"Are you rocking out the arenas?" Ryan asked.

"Of course," Dagger chuckled. "At least, I'd like to think I am."

"The reviews have been exceptionally good," Ryan said.

"You've been following up on me?" Dagger asked.

Ryan paused. It was his job to stay up to date on news in the music world and to do that required him to read dozens of different on-line news sources a few times each day. But since their initial meeting, Ryan had developed a more focused interest in Dagger, gone out of his way to find news bits on Dagger's shows; his whereabouts, and that wasn't the norm for Ryan. Once he completed an interview and wrote the review or article, it was usually on to the next artist. That hadn't been the case with Dagger and Dagger still continued to keep himself in Ryan's life, too; which also wasn't the norm for Ryan. After an interview, it was unlikely an artist would keep in touch with him – until the next time they needed some press. But Dagger wasn't the norm when it came to anything, so why should Ryan be surprised by the phone calls?

"I try and stay on top of who's touring and how it's going," Ryan said. His office was air-conditioned and yet he was sweating. What the hell was wrong with him?

"It's okay, Ry. I don't mind you following me," Dagger said. "Although, given a choice, I'd rather have you in front of me."

Dead silence.

Jesus. This thing with Dagger was heading in a direction that was foreign to Ryan and he didn't understand why. Had he led Dagger on in some way? In some twisted way did he want this kind of attention from Dagger?

"Over-thinking again?" Dagger asked.

"Yeah, probably."

Dagger laughed. "I'm sorry. I shouldn't be playing with your head like I do, but it's so much fun to mess with straight guys and watch them squirm."

"Thanks for that," Ryan said lightheartedly.

"I'll give you a call later," Dagger said.

"Sounds good."

Ryan had barely set down the phone when someone knocked on the door to his office. It was the new intern in the department, Sebastian Keating. Sebastian was tall and lean with thick, dirty blond hair and dimples; his full lips tilted up into a lopsided smile.

"Hey, Ryan. I'm Sebastian," he said, the slightest hint of an English accent hanging off each word he spoke. Sebastian crossed the room and reached over Ryan's desk to shake his hand. "Am I interrupting something?"

"Not at all," Ryan said.

"Oh, it was the expression on your face when I knocked," Sebastian said. "I thought you might be talking to your girlfriend."

Ryan laughed at that remark. "Male friend – and *just* a friend." He rubbed his face after he said it, unsure why he felt the need to elaborate at all to someone he was meeting for the first time. Why the hell did he care if Sebastian knew the gender of the person on the other end of his phone or the relationship he had with them? He was unraveling, and once again Dagger's two weighty words rang loudly in his head.

Over. Thinking.

And wasn't that exactly what Ryan was doing?

Sebastian nodded and dipped his head to hide a smile. "Well, thanks for clarifying."

"What can I do for you?" Ryan asked, eager to move Sebastian's unannounced visit along and hopefully get him back out into the hallway and on the other side of his closed office door.

"I've heard you're the 'go-to' guy for interview skills."

"Is that so?"

"It's been suggested I talk to you, maybe watch you work, so I can improve how I conduct an interview."

Ryan scratched his head. "Well, I don't have anything scheduled until next week. Then I'll be sitting down with Zander Metcalf and his band Ivory Tower."

"Damn! Ivory Tower? Their new album is their best yet."

Ryan nodded. "Well, you're welcome to tag along with me, if you want."

"I'd like that," Sebastian said. "Maybe you'll let me take you to dinner a few days before that and I'll help you outline your interview material?"

"I suppose that'd be okay," Ryan said.

They set a date for the following Monday night and Ryan went back to work – or at least he attempted to work. His ability to concentrate lately made working impossible. Too many things were rattling around in his head, things that didn't necessarily make him feel comfortable – things he'd rather not be thinking about at all, and every bit of it came back to Dagger. Why was this particular guy occupying so much space inside his head?

He left work an hour early and drove home. Once inside his two bedroom apartment he tossed his keys onto the kitchen table and grabbed a beer from the refrigerator. He popped the cap on the bottle and walked into the living room and sat down on the couch; using the channel selector to surf through several programs before settling on a baseball game. He wasn't sure which team was playing and he didn't much care.

The game ended and another one started and Ryan still had no clue what he was watching. If it wasn't for his stomach reminding him it was dinner time, he probably wouldn't have acknowledged that. He made a quick trip into his kitchen to heat up leftover takeout and returned to the couch again to stare mindlessly at the television screen.

A moment later his cell phone began ringing. The number was all too familiar to him now and a smile formed on his face. He lifted it to his ear and said hello but heard nothing but cheers and screaming coming from the other end of the line.

"I'm getting ready to take the stage in Atlantic City, Ry," Dagger said. "Can you hear all that noise?"

"Sounds like a helluva party," Ryan said.

"Not quite," Dagger said. "Party status can't be achieved without you here."

"Nice try, Dagger, but I've heard all about the parties you're able to achieve without me being anywhere nearby."

"Soon as I'm able, you and I are gonna get together and party," Dagger said.

"Is that a promise or a threat?" Ryan asked.

"A promise and then some," Dagger said. Another roar from the audience came through the phone. "I gotta go to work now," he said. "Wish me luck."

"Kill it, then tell me all about it."

The line went dead without Ryan being able to hear if Dagger had said good-bye or not. He relaxed back into the cushions on the couch and closed his eyes. It had been a long time since he'd had a close male friend and it felt good. He liked the fact Dagger had thought of him just before he took the stage; liked him checking in during the day, too. It made him feel like he mattered to someone and reminded him of what it was like when he was with Beth.

His beautiful, sweet, ginger-haired Beth.

The companionship is what he missed most about her, and having someone to go home to at the end of the day. Knowing that probably wouldn't please her, but it was the truth. She'd want him to say he missed the passion and intimacy the most, but that wasn't the case. The sex with Beth was adequate but no matter how hard they tried, what they shared in bed never seemed to escalate into the fiery hot category. In so many ways he felt he had failed her, but he simply wasn't feeling what she wanted him to feel.

She was right to leave, he thought. She'd moved on with her life, found a new boyfriend, said she was happy, and she certainly seemed to be, too. What remained between them was a close friendship without the daily conversations making him feel like he played a role in her life. He no longer did. Instead he represented a piece of her past, a relationship she'd remember with fondness and that was probably about it. Their talks were sporadic now and occasionally they'd meet for lunch or dinner if she was in town on business.

She knew him better than anyone; maybe too well, because it annoyed the hell out of him how easily she could read him. She saw things he preferred to ignore. It was easier that way. He was alone because he wanted to be. Case closed. No matter how analytic she wanted to be about it. Not everyone was meant to be coupled off with someone for life. With his erratic work schedule, it was better for him to be alone. That left no one at home to be pissed off at him when he was out nearly all night playing reporter to the music world.

It had been a while since he'd heard from Beth, he thought, rising up from the couch. He made a mental note to send her a text message in the next day or two, maybe see if they could meet. He stepped into the kitchen and tossed the empty cardboard container of chow mein into the trash bin and walked into his bedroom. A shower and bed sounded good.

He stepped beneath the warm shower spray and let the water pelt against his face and throat. He tipped his head back, feeling his cock responding to the sensation. Jesus, it'd been too long since he'd gotten laid. But to actually get a woman beneath him required a certain amount of interest and effort on his part and he lacked both. It just didn't feel all that important to justify the work involved.

Ryan crawled naked into bed and settled onto his back, closing his eyes. He tried to remember the last time he'd had sex with Beth and couldn't. Had it been so long he couldn't remember a single detail? It made him feel pretty pathetic, thinking of how long it had been since someone had touched him – or even excited him.

Talking to Dagger excited him, but that was because the friendship was new and why Dagger held his interest to such an exaggerated degree. There could be no other explanation beyond that, because there was nothing else between them, right?

His hand slipped between his partially spread thighs and cupped his balls, rolling them around beneath his fingers and his cock reacted quickly. He tried to remember the last time he had masturbated and nothing came to mind. Jesus, could his life possibly be that boring? He wondered if Dagger had to resort to such tactics of self-pleasure, and then scoffed at the idea. He sincerely doubted Dagger had to do anything by himself, then cursed himself for wondering what Dagger did at all. It didn't matter and he had no business caring; so why did he? And, why was he excessively thinking about Dagger? Was it simply a curiosity about a new friend – or a curiosity about his new friend's lifestyle?

The uncomfortable knot began to tighten Ryan's gut again. The closer he looked at this situation, the more uneasy he felt about it. He was spending far too much time thinking about Dagger, noting his whereabouts, reading up on him. The man had become a distraction in Ryan's daily life and he had no explanation for it.

Next chance he got, he would ask out the new girl in his department. Maybe he'd see what she was doing next weekend and they could go out to dinner – or something. The *something* he hoped would be her fucking him senseless – or least until he remembered what it felt like to fuck. What was her name, he wondered. Kaitlyn? Kathy? Kristen? All he remembered from their initial meeting was her name started with the letter K and she had a nice round ass.

Ryan was contemplating the girl's name when his phone beeped on the nightstand beside the bed announcing an incoming text message. He reached for it and saw the message was from Dagger.

"You up?" the text read.

Ryan glanced down at his semi-erect cock and smiled. Was he up? If Dagger only knew. He replied to the text message with a simple: yes. A few second later, Ryan's phone was ringing.

"How was the show?" Ryan asked.

"Fucking awesome," Dagger said. "Why are you out of breath?"

"I'm not out of breath."

"Then, you're breathing heavy for me?" Dagger laughed.

"You wish," Ryan said, and grimaced at the implication behind his comment.

"You're right, I do, but we both know that's not gonna happen," Dagger said. "Are you out for the night?"

"Nope, at home."

"Seriously? You're at home and it's not even ten o'clock your time."

"We've already established I don't have much of a social life, Dagger, so why would you be surprised to hear I'm at home in bed."

"Whoa! You're in *bed*? What the fuck are you doing in bed?" Then Dagger started laughing. "Holy shit! I caught you jerking off, didn't I? That's why you're breathing hard!"

"I was tired so I went to bed. It's not that big a deal."

Dagger was still laughing, not buying a single word Ryan said. "Hey, there's no shame in beating off, man. I do it at least once a day just to keep myself sane."

"What a line of bullshit!" Ryan said. "With the amount of willing … *partners* at your disposal, you expect me to believe you have to beat off?"

"For your information, I haven't been with *anyone* in quite a while," Dagger said, his tone lighthearted.

"And the guy I saw in your shower was there to clean the hair out of the drain?"

"All right, there was him, but there was no happy ending."

"Because I interrupted?"

"Yeah, pretty much," Dagger said. "I was too pissed off after you left – and panicked, so I sent Chris on his way."

"Sorry about that," Ryan said. "But I think you'll live."

"Yeah, I'll live."

Ryan could hear the smile in Daggers voice and he smiled, too. "Why is it every time we talk the conversation somehow turns to sex?"

"Because if I'm not *doing* it, I like to talk about doing it," Dagger teased. "Besides, I can tell you're falling for me, so it's obvious the sex talk is working like a charm."

Ryan pushed himself to an upright position against the headboard. The air caught in his throat and his face flushed. Falling for him? Is that what was happening? He pressed his thumb and index finger into his eyes until it started to hurt and a long moment of silence passed between them.

"Dagger, I'm straight," Ryan said quietly. "So, you're barking up the wrong tree."

"Is that some kind of metaphor for your cock?"

"You're crazy, you know that?" Ryan asked.

"That is true," Dagger said. "But I'm comfortable being the crazy artist type. Are you comfortable with who you are?"

I was until I met you, Ryan thought to himself. "Lately, I don't know what the hell I'm doing."

Dagger made a low humming noise. "That's because you're falling for me, Ry, but don't worry. I'll catch you long before you hit the floor."

"Is that supposed to make me feel better?"

"I don't know," Dagger said. "Does it?"

"I have to be honest, Dagger. When you say shit like that, it makes me feel a little uncomfortable."

"You're right and I'm sorry," Dagger said. "As much as I'd love there to be more, I really like talking to you, and I don't want to lose that. I'll make a bigger effort to behave myself."

Dagger reclined on his couch; the smile on his face turned serious. Shit. The realization he truly did want something more with Ryan – beyond the physical, slowly started to wrap around him. Then, the feeling enveloped him and Dagger bolted upright on the couch. It was insanity for him to consider going down that particular road again after such a long time. Even crazier for him to contemplate doing so with a straight guy like Ryan. He was fucked. How could anything good come from this? But, this was Ryan he was talking about, and Ryan was different.

"I should probably get going," Ryan said.

"Because of what I said?" Dagger asked.

"No, it's getting late and some of us actually work the day shift."

A soft laugh came through the phone, then Dagger sighed. "Okay, then I'll let you go," Dagger said. "Maybe we can talk tomorrow?"

"That'd be fine," Ryan said.

Ryan disconnected the call and exhaled the breath he'd been holding, feeling somewhat more confident he'd been heard. It wasn't that he found what Dagger was saying to him to be insulting or even disrespectful. It had more to do with how their conversations were making him *feel* and he wasn't quite sure yet if that was good or bad. The fact Dagger was making him feel anything at all, was disturbing. They were friends – nothing more, and no chance there could ever be more, so the flirting on Dagger's part was harmless. Right? Dagger's words merely stroked his ego and made him feel good about himself. Who wouldn't enjoy attention like that?

Still, Dagger's behavior was forcing Ryan to put his life under the microscope and dissect how he'd lived it so far. It was also making Ryan admit how excited he got anytime Dagger contacted him and how good it was to hear his voice. When he put it all together like that, it caused Ryan to question everything he thought he knew about himself. Was he attracted to Dagger beyond the normal perimeters of what defined a friendship?

In his entire life, he'd never had to question his feelings or attractions and lately it seemed he was doing that at least once a day. Since puberty, he'd only thought of being with girls and – once he hit high school, he wanted them in his bed. He always had a close circle of male friends, even had a gay friend in college, but never once had he spent a single second of time questioning the specifics of those friendships or if he wanted there to be more – possibly something physical.

Until Dagger.

Shit. Now he was more confused about himself than ever before.

CHAPTER FOUR

Sleep didn't come easy for Ryan that night. He tossed and turned for hours, eventually falling asleep with the sheets twisted around his legs and a pillow covering his head. The dreams that chased him throughout the night repeatedly woke him, bathed in sweat, only to drift off again to another onslaught of erotic visuals.

The most vivid of all of the dreams had him in the shower with Dagger. Their slippery bodies rubbing together in the heavy mist and steam of the glass stall, Dagger's mouth finding his, his tongue claiming him in a way no woman ever had, then Dagger dropping to his knees and taking Ryan deeply into his throat. So deep, Ryan thought he'd die from the pleasure. He watched from above, as Dagger's lips stretched around his thickness, taking more; bringing him closer to the edge with every suck and pull of his skin. Ryan shook himself awake moments before he came into Dagger's mouth, the image so disturbing and arousing, he wouldn't allow himself to finish it. He couldn't because that would mean … fuck! What did it mean? He didn't want the answer to that question spending any time in his head.

He hauled himself out of bed and stepped into his shower. He ran the water as cold as his skin could tolerate and scrubbed himself clean, refusing to acknowledge the enormous hard-on he had jutting out proudly, as if laughing at him; the freezing water not doing a damn thing to diminish it. Somehow he had to get the images from that dream out of his head. How was he supposed to face Dagger again after having such a dream – with Dagger playing a staring role? That was it; he simply wouldn't see Dagger again. Problem solved and Dagger would be forgotten.

He dried himself off and hit the speed dial on his phone to call Beth. She answered on the fifth ring, sounding sleepy and annoyed.

"Ryan, are you aware how early it is?" she asked.

Ryan glanced at the alarm clock sitting beside his bed. It was a full hour before he'd normally roll from bed to get ready for work and for a brief moment he felt bad for disrupting Beth's slumber. But Beth could sort out the worst of the worst of his problems and come up with a practical solution. More than anything, that's what he needed now.

"I'm sorry," he said, "But I had a really fucked-up dream and I wanted to run it by you."

"You're not serious," Beth said. "You woke me up to get a dream translation?"

"This wasn't just *any* dream," he said. "This one was … disturbing."

"Aren't they all? That's why they're called dreams," Beth said. "It's fantasy. Nothing more."

"I can assure you, this dream is *not* a fantasy for me!"

"All right, Ryan. I'll bite. What was your dream about," she said in a sarcastic tone.

Ryan opened his mouth to speak and stopped. A long moment passed and Beth sighed loudly.

"You woke me up and now you won't talk?" Beth asked. "You've got five seconds to start talking or I'm hanging up."

"Okay, okay," Ryan said. "I was in the shower … with – with a man."

The silence spilling from the phone made Ryan sway on his feet. He sat down on the edge of his bed. "Beth? Are you still there?"

"I'm here," she said. "Is the man someone you know?"

"Yes."

"Are you physically attracted to him?"

"Fuck no!" Ryan said.

"Then don't worry about it," Beth said. "Now, go back to sleep."

The next thing Ryan heard was the buzz of dial tone.

Two days passed without a phone call from Dagger. Maybe that was for the best, Ryan thought. Since Ryan had that dirty dream about Dagger, his head was in a very weird place and the idea of talking to him made Ryan nervous, as if Dagger would somehow know he'd had this dream. Even still, the absence of their conversations seemed to bother Ryan more than the unusual emotions he was experiencing when he did talk to Dagger.

Ryan found himself continually checking his phone throughout the day, seeing if he'd missed a call, even though the phone was never out of his sight long enough to miss one. He began to wonder what Dagger was up to, if maybe he'd found someone else to entertain him late at night. The idea of that upset him, too.

It felt a lot like jealousy and Ryan knew he had no right to feel it. He had no claim on Dagger. They were friends and friends didn't give a shit about such things, nor did a friend act like a school girl when they thought they were being ignored. Compounding all that with his twisted dream, it added up to a boiling pot of fucked-up stew.

Ryan picked up his cell phone for the umpteenth time and stared at it; almost willing it to ring, or at the very least beep to announce a text message. Complete frustration caused him to flip open the cover of the phone to reveal the text pad. His fingers moved quickly over the letters as he punched in his short message, then sent the text before he had a chance to change his mind.

"You OK?" Ryan's text message asked.

Five of the longest minutes Ryan could remember passed before the phone beeped.

"Yes. Why? Miss me?"

Ryan snorted. Actually he did miss Dagger, but he wasn't ready to admit that to the man.

"Been a while. Wanted to make sure you were OK," Ryan typed.

A moment later Dagger replied, *"I miss you, too."*

Smart ass, Ryan thought, and smiled. At least Dagger hadn't altogether sidelined the flirting. Ryan knew he was rusty in that department, but he was fairly certain that's what Dagger was doing. And if he were to be completely honest, he was a little grateful for it. He was turning into one messed up dude and damned if he knew how to fix it.

"On way 2 see mgr. Call U ltr.," Dagger's message read.

"OK. Talk soon," Ryan answered, and tossed the phone back on his desk.

Ryan was placing his take-out dinner onto a plate when Dagger called back. He took the steaming eggplant Parmesan into the living room and made himself comfortable on the couch.

"How've you been?" Ryan asked.

"Busy," Dagger said. "I haven't even hit the halfway point of this tour and management already wants to talk about the next tour and the merchandising for it."

"You're forgetting Black Ice is a very marketable commodity," Ryan said. "They want to make as much money off you as they can – while they can."

"I suppose so," Dagger said with a sigh. "But, I hate the business end of this."

"Every band feels that way," Ryan said.

"It's nice to know you missed me," Dagger said, his voice deepening ever so slightly.

"Who said that?" Ryan laughed.

"Deny it all you want, Ry, but I know the truth."

Dagger's intonation wasn't accusatory and that put Ryan somewhat at ease, even still, he could feel himself heating from the inside out. "Admitting I missed talking to you would do nothing but inflate your already over-sized ego."

"There are a lot of things about me that are over-sized," Dagger said. "And on occasion some are prone to inflate, too."

"Over-sized? Really?" Ryan laughed. "You're forgetting I've seen you in a towel."

"Ummm, yes, you have," he said. "And that image must have left quite an impression because that's the second time you've mentioned it."

"It's not every day I see two men in the shower."

"Intrigues you though, doesn't it?"

Ryan nearly dropped his plate onto the coffee table in front of his knees. It was as if Dagger could read his private thoughts. Impossible, Ryan thought, but once again, his palms were sweaty, all because of a conversation with Dagger.

"You're doing it again," Ryan said.

"Doing what?" Dagger asked. "Arousing a healthy curiosity within you? Is that such a bad thing? And here I thought life was all about experimenting with new things."

"New foods, clothing, or perhaps music, but not typically with one's sexuality," Ryan said.

"That's not necessarily true," Dagger said. "Sometimes people bury shit so deep inside themselves because they're afraid to look at it – until someone scratches the itch and it all comes to the surface."

"I'm not itchy, Dagger."

"Are you sure about that?"

"Positive," Ryan said.

"That's too bad," Dagger said. "Because I'd sure love to be the one to scratch your ... itch."

"Are you drunk?" Ryan asked.

"Not drunk, but I've had a few," Dagger said.

"So, you 'drunk-dialed' me? Is that it?" Ryan asked.

A few moments passed and Dagger was quiet, but Ryan could hear him breathing; slow and rhythmic intakes of breath; which for some stupid reason Ryan found sexy. Ryan could almost picture him reclined with his eyes closed, contemplating his answer.

"I needed to hear your voice," Dagger finally said.

It wasn't what Ryan expected to hear coming from Dagger's mouth and the emotion behind the words were just as startling. Nonetheless, it could not be ignored.

"Dagger, are you okay?" Ryan asked.

"Yeah," he said. "Just lonely. I bet that sounds pretty crazy to hear from a guy that is surrounded by people on a near constant basis."

"Where are the guys from your band?"

"I was with them earlier," he said. "Got bored and came back to my bus to call you."

More silence fell between them, then Ryan spoke again.

"It sounds like you need a boyfriend," Ryan said, attempting a laugh that sounded more like a cough.

"I haven't had a real boyfriend in over a decade," Dagger said. "I've had my share of one night hook-ups or maybe as long as a weekend, but no one that would qualify as a boyfriend."

"That's too bad," Ryan said. "I think it'd be good for you."

Dagger made a humming sound. "I'd love to find someone to share my life with – my bed; my heart." His words were beginning to slur.

"Dagger? Maybe you should get some sleep," Ryan said.

Another long minute passed.

"Ry, I need to see you," Dagger said slowly. "Would you consider flying out to see me?"

Ryan's head was spinning from Dagger's request and all his words leading up to it. This felt like it was coming from left field, but maybe that's what they'd been dancing toward since the night they met. Who knew what was going on? Certainly not Ryan. The whole situation with Dagger was an adrenaline rush, as much as it scared the shit out of Ryan.

"That's probably not a good idea," Ryan said.

"I can send a plane; have a car pick you up at the airport," Dagger said. "How's that sound?"

"Dagger, I have a job. I can't just up and leave in the middle of a work week."

"I hadn't thought about that," Dagger said.

"When's the tour end?" Ryan asked.

"Not for a few more months, but eventually the tour brings me closer to Los Angeles. Maybe when I get near California you'll consider coming out to see me?"

"I'd have to give that some thought," Ryan said.

"Don't over-think it, Ry. It's a simple invitation," Dagger said. His voice was serious and steady. "We obviously enjoy talking to each other on the phone. It makes sense to me that we might try and spend more time face to face doing the same thing."

Is that *all* Dagger expected from him: entertaining conversation? If he were to visit Dagger, was there no intention of pushing him for more, perhaps something physical? Dagger was very serious when he asked for the visit. Maybe Ryan owed him to at least give the gesture some thought for what Dagger was implying it was: a friendly visit. Did Ryan want something more with Dagger? And what would *more* mean to each of them?

"I promise not to over-think it," Ryan said.

"Good," Dagger said and yawned. "Ry, will you talk to me for awhile – maybe till I fall asleep?"

"Or pass-out?" Ryan teased.

"I won't pass-out," Dagger said. "Are you at home alone again?"

"Eating take-out and sitting in front of the TV," Ryan said. "Me and my exciting life."

"Well, at least I didn't catch you with your cock in your hand again."

"I wasn't holding my cock, Dagger. You assumed that all on your own."

"I told you there's no shame in jerking off, Ry," Dagger laughed. "I did it this morning and I'll probably do it again after we hang up."

"Maybe that's because you're always talking about sex," Ryan said.

"Or maybe it's your voice," Dagger said.

"*My* voice? You're the one with the raspy singer voice."

"Do you think it's sexy?" Dagger asked.

Ryan swallowed hard. Truth was, he found everything about Dagger sexy – especially his voice. There was definitely something primal about the man and it was no surprise Dagger had the appeal he did with both men and women.

"It doesn't make you gay admitting that," Dagger said.

"I didn't say it did," Ryan said.

"You hesitated with your answer, so I assumed you were probably over-thinking again."

"Well, there is that," Ryan said.

"I have no problem admitting I find you hot," Dagger said.

"You've mentioned that before," Ryan said. "Along with numerous other comments and innuendos." Christ, he was starting to seriously overheat. Was the air conditioning in his apartment malfunctioning? He pulled at the collar of his dress shirt, then undid a few buttons, but it made no difference. The sweat was still beading on his forehead and nearly every other spot of his body. If Dagger kept this up, Ryan's clothing would be drenched with sweat by the time he got off the phone.

"Do my comments really bother you?" Dagger asked.

"No, not that much," Ryan said. "It's a little weird though."

"Weird, how?"

"You're the first guy that's ever talked to me like this," Ryan said.

"I'm certain there were others that wanted to," Dagger said in a soft voice.

"I have my doubts on that," Ryan said.

"I, on the other hand, can appreciate the beauty in both men and women," Dagger said.

"Of course you do," Ryan said. "You sleep with both sexes."

"You've never fooled around with a guy?" Dagger asked.

"Nope. Not once. Not even close."

"What about back in junior high?" Dagger asked. "You know, back when you were young, dumb and full of come."

Ryan hesitated, suddenly remembering something he hadn't thought about in many years. He was quiet until Dagger started laughing.

"I knew it!" Dagger said. "You experimented, didn't you?"

"I wouldn't really call it that," Ryan said.

"Let me be the judge," Dagger said. "Tell me what you did."

"I don't think it matters what I did that many years ago."

"Yeah, I think it kinda does," Dagger said.

"It doesn't change who I am now," Ryan said.

"What the hell did you do, Ry?" Dagger asked. "Did you play a little slap and tickle with one of your buddies?"

"We kissed – that's it, and it was a one time thing, never to be repeated," Ryan said.

"What kind of kiss?" Dagger pushed. "Was it a quick peck on the lips or was there tongue involved."

"Stop it!" Ryan said. "It doesn't matter."

"Oh, it definitely matters if there was tongue," Dagger said. "That makes it a *real* kiss."

"I'm not offering the details," Ryan said. "It was a kiss. Nothing more."

"That's okay, Ry. You not wanting to talk about it, tells me exactly what kind of a kiss it was and I'm also willing to bet you liked it, too – since you're unwilling to share the details. I have to say, I was hoping your *experiment* had gone further than just one kiss, like maybe a little circle jerk action or something."

Ryan laughed out loud. "Don't tell me you've done that!"

"I did all sorts of crazy shit," Dagger said. "Especially during that period of time when I was trying to figure out who I was and what I preferred."

"When did you know?" Ryan asked in a soft voice.

"This isn't part of your interview, is it?"

"The interview is done," Ryan said. "This is off the record."

"Friend to friend?"

"Yeah, something like that," Ryan said. He heard things rustling around on Dagger's end of the phone and assumed he was settling in and getting comfortable. Ryan figured he better do the same and stretched out his legs on the couch, since it looked like this was going to be another very long conversation with Dagger.

"I fooled around with a few girls in junior and senior high school and it was okay," Dagger said. "It was the usual finger-fucking hand-job sort of games. I had no clue what I was doing and it always felt a little awkward. In my freshman year of high school, I was flunking science. My teacher hooked me up with a geeky kid named Carl Speen. I'll never forget him," Dagger chuckled. "He asked me over to his house after school so he could tutor me and we went up to his bedroom. He's sitting beside me at this desk and I notice he had a boner that he's trying to adjust in his pants. So I'm staring at his lap and my dick starts to grow. Next thing I hear is Carl asking if I wanted to jerk off with him."

"He really said that?" Ryan asked.

"Yeah, he did," Dagger said. "He looks right at me and explains how he beat off every day after school and he wouldn't be able to concentrate unless he did. Then he got up and walked to the floor beside his bed and waved me over to join him. He sat down on the rug, leaned up against the bed and unzipped his pants, pulled out his cock and just started working on it. I stood there in shock. I'd never seen anyone do that, except myself, and he didn't seem embarrassed by it at all; like it was the most natural thing in the world to do in front of someone he barely knew."

"Dare I ask what you did next?" Ryan asked.

"I sat on the floor beside him and watched for a while. Eventually, my dick was so hard I had to relieve the pressure, so I pulled it out and we both sat there and jerked."

"And that's how you knew you were gay?" Ryan asked.

"Hell no! That was just good clean fun," Dagger teased. "Carl and I didn't do anything beyond the jerking sessions. His father got a job transfer and Carl ended up moving part way through the year. I never saw him after that. Then I met a kid in band class. His name was Billy. He was a stoner, like me, and we started hanging out, playing guitar together, and smoking a lot of weed. We'd sit in his tree fort and just get obliterated on the stuff, barely able to move. The smoke would be pouring out the windows and through the cracks in the floor boards of this fort. It was funny as hell. One day it was hot as an oven up there. I couldn't take the heat so I stripped down to my underwear to try and cool off. One thing led to another and I got the urge to jerk off. I guess in my stoned haze I thought I was with Carl and this was an okay thing to do. So I'm working on myself and Billy's watching me the whole time, never took his eyes off my hand movements. I have to say, knowing he was watching made me come all the faster. After that, I just started doing it in the fort all the time and eventually Billy did, too. Sometimes we'd steal porn magazines and stuff to jerk off to. I think I had an idea Billy was more like me than Carl was, but he waited for me to make the first move."

"I had a feeling this is where your story was headed," Ryan said.

"It was an accident," Dagger said.

"An accident? I doubt that."

"The day it happened, I think we'd smoked about a pound of weed. Somehow I managed to shoot come all over my underwear so I took them off, then tossed them at Billy. He got pissed, stripped off his tighty-whities and shot them at me. From there we started wrestling. Naked. I had him pinned to the floor on his back. Chest to chest. Cock to cock. It was at that point I realized he was as hard as I was, so I started moving my hips; sort of like dry humping, but we were both leaking so much it was hardly a dry hump."

Ryan couldn't believe the story Dagger was telling him. Nor could he believe how aroused he was from listening to it. He unzipped his pants and freed himself, allowing his cock to grow the final few inches to its full eight inches of glory. He stared at it, watching it pulse on his lower belly.

"Are you still there, Ry?"

"Yeah, yeah," he said. "I'm here. I was absorbing what you said."

Dagger laughed, a deep throaty sound that told Ryan he knew what the story was doing to him.

"Shall I continue?" Dagger asked.

"I think I know how it ends," Ryan said. He wanted to touch his cock, but he knew if he did he'd end up stroking it, and that would not be good with Dagger on the other end of the phone.

"It definitely led to a happy ending – for both of us," Dagger said. "After that day, anytime we hung out, we'd end up naked; which led to wrestling, and a happy ending. I'm guessing you've never experienced naked wrestling with one of your buddies?"

"Not quite," Ryan said. His hand had moved down to hip, so very close to his cock, he could feel the heat radiating from it. "I dry humped a few girl's though."

"Doesn't count," Dagger said. "Nothing like two hard cocks sliding back and forth against each other. Some of my best ... orgasms ever."

When had Dagger's voice become strained or was he imagining it? Ryan thought. Was Dagger already doing what Ryan was aching to do? Two of Ryan's fingers ran the long length of his shaft. He closed his eyes from the pleasure.

"Is that all you two did?" Ryan asked. Halfway through the question, his voice cracked but thankfully, Dagger didn't acknowledge it. Maybe he was too focused on his own task to notice. The thought of Dagger with his cock in hand while they talked, aroused Ryan even more.

"We started giving each other hand jobs and eventually we ended up sucking each other off," Dagger said, a soft moan escaping at the end of his thought. "That's when I knew I was hopelessly obsessed with dick and not pussy."

"I didn't get a blow job until I was eighteen," Ryan said. "You're a lucky man."

Ryan caved in to the need. His hand circled his shaft and started pulling off slow strokes. He could hear Dagger's breathing deepen. It was becoming more obvious what they were both doing and he was getting to the point of not caring if Dagger knew.

"Maybe you should have asked … a buddy," Dagger said.

"For a blow job?" Ryan asked. "Get serious."

"You'll never get it better."

Ryan could hardly hear Dagger's last comment. His fist worked faster on his cock, using the precome as a lubricant. His orgasm was so close. He twisted his hand, watching his cock squeezing through the tops of his fingers, and his balls lifted tight against him in warning. He wasn't going to last much longer.

Dagger made no attempt to hide his pleasure now. He was openly moaning, using heavy sighs and humming sounds, that managed to push Ryan even closer to exploding. The visuals he was creating of Dagger with his cock in hand was better than any porn he had seen.

"Holy, fuck! Ryannnn...," Dagger said, drawing out the last syllable of his name, like he was singing it.

That's all Ryan needed and he joined Dagger in one of the most intense orgasms he'd ever experienced. Soon as the last aftershock faded, Ryan wanted to crawl into a hole and die. He was too embarrassed to talk and thought of hanging up without saying another word.

"Ry? You still with me?"

"Yeah, I'm here," Ryan said.

"Don't over-think that," Dagger said.

"I ... I ah, have to go," Ryan said. A moment later, he hung up his phone and shut it off before Dagger had a chance to call him back.

CHAPTER FIVE

Ryan kept his dinner meeting with Sebastian. They left directly from work using Sebastian's car and drove to the outskirts of L.A. and parked behind a sport's bar called Sporty's. Ryan followed Sebastian inside. A quick scan of the large single room revealed about a dozen or so men. Most were alone, silently watching one of many flat screen televisions mounted around the wall space of the bar. A few men sat together at the tables and booths scattered around the darkened room. A few others perched on stools at the bar staring up at the television screens hanging above the bar. Only one man took notice of their arrival; giving both Ryan and Sebastian a lingering once over, then smiling warmly at them.

Ryan's stomach twisted, but still he walked behind Sebastian to a private booth in the corner of the room closest to the bathrooms. He slid in opposite Sebastian; his eyes making another nervous swipe of the room.

"You've never been here?" Sebastian asked.

Ryan shook his head and signaled the lone waiter taking drink orders. He ordered himself an imported beer and motioned to Sebastian to order something.

"I don't live far from here, so I'm in all the time," Sebastian said. "Sporty's is my home away from home."

"Are you originally from London?" Ryan asked. He pulled his cell phone out of his shirt pocket and set it on the table.

"A tiny village about two hours north east of London," Sebastian said. "Been here in L.A. about ten years now. How about you?"

"Suburb of Milwaukee," Ryan said. "We moved to California when I was about twelve."

Ryan's cell phone vibrated on the table. His eyes glanced down at the screen and read the text message coming through. It was from Dagger.

"R U avoiding me now?" Dagger's message read.

Ryan slid the phone further away from him and smiled at the waiter delivering their beers.

"Would you like menus?" the waiter asked.

"That sounds good," Sebastian said. "How about you, Ryan?"

"Yeah, I'll take a menu, please," Ryan said. He waited for the waiter to leave, then looked across the table at Sebastian. Powerful green eyes caught his blue and Ryan averted his eyes.

"You should know, I don't typically create a list of questions for an interview," Ryan said.

"Then how do you approach it?" Sebastian asked.

"I go into the meeting with an outline in my head and allow the conversation to lead the interview from there."

"Nothing more than a mental outline?" Sebastian asked.

Ryan shook his head. "I find anything too structured comes across being as such, and that doesn't translate very well in print." Ryan watched Sebastian scribble a few notes onto a small notepad and then his phone vibrated again. "You'll find musicians prefer to be exhibited in what they consider to be their natural environment. You'll also find that structure and musicians don't mix well at all."

"Come on, Ry! Talk to me," Dagger's next text message read.

The phone was slightly turned toward Sebastian, allowing him to read the printed message.

"Who's double D?" Sebastian asked. "A girlfriend with a pair of double D's?"

Ryan rolled his eyes. "Hardly. He's a friend," Ryan said. At that point he knew he should have shut the phone off to avoid further interruption, but he was waiting for a return call from Beth that he really didn't want to go to voice mail. Instead, he subtly covered the phone with his paper napkin and hoped to hell Dagger didn't continue to text message him.

The waiter returned to their table and Sebastian ordered the fish 'n' chips. Ryan went with the steak tips and a baked potato, then excused himself to use the men's room; forgetting his phone when he left the table. While Ryan was gone, Dagger sent him another text message. Sebastian lifted the napkin covering Ryan's phone and inched it closer; pressed a button and displayed the message.

"Damn it, Ry! We need to talk about this. Ignoring what happened doesn't make it any less real. Call me back, Dagger."

It was no secret at work that Ryan had landed the coveted interview with Dagger Drummond. It was partly the reason Sebastian had sought out Ryan to talk about honing his interviewing skills. But were these messages from *that* Dagger or was it a nickname for someone else? And what the hell had happened to make Ryan ignore the phone calls from double D? Sebastian pushed the phone back toward Ryan's side of the table when he saw Ryan returning from the bathroom.

"How'd your interview go with Dagger Drummond?" Sebastian asked.

The question felt awkward to Ryan, completely out of context to what they had been discussing prior to him leaving the table. Ryan's eyes dropped to the table and he saw his phone was no longer covered with the napkin. He reached for it and read the last incoming message.

"You read this?" Ryan asked.

"What happened?" Sebastian asked. "Why's he so intent on talking to you?"

Ryan shrugged and willed himself to keep the panic from his voice. "He's another nervous artist and wants to read my article before it prints."

Sebastian smiled and took a long swig from his beer bottle. The expression was smug and Ryan had a feeling his explanation hadn't been believable enough to satisfy Sebastian's over-active curiosity. Ryan drank from his beer bottle, not sure if he should give a shit what Sebastian thought or not. After all, he hardly knew this new intern so why did it matter?

"I was going to ask you out myself," Sebastian said. "You know, on a purely social level that doesn't involve work related stuff. But, if you've already got something going on with Dagger..."

"Where the fuck did that come from?" Ryan spit out.

Sebastian leaned across the wide wooden table. One side of his face lifted in a grin. "I got a vibe from you right away, Ryan," he said with a soft voice. "That's why I wanted to get to know you. I thought we might be a good fit."

Ryan's eyes narrowed on him. "I don't know what kind of *vibe* you got, but there is nothing about us that's ever going to fit."

"I like your word choice," Sebastian said with a chuckle.

Ryan stood up quickly and pulled his wallet from his back pocket. "I think this meeting is over," he said, and tossed a few bills onto the table to cover his tab. He grabbed his phone and left the bar.

When he got out on the sidewalk he hailed a taxi to take him back to his car parked in the lot behind his office building. Once he was in his own car and on the way home, he called Beth and left another message. He needed to talk to her more than ever now. If anyone could figure out what the hell was happening to him, it would be her. She had a special way of deciphering bullshit better than anyone he knew. And that's exactly what this felt like: bullshit.

Ryan was unlocking the door to his apartment when Beth finally called him back.

"I'm sorry Ry," she said. "I've been in and out of meetings for the last couple of days. What's going on with you? Did you have another man-dream?"

He ignored her last question and shut the door behind him. "Are you headed up this way any time soon?" he asked, then tossed his keys onto the kitchen table.

"Sounds serious," Beth said.

Ryan sat down in a recliner chair in the corner of his living room and sighed. "I need your perspective on something, that's all."

"Does this have anything to do with your wet dream?" she asked.

"First of all, that dream wasn't *wet*," he said.

"Do you want to talk about something now?" she asked. "I won't be up in L.A. until later on this week."

"I'm coming unglued, Beth."

"Don't tell me you think you're gay, just because you had one stupid dream?" she asked.

"I don't know what is is," Ryan said. "All I know is it's stressing me out, like you wouldn't believe."

"Hmmm, that's a pretty big topic, Ry. Maybe we should wait until I get up to L.A."

"All right," he said. "I can wait until you get here."

"Okay, I'll call you back when I know my flight times."

"I'll look forward to seeing you," he said and disconnected the call.

He left his phone on the coffee table and went into his bedroom, then undressed and stepped beneath the shower spray letting it pelt his body. His thoughts went back to Sebastian and his questions about the relationship he had with Dagger. There was no relationship, just a twisted late night chat fest between two lonely people. Right? And what the fuck was wrong with Sebastian? Why would he suspect there was anything between him and Dagger beyond professional? Jesus! Had the whole world gone mad? Exactly what kind of *vibe* was he putting out to make men like Sebastian – and Dagger, think hitting on him would be well received?

He stepped from the shower more tense than when he started. He was towel drying when he heard his cell ringing again. He ran into the living room and pressed the phone to his ear. Soon as he heard the baritone voice, he cursed himself for not checking the caller I.D. before answering.

"We need to talk," Dagger said.

Ryan felt his shoulders slump. He tied the towel at his waist and sat down on the couch. "I'm too tired to do this now, Dagger."

"You freaked out, Ry. Needlessly. It's not that big a deal."

"That's your opinion," Ryan said.

"What's going on with you?" Dagger said.

"That's a good question," Ryan said. "When I figure it out, I'll let you know."

"I doubt this will help, but I think I understand where your head is at."

"Doubtful," Ryan said.

"You're confused by things you're feeling," Dagger said, "Things you think you *shouldn't* be feeling."

Ryan held his breath. How was it possible Dagger would know what was keeping him up at night and distracting him so much during the day he could barely do his job? He felt lightheaded, unable to draw in a full breath.

"I'm right, aren't I?" Dagger asked.

"Dagger, you don't have a clue what I'm feeling," Ryan finally said.

"Hmmm, and I disagree."

"Why the fuck would you give a shit about what I'm feeling?"

There was a heavy pause from Dagger's end of the line. "Because I care that you're struggling with this."

"What are you talking about?" Ryan asked, his voice going soft.

"I need to see you, Ry," Dagger said. "You and I need to sit down and talk – face to face."

"That's not going to happen."

"I get why you're fighting this," Dagger said. "I do, and I know I can't force you to look at it, but I'm hopeful you'll decide to explore it all on your own."

"Dagger, I gotta go."

"Don't hang up, Ry!" Dagger said, but Ryan was already gone.

Ryan worked from home the next day; unwilling to face Sebastian, and to his surprise, Dagger hadn't attempted to contact him once. He did his best to convince himself that it was for the best. He needed to get this *thing* with Dagger back on a professional track. The less he allowed Dagger to be a part of his private life, the better. No more long, personal conversations – at any time of the day. From now on he'd keep their contact to business related text messages and that was it. There was no reason he needed to hear the man's voice, because it had been established doing so did strange, fucked up things to his brain. It was almost like Dagger had some sort of power over him and he didn't like it. It made his thoughts drift into places he had no interest in going. Ever. And especially with the likes of Dagger Drummond.

Ryan sat in front of his laptop all day. It took hours of fine-tuning, but he finally completed the article on Dagger. He double checked his notes and all his research facts and did a final read-through, then saved the file. He'd email the file to his editor in the morning for approval. He ran his fingers through his hair and tipped back in his swivel chair. A smile relaxed his face. He was confident the article would please his editor, the readers, and also Dagger.

Dagger.

Ryan said the name out loud and growled in irritation. He'd promised to send a copy of the finished piece to Dagger before it went to print. Maybe it'd be best if he used this as an opportunity to make that their last contact? He could email the article to Dagger and be done with it ... whatever the hell *it* was, and get on with his life. That would work, right? The interview was over and the article was done. There was no reason beyond that for them to stay in contact. Dagger had plenty of friends and Ryan did, too. Certainly, neither of them needed to be a part in the other's life. Right?

Oh, who the hell was he kidding? Ryan thought, and tossed a ballpoint pen across the room.

At dinner time, Beth called and let Ryan know she'd be in town late the next afternoon. He agreed to pick her up at the airport and hung up; wondering if he'd be able to wait that long. The final touch for Ryan was to make dinner reservations at Beth's favorite diner called: Sidecar; a retro fifties-themed diner that served breakfast all day and for some reason Beth adored the dated decor. Ryan made it a point to share a meal with her there whenever she was in town. It felt like a date, he thought, which was something he desperately needed with a woman – even if it was with his ex.

Ryan went to work the next day and walked straight into his office; shutting the door. He hadn't even sat down before Sebastian knocked and opened the door before Ryan had a chance to say anything.

"Hey, I'm sorry about the other night," Sebastian said. "I thought you might be interested in dating but I guess I misread the *radar*."

"Forget about it," Ryan said, and sat down in his leather chair. He opened up a file and spread the papers over the top of his desk, then he realized Sebastian was still standing in the doorway.

"I didn't mean any disrespect," Sebastian said.

"I understand," Ryan said. "But, now you know, so we're cool."

Sebastian nodded and started to leave, then stopped. "Did you manage to work things out with Dagger?"

Was this guy serious? Ryan thought. He vigorously rubbed at his face, then met Sebastian's gaze. "Leave it alone, Sebastian."

"Well, if you ever want to talk about it..."

"There's nothing to talk about," Ryan said; cutting him off mid-sentence.

Sebastian nodded again and stepped into the hall, shutting the door to Ryan's office behind him.

Ryan glanced at his wall clock. It wasn't even nine o'clock and he was ready to go home. He turned on his computer and glanced out the double windows occupying one wall. His office wasn't very big and on days like this, it felt smaller than a closet with air just as stuffy to breathe. But at least it was an office with real walls and a door with his name on it and not a cubicle like many of the reporters had in the department. This was probably the only perk he had earned in the eight years he'd had the job.

Ryan looked around the ten by twelve foot room. He took note of the dying Christmas cactus sitting on the window sill and promised to give it a drink of water before he left for the day. The file cabinet was ajar and needed to be neatened up a bit, as did his desk. His desk was the worst of the mess but he didn't feel like cleaning it. He didn't feel like doing much of anything.

His fingers rubbed at his temples. He desperately needed to get his life on track again and headed straight back to vanilla-town. *Straight?* Interesting word choice, he thought, when everyone around him seemed to think he was gay – or at the very least: curiously bi. He started thinking about the conversations he'd had with Dagger over the last few days and remembered discussing his kiss with a childhood friend. It had been the first kiss of his life and it hadn't been with a girl – it was with a boy.

The kid's name was Tommy something, Ryan thought, trying to remember the last name. Singer. That was it. Tommy Singer. Jesus! That was a long time ago. He was fourteen at the time, he thought. Maybe thirteen. He wasn't exactly sure. It was the Summer before freshman year and he and Tommy, a neighborhood kid, were inseparable. Not a day went by where they didn't see each other. They rode their bikes everywhere, mostly just the two of them, but sometimes other kids came along, too. They hiked endlessly through the woods behind both their houses, fished in the town reservoir – even though they knew it was illegal, and sometimes played baseball with the older kids in the neighborhood. And they talked for hours and hours about their dreams for the future.

"I want to be a journalist," Ryan had said. *"Maybe for CNN or something cool like that."* Even at that young age, Ryan had realized his passion for writing and saw it as a gift.

"Good luck with that," Tommy had said. *"I'm gonna stay right here and teach something and maybe coach a team sport. I don't know what, yet, but it'll be just as cool as CNN."*

Christ, they had been so young and stupid back then, Ryan thought. Looking at it now, Ryan was starting to see a new truth about his friendship with Tommy emerging through that haze of youth, a truth Ryan was pretty sure Tommy already understood back then, even though Ryan was too blind or ignorant to see it.

Tommy was gay and had a full-blown crush on Ryan.

Why hadn't I seen that? Ryan asked himself. He spun around in his office chair and faced the windows looking out across the city skyline. He pulled his hands through his hair and squeezed his eyes shut. Suddenly, so many things in his adult life were sliding into place and becoming focused.

Ryan massaged his scalp. Remembering that summer now as an adult, Ryan could see so many clues he'd missed back then as a young teenager. The many times he'd caught Tommy staring at him for no reason, the almost possessive way he insisted he be close to Ryan – no matter where they were.

Tommy had started to bulk up with muscle that summer, too, and Ryan had found himself noticing it. Ryan's own physique at that age was still on the scrawny side, with very little body hair. Tommy had already developed an interesting thin line of dark hair leading from his belly button down to his groin and had patches under both arms. Ryan had seen that line of hair on display many times, when Tommy was in his underwear, swimsuit, or shirtless in his jeans. Ryan also remembered the fascination he had with it, wondering if that line led to a bigger area of pubic hair around Tommy's cock.

Then, Ryan remembered when things started changing with Tommy during that hot August. Tommy had become clingy, wanting Ryan to sleep over his house sometimes during the week – in addition to the occasional weekend night. And

Tommy was always needing to sit a little too close to him; whether on the couch, the floor, or outside, and Ryan remembered wanting to put more space between them. It was toward the end of that month that Tommy's crush took a turn.

And then there was that kiss.

Their first day of high school was still two weeks away and Tommy suggested Ryan join him for a bike ride to Benson's field. This was a favorite spot for them, offering views of the nearby rolling farm fields and privacy to hide them when they wanted to sneak a cigarette. Inhaling was a task they hoped to master before starting school and Benson's field was the perfect location to smoke, not get caught doing it, and cough your head off – if need be.

Benson's field was on the outskirts of town. It bordered other farms, with boundary lines distinguished by stone walls or groves of trees. The part of the field Ryan and Tommy liked best was the unused, lower sloping portion. This section was bordered on three sides with trees and had been unmaintained for years. Tall grass with random outcroppings of rocks now occupied it. About a third of the way up the slope was an enormous maple tree. The tree stood proudly alone on the slope, surrounded by nothing but the knee-high, swaying grass all around the massive trunk. It must have been over a hundred years old, with thick limbs that offered shade beneath its leaves and on a hot day like today, the shade was a welcome sight.

Ryan followed on this ten-speed bike behind Tommy. They peddled quickly over the familiar dirt pathway traversing the slope toward the tree, then laid their bicycles down on the visible tree roots bubbling up from the ground around the trunk.

Ryan collapsed in the tall grass with a loud sigh, then pulled himself to rest up against the tree trunk. Tommy scanned the field first, before sitting down beside Ryan. Once again, Tommy sat a little too close and Ryan gave him a playful push on the shoulder to try and create more space between them, but it didn't work. Tommy remained in the same spot.

"Have you seen the new girls that moved in over on Clover Street?" Ryan asked Tommy.

"Yeah," Tommy said. "They look like sisters and they're old." Tommy slid a long piece of grass between his lips pretending it was a cigarette.

"Old? What makes you say that?" Ryan asked. "Besides, why would age matter? They're cute and the short one has big tits."

Tommy shrugged. "Whatever," he said. "I think they're too old."

"I think you're being picky," Ryan said. "With that attitude, you're likely to be a virgin when you get to college."

Tommy turned toward Ryan and that weird expression floated across his tanned face. Ryan had seen this transformation take place several times over the last couple of weeks. Each time he saw the look appear on Tommy's face, a knot twisted Ryan's stomach and every one of his senses became heightened. Usually, Ryan would back away as soon as he saw this expression on Tommy. For some reason today, with their shoulders almost touching, he stayed put. He saw Tommy lick his lips and Ryan felt his breathing deepen.

"How old do you think they are?" Ryan managed to say.

"Who?" Tommy asked. He tugged the piece of straw from the corner of his mouth and tossed it aside.

"The new girls," Ryan said.

"Dunno. Don't care."

Tommy leaned closer, pressing the meat of his shoulder into Ryan's. His pale blue eyes continued to hold Ryan's gaze. Ryan watched the color in Tommy's eyes darken and the pupils dilate. He saw Tommy shift another inch toward him, leaving no space between them. Ryan knew he should move away, but something held him cemented to that space – that very close, heated, sliver of space separating his mouth from Tommy's. It certainly couldn't be much more than a few inches, Ryan thought. One flinch on either of their parts and their lips would connect. Is that what he wanted, Ryan thought? Did he really want to feel the press of Tommy's lips against his?

Ryan blinked once, then his eyes widened, when his brain registered the answer: yes. He *did* want this and he could already feel his cock flexing inside his shorts.

Tommy's move was quick; his lips hitting Ryan's a little too hard. Ryan felt himself jump at the sudden contact, but he didn't push him away. As Ryan's body relaxed to the touch, Tommy's lips softened against Ryan's; rubbing small, slow circles against their plumpness. Ryan kept his lips pressed together. He shouldn't be allowing this to happen and Tommy had to know it wasn't cool to be kissing your best friend. So, why did it feel good?

Tommy kept a gentle pressure against Ryan, his lips parted slightly; the tip of his tongue flicking against the seam of Ryan's closed mouth. The new touch turned into a soft stroke of tongue against lips and Ryan felt himself open for

Tommy; allowing Tommy's tongue to slip between them. A sensation Ryan had never experienced exploded inside his head, causing him to moan. The taste of cherry jelly-beans and a hint of earthy grass met his taste buds and Ryan was swept away in it.

Tommy opened his mouth further, capturing Ryan's moan of pleasure in his throat and fully covered Ryan's mouth. His tongue delved deeper, stroking along the side of Ryan's, then curling over the top and flicking it at the tip. Ryan sighed and Tommy slipped his hand around the back of Ryan's neck; giving their kiss a tighter connection.

Ryan slumped against the tree and Tommy followed, resting with Ryan against the bark. He pressed his chest to Ryan's; their mouths still fused together, tongues continuing to explore. This kiss seemed endless; a rising tide of new sensations flooding through both of them. Tommy sucked on Ryan's tongue, gentle tugs that had Ryan coming unglued. The sensual energy Tommy offered, Ryan gave right back to him, and the kiss deepened further.

Minutes passed, too many to count, and Ryan thought he'd come in his pants from nothing more than this kiss from Tommy. A kiss he wasn't sure he wanted to ever stop. Ryan's fingers curled around Tommy's neck; slick now with sweat, and squeezed the muscles. If Tommy had pushed him down onto the grass and climbed on top of him at that moment, he would have let him. He was that lost in this kiss.

It was Tommy that finally broke the seal. He pressed his dampened forehead to Ryan's. His hot, panting breaths washing over Ryan's face.

"Wow," was all Tommy could manage to say, as he continued to try and catch his breath. Then, a heartbeat later, he rose to his knees and turned away from Ryan as he stood. "I have to take a piss," he said.

Ryan watched Tommy walk through the tall grass and wiped the moisture from his lips. Tommy stopped about forty feet away with his backside facing Ryan and unzipped his shorts. The motion of pulling his cock from between the flaps of material had Tommy's body turning slightly, giving Ryan a slight side view. Ryan's gaze was fixed on Tommy. He expected to see a stream of urine arc out from Tommy's groin but didn't. Instead he saw the jerking movements of Tommy's fist around an erection; three short strokes at the tip followed by one long stroke all the way to the base, then back up to the tip.

Ryan was quite familiar with the action. He had been doing it to himself for a couple of years. But, he was shocked to see Tommy doing it such a short distance away in full view of him and in the middle of the day. It wasn't like anyone could see Tommy – except for Ryan, but still, Ryan had never seen anyone masturbate like this in public. He also couldn't deny how turned-on he was at that moment. Between their long kiss and now seeing Tommy pleasuring himself, it was an overload of stimulation for Ryan.

Ryan tipped his head back on the trunk and looked up at the intricate crisscross pattern of tree branches overhead and the glimmers of sunshine piercing through the spaces between the leaves. He didn't think he could stay and face Tommy when he returned to the tree, knowing Tommy had just masturbated. What would Tommy have to say? Would Tommy want to kiss him again?

Ryan lifted his head off the tree trunk in time to see Tommy ejaculating into the grass. Before Tommy could get himself tucked back into his shorts, Ryan had straddled the seat of his bike and was preparing to leave.

"Hey, Ry!" Tommy hollered to him. "Where you going?"

"I got stuff to do," Ryan said, and started peddling his bike down the path.

Ryan took the long way home, knowing that would be the first place Tommy would look for him. He hoped by the time he did get home, Tommy would have given up and left. Ryan peddled a good two miles out of his way and it was nearly dinner time when he finally turned into his driveway. Luckily, he was home before either of his parents. He jumped off his bike at the entrance of the open garage and pushed it inside to lean against the wall next to another bike. When he turned around Tommy was standing inside the garage. Ryan flinched at the sight of him.

"Why'd you run away?" Tommy asked, stepping closer.

"I told you, I had some shit to do," Ryan lied. He spun to leave the garage through a side door and Tommy grabbed him by the arm.

"Are you mad at me?" Tommy asked.

Ryan shook his head and looked toward the street, making sure no one could see them. "I'm not mad, Tom, but you really shouldn't have done that."

Ryan tried to pull away from Tommy's hold, but Tommy moved with him. "It wasn't just me, you know," Tommy said. "You were kissing me, too."

"Shhhhh! Don't fucking say that," Ryan said, lowering his voice.

"You gonna deny it?" Tommy asked.

"I don't want to talk about it," Ryan said.

Ryan tugged hard and escaped the hold Tommy had on him, but Tommy reached for Ryan again, this time pushing him up against the garage wall making the coffee cans his father filled with nails rattle on a shelf above their heads. Tommy used his body to pin Ryan beneath him. They were close enough for Ryan to feel the heat of Tommy's breath on his face and the hardness of Tommy's growing erection pressing into his hip.

"You liked it," Tommy whispered. "I know you did."

Ryan dug his fingers into Tommy's chest and pushed. "Tommy, listen to me," he said, trying to make eye contact with him. "I'm not gay. I don't know what happened or why it happened. All I know is that it *shouldn't* have happened and it can't happen again. Do you hear me? It *can't* happen again." Ryan gave a final shove at Tommy and sent him stumbling backward.

"You liked it," Tommy said. "You liked it as much as I did, and now you're gonna pretend it didn't happen?"

Ryan held Tommy's gaze, noticing the pained look in his eyes, and he nodded. "Yeah, I am." Ryan started to walk from the garage and stopped, glancing over his shoulder at Tommy. "Look, I don't think we can be friends anymore."

The very next weekend, Ryan attended an 'End of Summer' house party and hooked-up with a girl named Dana. Although their kisses weren't as arousing as Tommy's, Ryan knew this was the right path for him. Besides, Dana let him touch her boobs. Case closed, as far as Ryan was concerned.

A week later school started and Tommy gravitated to a new bunch of friends; a few Ryan suspected were gay, just like Tommy, and Ryan began to work through a quick succession of girlfriends none of them lasting more than a few months time – and not a single one of them could kiss him like Tommy. That was a fact Ryan had no intention of sharing with anyone. Ever.

Ryan sighed loudly at his desk and rubbed his face. His office was suffocating him; eating him alive. He hated reliving that memory of Tommy, hated the way he had treated Tommy, and there wasn't shit he could do about it now. Seventeen years later, it seemed Tommy was finally having his revenge and Ryan was once again struggling with a feeling inside him that didn't make a damn bit of sense. Yet, somehow it made all the sense in the world.

Ryan remembered the last time he had seen Tommy. It was at an after-graduation party in a meadow behind their high school football field. A live band played on a handmade stage and the beer was plentiful. Ryan had consumed his fair share of beer and had wandered away from the noise of the band to find a quiet place to take a piss. He found privacy behind a large tree and began urinating against the trunk. He heard footsteps coming up behind him and glanced over his shoulder to see who it was.

Tommy came into view and stood a few feet away from Ryan and nodded at him. He unzipped his pants in full view of Ryan and aimed his stream of urine at the same spot Ryan was hitting, then looked up at Ryan's stunned face.

"Great location for a party," Tommy said. "Reminds me of Benson's field. You remember that spot, don't you, Ry? It was one of our favorites."

Ryan stood in shocked silence. No words connected his brain with his tongue. He finished urinating and quickly tucked himself back into his jeans. Tommy did the same, then came up along side Ryan – close; too close, and squeezed Ryan's shoulder.

"I heard you got into Stanford," Tommy said toward Ryan's ear. "Good luck with that."

A moment later, Tommy disappeared into the darkness and Ryan exhaled the breath he was holding and that was that. The end of an era on a level that far exceeded them leaving high school. Ryan wasn't sure what to call it, but he felt real pain watching Tommy walk away that night and wondered if their paths would ever cross again.

Almost two decades later, Ryan was feeling new pain for never taking a moments time to think of Tommy before now. He wondered what had happened to his old friend, wondered if life had been kind to him. Then he tried to imagine if Tommy was happily in a relationship with a man or if he was muddling through life trying to find himself as Ryan felt he was doing now.

Fuck!

Funny how fate had a way of kicking you in the ass, Ryan thought. He spun his chair around to face his desk and the computer resting on top of it. He needed to wrap his head around work again. He'd sort through the mud bowl that had become his life later.

He clicked a few buttons on the keyboard and opened up his email account, then began deleting the spam mail that continuously clogged it. There was no way he could respond to hundreds of emails in one day. He saved the few that seemed relevant and trashed the rest. Then he emailed the Dagger Drummond article to his editor and created a second email to send the article to Dagger.

Ryan thought about adding a short, personal note for Dagger in his email, then changed his mind. He merely attached the article he written and that was it. He hit the send button before he could change his mind and sat back in his chair with a sense of relief. It was done. Maybe it was better to close that chapter before it had a chance to get started and move forward – just like he'd moved forward after Tommy. Wasn't it easier to walk away from a situation that made you uncomfortable than stick around and face it?

Christ! He sounded like a chick trying to dump her boyfriend, he thought. Except he wasn't a chick. He was a man attempting to end a friendship with another man for no other reason beyond the fact this man made him feel uncomfortable – exactly as he had done with Tommy. What the fuck was his problem?

Ryan looked down at the open file on his desk. He needed to switch his focus to his next project: his interview with Zander Metcalf and Ivory Tower. He had three days to prepare for it and get all his background research done. Nothing better than the daunting task of research to distract yourself from something your mind refused to let you forget.

The office phone on his desk rang just before lunch. He lifted it to his ear and said his name.

"You sound so professional," Dagger said.

Ryan spun his chair away from the door in his office, almost as if he felt the need to hide the fact he was on the phone.

"Since when do you call me on this line?" Ryan asked.

"You no longer take my calls on your cell phone, so I was left to this method of reaching you."

"What can I do for you?" Ryan asked.

"The article," Dagger said. "You really pulled it off, Ry. Made me sound almost human."

"I'm glad you liked it."

"I loved it," Dagger said. "And, it means a lot you kept your word."

Dagger's voice was already working its magic on Ryan. His heart was pounding heavily beneath his ribs and a thin sheen of sweat was gathering on his forehead. "It served no purpose to disclose your private life in an article based on your music."

"A lesser man would have used that secret to launch his career; never giving any thought to how exposure like that might effect my life," Dagger said.

"I'm not like most men," Ryan said.

"I know," Dagger said. "And I thank you for that."

"You're welcome."

"Come visit me," Dagger said on a sigh. "Let me take you to dinner and properly thank you."

"You know I can't do that," Ryan said.

"But, you want to, don't you?"

Ryan pressed his thumb and index finger into his eye sockets. Why didn't anything in his head make sense to him these days? Why did he always question himself when he was talking to Dagger? What was it about *this* man that got to him? Or, maybe it wasn't just Dagger that got to him, but *all* men, and somehow he'd managed to keep that buried inside himself until Dagger brought it to the surface – just like Dagger had suggested was the case.

Damn it!

"Will you at least think about it?" Dagger asked. When Ryan didn't answer, Dagger asked again. "Please, Ry. Consider my invitation. No strings. I swear. No expectations or hidden agendas; just us hanging out. Is that so terrible?"

"I'll think about it," Ryan finally said. "But, no promises."

"Thank you," Dagger said. His voice was thick with relief.

"Talk to you later," Ryan said and hung up the phone.

He sighed loudly and cursed. His life was changing faster than Ryan could possibly keep up with, and there was no slowdown in sight.

CHAPTER SIX

By the time Beth appeared by the baggage claim carousel, Ryan was jumping out of his skin. He was beginning to think she wasn't on the plane. Soon as he could reach her, he pulled her to his chest and sighed her name in her ear, rocking her gently back and forth.

"So good to see you," he said.

"Thanks for meeting me here at the airport," Beth said, rubbing Ryan's back.

"I'm the one that should be thanking you," Ryan said.

He stepped back and did his best to absorb the fact she was really here, standing in front of him. Her long auburn hair was pulled into a ponytail, exposing the slender column of her throat. His eyes dropped lower. Her button-down blouse revealed the slightest hint of the deep cleavage he remembered.

"You look tired, Ryan," Beth said, accepting the hand he held out for her to take.

"Thank you for noticing," he replied, with a roll of his eyes.

Ryan led her through the throng of people at LAX, outside, and back to his car as quickly as he could. They shut the car doors and the silence blanketed them. Beth turned to him. A brilliant smile making her luminescent blue eyes sparkle.

"Okay. Start spilling," she said.

"Not here," he said. "I need to concentrate on getting us out of the airport. When we get to the diner, we can talk there."

"The diner? You're taking me to Sidecar for dinner?"

Ryan smiled at her. "Of course. Isn't that our *thing*?"

The smile never left his face for the entire trip to the restaurant. Listening to Beth chat endlessly about her new life made the drive through the heavy traffic seem almost stress-free. Before he was ready, they were sitting at the small booth they always occupied at the front window of the diner. The same cracked vinyl bench seats scratched the backs of their thighs as they slid in to face each other. Not one thing had changed about the experience at the diner, except for them.

Beth reached across the Formica table top and took his hands. "Talk to me, Ryan. You haven't said one word yet about what's bothering you."

"I like listening to you," he said. He rubbed his thumbs over the back of her hands.

"What's got you so troubled?"

"Life," he exhaled. "It's really fucked up."

"Is it work that's got you down? A woman?"

Ryan forced a laugh and glanced around the diner at the other patrons. Many were couples looking like they were on causal dates, while others were businessmen probably getting a quick bite to eat before heading home from their jobs.

"Work is fine and it's not a woman," Ryan said.

"It's okay if it is, Ry. I don't mind talking to you about another woman. I want you to move on and find someone that makes you happy."

"Like you did," he said.

"Yes, like I did."

Ryan looked out the window and watched the cars stopped at a red light in front of the diner. "Why didn't we work, Beth? I've been thinking about that a lot lately."

She tipped her head to him. "We've been over that," she said. "I thought you understood the reasons. You agreed separating was the *right* thing to do."

"I know, I know," he said. "And I get it. I do, but I miss *us*."

"Me too," she said. "But you'll always be my best friend. Always."

He held her gaze, willing the answers to his problems to appear in the depths of her eyes. Beth tugged on his hands, urging him to speak and he looked away.

"I had a business meeting the other night with a new intern from my department," Ryan said. "He wanted to pick my brain about interview skills."

"I know you hate that sort of thing," Beth said. "So, I'm guessing this guy pissed you off."

Ryan nodded. "Big time."

Their conversation was interrupted by the waitress. They gave the woman their orders of two black coffees, a plate of scrambled eggs and toast for Ryan and Belgian waffles with strawberries for Beth.

Beth waited until they were alone again, then prompted Ryan to continue talking with a gentle kick under the table to his shin.

"Go on," she said.

Ryan ran his hands along the length of his thighs. "Part way into this meeting, the guy started hitting on me." He nearly choked on the words, then sat back in the seat. He watched Beth's face waiting for a response. Finally she smiled at him.

"You think that's funny?" Ryan asked.

"You're a very good looking man," she said. "It doesn't surprise me another man would find you attractive."

"It's never happened to me before," he said. "Not once in my entire adult life, so why now – and why suddenly by two different guys?"

"Wait a minute. You said the intern hit on you. Who's the second guy?"

"I can't say," Ryan said softly.

"Why not?"

"Because... I can't."

"Ryan, you can tell me anything and you know it goes no further. After all this time, you should know better than to think I'd repeat something you said to me."

"This is different," Ryan said.

"How so?" Beth asked. "Is it different because you had that dirty dream about a guy?"

"It's different because it's fucking me up," he said. "That's why."

"Do you like this intern?" Beth asked.

"Hell no! He's too..."

"Too, what?"

Ryan rubbed his face; exhaling loudly. Her questions were annoying him, yet he knew she was sitting across from him because he had asked her to and for no other reason. She was already seeing through the bullshit, just as he knew she would.

"Ryan, don't you dare check out of this conversation," she said. "You wanted to talk, so talk."

"I'm not *gay*." He said the last word like it was a curse rolling off his tongue.

"I didn't say you were," she said. "And simply being attracted to a man doesn't make you gay."

"I'm not *attracted* to the intern."

"What about the other guy? Are you attracted to him?"

He wanted to bolt, push himself away from the damned booth and run; never stopping until he ran the entire ten miles back to his apartment. Maybe then exhaustion would make him sleep to forget he was having this particular conversation. Sweat was pouring from every pore in his body. He wiped his brow and kept his eyes anywhere but on Beth.

Finally, Beth leaned closer to the table and lowered her voice. "Look, Ry. I can tell talking about this makes you very uncomfortable, but there's no need for you to feel that way. It's not unusual for people to have random attractions to someone of the same sex."

"You're telling me you have?" he asked.

Beth nodded her head. "A few months after we broke up, I had sort of a... fling with a female co-worker. We were away on business, had a little too much to drink with dinner, and it just happened." Beth cleared her throat, cutting off a laugh. "And, then there was this one time with Jake. He wanted to do a three-way, and I had never done one, so I figured: why not?"

"Are you fucking kidding me?" Ryan asked. He wasn't sure if he was more shocked, pissed off, or jealous from Beth's stories. "How is it, you seem to have lived three lifetimes in the year since we broke up while I've been stuck treading water?"

"First of all, it's been closer to two years and you not dating is your own choice," she said.

Ryan shook his head. "I can't believe you had a threesome!"

"Never mind that," Beth said. "Tell me about the guy."

He looked at her, opened his mouth, then shut it. A long silence hung between them; awkward and bordering on tense.

"It's more than just that guy," Ryan said. "I also recently remembered something that happened back when I was in my early teens. Putting it all together, it's freaking me out."

Beth nodded her head stiffly. "You said you're not gay, but do you think you might be bi?"

"I don't know," Ryan said. "Possibly. Fuck! I can't believe I just said that – out loud."

Beth lowered her head. "Wow," she said softly. "The dream I could easily shrug off, but now you say there's an attraction to a man and something happened in your past. What the hell, Ry? Do you think maybe that's why our sex life was less than..."

"Beth, don't say that. Please. This has nothing to do with you or how we were together."

"What happened when you were younger?" she asked.

"My best friend," Ryan said. "We kissed – but that's it."

Beth's eyes began to fill with tears and she looked toward the kitchen. "Did you like it?"

"Does it matter?"

"Yeah, it matters a lot," Beth said.

Ryan glanced around at the busy diner. "Honestly, I hadn't thought about it in seventeen years until a few days ago."

"Why do you think you thought of it now?" Beth asked.

Ryan shifted on the bench seat. "The other day I had a conversation with … that guy. He asked if I'd ever experimented. I said no at first, then I remembered that one time with Tommy."

"Tommy was your friend?"

"Yeah, best friend. We hung out for a couple of years, until … he kissed me. After that, I figured things would be too weird for us to see each other, so I ended the friendship." Ryan looked across the table at Beth and saw the emotion in her eyes. "Beth? Why are you getting upset?" he asked.

Beth wiped at the corner of her eyes. "Everything you're telling me makes me realize why things couldn't have ever worked for us. It makes me even more certain I made the right decision when I walked away from you and that makes me sad. It makes me wonder if… Never mind."

Ryan could feel tears biting at his eyes. "Say it, Beth. It makes you wonder what?"

"This hurts, Ry," she whispered. "But, there were times when we were together I thought you might be bi or at least bi-curious."

Ryan shook his head sharply. "No way, Beth. I was not feeling this back then."

"I'm sure you weren't conscious of feeling it, but I think it was probably there, only buried."

"I wish I could articulate how fucked up my head has been these last few weeks," Ryan said. "It feels like I've been walking around in a fog. I can't sleep and nothing makes sense anymore. Things I thought I knew about myself no longer seem real and I'm at a loss as to what I should do about that."

"Stop it, Ryan," Beth said in a terse voice. "I think you already know what you want to do, and you're just looking for me to high-five you or something. You don't need my permission to go after this guy! Maybe me leaving you has set you free in more than one way?"

"I'm pouring my heart out here, sharing something so personal to me it makes me want to vomit, and you're pissed off? Ryan stood up from the table. "Maybe talking to you about this was a mistake."

Beth grabbed him by the wrist. "Ryan. Please, sit down," she said. She waited a minute and when he didn't move she tugged on his arm. "I'm not mad. I'm hurt. There's a big difference." She tipped her head and twisted her hands in her lap. "I'm hurt because it makes me feel like all the time we were together was a lie – like I was wasting my time thinking I could have a happily-ever-after with you, when that was never possible."

Ryan reached for her and she offered him her hand to hold. "Beth, my love for you was – and still is very real, and our time together was *not* a lie." He shook his head and sighed. "I can't explain what's happening to me right now, but I don't think I can ignore it anymore, either. It's consuming me and I need to settle it – one way or another." He paused for a moment, then pulled her hand to his mouth to kiss her knuckles. "I'm so sorry, babe. I've been so fucked in the head over this, I never considered how this might effect you."

Beth blinked and sent a trickle of tears down her cheeks. "It's okay, Ry."

"Pretty twisted, isn't it?" he said, trying to laugh.

"I wouldn't call it twisted," she said. "You're obviously conflicted about what you're feeling for this guy. Throw it all out on the table and let's see if we can sort through it. Together."

He slumped in the booth. How had his life turned in this direction? Why had he let such a perfect woman leave him? She was living life to its fullest and it pained him to think of what he was doing with his. Nothing.

"So, you like him?" Beth asked.

Ryan nodded, unwilling to name names. It didn't seem fair to Dagger to do that, especially since the man had no clue what he meant to Ryan.

"We talk a lot on the phone," Ryan said. "But, that's about it."

"Do you want more?" she asked.

"More?"

"Yeah, you know, spend more time together and maybe move on to something physical," Beth said.

"Shit, this is so fucked up," he said.

"That doesn't answer my question."

A long moment passed and finally Ryan responded. "I honestly don't know. Maybe," he said in a voice so soft he wasn't sure she'd heard it. Shock registered on his face. *Had he just admitted that out loud – and to Beth?*

"Do you think he'd like there to be more?" Beth asked.

"He's gay, but nobody knows it," Ryan said. "And he's made it abundantly clear he'd like there to be ... more with me. He's asked me to come visit him – twice."

"He doesn't live around here?"

"He's on tour," Ryan made the comment and froze. "I didn't mean to say that."

"Is this someone in the music business?" Beth asked.

"I can't say who it is, Beth. Please. I promised him I wouldn't."

"Okay, so he's gay, and you're... curious. Why *not* visit him? It would give you an opportunity to explore these feelings and see if you really are interested in something more."

"You're forgetting the fact I'm not into dudes," Ryan said.

"Maybe not *all* dudes, Ryan, but you're obviously into *this* particular dude."

When Ryan saw the waitress returning to their table with plates, he let an audible sigh of relief leave his mouth. The steaming food now had Ryan's full attention. He sprinkled salt and pepper over his eggs and grabbed his fork to start eating. The fact that Beth sat staring at him and not eating caused him to set his fork down beside his plate. His eyes slowly lifted to hers.

"Are we talking about the guy from your dream?" she asked.

"Yes, same guy," Ryan said.

Beth was quiet for a moment, then looked at him. "Besides the fact I feel like I held you back on some subconscious level, you know I'd never judge anything you did or attempted to do with this guy, right? Don't put a damned label on it, Ry, and for God's sake, stop over-thinking it. If you want to go see him on tour, then go! You've got to follow it through or you'll live with the regret you didn't. Is that what you want?"

"Pretty messed up, isn't it?" Ryan asked.

"Sometimes it's not our choice where we find our happiness," Beth said. "Does talking with this guy make you happy? Does the idea of spending more time with him appeal to you?"

Ryan lowered his head and stared at his food until his vision blurred. "Yeah, I think I'd like to spend more time with him."

"Then, do it," she said, and lifted her fork to eat, satisfied she had solved Ryan's problem. "And next time I visit, I want a full report on you and this mystery man."

"You know it's weird I can talk to you about shit like this," he said.

"We're best friends, Ry. That's what we do," she said. "I'll always be here for you."

"And I for you," he said, reaching across the table for her hand and squeezing it.

After dinner Ryan brought Beth to the Radisson hotel downtown and pulled against the curb in front. A bellman came out to greet them.

"Are you sure you'd rather stay here than with me at my place?" he asked.

"You're not gonna want to drive me back across town for my seven o'clock meeting in the morning," she said. "But, it's nice of you to offer."

"Business is good?"

"Every quarter we're doubling our revenue," she said.

"Who would have thought hemp clothing would net such healthy profits," he said. "I'm really proud of what you've accomplished."

"Thank you for saying that, Ry," she said, and leaned across the car to kiss him on the cheek. Her fingers caressed his face, then moved down onto his shoulder. Her touch was comforting and welcomed.

Ryan set his hand on her thigh and tipped his head to get closer to her mouth. "If I knew you weren't happy with Jake, I'd invite myself up to your room," he said, his voice deepening.

Beth gently pressed on his chest and created more space between them. "Best friends don't sleep together," she said. "Besides, I don't think you're really interested in having sex with me. I think this has more to do with you trying to see what you'll feel – or what you won't."

The honesty in her answer irritated him. He didn't have to like the truth, but nonetheless, there was truth to what she was saying. He didn't want to feel anything for Dagger and a large part of him was thinking a roll between the sheets with Beth would make him rethink the connection he felt with Dagger all together. It made sense, didn't it: fucking a woman to forget a man? But that wasn't fair to Beth and he wouldn't use her like that.

Beth kissed him one more time on the cheek and slid out of his car. "Let me know what happens, Ry. Okay?"

He nodded and watched her disappear inside the hotel lobby, then pulled away from the curb and back out into traffic. There was something a little twisted about an ex-girlfriend giving her blessings for him to pursue a curiosity with a man. Why was it everyone around him seemed to possess more wisdom about his life then he did?

The drive home was a blur. He was so lost in thought he drove past the parking lot for his apartment building and had to turn around in the next driveway to get into it. He kept replaying his conversation with Beth in his head. She had seriously thought he might be bi-curious? How could that be? He'd never once had a male fantasy or even so much as looked at another guy *that way*.

Until Dagger.

Why now and why him? It made no sense at all. But Beth was right. If he didn't at least take a closer look at this, he'd spend the rest of his days wondering: what if.

CHAPTER SEVEN

The next day Ryan received another text message from Dagger. It was a welcome sight to see the double D name code pop up in the I.D. box on his phone.

The message read: *"The tour brings me near Cali in about a month. Have you had time to consider my invite?"*

Ryan toyed with his response. The answer he had in his head was rather long-winded, so he changed his mind and went with a simple: yes. Moments later his cell phone was ringing.

"Is your answer yes to visiting or yes you've had time to consider the invitation?" Dagger asked.

"I'll visit," Ryan said. "But you don't need to send a plane. I'll fly commercial."

"No way you're flying commercial, Ry," Dagger said. "That puts you at the mercy of their schedule. I'll charter a plane and you can fly when it's convenient for you."

"That's not necessary, but if you're insisting, then fine."

"I'm insisting," Dagger said.

The pause between them made Ryan nervous. His mouth suddenly felt dry, like he'd attempted to swallow a spoonful of cinnamon.

"I'm really glad you decided to see me," Dagger said. "I just wish you hadn't spent so much time agonizing over the decision."

"What makes you think I agonized?"

Dagger laughed. "One of the first things I learned about you is your tendency to over-think everything. Sometimes it's better to just jump into the deep end."

"And hope the pool has water in it?" Ryan asked.

"Leave it to you to think of that," Dagger said.

"I did give the trip a lot of thought, Dagger, and I also ran it by my ex and got her opinion."

"You're still friendly with your ex?"

"She's living with a new guy now, but we're still close," Ryan said. "Best friends, I guess you'd could call it."

"With benefits?"

Ryan smiled. The questioning tone in Dagger's voice teetered on the edge of jealously and Ryan liked that. "No benefits, and it wasn't for my lack of trying."

"You tried to get into her panties and she turned you down?" Dagger asked.

Ryan shifted in his chair and spun away from his computer screen. The mid-afternoon sun was streaming into his office window and the room was getting hot. Either that, or talking to Dagger was once again overheating Ryan's core temperature.

"Beth was never a cheater," Ryan said. "And sleeping with me would mean she'd be cheating on her boyfriend. Honestly, I was more interested in talking to Beth than fucking her. All in all, it's been one hell of a week – emotionally speaking."

"How was the week emotional?"

Ryan thrummed his fingers on this desk. "Just crazy shit, that's all. Stuff I've never had to deal with before and it's been mentally exhausting."

"Ry, if my invitation is weighing that heavy on you, then don't do it. I mean, really, I'm not expecting anything physical with you. I may joke about it, but I'm not in the habit of pushing myself onto straight men."

"It's more than your invitation," Ryan said.

"Then, what is it?"

"A combination of many things, all piled up into one looming tower of bullshit."

"Do you want to tell me about it?" Dagger asked. "I'm happy to listen if you feel like venting."

"I had dinner the other night with a guy from work," Ryan said. "Part way through the meal, he hit on me and asked me out – just like that. He said he got some kind of *vibe* from me; thought I might like to spend more time with him. I came close to punching him in the face."

Ryan held his breath waiting for a response from Dagger. The silence from the other end of the phone was unnerving; made him wonder if he'd said too much. He hadn't really planned on telling Dagger about any of it, but it had slipped out before he could stop it.

"It sounds like the guy made an honest mistake," Dagger finally said. "I hope you politely turned him down?"

"Yeah, I said no," Ryan said. "But, I told Beth about what happened and she decides to use that opportunity to tell me she's long suspected I might..." Christ! If he couldn't say it, how the hell did he ever think he'd have the nerve to explore it.

"She thinks you might be bi?"

"Yeah, that's what she said," Ryan said.

"How'd that make you feel, Ry?"

"I was pissed off at first, then a little insulted, but... in the end, I don't know. Look, I don't know what I'm saying here. Forget I mentioned it."

"No. I won't forget it," Dagger said. "Are you upset because you think there might be a little bit of truth to her comment?"

"There's more," Ryan said, "Something I recently remembered in vivid detail."

"What's that?" Dagger asked.

Christ! Why did his voice have to be so damned soothing, Ryan thought?

"I remembered what happened with my friend," Ryan said. "The kiss. It was very real and..." Ryan swore and stopped talking.

"Ry, it's okay," Dagger said. "I'm guessing you're upset because you liked it."

"Listen, I need get back to work," Ryan said.

"Running from this doesn't make it less real."

"Yeah, one of your text messages referred to something along those lines," Ryan said.

"Call me later when you get home," Dagger said. "I'll have some time to talk before the show."

Ryan said good-bye and disconnected the call. He knew then he wouldn't be calling Dagger later. He needed time; time to think – time to breathe. If he kept on this course, he'd have a heart attack from the mounting stress he had in his life.

Two days passed and Ryan continued to struggle with the reality of what was before him – with Dagger or without. He had talked to Dagger on the phone a few times, but Dagger hadn't pushed the subject of them being together outside of friendship. They kept their conversations non-personal, talking about work related things and even politics. Only once did Dagger mention he'd be in Vegas at the end of the month; the closest stop to California on his tour, before he went up to Canada for dozens of shows across the provinces in that country.

It was late Wednesday afternoon and Ryan was already contemplating another boring night at home. He was packing up his laptop bag in his office when his cell phone rang.

"Do you have plans for dinner tonight?" Dagger asked.

Ryan smiled at the sound of Dagger's velvety voice. "The usual," Ryan said. "Take-out at home with a beer."

"Not anymore."

"What do you mean?" Ryan asked.

"Would you consider having dinner with me?" Dagger asked

"You mean, talk to you on the phone while I eat my take-out?"

"No, I mean sitting down face-to-face with me, while we *both* have dinner," Dagger said.

Ryan stuttered something incoherent, then cleared his throat and tried to speak again. "How is that possible?"

"I just landed at LAX," Dagger said. "I can be at your office in about hour."

"No!" Ryan regretted his tone as soon as he said the word. He did his best to tamp down the panic threatening to choke him. "Too many people will see you if you come inside," Ryan said, using a softer voice this time. "Park in back. I'll meet you there."

"Are you embarrassed to be seen with me?" Dagger asked, with a lilt to his voice.

"Not at all," Ryan said. "I was thinking it would save you having to sign autographs or talk to people you'd rather not."

"Good point," Dagger said. "I'll be in a black stretch. Kinda hard to miss that."

"Right. I'll see you then."

Fuck! Fuck! Fuck! What the hell was he going to do now? He wanted to throw-up; run, anything but face the man inside that black limousine. Agreeing to meet Dagger for dinner was the stupidest thing he'd ever done. And what the hell was Dagger doing here in the middle of the tour? Ryan knew how tight the tour schedule was; he'd memorized every city and date, and tonight Dagger should be in New Orleans – not in L.A.

Ryan exited the elevator in the lobby of the high rise office building where Music Spin occupied the tenth floor. He walked to the back door and stepped out into the parking lot. His eyes nervously canvassed the area. Tucked in a back corner of the lot, Ryan saw the long, shiny car parked along the fence.

Waiting. For him. With Dagger inside.

He tried to move forward but his feet refused to take that first step. He adjusted the strap of his laptop bag and tried again. A dozen feet from the car, the driver stepped out of the front seat; dressed in a black suit, white dress shirt and tie, and stood beside the car.

"Good evening, Mr. Pierce," the driver said, and moved to open the rear door for Ryan.

Ryan's eyes went to the darkened opening. He saw no movement inside the car and for a moment he wondered if Dagger had merely sent a car for him and he'd be meeting him somewhere else. Ryan looked at the driver for confirmation.

"Mr. Drummond is waiting inside for you, Sir."

Ryan bent at the waist and eased his frame inside the car. His ass found the corner of the leather seat and he sat down, leaning forward to place his laptop bag onto the upholstered floor. It wasn't until he sat back into the plush seat that he noticed Dagger seated at the opposite end. Ryan's breath caught in his throat.

"You're supposed to be in New Orleans," Ryan said, finding his voice. Panic and fear almost making him open the back door and retreat to the safety of the office building. But more than all of that was the undeniable excitement he felt in seeing Dagger in the flesh; dark straight hair framing eyes that bore into him, black jeans, burgundy dress shirt with the sleeves rolled to the elbows; the spicy scent of his cologne filling his nose. The moment was powerful. He swallowed hard, wondering if Dagger was feeling it, too.

"You're right, I should be in New Orleans," Dagger said. "But I have a close friend struggling with a difficult truth in his life. I thought I'd be a good friend, spend some time with him, and show him my support."

Ryan looked out the side window. The muscle in his jaw twitched and sweat begin to build on his palms. Beside him, Dagger slid over, placing his muscled arm across the back of the leather seat. The tips of his fingers came to rest just a few inches from Ryan's shoulder. Ryan didn't have to look to know Dagger was close. Very close. He could feel him; his heat, the huge presence of him was everywhere.

"I'm worried about you, Ry," Dagger said. His voice a comforting purr.

"Don't be," Ryan said. "I'll figure this out in my own way; my own time."

"It's really good to see you," Dagger said, and squeezed the tight muscle in Ryan's shoulder.

Ryan willed himself to bristle at the touch, but he didn't; he pressed into it. He didn't want to feel this; didn't want there to be anything there between them, but there was, a palpable pulse pounding so strong Ryan could feel it all the way to his fingertips and toes. He grabbed on to his thighs to steady himself.

Dagger turned to Ryan; the wall of his chest brushing Ryan's arm. Dagger shifted again, his face making contact with Ryan's and slowly slid his cheek along Ryan's jawline. The scrape of whiskers against whiskers was audible; like sandpaper moving across wood. Ryan bit his bottom lip to prevent the moan in his throat from leaving his mouth and closed his eyes.

Daggers lips teased the shell of Ryan's ear. The closeness of the man was overwhelming for Ryan. He could feel the heat and moisture of Dagger's breath on his skin and a shiver shot through him.

"I can't stop thinking about you," Dagger whispered. "Not since the night we met and it doesn't usually happen like that for me," Dagger pressed a soft kiss to Ryan's temple. His fingers lifted to Ryan's face and stroked; feathery light touches over a days-worth of stubble on his unshaven chin. "I know you don't want to hear that, but it's true." Dagger leaned back, his eyes connecting with Ryan's. His hand still held on to Ryan's chin; his thumb skimming across his bottom lip. "You feel this, too, don't you?"

Ryan nodded. His heart was ready to explode from his chest.

"I'm also sensing you don't *want* to feel this," Dagger said, his eyes half-mast and lazy with lust. "But, it's too powerful for you to ignore. Isn't it?"

Dagger watched Ryan nod again. He dipped lower; his mouth hovering over Ryan's. "And, this is so powerful, Ry – even for me," Dagger breathed against Ryan's lips. "I can't stop myself."

Dagger's lips brushed first; a teasing stroke, then he heard Ryan moan and Dagger moved, capturing the sound as it rolled from Ryan's mouth. The physical touch sparked an energy between them, quickly flaming with each swirl of Dagger's tongue.

Ryan opened himself to it, allowed himself to feel and respond to the kiss – and he kissed back. He reached for Dagger, held on to his face with both hands and gave back every stroke of tongue Dagger offered. His boldness stunned him but he couldn't stop; the headiness of the moment was sweeping him away. It was like kissing Tommy, but a hundred times better, and so very, very real.

Dagger's arms circled Ryan and the kiss grew deeper; hotter. He nipped and sucked at Ryan's lips and hummed his appreciation when the flat plane of Ryan's tongue slid along the length of his. Dagger cursed and opened his mouth over Ryan's chin; his tongue tracing along his bristly jaw line, then dipping below to the soft hollow of his throat. Ryan's fingers tangled in Dagger's hair, then he lowered his face to capture Dagger's mouth for another kiss.

Dagger finally came up for air, his forehead resting against Ryan's. Both men were panting heavily.

"Holy fuck, Ry," Dagger sighed, trying to catch his breath. "You're killing me."

Ryan sat back, adding more space between them, and a veil of fear fell all around him. His lungs felt starved for oxygen from Dagger's closeness. He pushed off the seat and knelt in front of the mini bar positioned halfway down one side of the long car. He held onto the shelf displaying the beverage glasses with outstretched arms. He looked through the darkly tinted window and saw the vehicles racing by them on the street.

When the hell had they started moving, he thought? Had he been so aroused by Dagger's kiss that he hadn't noticed the limousine had left the parking lot and pulled out into traffic? Then his eyes dropped to the alcohol bottles, neatly lined up one next to the other. He stared mindlessly at them for a moment. Whiskey. Gin. Rum. Vodka. Every imaginable liquor and mixer was there for the taking.

"I need a drink," Ryan said softly. "Something really strong."

He took the bottle of Jack Daniels and poured himself a shot, tossing the liquid into the back of his throat. The burn of the whiskey felt wonderful, searing his insides all the way to his stomach. He set the glass down on the shelf and poured another. This time he held the glass in front of him and swirled the amber colored liquid around the sides of the glass before gulping it.

The booze was offering Ryan a nice distraction from the man he knew was sitting behind him waiting for him to turn around. He could feel the heat of Dagger's gaze burning his back. He should have been repulsed, angry, even disgusted by his actions, but he wasn't. Scared shitless, yes, but fear was healthy, wasn't it? He sat back on his haunches; his hands resting on his thighs, head lowered, trying to fully assess the emotions pumping through his veins. Every nerve ending in his body was on fire. Being with Dagger was the best adrenaline rush he'd ever experienced. It made him feel alive.

"I'm really sorry, Ryan," Dagger said. "I probably shouldn't have done that, but I hadn't expected it to feel that good – or that you'd kiss me back. Jesus! It felt like you were right there with me in that moment; enjoying it as much as me. I'm so sorry."

"I wanted the kiss," Ryan said in a soft voice, his eyes still focused on the liquor bottles.

"What'd you say?" Dagger asked, and slid forward on the leather seat.

"I wanted you to kiss me," Ryan said. He glanced over his shoulder at Dagger and shrugged, then looked back at the mini bar. "If you hadn't done it, I would have been disappointed. And, that's me being painfully honest with you and myself – maybe for the first time in my adult life."

Dagger came to the center of the car and dropped to his knees beside Ryan. "Honesty is always best and I appreciate it," he said. "I was nervous I freaked you out."

Ryan smiled shyly, his eyes briefly meeting Dagger's, then moving away. "I didn't say I wasn't freaked out," he said. "Trust me. I'm sufficiently freaked out, but probably not for the reasons you're imagining."

Ryan felt strong fingers press into the muscles of his back, then slide up to grip the back of his neck. He swayed from the touch and turned to Dagger, and as he hoped, Dagger was right there to take his mouth again. His heart lurched in his chest, going from zero to one hundred in half a second. How was it possible to feel this much heat and passion from another man?

Ryan fell back against the other bench seat in the car and Dagger moved with him; effectively pinning him with the bulk of his body and his mouth. This kiss was more aggressive, each scratch of beard stubble across their faces igniting fires, tongues more confident, both taking what they wanted from the connection their mouths shared. It was intense and all Ryan could do was hold on and enjoy the new sensations flooding his system.

Dagger came up on his knees and lifted Ryan with him onto the bench seat. His lips ran over Ryan's, then softly pressed; his tongue ran along the seam until Ryan opened for him and allowed Dagger's tongue to slip inside. Ryan reclined, resting his back on the seat cushion and Dagger moved over him; bearing his weight on his elbows, his face just a few inches above Ryan's.

"What about the driver?" Ryan asked, in a breathless whisper.

"He knows better than to breach my privacy."

Dagger slid one long leg over Ryan's thigh.

"Where's he taking us?" Ryan asked.

"The Grove," Dagger said. "We have dinner reservations, but I'm not all that hungry for food right now, and I'm really not sure I feel like sitting in a crowded room."

"Me neither," Ryan said, his chest beginning to heave.

Dagger nipped at Ryan's bottom lip. "We could drive around for a while, but this car isn't all that comfortable." He lifted himself up into a sitting position and paused. "I've got a better idea," he said, and hit the intercom for the driver. "Oleg, take me home," he instructed.

"Yes, sir," the driver's voice called out, and then the back of the limousine went quiet again.

Ryan could feel the car switch directions and looked up at Dagger in the dim light. Dagger was staring at him, a half grin lifting one side of his mouth. Then Ryan watched Dagger carefully crawl up and over him, settling on top. His long hair swung forward and tickled Ryan's face.

Dagger pitched his hips slightly and, for the first time, Ryan felt it; the solid length of Dagger's arousal pressing against his own. Ryan moaned and Dagger bent and covered his mouth. This touch was softer, less desperate, but just as hungry. Dagger rolled forward again, the long arc of his erection rubbing along the length of Ryan's. The friction of fabric made Ryan's cock lurch beneath his jeans. The kiss deepened, with Dagger sucking on Ryan's tongue; his hips continuing to grind against Ryan.

"Stop! Stop moving. Please," Ryan said.

Dagger's face lifted, his dark eyes studying Ryan. "Stop?"

Ryan desperately gulped in air as fast as he could. He used his hands to lightly push against the firm center of Dagger's chest. "You move one more inch and I'm gonna come."

The smile Dagger offered to Ryan melted him from the inside out.

"You had me worried," Dagger said, shifting to an upright position. His gaze went to the window. "Just as well. My house is about a mile more on the left."

Ryan sat up and adjusted his shirt. He ran his fingers through his tousled hair, then bent forward to rest his forearms on his thighs.

"How long are you in L.A.?" Ryan asked.

Dagger glanced at his wrist watch. "Only a few hours, then I go back to New Orleans and face the wrath of my manager."

"Why wrath?"

Dagger threw his head back and laughed. "I blew off a pre-show meeting and a walk-through of the stage set-up at the arena to come here. And in the short time I've been in L.A. my manager has called and left several messages. He's pretty pissed off, but he'll get over it."

Ryan's eyes slammed into Dagger. "Tell me you're not serious."

Dagger slowly nodded. "I'm very serious."

Ryan heard the words and realized Dagger was no longer talking about work. The heat radiating from Dagger was intense. The man oozed carnal vapors from every pore in his body. It unnerved Ryan and excited him all at the same time.

"Can I ask you something?" Ryan asked, sitting back in the seat.

Dagger turned and nodded. "Of course."

"Does it always feel like this, you know, whenever you're with a new guy?"

Dagger rubbed his chin and smiled. "I'm going to tell you the truth, but I doubt you'll believe me."

"What do you mean?"

Dagger relaxed into the seat; his head rolled on the headrest and faced Ryan. His smoldering gaze held Ryan for a long moment before he spoke.

"I've never had a first kiss like that," Dagger said. "It's *never* felt that good. Ever."

Ryan looked away and grinned. "I feel the same way," he said, and his face turned serious.

Dagger leaned closer to Ryan, nudging his shoulder to Ryan's. "What's going through your head?"

Ryan set his head back to the seat and rubbed the heels of his hands into his eyes. "This is so fucking surreal right now. I'm not supposed to be..."

"Turned on from kissing a guy?" Dagger asked, finishing Ryan's thought.

Ryan lifted his head and looked at Dagger. "This is easy for you, but for me it's... complicated."

The car stopped in front of the security post at the entrance to Dagger's estate. Ryan watched two huge cast iron gates electronically swing open and then the limousine escalated again, winding up the long driveway.

"How do you see this being easy for me?" Dagger asked.

"Because you're with guys all the time," Ryan said.

Dagger's response was delayed when the back door to the limousine opened, flooding the passenger compartment with fresh air and the sounds of singing bugs. Dagger stepped out first and waited for Ryan to follow him. They walked up the three steps under a stone portico and approached the front door. Dagger punched in the security code on the key pad mounted next to the double mahogany doors and an alarm sounded. The shrill noise made Dagger curse.

"Oleg," Dagger yelled back to the car. "Call the alarm company and tell them it was me that fucked up the security code, and ring the doorbell when it's time for me to head back to the airport." Dagger turned back to the key pad. "The last thing I need tonight is the fucking cops showing up."

"Cops would come for that?"

Dagger punched in a different sequence of numbers and the alarm silenced, then Dagger used his key and the front door opened. Dagger stepped inside and held the door for Ryan, then shut the door behind them.

"The security company knows I'm on tour and no one is supposed to be in the house; except for my housekeeper," Dagger said.

The house was eerily quiet. The silence magnified the sound of their feet walking across the polished Italian marble foyer. Dagger's path brought them between two curved

123

staircases to the second floor and two rooms off each side of the foyer with closed French doors.

"Typically, I don't use the front door of my house," Dagger said. "I usually come in from the kitchen in the back."

Dagger began switching on lights as they made their way deeper into the house. They ended up in an expansive kitchen with Spanish tiles and accents, granite counter tops, a large island area near the sink and an industrial sized gas stove any professional chef would love to own. Custom-made cabinetry rose from the floor to the ceiling in the cooking space of the kitchen. A bump-out area at the far end of the room had an oval shaped kitchen table and six chairs around it; which made for a comfortable eating area. Behind the table were huge windows that faced what Ryan imagined was the backyard. The room appeared homey but hardly used – if ever. Ryan figured that was probably due to Dagger being gone for long periods of time each year.

Dagger walked to an enormous restaurant-sized refrigerator and pulled out two imported beers, removed the caps, and offered one to Ryan. He leaned against the island area and took a long swig of the beer.

"Just so you know, I fucked up the security code out front because of you," Dagger smiled. "You make me nervous."

"I make *you* nervous? How is that possible?" Ryan asked.

"You know I've been... around the block a few times," Dagger snickered. "But being with you is different – a *lot* different."

Ryan shook his head. "Well, this is definitely different for me." He raised his beer bottle to Dagger, saluting him, then took a long gulp.

"You already know more about me than most of the people I've known for a decade, Ry. I've never been one to give away too much of myself too soon, but for you, I've already broken so many of my self-imposed rules. For instance, I don't bring guests back to my house. No one sees this. It's for me, my own safe place," he said, waving his arms around in the air.

Silence fell between them as Ryan tried to absorb Dagger's words and what it was he was feeling standing in this man's kitchen. His throat felt thick; his chest tight, his lips still raw from kissing Dagger in the back of the car only a few minutes ago.

"Say something," Dagger said.

Ryan leaned against the cabinets; his head fell back and hit the wood. "For me, this is having to rethink everything I've ever known about myself. It's more than a little fucked up."

"I get that, Ry, really I do, but please don't over-think this," Dagger said.

"Easy for you to say," Ryan said. "You've known your whole life who you are and what you want. Me? I haven't spent one second of my adult life imagining myself with a guy."

"Until me," Dagger said, his voice deep and heavy with sexual tension.

Ryan nodded. "Yeah, until you."

Dagger's heart flooded with something he hadn't felt in a very long time and it went far deeper than arousal. Did he actually have a chance with this gorgeous man? Did Ryan really want him – the same way he wanted Ryan? Dagger's eyes scanned the long length of Ryan's physique, then lifted to his eyes – those intensely blue eyes that seemed to change color with every new emotion the man expressed. He could see the fear in them, too, mixing with a hint of smoldering sensuality that when Dagger thought of being unleashed on him, it made his chest tighten. There was no doubt he wanted Ryan in his bed, but Dagger wasn't thinking this could be a one-time thing for him. The feelings were already too intense. For the first time in over a decade, Dagger was thinking he might want this to be more than physical, and that was something he doubted Ryan would ever want with him.

Ryan watched Dagger set his beer down on the counter top, then push himself away and slowly move toward him. His swagger was primal; almost predatory, the smirk on his face displaying his full intentions and every nerve ending in Ryan responded to the heated gaze Dagger was giving to him. He stood upright against the cabinet and licked his chafed lips. Christ! How much more could he handle from Dagger? How much more would Dagger want or expect?

Dagger stopped in front of Ryan. Their eyes almost level with each other. Ryan swallowed hard, his eyes canvassing Dagger's very masculine features. There was something about him that made Ryan want to touch and feel the man's skin beneath his fingertips; his tongue. He felt his cock beginning to harden again – or maybe it was still hard from the car. He wasn't sure.

"You gonna give me the grand tour?" Ryan asked, trying not to focus on Dagger's mouth.

"Not tonight," Dagger said.

"Wasn't that the point in bringing me here?"

Dagger shook his head. He leaned forward and set his hand on the cabinet beside Ryan's head. "I don't trust myself to bring you upstairs, Ry," Dagger said, and inched forward, his mouth moving close to Ryan's ear. "If we get anywhere near my bedroom, all bets are off," he whispered into the hair at Ryan's temple. "And I don't think you're anywhere near ready for that."

Dagger pulled back; eye to eye again with Ryan. He removed the beer bottle from Ryan's grip and set it beside them on the counter, his eyes never leaving Ryan's. The moment was heavy with anticipation.

Ryan touched Dagger's chest; his eyes followed the movement, watching his fingers press into the plane of muscle hidden beneath Dagger's shirt. Dagger responded, tipping his hips forward and pinning Ryan to the cabinets with his groin. It was the second time in an hour, Ryan was rubbing against another man's erection. Ryan lifted his gaze to meet Dagger.

"You want this, don't you?" Dagger asked. He waited for Ryan's nod, then folded his arm, resting his weight on his elbow beside Ryan's head, bringing his face closer to Ryan's. His lips brushed Ryan's, then sucked the bottom lip between his teeth, lightly nipping Ryan. His free hand pressed Ryan's shoulder into the cabinet, his chest to Ryan's, and a fiery kiss began.

Dagger's hand slid down onto Ryan's chest, then lower to his hip, and stopped between their bodies. He gripped the long length of Ryan's cock harnessed beneath his jeans and both men moaned into the others' mouth. Dagger deepened the kiss; tongues wrestling for the upper hand, and Ryan struggled to breathe. The hand on Ryan's groin continued to rub slow strokes over the fabric.

"Let me take out your cock and jerk it," Dagger said against Ryan's mouth. "I want to feel you come in my hand."

Ryan's arm curled around the back of Dagger's neck, pulling him closer; his breathing erratic and strained. Dagger took his mouth again, his fingers working at the button on Ryan's jeans. Ryan felt the button release and his zipper inching down.

"Dagger, don't," Ryan said. "I'll come."

Dagger licked at Ryan's lips, his hips rocking against Ryan. "Don't worry, Ry. I love come."

Ryan closed his eyes and groaned loudly, his head fell back against the cabinet with a thud. Dagger leaned back, making his groin the only connection to Ryan. His hips continued to apply the perfect friction against Ryan's aching cock; grinding and rolling back and forth over the rock hard ridge.

"Oh, God! Dagger," Ryan said, and then Ryan stilled, a deep sigh escaping his mouth.

"Christ! You're sexy when you come," Dagger said, softly kissing the side of Ryan's mouth. His fingers curled over the waistband of Ryan's partially opened jeans and dipped inside the heat of his boxer briefs. His index finger dragged along Ryan's still pulsing shaft, collected a bit of the warm sticky fluid, then pulled his hand out and brought it to his mouth to taste.

Ryan lifted his head and watched Dagger licking his finger. Embarrassment flushed his cheeks. He stood up straight against the cabinet and Dagger had to take a step backward to keep from falling.

"That's never happened to me," Ryan mumbled.

"First time for everything, right?" Dagger asked.

Ryan rolled his eyes at Dagger's attempt at humor. "Where's your bathroom?" he asked.

"Down the hall. Second door on the left," Dagger said.

When Ryan returned to the kitchen, Dagger was straddling a pull-out trash compactor drawer, stroking his over-sized cock and then ejaculating into the bin. Ryan stood mesmerized by what he saw, unable to take his eyes away. Dagger tossed his head back over his shoulders when he came and sighed.

A moment later, he straightened up and tucked himself back into his pants, then used his foot to push the trash drawer back into the cabinet. He turned around and saw Ryan standing there, and instead of showing any sign of shame, Dagger gave Ryan the most amazingly sexual smile. The man truly was comfortable with himself, no matter how intimate the situation.

"My housekeeper is *not* gonna be happy with me tomorrow," Dagger said, the smile never leaving his face.

Before Ryan could respond, the doorbell chimed and echoed around the space of the kitchen.

"Shit, I lost track of time," Dagger said. He finished zipping up his pants and walked to Ryan; gripping the back of his neck. "Come on," he said. "I'll give you a blow job in the car."

Ryan came up short, disbelieving what Dagger had said, then he heard Dagger's dirty chuckle and knew it was a joke. Relief washed through him and then a little bit of something else. Perhaps disappointment?

"I know saying shit like that messes with your head, Ry, but I can't seem to help myself. It's so much fun to do!"

He followed Dagger outside and watched him slide first into the backseat of the limousine. Ryan settled in beside Dagger. He looked across the sitting area and at the opposite seat. Visuals of him dry humping Dagger there ran through his head and his heart began to thump a little harder in his chest.

"Where do you want Oleg to drop you?" Dagger asked, the back of his hand brushing against Ryan's resting on his thigh. The short bristles of hair on Dagger's hand brushing his skin made him shiver.

Ryan looked at him. "My car is in the office parking lot."

Dagger nodded and pressed the intercom button to instruct the driver, then he leaned into Ryan. "I'm sorry we never had dinner," he said. "I'm not leaving you with a great impression of a first date, am I?"

"Is that what this was – a date?" Ryan asked.

"I'd sure as hell like it to be," Dagger said.

Ryan nodded but couldn't find the right words to respond to Dagger. Finally Dagger squeezed his hand. "You'll still come visit me in Vegas, right?" Dagger asked.

"I don't know," Ryan said. "I guess so."

"Hmmm, that doesn't sound very convincing, Ry."

"I know and I'm sorry," Ryan said. "But I need time to digest... everything."

Dagger laced his fingers with Ryan. His thumb rubbed against the back of Ryan's hand. Ryan watched the connection for several moments. Their hands tied together like that looked nice, almost normal, but Ryan knew differently. He tried to focus on the smooth texture of Dagger's fingers, the beautiful dark color of his skin, and how comforting the touch was for him. But, it was way more than comfort he was getting from Dagger's touch. He was also feeling arousal. Again. It seemed Ryan no longer had control of his cock whenever Dagger was nearby. He felt his cock start to thicken and lifted his eyes up to Dagger's.

"I wish I didn't have to leave right now," Dagger said. "I'm concerned once I'm gone, you'll spend way too much time obsessing over what happened between us tonight."

Ryan forced a smile and Dagger squeezed his hand again.

"Promise me one thing, Ry," Dagger said. "When you do think about this, promise me you'll remind yourself of how good it felt when we were together. Okay?" Dagger leaned closer to Ryan and pressed his lips to the corner of Ryan's mouth. "Our kiss was very real and you were just as much a part of it as I was; right there with me, getting off from my touch. Remember that."

Dagger's hand untangled from Ryan's fingers and slid up the inseam of Ryan's pants to cup his bulge. A throaty hum left Dagger's mouth. He tipped his head against Ryan's. "You're hard again – from my touch," he whispered. Then he took Ryan's hand and pressed the palm to his own erection. "And, see how hard you make me?"

Ryan kept his hand on Dagger's cock and turned his head to face him. His breathing was beginning to quicken. Dagger's head rolled, too, their noses making contact, each of their mouths opening and inched closer.

"I promise to think about Vegas," Ryan said. "But, you need to promise me something, too. Remember, this is all new for me. It's a lot to process and I'm not even sure I'll be able to figure out how to process it. Promise me you'll give me time to at least try and sort through it. Okay?"

"Anything," Dagger said, his lips connecting with Ryan's. "Anything for you."

Ryan responded quickly; his head dropping back to the cushion. Dagger deepened the kiss; his hand still rubbing Ryan's erection.

"I could fall so easily for you, Ry," Dagger said. "Do you think you could ever fall for me?"

Ryan pulled back from the kiss and held Dagger's gaze. Could he fall for him? He was no longer sure what he was capable of when it came to Dagger. A few weeks ago, he wouldn't have thought it possible for him to be kissing a guy – and enjoying it. So, where did that leave him now?

He carefully removed Dagger's hand from his lap. "I've never come in my pants before tonight and you're about to make me do it a second time. That would be pretty pathetic, don't you think?"

Dagger smiled. "Not pathetic, but it would be a shame to waste," he said. "How about I call when I get back to my hotel and we'll jerk-off together over the phone again?"

Ryan shook his head and grinned. "I doubt I'll be able to wait that long."

Dagger chuckled. "You'll probably do it in your car on the way home." Then his smile turned serious. "It's nice to know I effect you like that, Ry. I wasn't sure I'd be able to, considering you've always thought of yourself as being straight." He ran his fingers over the dark stubble on Ryan's chin. "I know better than to mess around with straight guys," he said. "It hurts too much in the end when they realize they're *not* gay... but, there was something about you I simply couldn't resist – I couldn't stay away."

The car came to a stop and Ryan reached for his laptop bag on the floor. "Thanks for the surprise visit," Ryan said.

"I'm glad I did it," Dagger said. "I'm even happier we cleared up that other burning question, too."

The car door opened and Oleg was standing on the pavement beside it. Ryan saw Dagger lean in for a kiss, then changed his mind and pulled back. Disappointment at that missed opportunity clenched Ryan's heart. He smiled at himself; thinking how odd it was for him to even acknowledge having such an emotion, when it was brought on in regards to not being able to kiss another man.

Ryan offered Dagger a wave and slipped out of the car, then Dagger called his name and Ryan poked his head back into the passenger compartment.

"Think about Vegas, but don't *over*-think it," Dagger said. "No pressure. We'll hang out and... have fun."

"Yeah. Fun." Ryan waved again and walked to his car. Behind him he heard the limousine exit the parking lot and that's when Ryan's hands began to shake. He dropped the car keys on the ground trying to unlock the door, then again once he got inside while attempting to start the car. He stared at the steering wheel and tears began to pool in his eyes. What had happened to plain ol' beige Ryan, the man that never veered too far off the center line in the middle of the road?

CHAPTER EIGHT

Ryan drove home in a haze of emotion; an erection still straining against his pants. After the release he'd had earlier he expected to feel sated, but his body was still on fire and yearning for more. Dagger was the first person with whom he had been intimate that had the ability to leave him in such a breathless state of arousal. The thought of that was as upsetting as it was gratifying.

He shut the door to his apartment and rubbed his forehead. He realized there were parts of the trip he couldn't remember at all. He set his laptop bag on the kitchen table and stood there, stunned. He was hungry but didn't feel like eating. He decided on a shower and walked into his bedroom and started peeling off his clothing. The wet spot on the front of his underwear was still obvious. He shivered at the memory of what had caused it and pulled the garment off his hips; his cock slapped against his lower stomach. If he so much as brushed the back of his hand against it, he was certain he'd come. He was just that hyper-sensitive right now.

He turned on the shower and waited for the water to heat, then he caught his reflection in the mirror above the sink. A raised red whisker burn was evident on his face, chafed raw from Dagger's arduous kissing and the beard stubble covering the man's chin. That erotic reminder made Ryan sway on his feet. He stepped beneath the shower spray and held his breath as the water hit his face.

Could he fall for Dagger, Ryan questioned himself? Did he want to fall for him? Maybe he already had. These were questions he couldn't answer. What he did know was, he wanted more – more kissing; more touching, more of Dagger. How screwed up in the head did he have to be to even allow that thought to linger in his mind? He could not believe what he was feeling, what he wanted – and from a man. He tried to remember the last time he felt this sexually charged. Junior high, he thought. Back then, it didn't take much to get him hard. And now? All it took was the sound of Dagger's voice and his cock was thickening.

Ryan looked down the length of his chest and stomach to the throbbing member jutting out from between his legs. His hand curled around the swollen shaft of his cock and started working on the flesh; twisting, pulling. It took less than six strokes to get him where he wanted to be. The first ribbon shot out the tip and hit the shower wall where it creased and met the floor. Watching himself come reminded him of seeing Dagger shooting into the trash compactor at his house. The scene so raw and sensual, Ryan grunted and shot another thread of his thick liquid; this time hitting the drain. Two more strings shot before Ryan leaned against the wall, trying to recover his breathing; his sanity, if that was possible.

He finished his shower and toweled dry, then made his way to his bed and flopped naked onto his back. His cock remained semi-erect, like he still wasn't sated, even though he knew he should be. Ryan stared at the ceiling. He wondered where Dagger was in his trip back to New Orleans and if he'd call when he got back to his hotel. He closed his eyes for a moment and his cell phone rang. Ryan reached for it and smiled when he saw that it was Dagger.

"Did you already relieve the pressure?" Dagger asked.

"I had to," Ryan said with a chuckle.

"That's too bad," Dagger said. "I was hoping we could do it together."

"Are you back at the hotel?"

"I wish. I'm still in flight; about halfway – or so they tell me." Dagger's voice deepened. "Where are you?"

"In bed. Naked," Ryan said. *Was he really talking like this to another man?* He couldn't believe the words spilling from his mouth, nor could he seem to stop them. When had he gotten so bold?

"Sounds nice," Dagger said. "I'm in the bedroom at the back of the plane ready to sexually abuse myself."

"No one there to help you with that?" Ryan asked.

Dagger exhaled loudly. "Listen, Ry, if you and I are going have something between us, and after tonight that's the way it seems, then there won't be anyone else in my life and I'd expect you to do the same for me. Otherwise, this won't work. I get tested every six months and I'm happy to show you the documents to prove I'm clean and I always wear condoms. Trust and respect run both ways, Ry, so I'd want you to be tested, too. Does all that sound like something you can handle?"

Hearing Dagger's words made everything seem so much more real and what he said was a huge relief. It made Ryan feel safe, and for that, he was willing to be tested. If this *thing* with Dagger was going anywhere, he really had no intention of sharing Dagger with dozens of nameless partners he picked-up while out on tour.

"Trust is everything," Ryan said.

"So we're cool?"

"Yeah, we're cool," Ryan said. *What the fuck had he just agreed to? Fuck. Fuck. Double fuck.*

"Good, I'm glad we straightened that out," Dagger said. "Because now I want to play."

"Play with yourself?" Ryan teased.

"Well, yeah, but I also want to talk dirty to you; get you nice and hard, like you were at my house and in the car."

Ryan closed his eyes. The memories Dagger was stirring up made him flush with heat. It was difficult to believe he had been a willing participant in all of it. It made him wonder how far he would have gone if Dagger didn't have to leave, made him wonder how far he *wanted* to go. He couldn't remember ever being that turned on so quickly and for such an extended duration of time – long after getting off. Ryan's toes curled on the bed at the memory of Dagger's touch, the way he stroked him through the pants, then dipped his finger inside to taste his seed. Watching him do that was extremely intimate and so very arousing – and something he never imagined he'd be doing with a man. He just couldn't get past that fact. Dagger was a man, a man Ryan was seriously attracted to, a man he couldn't wait to kiss again.

"You have an amazing mouth, Ry. I could kiss you for hours," Dagger said. "The way you respond to me; to my touch. It's so... hot."

All Ryan managed was a soft moan. He could hear similar noises coming from Dagger's end. It was obvious they were both pleasuring themselves and neither of them seemed to care the other knew. Before he met Dagger, jerking-off while talking on the phone wouldn't have been a consideration. Ever. Now with Dagger, it seemed to be a consistent thing.

"Are you stroking your cock, Ry?" Dagger asked. "I wish I was there so I could touch you, like I did in my kitchen earlier. Fuck! I was very close to dropping to my knees and taking you in my mouth right then, but I thought you might freak if I tried."

"I might have," Ryan whispered. "But, what you were doing felt good."

"Christ! I want to suck you so bad; taste you on my tongue."

Ryan hummed. His hand stilled on his dick. "I thought there was no pressure?"

"When we're together there will never be pressure. I won't ever push you to do something you don't want or feel uncomfortable doing. But right now, this is play. I'm merely using the visual of you fucking my mouth to get me off. That's all."

"Kinky."

Dagger laughed. "You have no idea."

"Should I be afraid?"

"Never with me."

"I am a little afraid," Ryan said.

"Why?"

"Because I don't know what I'm doing... and you do."

"I'd never have guessed that, Ry. The way you acted in the car and in my kitchen; you seemed to know exactly what you were doing and what you wanted."

Ryan hadn't spent this much time with his cock in his hand since he was a teenager. If he kept on this pace, he'd likely rub the foreskin right off. Dagger was inspiring him to feel new things and his once dreary life was slowly becoming bright. Fun. He felt whole.

"Ry? You already come?"

"No, not yet."

"Good. I want to hear you get off, like in the kitchen, only this time I won't be able to see your face."

"That was embarrassing."

"It was fucking hot."

"Watching you at the trash can was... hot."

"You liked that?" Dagger asked. "Next time we're together, Ry, let's watch each other, or better yet, let me do it to you." Dagger groaned. "Then again, if I had your cock in my hand, I'd have to push it into my mouth, feel you come down my throat."

Ryan's hips started rocking, thrusting his cock into his fist. He was close to losing it. Sweat began beading all over his body. "I'm gonna come."

"Do it with me, Ry. Imagine your cock deep in my throat when you release and I'll visualize my come shooting all over your stomach."

"Oh, my god," Ryan said, and arched off the bed, his fist pulling off one final stroke. He heard Dagger grunting on the other end and knew he was coming, too. A moment later, Ryan heard laughter.

"You should see the mess I just made," Dagger said, his throaty chuckle vibrating through the phone. "I gotta take a picture. You need to see this."

"That's not necessary," Ryan said, glancing down at the pool of wetness sprayed all over his own stomach and chest.

"I just sent it to your phone," Dagger said. "The file should pop up any second."

Ryan's stomach did a flip-flop. A photograph of Dagger on his phone? He looked at the face of his cell phone and saw that a new file was there. All he had to do was hit one button to open the file and view what Dagger had sent, but did he really want to see it?

"I can't look at that photo, Dagger."

"Are you afraid to see my cock?" Dagger asked, in his ultra masculine voice.

"I don't know," Ryan said. "Maybe."

"Okay, then save it on your phone until you get the nerve," Dagger said. "I'm guessing the answer would be no if I asked you to send me a photo of you, right?"

"You're unbelievable," Ryan laughed.

"From what I was able to feel, you have a nice piece of meat, Ry. I hope one day you'll let me see it... up close, and very personal."

"But, no pressure. Right?"

Dagger laughed. "Nope, no pressure at all."

Ryan went to work the next day, his face raw from making-out with Dagger the night before. He hoped no one noticed – or worse, made a comment that would have Ryan coming unglued. He went into this office and turned on his computer. He needed to finalize the research on Zander and Ivory Tower for the interview scheduled the next night. He never got too excited about doing the research required with his job, but it was a necessary part to do, and he was good at it.

His thoughts shifted to Dagger and what happened between them last night; how good it felt, how good the memory of it felt to him even now. He remembered Dagger's request for Ryan to get tested at a clinic before anything went further than it already had between them. He'd never been tested before; had never felt a reason to do it. He'd always practiced safe sex, but if Dagger was willing to subject himself to testing for him, he'd do the same for Dagger.

He picked up his office phone and called the clinic near his apartment building and set up an appointment for the following day after work. When he hung up the phone, his hand bumped his cell phone on the desk and he remembered the unopened picture file Dagger had sent to him. He had come close to looking at it so many times already, but had somehow managed to stop himself. It felt weird, like he was spying on something he shouldn't; even though it was Dagger that had sent the photograph to him and asked him to look at it.

He picked up the cell phone and held it in his hand. His thumb rubbed over the button that when pressed would reveal the photograph to his eyes. A part of him wanted to look at it, for curiosity sake. Arousal was already starting to knot his groin. His hand skimmed over his chin and he felt the burn of the whisker rash on his skin; another reminder of Dagger.

Before he could change his mind, Ryan hit the button on the phone to begin the process of downloading the picture file. A moment later, the photograph appeared. The shot was taken from above, with Dagger sitting up in bed leaning against the headboard and pointing the camera down toward his groin. A good portion of Dagger's chest and stomach was displayed with enticing swirls of trimmed brown chest hair; as well as, most of his erect cock and that mysterious tattoo Ryan still couldn't figure out.

Ryan could see the pearly white fluid pooled all over Dagger's muscled stomach and his cock laying off to the side of it. The angle of the camera exposed the full length of Dagger's thick cock, a perfectly shaped head with another drop of come seeping from the slit, a dark strip of trimmed pubic hair, and a small glimpse of his balls. It was all there. Nothing left to the imagination at all and Ryan could not deny how aroused he became looking at it. Dagger exposed in this raw, intimate pose drove home the point of how male he was inside and out.

Ryan set the phone back onto his desk. His cock was painfully bent in his pants. The photograph should have turned him off, instead he found himself wanting to see it up close. What might it be like to touch Dagger's chest and stomach; hold his cock? He was curious to what the weight of it might feel like in his hand. He picked up the phone again and stared at the photograph. His other hand dropped to his lap, attempting to adjust the hardened column to a more comfortable position.

A knock on his office door made Ryan jump in his seat and he dropped his phone. The door opened as Ryan was grabbing it from the floor.

"Hey, Ryan," Sebastian said. "Am I still invited to tag along with you to the Ivory Tower interview?"

Ryan sat upright in his seat, holding on to his phone; his face flushed red.

"Whoa! What the hell happened to your face?" Sebastian asked.

Leave it to Sebastian to notice his chafed skin, Ryan thought. But the rash on his face was the least of his worries. He said a silent prayer that Sebastian wouldn't cross the room and see the enormous erection tenting his pants. He shut off his phone and set it inside the top drawer of his desk.

"I think I'm having a reaction to a new shaving cream," Ryan said softly.

"Hmmm, but it doesn't look like you've shaved recently."

Good call, dickhead, because I haven't, Ryan thought. "Maybe it's from cologne, then," Ryan said.

"Looks like beard burn to me," Sebastian said. "I've had the pleasure of receiving a few of those, myself."

Ryan felt his face grow redder. "Definitely not beard burn."

Sebastian studied him and smiled, like he knew the secret Ryan was so desperate to keep to himself.

"Whatever," Sebastian said. "May I join you tomorrow night or not?"

"Yeah, yeah. Fine," Ryan said. "I'll let you know what time."

Sebastian nodded and turned to leave. "Oh, I almost forgot," he said. "Rumor has it, you were picked up from work last night in a limousine. Any truth to that?"

"I needed a ride downtown."

"A ride, huh? Maybe that's when you got your beard burn?"

"Don't push it, Sebastian."

Ryan collected his mini-tape recorder from his desk drawer and replaced the tape with a fresh cassette for the interview with Ivory Tower. He set the old cassette on his desk and then remembered this was the tape with Dagger's interview on it – and the conversation between Dagger and Chris that was recorded after he left. His gut clenched at the memory. He grabbed a pen and labeled it: DD, and locked it in his desk. Hearing Dagger flirting with another guy on that tape didn't exactly sit well, now that he was with him.

With him? Where the fuck did he get the notion he was with Dagger? Just because Dagger had told him there would be no one else in his life, did that mean they were a couple? They'd made-out a little bit and talked dirty to each other on the phone. Did that translate into them being a couple? Dagger said he wanted last night to be considered a date but with his touring schedule, how many dates would they ever be able to have? And more importantly, why did he care so much?

Ryan grabbed his note pad and pen and left his office. He walked to his car and sat in the front seat while he waited for Sebastian. He decided to text Dagger his whereabouts so he wouldn't try calling him later while he was in the middle of the interview.

"On my way to the venue to interview Ivory Tower. Shall I say hi to Zander for you?" Ryan's text message read.

"Zander is into dudes, Ry. Watch your back... or he'll be all over it," Dagger's text reply said.

"He has a runway model for a girlfriend," Ryan typed.

"Yeah, and I've been known to jump the fence, too, but I'm into dudes... as you very well know. Just watch the vibe you're putting out around him."

There was that word again: vibe. Ryan needed to take a hard look at that and see if there was any truth to it. If there was, that was news to him.

"Jealous?" Ryan typed.

The pause that came after his text felt too long and Ryan wondered if he had struck a nerve with Dagger.

"Yeah, I'm jealous. Do you blame me? You're fucking hot and oblivious to the fact... which is a lethal combination. I should have a security detail watching your ass." Dagger's next text read.

146

"You're forgetting I'm not into dudes... just you." Ryan's finger hovered over the send button, trying to decide if he should send it. Wasn't it already obvious to Dagger he liked him? Was it necessary for him to articulate that sentiment in print? Fuck it, he thought, and hit the send button.

Dagger's next message came quick. *"I'm into you, too, Ry, and I'm pretty sure we both made it clear just how much the other night. Be safe and call me later – if you can. XXOO"*

Had Dagger just signed his text message with X's and O's? Christ! What he wouldn't do for one of his kisses right now?

Sebastian opened up the passenger side of Ryan's car and sat in the front seat. Ryan jumped from the sudden intrusion to his private thoughts about Dagger.

"I thought you left without me," Sebastian said.

"I said I'd meet you at my car," Ryan said. "Don't worry, I would've called before I left."

Sebastian smiled at Ryan. "Thanks for bringing me," he said. "I know we got off on the wrong foot, so I appreciate you giving me another chance and I promise not to hit on you – again."

Why did everything that came out of Sebastian's mouth piss off Ryan? Was it the English accent that bothered Ryan, or the way Sebastian looked at him; that smug, knowing look was more annoying than the one his mother had perfected decades ago.

"Are we doing this interview backstage?" Sebastian asked.

Ryan sighed. "Afraid so. I'd much rather meet a band on neutral ground than at a venue. It's never a good idea to allow them too much power with these interviews. You give them any leverage, and they will run with it, and then it won't be your interview – it will be theirs. Remember that."

"How was the interview with Dagger Drummond? You did him on his tour bus, right?"

Sebastian's words swirled and then settled in Ryan's head. *Did him on his tour bus?* He didn't like the tone of the question or the direction it seemed to be heading.

"Do you have a *thing* for Dagger Drummond?" Ryan asked, driving out of the parking lot and into city traffic. "I'm asking, because you keep bringing him up in conversation."

"He's huge in the business," Sebastian said. "I was curious to know if he's as nice a guy as he seems?"

"Yeah, he's a nice guy." Ryan said. *Real nice, and I can't wait to swap some more spit with him.* That's what Sebastian really wanted to hear, but there was no way in hell Ryan would ever divulge that to him or anyone else. Dagger would have to remain his dirty little secret.

Ryan met with their liaison at the Staples Center. He displayed their press credentials around his neck and collected their laminated backstage passes. The liaison ran through the schedule for the evening and then escorted them to the backstage holding area for press. There were reporters from a dozen or more news outlets, even Rolling Stone Magazine was there to cover the concert. It pleased Ryan they had an early time slot with the band. With any luck, Ryan could get what he wanted from Ivory Tower and be home before midnight.

"You nervous?" Sebastian asked him.

Ryan scoffed at the idea. "Not in the least," he said. "I'm grateful we'll be out of here before the insanity starts."

The door to the press room opened briefly and Ryan could hear the band running through a sound check out on stage.

"They sound incredible," Sebastian said. "I wish we could go out front and watch."

"Another time," Ryan said.

"Zander is sexy as hell. Don't you think?"

"Maybe to a woman – or someone like you," Ryan said.

"You prefer the tall, dark, and brooding type, like Dagger?" Sebastian asked.

Ryan's head swung toward Sebastian and his eyes narrowed. "Don't. Go. There."

"It was a joke, Ryan," Sebastian laughed. "Nothing more."

Ryan drummed his pocket sized notepad against his thigh; a habit he had whenever he was tense or irritated. If he had to listen to Sebastian talk much longer, he might walk-out and have him do the interview by himself. He glanced around the room. He knew a few of the reporters in the room, but really had no desire to chat them up, instead he settled for a quick nod in their direction and let it go with that.

A few minutes later, the band manager for Ivory Tower entered the press room and signaled Ryan to follow him.

"Game time," Ryan said, and tapped Sebastian on the arm.

Sebastian hurried to catch up with Ryan; trying to match his stride; which was near impossible with Ryan's long legs.

Ryan turned the corner with the band manager and followed him into another backstage room. One by one, the guys in Ivory Tower slowly entered.

"Ryan Pierce, right?" Zander asked, and extended his hand.

Alexander Metcalf, or Zander, as he was known in the music business, was well over six feet tall with straight shoulder-length light brown hair pushed behind both ears. The overhead lights illuminated golden streaks in it that any woman would envy and Ryan wondered if they were natural. Tattoos went up both forearms; a dragon on one arm with a curling tail and a centaur reaching for what looked to be a naked man on the other. Ryan couldn't see the entire design to know for sure. A delicate silver hoop pierced one nostril and a rod went through his eyebrow. He had multiple earrings in both ears and a goatee outlined his mouth and chin in whiskers a much darker shade than his hair. As rough as he looked, his smile was killer perfect, with straight white teeth that accentuated his green eyes.

Ryan had met him a few years back at a heavy metal music festival, but their conversation had been brief due to the backstage chaos swirling around them.

"Nice to meet you," Ryan said, shaking Zander's hand.

"Actually, we met backstage a few years ago," he said, his eyes scanned Ryan from head to toe. "It was a short chat, so you probably don't remember."

Ryan nearly fell backward at Zander's admission. Their conversation couldn't have lasted more than ten minutes and even he couldn't remember the entire context of it. The fact that Zander did, shocked him.

"Yeah, we were both gushing about the new Gibson guitar that had launched that week," Zander said. "I was impressed you knew so much about the instrument."

"You have quite a memory," Ryan said.

"I remember what's important and I never forget a face," Zander said. A second once-over glance came after Zander's comment and Ryan began to feel uncomfortable. Zander had that hungry look in his eye; similar to the look Dagger had when they were together. The difference was, with Dagger that look was welcomed, and with Zander it was not.

Sebastian cleared his throat and Ryan finally acknowledged him standing there. "Zander, this is our new intern at the magazine. Sebastian took Zander's hand and laid his second hand over both.

"Really nice to meet you," Sebastian said, but Zander's warm green eyes were still on Ryan.

"So, where do you want to do this?" Zander asked Ryan.

"I guess we'll set you up over there on the couch," Ryan said.

Sebastian leaned into Ryan's ear and whispered, "Shall I get a fire extinguisher?"

"What the hell for?" Ryan asked.

"To put out the fire between you and Zander." Again, that same smug smile crossed Sebastian's face.

Ryan got into Sebastian's space. "You just don't know when to quit, do you?" he seethed in as low a voice as he could manage, and gave him a small shove. "If we weren't here right now, I'd punch your fucking face."

Sebastian laughed and retrieved two chairs and set them in front of the couch. Ryan sat in one and Sebastian took the other. The tape recorder was set on the coffee table and Ryan pressed the record button.

Thirty minutes later, Ryan had the material he needed to write the article and stood up to thank the guys in Ivory Tower. Zander lingered behind to personally thank Ryan.

"I always make a point of reading your articles, Ryan," Zander said. "Top notch in every issue. I'm excited to see what you'll do for us."

Ryan nodded. "Thank you."

"I read in the magazine you have an article coming up about Dagger Drummond," Zander said. "Dagger's a friend. We go way back."

Ryan's eyes narrowed on Zander. Exactly how well did they know each other? Was Zander one of Dagger's random hook-ups? Maybe that's how Dagger knew Zander was into guys? Ryan shook the thoughts from his head and turned to step away. Zander's hand curled around his forearm and stopped him from moving.

"You got a business card with your contact info on it?" Zander asked.

Sebastian stood behind Ryan and snorted, mumbling something about the fire extinguisher again.

"Why do you need my card?" Ryan asked.

"In case I have a question or something," Zander said, flashing another killer smile that would have stopped the traffic out on the freeway.

Ryan reached into the back pocket of his jeans and pulled out his wallet. He removed a business card and handed it to Zander. "My email address and cell number is at the bottom."

"Nice. Thanks," Zander said. "Hang back after the show and we'll have a drink."

"Sorry. Can't," Ryan said. "I have an early meeting in the morning."

Zander nodded in understanding. "Maybe next time."

Ryan stepped into the hallway and started toward the exit but Sebastian wasn't beside him. He turned to see what had detained him and saw Sebastian inside the interview room still talking to Zander. Then he saw Sebastian pass another business card to Zander, leaning in to talk to him, and pointing out something on the card. Anger rose again inside Ryan. This guy really had no clue how to act in these situations.

Several minutes passed, while Ryan remained out in the hall, leaning against the wall waiting for Sebastian to finish working his charm on Zander. Ryan finished jotting down a few additional notes into his notepad and looked up. Zander was looking at him, even though it was Sebastian that was talking to him.

Finally Sebastian came out of the room with a confused look on his face. "Why are you standing out here?" he asked. "Zander wanted us to stick around and party, well, really with you, but you had left the room."

Ryan didn't say a word. He just pushed his way through the crowed hallway toward the nearest exit he could find.

"Hey! Where're you going?" Sebastian asked.

"My car," Ryan said.

"I thought we were staying to see the show."

"You can go ahead and stay, but I'm leaving," Ryan said.

Sebastian lifted his chin. "I want to stay."

"Perfect. Get your own ride home," Ryan said and stalked from the arena.

Ryan drove home tired and angry. If Sebastian was going to suck dick on his way to the feature article department, he wouldn't last long at the magazine. Ryan was determined to make sure there was no way in fucking hell he'd be working anytime soon with Sebastian. And what the Christ was up with Zander, wanting his phone number? That was not the typical outcome of an interview. If Zander had questions he could present them through the proper channels and have his band manager contact the magazine.

Ryan pulled into the parking lot of his apartment building and shut off his car. He couldn't shake the feeling that Zander was hitting on him. What the fuck was up with that? Did he have some kind of gay bulls-eye painted on his back? He took the elevator to his floor and stomped down the hall into his apartment.

He glanced at the wall clock. It was a little after ten o'clock. He knew Dagger was in the middle of a show in Albuquerque, but he still pulled out his phone to send him a text.

"Interview is done. Zander says hi," Ryan typed.

One hour turned into two and Dagger still hadn't contacted Ryan. He showered, forced down some leftover Italian food, then lay in bed while staring at the ceiling trying to figure out his life. Nothing was as it used to be and every day brought new challenges and truths for Ryan to face. He didn't feel the same, like he was living inside someone else's body.

A little after midnight Dagger's text message to Ryan came in saying, *"Is it too late to call?"*

Ryan wasn't sure he wanted to talk to Dagger while he was in such a negative and confused mood. Even still, he couldn't stop himself from responding. *"I'm awake,"* Ryan said, and a moment later his cell phone was ringing.

"How'd it go?" Dagger asked in his whiskey rough voice.

Ryan rubbed at his face. Fatigue was weighing on him but anger kept him wide awake. "Fine, I guess."

"Did Zander hit on you?"

"Of course," Ryan sighed. "Would you expect anything less?"

"I suppose not," Dagger said. "Was he disappointed when you shut him down?"

"What makes you think I turned him down?" Ryan asked in a tight tone.

A long pause fell between them.

"What's going on, Ry?" Dagger asked. "You all right?"

Ryan exhaled loudly. "I had to bring that asshole intern with me to the interview. On top of asking me out last week, he had to make a remark about the whisker burn you gave me the other night, then asked who was in the limo! Plus, he keeps asking questions about you."

"Do you think he knows I was the one with you?"

"I doubt it, but he's driving me nuts. Every time I turn around he's there with that stupid smug smile of his, like he knows something. I was in my office yesterday looking at your photo..."

"Whoa! You finally worked up the nerve to look at it?" Dagger asked. "And you did it your office, Ry? That's a little dangerous, isn't it? I thought you'd use that for inspiration for your 'spank bank' at home – not to use at work."

Dagger's words made Ryan smile and a little bit of his anger disappeared. "Never mind about my shitty night or the photographs in my spank bank. How was the show in Albuquerque?"

"Killer," Dagger said. "Wish you could be here. I miss you."

Ryan made a humming sound. "I miss you, too."

"Do you?"

"Yeah. I do."

"Couple more weeks, Ry, then we can be together for a few days."

"A few days?"

"You can stay as long as you want," Dagger said. "Is that what you mean?"

"I figured we were only talking about one day," Ryan said.

"That's it?" Dagger asked. "I was hoping you'd want to stay for a couple of days... and nights."

"The Vegas show is on a Thursday," Ryan said. "I was thinking I could fly out that morning, spend the night, and fly back to L.A. Friday morning."

"How about we start with that schedule but leave your departure date... open ended. How's that sound?"

"You're persistent," Ryan said, a full smile on his face removed the last bit of anger he held inside. Once again, Dagger had managed to relax him.

"What can I say? I miss you, and I want to give you another whisker burn to mark you as mine."

Ryan swallowed hard. "Yours?"

"Does that status interest you?" Dagger asked. Silence poured from the other end of Dagger's phone. "Still trying to process this, Ry?"

"You know me too well."

"I got two words for you: just feel. That's all you need to focus on. How do you feel when we're together or talking on the phone? If your answer is the same as mine, then I think we need to follow this through; see where it takes us."

"I'm over-thinking this, I know, but..."

"Come to Vegas and we'll talk about it some more," Dagger said.

"Talk? I thought you wanted to give me another whisker burn?" Ryan teased.

"We'll talk first, then I'll give you that whisker burn all over your body. See what your little intern has to say about that."

"The little intern won't be seeing any whisker burns I may or may not come home with, Dagger."

Dagger laughed, a rich throaty sound that was almost a growl. "I'm hoping no one but me will get to see the chafe I give you, Ry."

"Only you," Ryan said.

"I like the sound of that, Ry. A lot."

"I gotta get some sleep, Dagger. "I'll talk to you tomorrow."

It was after lunch when Sebastian stood in the open doorway of Ryan's office. He looked disheveled and exhausted, the dark circles below each eye a sharp contradiction to the wide, goofy grin on his face. Ryan couldn't remember what Sebastian wore the previous night, but he suspected he was still wearing the same clothing.

"You just rolling in?" Ryan asked, barely acknowledging Sebastian's presence.

"What a night!" Sebastian said. "I stayed for the show, then partied with Zander after." Sebastian scratched his rumpled hair and smiled. "He showed me his tour bus," he said with pride.

Ryan's gaze lifted from the paperwork on his desk and hit Sebastian. "You partied with Zander on his tour bus?"

"Yeah, why? Are you jealous or something?"

Ryan's expression turned dark. "Come in and close the door," he said. He watched Sebastian do as he was told and leaned back in his leather chair, contemplating his words before he spoke. "If you want to hang around backstage and act like a fucking groupie, you do it on your own time. When we're out on assignment we're representing the magazine and you act accordingly. And you're sadly mistaken if you think sucking dick will get you anywhere in this business. It will do nothing but get you fired. Something to think about, Sebastian. You're young. I suggest you learn from this and grow the hell up."

Sebastian came closer to Ryan's desk. "Sounds to me like you're pissed off I was with Zander and you weren't," he said. "But, I thought you were Drummond's toy, so why would you give a shit about me and Zander."

Ryan rubbed at his face. "Sebastian, for the last time, I am *not* Dagger Drummond's *toy* or anyone else's!"

"Right, and according to what the media knows about Zander, they think he's straight, too. But, I can assure you, he's into dudes. I've got the love bites to prove it."

Sebastian winked after his final statement; which infuriated Ryan. He slammed his fist on his desk. "You and I won't be working together again," Ryan said. "And consider yourself warned about partying while on the job. That was your one and only free pass."

"Hmmm, looks like I hit a nerve with the Dagger Drummond comment," Sebastian said.

"Get the fuck out of my office."

CHAPTER NINE

Could the week take any longer to end, Dagger silently asked himself. The days seemed to be dragging and Dagger found himself counting the hours until he saw Ryan. He smiled at the thought of Ryan joining him in Vegas. After his whirlwind visit back to L.A. to see Ryan and their erotic limo ride, he hadn't been able to concentrate on a damn thing. Every thought brought him right back to Ryan.

Dagger couldn't remember the last time he was this excited about a man and the potential for a relationship. A *relationship*? Dagger didn't do relationships – ever. He wasn't interested in the work involved in maintaining one and he certainly hadn't met anyone worth the effort, either.

Until Ryan.

Having Ryan in his life, all Dagger could think about was a full-blown relationship – right down to the white picket fence. He wanted that day-in-day-out connection with a real partner. Someone he could share every aspect of his life with – including his bed. Damn! He wanted all that with Ryan, and then some. Problem was, Dagger wasn't sure if Ryan would ever want the same things with him.

The long phone conversations they'd shared had confirmed how much they had in common; the core values they shared and their desire to have someone special in their lives. They seemed to be a perfect reflection to each other. And after the kisses they'd exchanged in the back of Dagger's limousine and inside his kitchen, Dagger knew the physical connection they shared was like nothing he'd ever experienced. Explosive. It was the one word Dagger felt adequately described the chemistry he felt with Ryan and he wanted a whole lot more.

Getting Ryan to that same place in his head and heart would be a challenge, but Dagger wanted to do the work involved to prove he was worthy of Ryan's love and commitment. He'd give it everything he had, to try and open Ryan's mind to simply be in the moment with Dagger and *feel*. If he could get Ryan there, he was quite certain they could be together in every sense of the word. A niggling little voice inside Dagger's own head told him Ryan could very well be 'the one' and that was something Dagger couldn't walk away from – no matter how much work was involved in getting Ryan to embrace the idea of having a real relationship with him.

Dagger closed his eyes and reclined on the bed inside his tour bus, remembering the warmth of Ryan's lips pressed to his, and every nerve ending in his body sparked to life. He glanced at his cell phone, aching to hear Ryan's voice, but it was too late to call him. He knew Ryan would be sleeping. If Ryan had any idea of the feelings Dagger was developing for him, he'd run hard and fast in the opposite direction.

The cell phone in Dagger's hand buzzed, announcing an incoming text message. He looked at the display panel and read the name of the sender. Gyro. He should have known without looking at the caller I.D. who it would be. Anytime he was in Phoenix performing, it was nearly guaranteed he'd be hooking up after the show with Gyro, an exotic, slender man, Dagger had known for a few years and the sex was nothing short of amazing every time they got together.

"R U hiding on your bus?" Gyro's text message asked.

"*It's late,*" Dagger typed back.

"*You're turning down an opportunity to fuck?*" Gyro asked.

Dagger contemplated Gyro's question for about half a second before he knew his decision was final. Christ, his head – and heart, really must be with Ryan if he was turning down some hot, no-strings sex with Gyro.

"*I'm involved with someone,*" Dagger typed and hit the send button, before he changed his mind.

"*Is he with you now?*" Gyro asked.

"*Don't push it, Gy. I can't – I won't do that to him.*"

"*Must be love if you're getting all monogamous on me,*" Gyro responded.

Dagger smiled at that. It was a little too early for love to be a factor with Ryan, but it sure as hell felt like he was well on his way to falling in love with him. And, damn, if that didn't feel like bliss!

"*Have a good night, Gy,*" Dagger typed and shut off his phone.

He'd have to go back to counting down the hours until he could see Ryan again; hold him, and stare into his blue pools of liquid sapphire. Dagger made a humming sound in the back of his throat. What he wouldn't do to hear the soothing sound of Ryan's voice that very minute, Dagger thought.

Would this week ever end?

The flight to Las Vegas was stressful for Ryan. Being the sole occupant on this private jet was unnerving in itself, but flying out to see Dagger upped the anxiety level by ten. He shifted in the leather seat and went through a mental inventory, double-checking to make sure he remembered to pack everything he wanted for this trip. His hand touched the pocket of his shirt where he had stashed the letter from the lab with his test results. It felt weird bringing it along on this trip. He wasn't sure he needed to, or if Dagger would want to see the letter with his own eyes to know Ryan was clean or not.

Ryan rolled his eyes at himself. It bothered him that he didn't know how these things worked and he hated feeling stupid. Instead of allowing his insecurity to swallow him alive, he tried to focus on how excited he was to see Dagger – face-to-face, and hopefully, mouth to mouth. He smiled at that thought. Yeah, he definitely hoped there'd be more kissing, maybe more touching, too. Beyond that, he wasn't sure what he wanted, and he refused to let himself get too hung up on it, either. He wanted to let things unfold as they were meant to, and maybe they wouldn't? Who knew. All he could do was sit back and try not to over-think this. If he could pull that off, it would be a fucking miracle.

Ryan left the arrival gate of the charter flight area at Henderson Executive airport south of Las Vegas. A driver wearing a black suit and tie waited just outside the door holding a sign bearing Ryan's name on it. He walked toward the man and managed a weak smile, feeling more like a man being led to slaughter than a man on a mini vacation. If he was the lamb did that make Dagger the big bad wolf?

"I'm Ryan Pierce," he said to the driver.

The man nodded. "Please follow me."

Ryan walked behind the driver down the crowded sidewalk outside the terminal toward the limousine. It was hot for a mid-morning in October in Vegas. Ryan was sweating and his heart was beating in his chest like he'd finished a marathon. He wanted to believe all of that was due to the heat, but he was pretty sure it had more to do with who he was meeting in Las Vegas. He was tempted to ask the driver to give him a scenic tour around the city so he had a little more time collect himself before meeting Dagger at the hotel.

The driver stopped beside the long, black limousine and opened the rear door. Ryan crawled inside and set his backpack on the carpeted floor beside the seat and the door shut behind him. A moment later his eyes adjusted to the change in lighting and he realized Dagger was sitting on the seat across from him; his backpack sitting on one of his booted feet. Ryan gulped in air at the sight of him. Deep brown hair feathered around his face and neck, a few strands fell over his forehead. He wore a silky, white shirt unbuttoned to his navel, rolled up to the elbow, and tucked into a pair of black leather pants. Ryan took several seconds to canvass every inch of Dagger; his partially spread thighs brought his eyes to Dagger's groin and what appeared to be the beginning of arousal. Ryan's eyes dragged up to Dagger's face and his heated gaze and Ryan felt his chest tighten.

"Good to finally see you, Ry," Dagger said. His smile was endless.

Ryan swallowed. "I didn't think I'd see you until the hotel."

"I couldn't wait," Dagger said. "Sorry to surprise you like this."

"No, no. It's fine."

Dagger swung himself over to Ryan's side of the car and sat beside him. His large hand touched Ryan's thigh and squeezed; his shoulder nudged Ryan's. "You look scared to death," Dagger said. "Am I really that scary?"

Ryan watched Dagger's hand on his leg and closed his eyes trying to tamp down the fear and simply be in the moment. Dagger's closeness and touch spread warmth through him. It felt comfortable; right, and his cock began to stretch the front of his pants.

"What I'm feeling is overwhelming," Ryan said in a soft voice.

"And, that scares you?"

"Fear of the unknown, I guess," Ryan said.

Dagger turned himself slightly on the seat; his face easing in close to Ryan's ear. "Maybe the unknown you fear is crazy good. Think you could handle crazy good?"

Dagger's voice vibrated against Ryan's exposed neck. The passenger compartment felt like it was closing in around Ryan. His throat was dry; constricted, and he felt like he was drowning. Ryan dropped his head against the back of the seat and rolled it toward Dagger. Their eyes met and Dagger's fingers caressed Ryan's face. "I'm glad you didn't shave," he said. "I love the scratch this gives me," then his fingers moved down onto Ryan's throat. His index finger teased the soft hollow at the base and his eyes met Ryan's.

"I don't want you to fear my touch, Ry," he said. "I want you to lose yourself in it and allow yourself to feel."

Dagger's fingers slid around the back of Ryan's neck and pulled him closer. His lips brushed and his tongue swiped a teasing lick at Ryan's bottom lip, then Ryan opened his mouth and took the kiss Dagger was offering. Heat raced across Ryan's skin making him sigh loudly.

"Tell me how good this feels, Ry," Dagger said, dipping his tongue in Ryan's mouth again. "Tell me you feel it like I do."

Ryan pushed his fingers through Dagger's hair and grabbed the back of his head; firmly holding Dagger to him, and their kiss turned carnal. Hungry bites and strokes of tongue pushed Ryan higher. Flashes of light fired in his head. His hands slid to Dagger's chest. He massaged the muscles flexing beneath the shirt; solid and hot to the touch, but he wanted more – needed more. More contact, more of Dagger's mouth, and much more touching.

He pushed Dagger onto his back and rolled on top of him; the hard arc of his cock landing alongside Dagger's. Ryan pressed his hips forward, starting a slow grind, and covered Dagger's mouth for another kiss. Dagger's hands reached around and gripped on to Ryan's ass and both men moaned.

"You're working me very close to losing control with you, Ry, and here on this seat isn't the best place for that to happen."

Ryan's hips stilled. He lifted himself up onto his elbows. It felt like he was coming back from an out-of-body experience. He looked down at Dagger pressed beneath him and couldn't believe his own assertive behavior – couldn't believe he was capable of it. Ryan pushed off the seat and sat upright. His gaze went to the side window and the traffic passing by their car.

"I'm sorry about that," Ryan said.

"Are you kidding me?" Dagger asked. "I fucking loved it. Don't apologize."

The limousine pulled in front of the Mandalay Bay Hotel and stopped.

Dagger hit the intercom button to talk to the driver. "Give us a minute," he instructed, then his head turned to Ryan and he smiled. "I don't know about you, but I need a little time to let things... settle down."

"I'm not sure time will help me with that," Ryan said, glancing at his lap.

A moment passed and finally Dagger reached for the door handle. "Ready?" he asked.

"Does it look like I am?" Ryan asked with a laugh.

Dagger's eyes dropped to the front of Ryan's tented pants. The look of a starving man crossed his face. Unconsciously he wet his lips. He tried to speak, then stopped and cleared his throat.

"You may want to carry your bag in front of you, so you don't get arrested," Dagger said.

Dagger cracked the door seal and the driver was there to pull it wide open; flooding the backseat with sunshine. Dagger stepped out and waited while Ryan collected his backpack from the floor and slid across the seat to follow. His head came out of the car first and Dagger extended his hand. It was an intimate gesture and panic washed over Ryan. Dagger must have seen the look and retracted his hand, sliding it into his front pocket.

Two security guards met Dagger at the car and walked with him to the front entrance of the hotel. Ryan lagged behind, not wanting to make it obvious they were together. The guards rode the elevator with them, too, each second making it more difficult for Ryan to accept where he was going and with whom. Dagger's head turned to him and his eyes, always so serene and warm, had an instant calming effect over Ryan.

They exited the elevator and followed the guards down the long corridor to the penthouse suite. Dagger used his pass key and opened the door. He waved goodbye to the guards and motioned Ryan to enter.

Ryan whistled approval at the vast expanse of living room space and the wall of windows facing the Vegas strip. He walked to the sliding glass doors and stepped out onto a private rooftop patio; one of three VIP suites facing the Vegas strip with similar verandas. Dagger was right beside him at the railing.

"Incredible view," Ryan said. "I bet it looks just as sweet all lit up at night."

Dagger's eyes were on him. "You'll be able to see for yourself later." He took the bag from Ryan's hand and started walking. "Come on," he said. "I'll show you the rest of the suite."

They went inside together with Dagger playing the dutiful tour guide, pulling Ryan by the hand as they passed a gourmet kitchen and down the hall into a large bedroom.

"This is the guest room," Dagger said. "Bathroom is in there," he said and pointed to a closed door. "You're welcome to stay in here, if you want," he said, facing Ryan. "Or, you can stay in my room with me."

Ryan felt his face flush and looked at his feet. Dagger tossed the backpack onto the bed, then reached for Ryan's hand again. He tugged gently and started moving from the room. He chatted as they walked, pointing out different highlights to the suite.

"Kitchen. Dining room. Exercise room," Dagger said.

"Exercise room?"

"State-of-the-art," Dagger said. "And sadly I won't have time to use it while I'm here."

The last room on the tour was Dagger's master suite. This room was almost as big as the living room, with a king-sized bed and a bathroom nearly as large as the bedroom. Another wide wall of windows in the bedroom opened up to a private patio.

Ryan stepped into the bathroom. A walk-in shower that could accommodate four was on the left, Jacuzzi tub on the right, separate room with a toilet and a wall dedicated to two sinks and a gilded mirror mounted above.

"Holy shit," Ryan said.

"I know," Dagger said. "Excessive and totally not me."

Ryan looked at him puzzled by his comment.

"Okay, so I lied," Dagger laughed. "I'm all about excess and my bedroom at home is at least this size – if not bigger, but definitely not with all these girly accents."

Ryan found his mind drifting to what Dagger's bedroom did look like and if he'd ever be standing inside it, as he was now with him in this bedroom in Las Vegas. His eyes darted to the bed; so roomy and comfortable in appearance. A part of him wanted to jump on it... with Dagger beneath him.

"I brought something for you," Ryan said, and left the room, walking back to the guest room. He removed a paper bag from his backpack on the bed and brought it out to the living room, sitting down on an ultra soft couch.

"A gift?" Dagger asked, siting down beside Ryan.

"Well, I'm not sure I'd classify it as a gift," Ryan said, as he handed it to Dagger.

"Hmmm, nondescript brown paper bag, Ryan, you know me too well," Dagger teased. "I'm having a flashback of my youth." He reached inside and pulled out the Music Spin magazine with a photograph of Dagger occupying the entire front cover. "Is your article about me in here?"

"Page ten," Ryan said. He leaned in to Dagger and watched him open the magazine and flip through the pages, stopping on page ten. Dagger's finger touched a full page shot of himself performing on stage; the camera angle shooting from his feet right up Dagger's long legs, making him appear twelve feet tall. Colorful lights illuminated his face and hair and spilled onto the stage below Dagger's feet.

"Really nice shot, Ry. This is from our Columbus show a few months back."

"It's one of my favorites of you," Ryan said.

Dagger looked at him. A slow smile relaxed his face. "Thank you," he said. "This means a lot." He flipped through the other six pages of the article, clearly excited about the layout of each page. "Did you pick out all these photographs of me?"

"Yeah, I had fun with that," Ryan said.

"Something tells me you don't give such personal attention to all your articles, do you Ry?"

"Typically, I email the finished text copy to my editor and I never see it again until it prints. Sometimes I don't even bother to look at it then."

Dagger set the magazine on the coffee table at their knees and turned to face Ryan. "Knowing that makes this even more special." Dagger reached for Ryan's hand and brought his fingers up to his mouth. He kissed the digits and then set Ryan's hand on his thigh.

"How long before you have to be backstage?" Ryan asked.

Dagger glanced at his watch. "Four hours," he said. "We have time to go get some lunch... or we could stay here, maybe get room service later."

Ryan lightly squeezed Dagger's leg and flashed him a nervous smile. "I like the sound of room service."

Dagger shifted closer to Ryan on the couch. "Me, too," he said. His hand cupped the side of Ryan's face, then his fingernails lightly scraped down the edge of Ryan's unshaven jawline then fanned over his throat. Ryan's breath was coming heavy, his chest rising quickly. The familiar ache Dagger caused had returned to his groin. He set a shaky hand to Dagger's chest above his heart. He could feel it pounding beneath his palm. Ryan watched his hand moving over the width of Dagger's chest and heard him moan. His eyes lifted and Dagger had settled against the back of the couch, his eyes closed, a satisfied smile on his face. When Ryan removed his hand, Dagger's eyes opened.

"Don't stop," Dagger said. "I love it when you touch me."

Ryan leaned back, leveling his face on the couch with Dagger's. Their eyes held; smoky and filled with carnal promise.

"Kiss me," Dagger whispered. "Like you did in the car."

Dagger slid another inch closer. His hand curled under the mound of knotted heat between Ryan's legs and squeezed. Ryan's breath caught in his chest and the fire between them lit. He closed the remaining distance between them and pressed his lips to Dagger. Soon as Dagger opened his mouth, Ryan was on him; loving the taste and perfect fluid texture of the man. No matter how he tried, he couldn't get enough. Ryan swirled his tongue around Dagger's again and Dagger dropped flat on his back on the couch; their mouths never separating.

Dagger's hands slid over Ryan's backside and settled on his ass, grinding himself to Ryan. Dagger's fingers dug into his buttocks, seemingly pushing through the fabric of his jeans, and Ryan heard himself moan again.

Dagger rolled onto his side and eased Ryan onto his; turning them to face each other. Dagger's hand ran over Ryan's chest and down onto his stomach. His fingers started pulling Ryan's t-shirt from his jeans, then went to the belt buckle. Ryan froze and Dagger calmed him with another mind-blowing kiss that nearly sucked the air from his lungs. The belt buckle released and Dagger's fingers went to the metal button and zipper.

Ryan felt the teeth of his zipper inching down and he started to squirm. If felt so good. He didn't want to stop, but knew he probably should, then asked himself why he'd question something that felt as perfect as this at all.

"It's all right, Ry," Dagger said gently, and offered him another slow kiss. "I won't do anything you don't want."

Ryan felt long fingers reaching into the front of his jeans and boxer briefs, then circle his cock. The hand clamped around his flesh and pulled off one stroke.

"Fuccckkk," Ryan said on a long sigh.

"Tell me you want this," Dagger said.

"Oh, my God, yes" Ryan said.

Their lips were touching but not fully kissing. Ryan's hands held on to Dagger's shoulders. It was becoming more and more difficult to draw in a breath. The pleasure of Dagger's fingers exploring him was bringing him close to release. Dagger's other hand was spreading the front of Ryan's pants further and trying to push them off his hips. Dagger's fist tightened and turned on Ryan's cock. Ryan threw his head back and groaned.

"You are so hard for me," Dagger hissed against Ryan's open mouth. "Come in my hand. I want to feel you shoot all over me."

"Oh, God – oh, God!"

Ryan's body tensed, then arched into Dagger's hand and he exploded all over both of them. Dagger continued to work Ryan's cock through the aftershocks until Ryan finally stilled. Dagger gave Ryan a soft kiss, then pulled his hand from Ryan's pants.

"You look so fucking hot when you come," Dagger said.

Ryan eased himself upright. His fingers pushed through his hair. He looked down at his stomach and saw the mess he had created all over his shirt, then glanced over at Dagger and saw a few drops of his come on Dagger's white shirt, too.

"Damn, I'm really sorry about that," Ryan said, and stood up from the couch.

"You're joking, right?" Dagger asked. "I love getting messy with you."

"Let me go clean up," he said, and started walking down the hall.

Ryan entered the guest bedroom and went to his bag. He carefully pulled off his t-shirt and wiped up as much come as he could from his stomach. Luckily, his shirt had taken the brunt of that release; very little had splattered anywhere else, except on Dagger. The thought of that made Ryan's face burn hotter. He was embarrassed by his lack of control. That made two times where he was unable to hold off ejaculating all over himself from Dagger's touch. At least this time he held off long enough to get his cock out of his pants. That was progress, right?

He sat down on the edge of the bed, holding his shirt in his hands, and feeling pretty stupid. Movement in the doorway lifted Ryan's gaze.

"You okay?" Dagger asked.

Ryan rolled his eyes and tossed his dirty shirt on to the floor.

Dagger had removed his shirt and was holding a terry cloth towel from his bathroom; wiping off his hands. He started walking toward Ryan sitting on the bed. His swagger had Ryan's complete attention; his eyes transfixed on his bare, muscled chest and stomach. His skin was tanned nicely and looked soft to the touch. Swirls of hair covered Dagger's breasts and a thin dark line of hair split the center of his sculpted stomach and disappeared into his tight, low-riding leather pants.

Dagger plunked himself down on the bed beside Ryan and draped his arm around Ryan's back. His fingers massaged the tight muscles there, then he leaned in and pressed his lips to the skin of Ryan's shoulder.

Ryan felt the heat of Dagger's tongue dragging over him. The smooth touch of tongue against skin was setting off electric charges in Ryan and his core temperature started pitching higher all over again. The effect this man had on him was incredible, like nothing he'd ever experienced. No one's touch compared to Dagger's. It truly left him breathless and lightheaded.

Dagger placed another feathery kiss against Ryan's collar bone. "You're freaking out, aren't you?" he asked.

Ryan exhaled. "I'm trying not to, but it's difficult. I'm completely out of my comfort zone."

Dagger lifted his head making his face level to Ryan's. "Do you want to go back to L.A.? I can have a plane fueled and waiting for you at the airport within the hour. No hard feelings. No worries, Ry. I don't want to stress you out."

Ryan flopped back onto the mattress and pressed the heels of his hands into his eyes. Dagger reclined on one elbow beside him.

"Do you want me to call the charter company?" Dagger asked.

Ryan rolled his head toward Dagger. "I'd like to stay," he said.

Dagger sighed and placed his hand on Ryan's bare chest, sifting his fingers through the soft hair. "I'm relieved to hear you say that, Ry, because I really don't want you to go." Dagger's hand slid over Ryan's breast; his index finger circled a light brown nipple; his eyes followed the movement of his hand. "My God, you're beautiful."

Dagger dropped his mouth over Ryan's nipple, his tongue curling over the tiny, hardened bead of flesh, tugging it into his mouth, and Ryan made an audible sigh. That sound seemed to be the only encouragement Dagger needed and he began kissing and licking his way all over Ryan's torso. Dagger's fingers explored, too, and had brought Ryan's body back to full arousal again.

Dagger's middle finger dipped into Ryan's belly button and found the wetness of leftover semen from Ryan's earlier release.

"Looks like you missed a little," Dagger said. He ran his tongue around the rim of Ryan's indent, then slipped it inside and lapped it clean.

The slurping noises from Dagger had Ryan coming unglued. His fingers combed through Dagger's long hair at the back of his head. The attention from Dagger's tongue had him on fire. Then Dagger's hand drifted into the front of Ryan's open jeans. Fingers clasped around his cock; rigid and straining again for release, as if the orgasm from a few minutes ago hadn't happened.

Dagger's mouth licked lower and Ryan thought he'd lose his mind. Dagger's mouth was so close to his cock, he could feel the heat of his breath on it. Part of him wanted to use the hand on Dagger's head to push his mouth onto his cock and feel the heat inside that his tongue only knew existed.

Was he really imagining his cock in a man's mouth? Wanting it so bad he couldn't think of anything else? The familiar inner turmoil began to churn in Ryan's gut. He could not let it take over his thoughts. Not now. He needed to stay present and be in this moment with this amazing man and just *feel*.

Dagger must have sensed his trepidation. He momentarily stopped licking Ryan's stomach and glanced up at him.

"Do you want me to stop?" Dagger asked.

Ryan shook his head. "No... I'm trying not to over-think."

"Over-thinking is not allowed, Ry." Dagger whispered against his skin. "Just breathe. I want you relaxed, so you can really feel this." Dagger pressed a soft reassuring kiss to Ryan's hip, then reached below his butt to slide his jeans down and off his legs. Ryan's cock sprang free and Dagger moved over it. He pressed his cheek to it first, slowly rubbing his face in circles. The chafe of whisker stubble electrified Ryan's already over-sensitized skin. Ryan could hear Dagger inhale, then felt the warmth of his incredible tongue against his shaft.

"Fuck!" Ryan cursed, lifting his head and looking down at Dagger. "I won't last."

"Yeah, you will," Dagger said. "I'll make sure of it."

Ryan dropped back onto the mattress and moaned, feeling Dagger's tongue swirl around the engorged head and slide down the length and back up the opposite side. He completely coated Ryan's cock with his saliva, then eased off one stroke with his hand before squeezing Ryan at the root.

A chuckle rolled from Ryan's mouth sounding more like a strained groan. "I almost lost it," he said.

"I could tell, Ry, that's why I'm giving you a minute," Dagger said, using teasing flicks of his tongue to keep Ryan right on the razor's edge of arousal.

Another long lap of Dagger's tongue had Ryan at the brink again and he arched on the bed. "This feels so good. Don't stop."

"I have no intention of it," Dagger said. "I'm going to have fun torturing you for a little while, then maybe I'll let you come."

Another moan came from Ryan. "You're gonna kill me."

"I'll be killing you with pleasure, Ry. I can't think of a better way to go."

Dagger took Ryan deeply into the back of his throat and held him there. Ryan gasped at the intense sensations ripping through him. The ache in his balls was increasing by the second. He wanted to scream out; arch into the embrace, but he remained still. Moving would bring an end to this new bliss all too soon and Ryan wasn't ready for that. If he could only make this one moment last forever.

Ryan tipped his head to watch Dagger; his straight dark hair spilled over his lower belly. Each subtle movement of Dagger's head swished the long strands on his skin. It felt cool like silk; a delicious contrast to the heat of Dagger's mouth.

Dagger pulled off Ryan's cock, holding the wide head between his lips; the glistening shaft visible to Ryan. The sight made him hum and then draw in a breath making a hissing sound through his teeth. His head rolled back on the quilt.

"Dagger, please."

Fingers tightly circled the base of Ryan's cock and then the wet heat lifted. "You want to come?" Dagger asked, dragging one teasing lick over Ryan's tip.

"Fuck! Yes," Ryan said.

Dagger's tongue swirled around the crest, then his mouth opened and took Ryan inside as far as he could in one fast stroke. Ryan cried out and reached for Dagger's head; holding it in place, his legs spread wider. He was on the edge and fearful Dagger would hold him off again. Strong fingers curled around his ball sac and massaged, while lips and tongue continued to deliver the most exquisite pleasure to his cock.

One finger slipped lower and found the puckered indent in his crease, then applied the slightest amount of pressure without entering.

Ryan saw stars, then brilliant kaleidoscopes of iridescent colors, exploding in front of him like fireworks on the Fourth of July. He wasn't aware an orgasm could feel this good and be survivable. His hands grabbed onto his head, as if to keep it from blowing apart; his back arched off the bed, the one remaining connection to Dagger was his mouth. The warm, moist suction milked him through the very last tremor, and Ryan exhaled. Slowly, the breath came out of him, like he'd been holding that one breath his whole life. It felt like his body had turned to liquid and was seeping into the bed.

Dagger dragged his tongue across Ryan's stomach and chest, up the length of his throat, and stopped on his chin. Ryan's mouth was open, eyes closed, and his hands still holding on to his head. Dagger licked Ryan's bottom lip, then rolled to his side.

"Say something, Ry," Dagger said, his hand touching Ryan's chest.

Ryan's head turned toward Dagger. His arm reached and pulled Dagger closer, just a few inches separated their mouths. Dagger moved first brushing his lips to Ryan's.

"You cool with that?" Dagger asked. "Or, are you freaking out?"

Ryan stared at Dagger with unblinking eyes. "I can't think of an adjective good enough to describe how that felt."

"Hmmm, that good?"

"The best," Ryan said.

"I told you, men give a better blow job."

Ryan laughed, then his expression turned serious. "I'm not sure I can give you back what you've given to me."

"I'm not asking you to go down on me," Dagger said. "I'm still amazed you're here with me at all; naked, and getting off from my touch. I call that a gift."

"I might call it a miracle," Ryan smiled.

"Or an awakening," Dagger said. He opened his mouth against Ryan's; his tongue slipping inside and stroking. Ryan rolled into the kiss, resting on his side; bare chest to bare chest, the hair from each causing the perfect friction.

Between them, Dagger's fingers went to work on his own pants; unzipping and pushing them off his legs. He moved back against Ryan, his fist beginning to stroke his cock.

Ryan could feel Dagger's hand shifting back and forth over his erection; each stroke pronounced when the back of his hand bumped into Ryan's stomach. He wanted to watch Dagger get himself off, but couldn't bring himself to give up the wonderful sensations Dagger's mouth had to offer with each new kiss.

Ryan cupped the back of Dagger's neck and pulled him tighter to his mouth; deepening their kiss. He could taste the lingering tangy flavor of his come on Dagger's tongue and it aroused the hell out of him, made his cock start to stiffen again.

The hand Ryan had behind Dagger's neck moved down onto his chest and across a nipple. Dagger sighed at the touch and it made Ryan grin. His fingers ran through the hair, trimmed short, then his hand dropped lower. His knuckles brushed Dagger's stomach and stopped at the point he could feel Dagger's hand banging into it with each new stroke on his cock. Ryan's fingers stretched and touched Dagger's hand and the jerking motion stopped.

Dagger broke the seal on their mouths and gazed at Ryan. "Do you want to touch me?" he asked in a soft voice.

Ryan nodded. "Yeah, I think I do," he said and swallowed hard.

Dagger removed his hand and allowed Ryan access to his cock. The hesitation was obvious and Dagger did his best to urge Ryan, relaxing him with his mouth. Ryan used one finger first, to run the long length of Dagger's cock; from base to tip, then his fingers curled under and around the thick shaft, slowly tightening. The heat and weight of it amazed Ryan. He explored every inch, reveled in each ridge and vein, mapping it to memory through touch. He reached the tip and felt the precome leaking from the slit, collected it with his index finger, and used it to lubricate the shaft. Feeling Dagger pulse against his palm was enough to make him start to leak himself.

"Yes, just like that," Dagger sighed.

Ryan smiled against Dagger's mouth, encouraged by Dagger's praise. He wanted to pleasure Dagger, make him come with an intensity like Dagger had done for him. He tightened his grip and continued stroking, spinning his palm around Dagger's shaft. Each groan that left Dagger's mouth gave Ryan more confidence. He added his other hand, moving it between Dagger's thighs, to massage Dagger's balls. It didn't take long for Ryan to bring Dagger to the edge; which surprised them both.

"Holy, shit! Ryan, you're gonna make me come," Dagger cried out.

Ryan turned his fist again and felt Dagger's cock pulse and his balls pull up tightly to his body. Then he heard the cry of relief as Dagger released. Ryan felt the first hot blast of come hit his stomach. A second string hit his forearm, then Dagger leaned in and finished right beside Ryan's belly button.

Dagger held on to Ryan, panting, the smile on his face so bright. It made Ryan's heart clench, knowing he had been able to give Dagger this. After Dagger's breath slowed, he looked down between them and saw Ryan's belly.

"Looks like I left quite a mess on you," Dagger laughed. "Reminds me of the picture I emailed to you, except this time it's all on *your* stomach."

Dagger ran his fingers through the thick fluid and coated them, then lifted them to bring to his mouth. Ryan took Dagger's wrist and diverted his fingers to his mouth instead; sliding the digits between his lips, his tongue curling around them to taste. Dagger sighed at the sight of his fingers in Ryan's mouth. Ryan watched Dagger's pupils dilate and the smile on Dagger's face turned hungry.

"That is the hottest thing I've seen you do," Dagger said. He removed his fingers from Ryan's mouth and pushed them into his own, then pulled Ryan to him for a kiss. Their arms wrapped around each other, gently at first, then the embrace turned more urgent as the kiss grew deeper.

"Tasting myself on your tongue makes me so fucking hard," Dagger said. He slid a leg over Ryan's thighs and stretched out over him; chest to chest and cock rubbing against cock. Dagger's come on Ryan's stomach offered the perfect lubrication as they started to rock together.

"Naked wrestling?" Ryan asked.

Dagger tipped his head and grinned. "Would you like that?"

The new position had an instant effect on Ryan. One rub from Dagger and something inside Ryan triggered. He laced his legs with Dagger's and flipped him onto his back, this time Ryan was the one pressing Dagger into the mattress using his chest. Ryan pinned Dagger's arms above his head and started to grind circles on Dagger.

Ryan stared down at Dagger. Lust made his eyes sparkle with fluid, his mouth partially opened, his body relaxed and giving in to every rotation of Ryan's hips. This was intimate beyond anything Ryan had experienced with a woman in his past. He bit his bottom lip trying to hold in the emotion this moment was pouring over him.

Both cocks were unrelentingly hard and straining again with each long thrust against the other. Chest hair raking over sensitive nipples and muscled thighs flexing together, it was an overload of sensory pleasure. Ryan threw his head over his shoulders and moaned loudly.

"You love having my cock under you, don't you, Ry?"

Ryan managed a grunt for a response and thrust again, making Dagger moan.

"I don't bottom for anyone, but I would for you," Dagger said.

Ryan's hips slowed and he let go of Dagger's arms on the bed. Dagger's hands lifted and curled around Ryan's biceps lightly squeezing, then he gently tugged Ryan down onto him bringing their mouths together. Ryan was now flat against Dagger, both men panting; cocks pulsing between them, then

Dagger opened his thighs and Ryan slipped between them, making for an even more intimate connection. The sudden shift made Ryan's breath catch in his throat.

"Do you like the idea of fucking me?" Dagger whispered. His hands dropped to Ryan's hips and eased Ryan across his cock and balls with perfect precision.

Ryan held onto Dagger's face and kissed him; a soulful kiss, the meaning so much more significant than Ryan could ever articulate with words. How could you express an emotion you didn't yet understand? Being with Dagger made no sense, and yet, it felt – perfect. Ryan sighed against Dagger's mouth and gave himself over to the feelings rising up inside him. Dagger's hands moved onto Ryan's buttocks; his fingers drifting into the crease in the middle, as he kept them rocking together. Dagger's fingers slipped lower in Ryan's crack and Ryan trembled. One more slow drag of hips over hips and Ryan arched in Dagger's embrace and climaxed between them. Dagger wrapped his legs around the back of Ryan's and joined him with his own release.

Ryan collapsed on Dagger's chest; his breathing, his head, and his heart slowly coming back to earth. Dagger shifted beneath him, his strong fingers skimming the muscles of Ryan's back. A sliver of uncertainty flickered inside him but he quickly pushed it down. He had no room for any of that negative bullshit right now. He closed his eyes and smiled. He felt peace, every nerve ending was alive and triggering an avalanche of sensation to every point of his body.

This felt right. He was where he was supposed to be. How long had he waited to feel this connection with someone? He'd given up years of his life endlessly working to make a relationship develop into *this*, but with Dagger it wasn't work.

It just was – and it worked. Did it matter this feeling came to him with a man attached to it? Did that make it any less real?

Ryan rolled off Dagger and on to his back and Dagger lifted his head to peek at his stomach. "Look at that, Ry," he said. "You and I mixed together. It doesn't get any better."

Ryan glanced down at his own stomach and the mess smeared all over it. The sight made him laugh. "I think we could both use a shower."

"Go ahead," Dagger said, "And I'll join you."

CHAPTER TEN

Ryan's body felt like rubber, as they made their way onto the elevator to head downstairs for Dagger's pre-show meet and greet. Between the long, hot shower they'd taken together – giving each other another stimulating body grind surrounded by a dozen water spigots pelting against them, and the blow job Dagger delivered after they finally stepped out of the bathroom – Ryan was completely exhausted. He leaned against the cool metal wall of the elevator and closed his eyes.

Dagger watched Ryan's sluggish movements and decided to hold off on selecting a floor number on the elevator panel inside the door which held the car in place. "You look like you're gonna slip into a coma on me," Dagger teased.

"I feel like I could," Ryan said.

Dagger took two steps toward Ryan and stood there with a predatory look on his face. "I'd love to maul you again right here, but there's too many cameras watching us."

Having Dagger standing this close had his body coming to attention. He slid upright on the wall and pressed his backside to it. He watched Dagger's eyes dance around his face, then settle on his mouth.

"Don't do that," Ryan whispered.

"Do what?"

"You're staring and it's making me..." Ryan's head turned to search for the concealed cameras.

"Hard?"

"Well, yes, there is that." Ryan smiled. "It will be a miracle if I survive this weekend without injury."

"Wait until later," Dagger said. The ring of Dagger's cell phone interrupted their flirting. He exhaled and lifted the phone to his ear.

"What, Tony?" Dagger asked.

"You're late for the meet and greet," Tony said.

"I'm aware of that, and we're on our way down to the lobby now," Dagger said.

"We're? Who the hell is with you?" Tony asked.

"Ryan Pierce."

"Are you doing another interview with him?"

Dagger laughed, using that devilishly throaty sound he was well known for when he was about to raise some hell or say something to raise a few eyebrows. He punched in the proper floor number on the elevator panel, the car briefly jostled them, then began an expedited descent to the lobby.

"He's off the clock this weekend," Dagger said, his eyes canvassing Ryan.

"Hmmmm, I don't like the sound of that," Tony said. "We'll have to talk about it later."

"Nothing to talk about, Tony. It's cool. I'll see you in a few," Dagger said. He disconnected the call.

"Is Tony questioning my visit?" Ryan asked. He watched the floor numbers quickly decreasing on the electronic panel above the doors.

A moment later the doors to the elevator opened and a security guard met Dagger as he stepped into the lobby. Camera flashes from a few photographers blinded them and an eruption of screams echoed in the lobby from the gathered crowd being held back behind velvet ropes. Most were women, jumping up and down and yelling Dagger's name to get his attention. Dagger gave them a broad smile and waved as the security guard directed him down the hall. Ryan stayed with him and did his best to avoid having his picture taken.

Tony met them in the hall and he took Dagger by the elbow, running through a few last minute changes to the schedule. Then his eyes hit Ryan.

"Make sure you stay out of the way," Tony said to Ryan.

Dagger touched Tony on the chest and gave him a light shove. "Don't be rude," Dagger said. "Ryan is here as my guest. Show some respect."

The meet and greet took almost two hours. Dozens of people practically crushed each other to get into the room to say hello to Dagger. How many women had Dagger hugged and kissed, Ryan thought. If they only knew where his lips had been just a short time ago. Ryan smiled at his joke and scanned the crowd. The fans loved Dagger; worshiped him. Some cried, some insisted they get a photograph with him. He autographed more than one bared body part, and Dagger accepted it all with grace. He wiped their tears, even sat down for a while to speak at eye-level with one young girl in a wheelchair.

Ryan watched it all from a distance, seeing a man known for his enormous stage ego and rock swagger show another side of himself. Ryan found it hard not to get emotional. This visit was supposed to be all about revealing themselves to the other and exploring what the found together. But the man Ryan was discovering was better than he imagined; more human and real, with an endless amount of compassion. There was a grace about Dagger that really spoke to Ryan, so far removed from the rock star enigma for which he was known.

Every once in a while, Dagger's eyes would find Ryan in the crowded room and hold. The heat Ryan felt from him was always smoldering. In those brief stolen moments from across the room, Dagger's eyes said so much. It made Ryan's heart begin race and his palms sweat. This new feeling he was experiencing with Dagger scared the shit out of him.

When the last fan was escorted from the room, Dagger approached Ryan. His hand touched Ryan on the shoulder, then his fingers swept down to his hip and across his ass. It was a quick glance of a touch, but Ryan felt every nuance of it as Dagger's fingers skimmed across his body. He looked around the room to see if anyone else had seen it, too. Thankfully the only people left in the room were stage crew and a handful of other personnel and none of them seemed to be paying attention.

"Come on," Dagger said. "I need to go to my dressing room and warm up."

Ryan walked beside Dagger down the hall and waited while he opened up a door. Dagger stepped inside and shut the door as soon as Ryan entered. Dagger remained leaning up against the closed door; his fingers turned the lock on the knob.

Ryan surveyed the small square room. There wasn't much for amenities, that was for sure. A couch and a couple of metal folding chairs sitting beside a long rectangular table and that was about it. No fruit baskets, lunch meat platters, or liquor bottle display; none of the usual items Ryan would expect to see in a backstage dressing room. Ryan spun around and faced Dagger.

"This isn't your dressing room," Ryan said.

"What makes you say that?" Dagger asked, still leaning against the door. He crossed his legs at the ankle accentuating the bulge between his legs.

"You're forgetting what I do for a living," Ryan said. "I've seen my share of backstage dressing rooms."

Dagger laughed and pushed off the door. He came across the floor toward Ryan. The smile on his face faded leaving behind the mask of an emotion Ryan hadn't seen on Dagger yet.

"What are you up to?" Ryan asked.

"I needed a moment alone with you."

Ryan didn't move. "Who's room is this?"

"I have no clue," Dagger said. "But for the time being, it's ours."

Dagger stood in front of Ryan. Only a few inches separated them. Ryan could smell the breath mint in Dagger's mouth, then heard the crunching sound he made as he chewed it. Dagger ran his fingertips across Ryan's cheek.

"Are you okay?" Ryan asked, seeing what looked like emotion building in Dagger's eyes.

Dagger exhaled and reached for Ryan, pulling him against his chest and Ryan wrapped his arms around him. The embrace was loose but there was nothing awkward about it. Ryan sensed Dagger needed his strength right then, and not his insecurities about their developing relationship.

"It's good to hold you," Dagger said, and pressed a soft kiss to Ryan's neck. He pulled back and rubbed his nose to Ryan's, then skimmed his lips with his. "That girl in the wheelchair really got to me," he said. "I almost lost it right there listening to her tell me about her cancer."

Ryan rubbed Dagger's back and felt him relax. "You were really good with her," Ryan said.

Dagger stepped back and wiped at his eyes. "I'm sorry," he said. "I didn't mean to dump this in your lap."

"What do you mean?"

Dagger hopped up on the table and sat down. "I had a kid sister," he said. "She was three years old when she was diagnosed with a rare form of leukemia. She passed a week after her fifth birthday; I was ten. A lot of my childhood memories revolve around her getting treatments. It wasn't pretty."

Ryan covered his mouth and walked to Dagger. He stood between his parted knees and hugged him tightly. "I'm so sorry, Dagger."

Dagger slid his arms around Ryan's waist; gripping at his shirt. "It's been a while since I've thought about it, but when I saw that little girl with no hair because of the chemo, it brought it all back."

"What was your sister's name?" Ryan asked.

"Meghan," Dagger said. "She was a pretty little thing. She'd be close to thirty right now, had she lived."

Ryan could hear the sadness in his voice and it killed him. "If she looked anything like you do, she'd be a beautiful woman."

"Thanks for saying that, Ry," he said. "We looked a lot alike as kids and despite the five year age difference, we were close."

The ring of a cell phone forced Dagger to let go of Ryan.

"I hate this fucking phone," Dagger said, lifting it to his ear as he stepped down from the table. "What can I do for you, Tony?"

"Where the hell are you?" Tony asked.

"None of your business," Dagger said. He walked to the door and motioned Ryan to follow him.

"You're supposed to be in your dressing room," Tony said.

"I got lost," Dagger said.

"Well, get a fucking map and find your way – soon," Tony said.

Ryan watched Dagger slide his phone back into his pocket. "You don't get along with Tony, do you?"

"Most of the time he's okay," Dagger said. "But tonight he's driving me nuts."

"Maybe he's pissed I'm here," Ryan said.

"Probably, but I don't give a shit," Dagger said. "I have the right to invite guests to my shows."

A moment later, Dagger opened the door to his dressing room and Tony was waiting. He rose from a lounge chair and approached them.

"You've got some time before you go on," Tony said. "Eat and warm up," was all he said before he left the room, slamming the door behind him.

Ryan watched Tony leave. By the time he turned back to Dagger, he was already filling a plate with macaroni salad and sliced roast beef.

"Damn, this smells good," Dagger said. "Either that, or I'm hungry enough to eat just about anything."

Ryan stood beside him at the food table. His mouth started watering at all the different food selections and realized he hadn't eaten much since he had arrived in Vegas. Dagger and he had barely taken the time to have a snack up in his room and now Ryan was feeling the full effect of that.

"We never really had lunch," Ryan said.

Dagger looked at him and smiled. "I guess we had better things to do," he said. He winked at Ryan and popped a cherry tomato into his mouth.

Ryan created a turkey sandwich using the breads and condiments displayed on the table and sat down in a chair to eat. They were quiet while they ate; uncharacteristic for Dagger, who never seemed to be at a loss for words.

"I want to do something for that little girl's family," Dagger finally said. "Maybe a trip or give them some money to help with the medical bills."

Ryan lifted his head from his plate and looked at Dagger. Once again, the man's big heart was surprising him. "I think that would be a nice gesture," Ryan said.

Dagger nodded, a nervous smile curling one side of his mouth. "I'll have Tony take care of it."

After they ate, Dagger began running through a series of vocal exercises, then warmed up his fingers by plucking cords on an acoustic guitar. A knock sounded on the door and Ryan glanced at his watch. He knew it must be time to head to the stage and stood up from his chair.

Dagger set the guitar back into a stand and walked to Ryan. He took his hand and tugged him against his chest. "I'm so glad you're here," he said.

"Me, too," Ryan said.

Dagger leaned in and pressed his mouth to Ryan's and they melted into each other. Dagger ran his tongue along the seam of Ryan's lips and he opened for him, nipping with his teeth. Ryan spun them around, pushing Dagger up against the wall. They hit with a loud thud and Ryan ground himself into him.

Dagger grabbed onto Ryan's ass and licked at his bottom lip. "I can't wait to get you upstairs to my room," he said. Ryan's cock flexed in his pants and Dagger smiled. "Feels like you're eager for that to happen, too."

"Never thought in a million years I'd admit this about a guy, but yeah, I am," Ryan said.

Dagger bent in to Ryan's ear. "That's because you're falling for me."

Ryan tipped away from Dagger and caught his gaze. He liked the way Dagger made him feel, but did that mean he was falling for the guy?

Another knock came at the door. Dagger stepped away from Ryan and swung open the door. The stage director was standing there.

"Fifteen minutes," the man said and continued down the hall.

Dagger shut the door and walked over to a rack of clothing in the corner of the room to sift through the choices he had for shirts to wear on stage. He pulled the t-shirt he wore over his shoulders and tossed it onto a chair. Ryan watched Dagger select a royal blue silk dress shirt and a second one identical in style and fabric, but wine colored. He held both up to his bare chest.

"What do you think?" Dagger asked.

Both colors looked amazing against Dagger's dark skin but Ryan was partial to how he looked without a shirt on at all. "The blue one," he said.

Dagger smiled and slid on the shirt, buttoning a few buttons at the bottom, then undoing his pants to tuck it in. He looked up at Ryan and raised one eyebrow. "Would you like to help?"

Ryan laughed and shook his head. "You don't need my help with that."

"No, but two sets of hands are way more fun."

Dagger finished getting dressed and walked over to a full-length mirror, he used his fingers to comb through his hair and fluff it up. There would be no pre-show hair and make-up tonight. He wanted to spend every minute he could alone with Ryan.

"That's as good as this crowd is gonna get," Dagger said. He turned toward Ryan and held out his hand, then waited for Ryan to come up beside him. Dagger threaded his fingers with Ryan's and pulled him in for a soft kiss that quickly flamed into something hard and hot. Dagger broke their seal and set his forehead to Ryan's and exhaled loudly.

"I figured I better do that now," Dagger said. "Once we get out there, I won't be able to touch you until after the show."

"Understandable," Ryan said.

Dagger opened up the door and dropped Ryan's hand. Ryan instantly missed the warmth and weight of it and how perfectly it fit against his. He followed Dagger down the hall, doing his best to stay in the background. A few doors down, Dagger met up with the four other guys that made up his band,

Black Ice. They hugged and talked briefly about the song list they'd be performing, then Dagger introduced Ryan to them, and they all proceeded toward the stage, pausing just short of the curtain area.

Ryan heard the introduction of the band and the audience roar in excitement. Dagger turned to Ryan and smiled.

"I'll see you in a few," Dagger said.

"Go kill 'em," Ryan said. He watched Dagger walk out to center stage and grab the microphone.

"Good evening Las Vegas!" Dagger yelled to the audience.

Ryan couldn't stop the smile that formed on his face. His chest swelled with pride, seeing Dagger in his element like this, and the last thread of uncertainty in his visit evaporated. This is where he wanted to be; where he needed to be, no matter what anyone else had to say about it.

"So, you and Dagger are together?" Tony asked, standing beside Ryan.

Ryan turned and looked at Tony. He wasn't sure why the man was insistent on being a prick to him, but he refused to allow Tony's negativity to diminish what he was feeling being here in Las Vegas with Dagger.

"Dagger invited me to the show," Ryan said. "That's it."

Tony laughed. "Dagger tells me everything," he said. "I know exactly what's going on between you two. I knew what he was up to long before you even knew."

"What the hell does that mean?" Ryan asked.

"You need to understand something," Tony said. "You 'out' Dagger and you'll be outing yourself – I'll make sure of it. Remember that."

"I have no intention of outing him," Ryan said.

"That's what you say, Ryan, but at the end of the day you're still a reporter. You report the news. Isn't that right?"

"I gave Dagger my word."

Tony smiled, but it came across his face looking more like a sneer. "Ah, yes, your word," Tony said. "And we should take you at your word and trust you, why?"

"What the fuck is your problem?" Ryan asked.

A smile twisted Tony's facial features. "It will be difficult to damage Dagger's reputation, when your own will be at stake; which is why he's with you," Tony said. "It's called insurance. You fuck him over in any way, and you can be guaranteed never work in this business again."

Ryan's head spun with irrational thoughts of dragging Tony into a room and beating his face to a pulp. What the fuck was Tony's deal? His eyes went to Dagger singing his heart out at center stage and his powerful swagger, as he moved around with perfect fluid grace. Their eyes connected and the smile Dagger flashed him made Ryan's chest cramp tight.

Was there any truth to what Tony said? Was this some kind of a game for Dagger? A sick joke? Was Dagger with him solely to save his own ass? Was there a special prize given when a gay man managed to get a straight guy into bed? What kind of fool did that make him, Ryan thought. He turned away from Dagger and watched the road crew shifting around crates and cables backstage. Ryan thought of leaving, but he wouldn't give Tony the satisfaction nor would he stalk off without talking to Dagger first. He had a few questions for Dagger and Dagger sure as hell better have the right answers for him and it would be done face-to-face.

Ryan swallowed hard. He knew all too well what happened whenever they found themselves face-to-face. It was a given, as neither of them seemed to foster any control when the other was nearby. It led to things – sexual things, that Ryan had discovered he loved doing – with Dagger.

Fuck.

Ninety minutes later and after three encores, Dagger left the stage with his band. Sweaty and panting, Ryan was the first person he hugged.

"Great show," Ryan said.

Dagger pulled back and met Ryan's gaze. "Thanks," he said, then grabbed Tony as he walked by. "Tony, I want to do something for that little girl in the wheelchair. Find out who she is and what her family could use; maybe a vacation to Disneyland or help with medical expenses. Make it happen for me," he said, then he walked over to his guitar tech to talk to him.

Tony turned toward Ryan. "I see Dagger's all cranked up over that kid in the chair."

"That doesn't surprise me," Ryan said. "Considering."

"Considering what?" Tony asked.

"Do you know the name of Dagger's sister?"

202

"Dagger has a sister?" Tony asked.

Ryan smirked at Tony, then patted him on the shoulder. "I guess Dagger doesn't tell you *everything* after all."

Ryan stepped away from Tony feeling satisfied with this minor victory. He had managed to dispel one thing with Tony: that Tony and Dagger weren't as close as he'd suggested. Even still, Ryan would ask his questions and if he wasn't satisfied with Dagger's answers, he'd be going home without any further intention of seeing Dagger again. Could he really walk away from Dagger – after everything they'd shared together? That was the million dollar question he had for himself.

CHAPTER ELEVEN

It was late when Dagger brought Ryan back to his suite. Dagger started stripping off his clothing, saying he needed a shower, and walked into his enormous bathroom. Ryan mentioned waiting out on the rooftop patio and went into the living room. He stopped at the bar and filled a glass with two fingers of whiskey and stepped outside to stand at the nearly chest-high railing.

Ryan stared at the brilliant lights blazing down on the Vegas strip below, making it seem almost daylight there. The night air was warm and dry, a soft breeze moved his hair around his head. Ryan drew in a long breath. His head ached from over-thinking every detail of the last few hours. What was he doing here? How did he ever think visiting Dagger on tour was a good idea?

He had always considered himself a rational thinking man, but in the few months since his interview with Dagger, he'd managed to become completely irrational. How the hell was this possible? Was he that desperate for human contact or a relationship that he'd risk his career, his sanity, and his heart by getting involved with Dagger? What the fuck was he thinking? That seemed to be the number one recurring question in his life these past few weeks. And it was a question he still hadn't been able to answer.

Ryan tossed back the last bit of whiskey from the glass into his throat and closed his eyes. He could smell Dagger's spicy, musk blend of cologne floating through the air and knew he was standing beside him without having to look. It was amazing how familiar the man had become to him in such a short period of time.

"Enjoying the view?" Dagger asked.

My God! That sexy fucking voice will be the end of me!

Ryan nodded, contemplated refilling his glass, then turned his head toward Dagger. He was bare-chested; wearing nothing more than a pair of loose fitting athletic pants. Ryan could see his toes peeking out from the hem of the pants. He lifted his gaze to Dagger's eyes. His hair was still damp from the shower and his face was freshly-shaved. Smooth and clean.

"What's wrong?" Dagger asked.

How was it possible for Dagger to know his moods so well? It was as if he had an inside connection to Ryan's personal thoughts. It unnerved Ryan a bit, but for some reason it also felt comfortable, like they'd known each other for decades instead of weeks.

"Looks like you've been out here over-thinking things, Ry, and that always makes me nervous," Dagger said. His hand gripped the back of Ryan's bicep, then his fingers started rubbing the tight muscle. "Talk to me, Ry. What's going through that over-active brain of yours?"

A long moment of silence passed before Ryan finally spoke.

"Why are you with me?" Ryan asked. "No bullshit. Tell me why. I really need to know. Why me, when you could easily have any guy you wanted?"

Dagger set his elbow onto the railing and rolled to Ryan. "Because to me, this feels right. You and I together feels *right*. Maybe I could have other men, but I don't want them. They're not you. They don't make me *feel* the way you do. They can't make me feel anything at all. It's that simple."

"It's *not* that simple," Ryan said. He started walking into the suite carrying his glass. "I need another drink."

Dagger followed him inside to the bar and watched Ryan pour another two fingers of whiskey into it. "You're pissed off because you don't want to feel anything for me, but you do. You can't find any logic behind that, so you'd rather find a way to dismiss it instead. It's easier that way, isn't it? It's easier to walk away from something that's uncomfortable for you to face. From what you've told me, that is how you've lived your entire life, and it's what you want to do now with me. Isn't it? You want to run back to Los Angeles because you can hide there and not have to feel things that are new and scary for you."

Ryan drained the glass and set it on the bar. Every word Dagger spoke rang true. It annoyed the hell out of him that this man had him figured out so clearly and had no problem calling him on it, either. He wanted to yell; punch something, anything to make what he was feeling go away, because in the end what he feared most was being hurt by Dagger.

Ryan rubbed at his face. "You're right," he said. "You're absolutely right. That's exactly what I'm doing, so why waste your time on someone as fucked up as me and afraid to live his life?"

Dagger ran the back of his fingers across Ryan's face. His eyes were painfully serious; appearing to glisten with emotion; the second time in one night Ryan had seen this in Dagger's expression.

"You're pushing me to reveal too much of myself, Ry," Dagger said, his voice a soft whisper. "If I admit exactly what I'm feeling for you, it will only hurt more when you leave."

Ryan swallowed around the lump forming in his throat. "What makes you think I'm leaving?"

"Because nice guys like you never go for someone like me – especially straight guys, and you happen to be both."

"I don't know what to say," Ryan said.

"Say you'll stay and jump into the deep end of the pool with me." Dagger said. He reached for Ryan's hand and squeezed it. "Don't think for one second I'm not scared or that I've got this all figured out. I don't. I'm feeling things I've never felt before and that scares the shit out of me, but I'm willing to face it because this feels right – *you* feel right. Stay and face this with me, Ry. We'll figure it out as we go."

"All or nothing?" Ryan asked.

Dagger smiled. It was the first sign of levity Ryan had seen on him since the concert ended. Dagger stepped closer; his bare chest almost pressing to Ryan, and he ribboned their fingers together. Their eyes held; Dagger's hazel brown iris's turned into a warm chocolate. He lifted Ryan's hand and set it against the firm pectoral muscle on his chest.

Ryan leaned into to the heat and smoothness of Dagger's skin. The pads of his fingers dug into the flesh, then sifted through the soft hair covering Dagger's breast. His eyes dropped to the spot he was touching. His hand on Dagger's skin looked natural; it felt natural, so much more arousing than anyone from his past.

"Will you stay?" Dagger asked.

Ryan lifted his gaze to Dagger. "I don't know what I'm doing," Ryan said. "And I'm afraid eventually you're going to become frustrated with that, but I love the way this feels – how *you* make me feel. If I wanted to, I don't think I could walk away."

"That's probably the most honest thing you've said so far, Ry." Dagger removed Ryan's hand from his chest and tugged on his arm. "Come on. Let's go to bed."

Ryan wasn't sure which of them woke first. One thing he did know: Dagger was wrapped around his naked body in a spooning position; his erection cradled between Ryan's butt cheeks, his face pressed to Ryan's shoulder blade. Ryan tensed at the sensation and pulled away from Dagger's embrace, turning onto his back. He cursed and draped an arm over his eyes.

Dagger pulled himself up onto an elbow and smiled down at Ryan. "I'm guessing this is where you do your damnedest to blame last night on too much alcohol," Dagger said. "But, here's the thing, Ry. Neither of us was anywhere near drunk, so you'll have to find another excuse to justify the fact you're waking up naked in my bed." Dagger lifted the sheet and peered at Ryan's outstretched form. "Deliciously naked."

Ryan's face flushed. "I'm not looking for excuses, Dagger," he said.

"Aren't you?"

Ryan shook his head. "I think I'm past the acceptable time limit to use them," he said. "Besides, any lingering reservations I may have my cock seems to be ignoring, so what difference does it make? I'm here because I want to be."

Dagger placed his hand on Ryan's chest, then starting sliding it down beneath the rumpled sheet. His fingers stopped just short of touching Ryan's erection. He bent down and pressed a soft kiss to Ryan's lips, then slid his mouth to his ear. "Liam," he whispered, then pulled back to watch Ryan absorb the information.

"Who's Liam?"

"I thought you might like to know who you're waking up with this morning."

"Your name is Liam?" Ryan asked.

Dagger nodded. "Liam Whitmore," he said. "Although back then, the friends I had called me Lee."

"Did you legally change it?"

"Yeah, I really needed to."

"Why's that?"

Dagger pushed himself up against the headboard. His shoulders shrugged. "It was time. New chapter in my life was starting and it required a new name."

Ryan's gaze dropped to the large tattoo inked on Dagger's right bicep. His index finger traced the intricate swirling pattern of a Celtic cross. The letters P and M occupied a small space in the center.

"Does this have any significance?" Ryan asked.

Ryan felt Dagger bristle and pull away and something closed down inside him. He watched Dagger slide from the bed and walk to the bathroom. His beautiful naked frame taking panther-like strides across the carpet. Ryan heard the sink water run and followed Dagger; stopping to lean against the door frame. He watched Dagger splash water on his face, then brush his teeth.

"Did I ask something I shouldn't have?" Ryan asked.

Dagger held on to the edge of the marble counter top; his eyes staring into the sink. "There's a dark period of my life that I'd rather not talk about," he said.

"I'm sorry," Ryan said. "I wasn't trying to be nosy."

Dagger looked at him over his shoulder and smiled weakly. "I'm not saying I'll never tell you about it, but I'm not ready to talk about it right now. Are you okay with that?"

Ryan nodded. "Of course."

Dagger turned and reached for Ryan. He held his face in his hands and kissed Ryan on the lips. "That was the first time in fifteen years I've said my real name out loud. No one knows what it is. Not even Tony."

"Are you kidding me?"

"No joke, Ry. No one knows – not even the guys in my band."

"Why not?"

"It's part of my past," he said. He left the bathroom and walked back to the bed. He sat on the edge of the mattress and Ryan went to him. Dagger wrapped his arms around Ryan's waist and pressed his face to his bare stomach.

"Then, why tell me?" Ryan asked. His fingers combed through Dagger's long hair. Ryan could feel Dagger's warm breath against his skin; feel his tongue moving through the soft hair on his lower abdomen, his teeth nipping. Ryan dropped to his knees between Dagger's parted legs to make himself eye level with him. He braced himself on the mattress beside Dagger's thighs and their eyes locked. "Why did you tell me?" Ryan asked again.

"I thought you deserved to know," Dagger said. "And I trust it won't go further than this room."

Ryan nodded, loving the sincerity in Dagger's hazel eyes. "You know I can be trusted."

Dagger fell onto his back and held on to his head. "I can't believe the chances I'm taking with you, Ry. Scares the hell out of me. Feels like free-falling without a parachute."

"That's exactly how I feel," Ryan said.

Dagger smiled at that and touched Ryan's face.

Ryan came up over him and pressed his chest to Dagger's; his hips settled between Dagger's parted thighs, and their cocks touched. A humming sound vibrated in Dagger's chest when Ryan slipped his hand between them and gripped Dagger's thickening organ. His face ran over Dagger's chest hair, then lower to his stomach. The appreciative noises coming from Dagger made Ryan bolder. He tried using his tongue and lips; shifting lower and lower on Dagger's muscled stomach, each touch eliciting another sound of thanks.

Last night in bed with Dagger felt different; touching Dagger in the dark was a *lot* different. There was an urgency to their moves then, getting naked and pressed together seemed to be of monumental importance, but it had been primarily Dagger delivering all the pleasure for both of them. Ryan had lost count of how many orgasms he'd had – most often in Dagger's very skilled mouth, and never once had Dagger suggested Ryan return that favor. He seemed content to have Ryan with him – in the moment, and enjoying every stroke or rub that was offered.

Now with the light of the new day bathing the king-sized bed, Ryan could clearly see the man laid out before him. His beautiful dark skin covered with a thin layer of chest hair was flawless. Muscles defined beneath the flesh made delicious ridges for Ryan to nip and taste. Ryan took full advantage of the light to explore Dagger inch by inch, reveling in everything that Dagger was: so very male. And, in his pursuit of discovering Dagger, he was able to deliver pleasure; same as Dagger had so selflessly done to him the previous night.

Ryan shifted again, licking Dagger's hip bone, then dragging his tongue up to his belly button; leaving a glistening trail of wetness on Dagger's skin with each new trail he created. He licked and tasted and Dagger groaned his appreciation for his efforts.

Ryan's chest cradled Dagger's over-sized cock. He could feel the heat of it pressed to him and smell his arousal. It was an intoxicating scent and Ryan's head began to swim in it. His mouth dropped again and Dagger's cock twitched, gently stroking the side of Ryan's cheek in the process. He ran his nose through the trimmed strip of pubic hair Dagger had around his cock and inhaled. Ryan used his hands to spread Dagger's thighs wider, then pressed his lips to his inner thigh. His tongue stole a taste then pulled upward to that mysterious tattoo inked right beside Dagger's pubic hair. Ryan kissed it first, then studied it with his eyes, and smiled when he recognized the cartoon character.

His fingers circled Dagger's sac and lightly squeezed. Dagger's hips pitched. He rose up on his elbows and looked down at Ryan. When their eyes connected, Ryan saw Dagger's flushed face, his eyes heavy lidded with lust. Ryan closed his and stole a quick taste of Dagger's shaft with his tongue.

"Ryan," Dagger said, his fingers laced through the short strands of hair on Ryan's head. "You don't have to do that. I mean, I'm not expecting you to..."

Ryan licked again, this time he covered the whole length right up to the broad head and Dagger cursed loudly.

"Fuck, Ry – please!" Dagger pleaded. "Don't."

Ryan sat back on his heels. "Why not?" he asked. His fingers skimmed through the saliva he had left on Dagger's pulsing shaft.

"It feels too good," Dagger panted. "I'll come."

Ryan smiled broadly. "Lie back and relax," he said. "You tortured me for hours last night. Now it's my turn."

"Oh, fuck," Dagger said, and dropped back onto the mattress.

Seeing Dagger spread for him like this in the daylight was intimate. The thought of it tightened Ryan's stomach. His heart began pounding against his ribs. He wanted this connection with Dagger; wanted to give Dagger something of himself, but he wasn't sure if he'd be good enough.

Ryan pressed his forehead to Dagger's hip and closed his eyes. He drew in a deep breath and did his best to tamp down his feelings of inadequacy. He could do this, right? He'd gotten head from countless women in his past and most recently from Dagger. All he had to do was mimic the techniques they'd used that made him blow a part at the seams. How difficult could it be?

Ryan lifted his head and ran his lips over the head of Dagger's cock. A groan rolled from Dagger and Ryan curled his tongue around the crest circling it in one slow sweep. He opened his mouth and took the head between his lips. Another soft moan from Dagger followed by words of praise had Ryan taking more of Dagger inside. His tongue worked down the sides of the shaft, while his fingers massaged Dagger's sac. Dagger's skin felt so hot in his mouth; the wide length pulsed against his tongue. The taste of him was like salty musk. It was heady and masculine like Dagger, and Ryan found himself wanting a whole lot more.

He eased two more inches of Dagger inside, feeling his lips stretching wider and causing a slight sting. Dagger was big, but Ryan was determined to take as much of him as he could into the back of his throat.

"Oh, god, Ry," Dagger said. "You keep that up and I'm gonna come."

Ryan did exactly that, and increased his suction.

"Sweet mercy," Dagger said, elongating the words making it sound like a sigh. "Unless you want a mouth full of my come, you better pull off."

Ryan swirled his tongue around Dagger's shaft again and tightened his grip on Dagger's balls. He felt them lift in his palm and knew Dagger was close; so very close, and that both excited and scared the hell out of him. What would Dagger's release taste like and what if he didn't like it?

"Ryan, please! I'm gonna unload."

Dagger's hips lifted off the bed, driving himself deeper into Ryan's mouth. He opened wide as he could and took it, loving it, and hoping for more. He felt the first hot blast hit the roof of his mouth; nearly choking him with the thick fluid. Dagger thrust again and sent the second shot directly down Ryan's throat. Ryan pulled back keeping the suction on the tip; fearful he might gag if he took Dagger too deep, but he kept working Dagger's shaft with his tongue and hand until Dagger finally stilled on the bed.

He let Dagger's cock slip from his mouth and crawled up onto the bed and reclined against the pillows at the head board. He wiped his lips and chin with the back of his hand and looked over at Dagger with his legs still dangling over the edge of the bed, thighs spread, his chest rising and falling quickly. He couldn't believe what he had just done; couldn't believe how much he enjoyed it, and hoped to hell Dagger had, too.

"You okay?" Ryan finally asked.

Dagger turned his head to see Ryan and smiled. "Are you sure you've never been with a guy? You are unbelievable," he said, and rolled his body to sit at the pillows beside Ryan.

His fingers skimmed over Ryan's lips, puffy from the work they'd just done, and then bent forward to kiss him. Dagger's lips gently nuzzled, then his tongue separated Ryan's lips and slipped inside.

Dagger's comments embarrassed Ryan, and he knew there was no way in hell what Dagger said was completely accurate, but it sure felt good to hear it. He was certain Dagger had gotten a better blow job in the past, but his first effort couldn't have been all that bad. He'd managed to get Dagger off – and relatively quick, too. That had to mean something, right?

"I can taste myself in your mouth," Dagger whispered. He curled his tongue around Ryan's and sucked it deeper.

Ryan grinned against Dagger's lips and pulled back from the kiss. "Tasmanian Devil tattoo?"

Dagger looked confused at first, then laughed. "Yeah. The guys in my band gave me that nickname years ago," Dagger said. "They say I act like one when I get pissed off."

Dagger provocatively ran his fingers down Ryan's breast bone and onto his stomach. Ryan's cock jerked to full attention. "What would you like me to do with this?" he asked, wrapping his long digits around Ryan's thick shaft.

"You've already done so much," Ryan said. "I'm not sure I'll ever come down from the high you've had me on for the last twelve hours."

Dagger slid his thigh over Ryan's; his hand cupped Ryan's balls. "I don't want you *down* for me, Ry. I prefer you up – just like this. Always."

Ryan's face went slack. Dagger saw the change and tipped Ryan's chin up with his index finger.

"You've got that look again, Ry," Dagger said. "Tell me what's on your mind."

Ryan leaned back into the pillows.

"Come on, Ry," Dagger said. "Say what's on your mind."

Several long moments passed as Ryan contemplated his words. He wanted to chose them carefully; make each one matter. "Being with you has been... so good," Ryan said, "For many reasons, but..."

"Damn it. I knew there'd be a but." Dagger's head rolled on the pillow. "I know better than to get involved with straight guys. It never ends well for either party, but it felt different with you, Ry, and that's the only reason I pursued you the way I did. Now I'm starting to feel a little guilty about that. Maybe I pushed you into something you're not feeling."

"You chasing me didn't turn me gay," Ryan said.

"And, you sleeping with me one night doesn't make you gay, either."

"Maybe not, but it does make me question the relationships I've had," Ryan said. "If this is who I really am, than what the fuck were the last fourteen years all about? Was all that a lie?"

Dagger held the side of Ryan's face and ran his thumb over his cheekbone. "Your past wasn't a lie," he said. "What you felt then was real – in that moment, but as we age we evolve. We discover new things about ourselves; preferences, and so on. It's all part of defining who we are – who we were meant to be. I think that's what's happening to you."

Ryan felt the sting of tears in his eyes. "I'm over analyzing again, but I don't know where I'm supposed to go with *this*."

"I don't want you to go anywhere," Dagger said, his back stiffening. "I want you here with me."

"I wasn't implying I wanted to leave you, Dagger. I'm just trying to figure things out, that's all."

Dagger pressed his hand to Ryan's stomach and spread the fingers. "I told you, we can figure this out *together*. You need to stop worrying. Okay?"

Ryan nodded and rubbed at his eyes. "I need a shower," he said.

"And while you're doing that, I'll order room service."

CHAPTER TWELVE

"After Vegas we fly up to Spokane and then on to Vancouver," Dagger said, chewing on a piece of bacon from the breakfast platter sitting in the center of the table. "I'd love it if you joined me."

Breakfast the morning after and it wasn't awkward, Ryan thought. This was a first for him. When he dated before Beth, he couldn't wait to get the hell home after a hook-up. Or if the girl stayed at his place, he wanted her out the door by first light. But sitting at the breakfast table with Dagger was entirely different. It was... comfortable. There was that word again. It kept floating around inside his head and spread warmth through his body.

Ryan smiled to himself, the two of them sitting side by side at an enormous dining room table for ten, bare chested, and acting like a couple who'd been together for decades. Ryan had doubts his time with Dagger would be anything more than an erotic fling and that thought made his heart flutter for a different reason. He loved spending time with Dagger, enjoyed watching him work, and there would never be enough time to touch the man, but the fantasy couldn't last forever. Could it?

"You know I can't stay," Ryan said.

"Don't you have vacation time?"

Ryan cut into his mushroom and broccoli omelet with a fork. He did have vacation time, more than enough to extend his weekend with Dagger into about ten days, but could his heart handle the emotional impact of it? He tried to remember the last time he took a real vacation and couldn't. His brain did a mental inventory of his appointments and job assignments for the next week and came up with nothing of importance. He had his laptop with him. He could easily work from the road with Dagger. So, what was stopping him?

Heartache.

He could feel emotions developing for Dagger and he didn't want to get hurt. Staying too long with Dagger could mean emotional disaster for him, but leaving Dagger was going to hurt, too – for both of them.

"You're hesitating," Dagger said. He reached across the table and held Ryan's hand. "Does that mean you're considering it?"

"Don't you think people will start to question why I'm still hanging around?" Ryan asked.

"Maybe, but I doubt they'll jump to the conclusion you're sucking my dick."

Ryan nearly chocked on the piece of omelet he was chewing. He reached for his cup of black coffee and took a quick gulp of the liquid to try and wash it down. Dagger watched him; the sly grin on his face told Ryan he enjoyed messing with his head far too much.

"You're doing it again," Ryan said.

"I know, and I'm sorry."

Dagger's cell phone rang on the table. "It's Tony," he said. "I gotta take this." He stood up from the table and started walking around the room while he talked.

It sounded more like an argument to Ryan, something about two interviews and a photo shoot that Dagger didn't want to do. What else was new, Ryan thought. He finished his breakfast and took his cell phone to the outside patio. He'd missed several text messages and one phone call from Beth and felt bad he hadn't made the time to call her back. She deserved at least that much, after all the coaching she'd given him on making this trip to see Dagger. He dialed her number, figuring he'd leave a message, and was surprised when she answered.

"It's about damned time you got back to me," Beth said, the softness in her voice told him she wasn't really mad.

"I'm sorry. I've been busy," Ryan said.

"You're not usually too busy to send me a text message, Ry. What's going on with you?"

"I'm out of town at the moment, but I had every intention of calling you when I got home," Ryan said.

"Oh, my god! Are you visiting your mystery man?" Beth asked.

"I'm in Vegas," Ryan said.

"With *him*?" she asked. "Come on, I need details, Ryan!"

"I can't give you details, Beth. You know that."

"I'm not asking for his name and address," Beth said. "I merely want to know if you've explored your... attraction."

The silence on the phone was louder than anything Ryan could have shouted at her. "I can't talk about this right now," he said, glancing over his shoulder and checking for Dagger's whereabouts. "He's in the other room."

"Okay, then answer me this: are you happy?" Beth asked.

Ryan smiled and again he felt those nagging tears biting at the corners of his eyes. "Yeah, I'm happy – very happy."

Beth let out a shriek on the other end of the phone and Ryan pulled the phone away from his ear for a few seconds. "I knew it," she said. "I'm thrilled for you, really, I am. I know you've been searching a long time, Ry. Maybe this is what you've been looking for?"

"Maybe."

"That's all you've got to say about it? I need more details than that! Do you think this could turn into something serious?"

Ryan rubbed at his forehead. Something serous? Was that even possible with a guy like Dagger? Did *he* want this to be something serious with Dagger?

Fuck. He did.

"I don't know, Beth. It's too early to tell and it's complicated."

"Complicated because you're both men, career conflicts, or what?"

"All of the above," Ryan said.

Another pause fell between them and Ryan heard Beth sigh.

"I'm really proud of you, Ry. I know visiting this guy wasn't easy for you to do."

"It was the most difficult thing I've ever done," he said. "But... it feels... right."

"Wow, you're making me cry," Beth said.

"Jesus, don't cry!" Ryan said. "This new situation also makes me question things from my past, Beth. If I had known then what I know now..."

"Don't go there, Ry," she said. "For whatever reason, you weren't meant to discover this about yourself until now."

"What we had was real," he said. "You believe that, right?"

Beth paused for a moment and collected her thoughts. "Since our conversation at the diner, I've thought long and hard about this. There were red flags in our relationship, Ry; which I chose to ignore. Even if I had somehow forced you to look at those red flags back then, I don't think it would have mattered. I think it was meant to be this particular man that opened your eyes to who you really are."

"You wanted something I couldn't give back and now,... I think I know why. I'm so sorry for that."

"Stop it. You didn't know, Ry, and I don't blame you for that."

The emotion stinging Ryan's eyes had blossomed into full blown pools of tears threatening to spill at any minute.

The lump in his throat was constricting, making it nearly impossible to talk.

"Can I call you when I get home?" Ryan asked.

"You better, or I'll be calling you!"

"Thank you – for everything," Ryan said softly, and ended the call.

Ryan slid his phone into the back pocket of his jeans and leaned forward, setting his elbows on the railing. His shoulders slouched and his head hung between them. What the hell was he doing? And why did this thing with Dagger have to feel so fucking perfect?

A warm hand sliding up his bare back pulled him from his trance and he stood up straight. Dagger's hand squeezed the back of his neck. His touch was always just right, exactly what he needed in any given moment, and he bent into it.

"Someone on the phone upset you?" Dagger asked. He pressed himself to Ryan's back and kissed the nape of his neck.

"I was talking to Beth."

"Your ex?" Dagger asked. He rolled to Ryan's side to rest against the railing. "I guess you weren't kidding when you said you two were still close."

"What do you mean?"

"You talk to her a lot."

"Maybe once every couple weeks," Ryan said. He looked at Dagger and saw the furrow in his brow; the pout of his lips. God! He wanted to kiss the pout right off of them. "You're not jealous of Beth, are you?"

"Why wouldn't I be?" Dagger said. "It was only a few weeks ago you said you tried to get her into bed again. Maybe you still have a *thing* for her?"

Ryan's hand harshly cupped Dagger's jaw almost like a slap to the face. The touch was rougher than he wanted it to be, but the arousal he saw flare in Dagger's eyes prevented him from apologizing for it. He inched closer to Dagger, their lips so close to touching; hot breath bounced between them, their chests rose and fell together.

"I have a *thing* for you," Ryan said. "Only you." His lips brushed once, then took total possession of Dagger's mouth and there it was again. Zero to one hundred in a heart beat, with both their cocks straining against their zippers.

Ryan's hand slipped behind Dagger's neck and pulled him tighter to him; his tongue diving deeper inside Dagger's mouth. Hearing Dagger moan made Ryan sway on his feet. He pushed his hand between them and gripped Dagger's erection through his pants. His fingers went to the zipper and started tugging, then slipped inside to stroke the heated flesh. Dagger responded by pressing Ryan's back to the railing and grinding against his palm.

"You make me so fucking hard," Dagger said. His tongue licked at Ryan's bottom lip. "There's no doubt I want you again, but not out here."

Ryan's hand slid inside Dagger's pants, across his hip and onto his ass. His hand firmly clamped onto the tight muscle of Dagger's butt cheek making him wince. Dagger reacted with a sharp bite to Ryan's lip drawing a small amount of blood that both men could taste.

"You wanna play rough?" Dagger asked in a whispered hiss. "I'll give you rough. Come on, let's go inside."

Dagger pushed off Ryan's chest and made no attempt to redo his pants. He walked inside the suite and directly into the master bedroom with Ryan following close behind. Soon as Ryan cleared the threshold, Dagger was on him with an embrace so tight, it constricted Ryan's normal breathing. The kiss he offered Ryan was fierce, but so erotic it made Ryan's knees weak. He'd never craved anyone's touch the way he did Dagger's.

Dagger's fingers worked quickly at Ryan's jeans and pushed them off his hips. He sighed when he heard the thick length of Ryan's cock slap against his stomach. Dagger shoved his own jeans down his legs and kicked them off his feet. His fingers caressed Ryan's balls, then squeezed to the edge of pain.

"Oh, god," Ryan said.

Dagger pressed closer, aligning his cock to Ryan's and used both his hands to circle their combined thickness. He pulled off one stroke and Ryan made a choking sound in his throat.

"You like that, don't you?" Dagger asked. He sucked a spot on Ryan's throat then bent to lick a light brown nipple. He pulled the tiny bead with this teeth and nipped it. Ryan cried out but it wasn't from pain. Dagger repeated the same treatment to Ryan's other nipple then moved down onto his stomach. His fingernails dragged the length of Ryan's torso along his ribs, as he dropped to his knees.

"Mother fucker," Ryan said through clenched teeth. It felt like Dagger had drawn blood. At the very least, he'd have long red lines all the way down to his hips. The pain jerked every nerve ending in his body alive in one quick swipe. Then the stinging turned to exquisite pleasure when Dagger's tongue licked a circle around the head of his cock. Ryan's fingers dug into Dagger's scalp and plunged into his mouth. His fingers laced through the long strands of Dagger's hair, as he held him at the root of his shaft, slowly rocking his hips. Dagger pulled back long enough to draw in a breath and Ryan thrust in again.

"Fuck my mouth," Dagger said, looking up at Ryan.

Their eyes held; the longing between them palpable. Dagger's fingers dug into Ryan's ass cheeks, forcing Ryan's thrusts deeper into his throat. Two long fingers traced the crease until they found the puckered indent. Dagger coated his index finger with saliva then started pushing it inside Ryan's ass, his mouth still bobbing on Ryan's cock.

Ryan's head fell back over his shoulders as he cried out again. Dagger eased a second finger into the heat and Ryan swayed.

"Spread your legs," Dagger said.

Ryan complied and widened his stance, resting his hands on Dagger's shoulders for balance. Dagger's mouth and tongue brought him right to the edge and held him there; Ryan's pleading doing nothing to convince Dagger to expedite his release.

"I swear I'm gonna pass out," Ryan sighed.

The flat plane of Dagger's tongue made another destructive pass over the pulsing head of Ryan's cock making him wobble again. Dagger's hand twisted beneath Ryan's ball sac, effectively spinning the fingers inside his ass and pressed against the swollen gland. Ryan's hips started thrusting.

"What are you doing?" Ryan asked. "Jesus! Don't stop. Don't stop."

Ryan felt Dagger's finger stroking the hidden spot and lost all control. The orgasm tore through him and Dagger swallowed it all until Ryan began staggering backward. Dagger grabbed Ryan by the hips to steady him and drove Ryan's cock as far into the back of his throat as it would fit.

Ryan continued to ride the crest, disbelieving it was possible to have what seemed to be an endless orgasm. When his hips finally stilled, Ryan stumbled sideways and flopped onto the bed. Dagger walked to the bed and crawled across the quilt to lay beside Ryan, running his fingers through his chest hair.

Ryan rolled his head on the pillow toward Dagger. "What the fuck did you do to me?"

Dagger laughed. "I can't give away all my secrets."

"Tell me, so I can do it to you," Ryan said.

"Well, aren't you an eager student."

Dagger slid a thigh over Ryan's lap and stretched out on top of him; pinning his arms above his head. He lowered himself and offered Ryan a kiss, rubbing his groin against Ryan's. "You can do it to me, Ry, but I don't want your fingers," he said. "I want your big, fat cock. Think you can handle that?"

"You said you don't bottom," Ryan said. The word 'bottom' awkwardly rolled from his lips.

Dagger slid off Ryan and rested on his side pressed to Ryan; facing each other on the pillow. "You know what bottoming means?"

Ryan nodded. "I think I have a pretty good idea."

"Straight guys typically don't."

"Why don't you bottom?" Ryan asked.

Dagger shrugged. "I did – a long time ago."

"But not since?"

"It hasn't felt right," Dagger said. His voice becoming softer with each word. "I top. You want me to top you?"

Ryan searched Dagger's eyes trying to read him and then he saw Dagger's smile. "I'm not sure I could top or bottom," Ryan said. "It sounds like it hurts and I don't want to hurt you or be hurt myself."

Dagger's hand reached between them and gripped on to Ryan's expanding organ. He stroked him until he was granite-hard again, then turned onto his back; pulling Ryan on top of him.

"You won't hurt me," Dagger said. "I promise, it'll be good for both of us."

"You want *me* to fuck you... but not the others?" Ryan asked.

"You still don't get this, Ry, do you?" Dagger held Ryan's face in his hands, stroking his cheekbones with his thumbs. "I've been with lots of guys and it was fun to fool around with them, but it never felt like this. With you, every touch and kiss... is enormously powerful."

Ryan gently rocked against Dagger and smiled. "That's because you're falling for me."

"Fuck you," Dagger said with a grin.

"Apparently, you seriously want me to fuck you," Ryan said, and the smile fell from his face.

"Yeah, I do, but I know you're not ready to give me that."

"What if I'm never ready?"

"It doesn't matter," Dagger said. "I still want to be with you."

Ryan pressed his chest to Dagger's and sought his mouth. The kiss started soft, but turned hungry in a matter of seconds.

"I'm nervous about you going back to L.A.," Dagger said.

"Why's that?"

Dagger held Ryan's gaze. "I don't want to share you, Ry – not unless you want to do it together, maybe with a chick or something. Even then, I don't think I could handle watching you get off with anyone but me. And I *really* don't want you going with any other guys."

"I'd be lying if I said I wasn't worried about you being on the road," Ryan said.

Dagger ran his fingers across Ryan's lips. "We both agreed in the beginning they'd be no one else. You're still cool with that, right?"

"More than ever."

The smile Dagger offered Ryan lit the room. Damn, he was falling for this guy in a big way and he wasn't sure he wanted to stop himself, either.

Dagger's cell phone starting ringing on the nightstand. He pulled away from Ryan and glanced at the caller I.D.

"It's Tony again," Dagger said. "He can fucking wait." He tossed his phone down and pulled Ryan back to his mouth and Ryan devoured him. One kiss rolled into the next and Ryan started rotating his hips over Dagger.

Dagger moaned then heard movement inside the room.

"Wow!" Tony said, his voice slicing through the heady sex haze hanging in Dagger's bedroom like a thick harbor fog. "You two look amazing together, like a Grecian sculpture."

"What the fuck are you doing in here?" Dagger screamed, moving out from under Ryan.

"Your bedroom door was open," Tony said. He made no effort to turn away or hide the obvious erection tenting his pants.

"But, the door to the suite was CLOSED!" Dagger yelled.

Tony waved his pass card key above his head. "You know I always have a key to your room, Dagger. It's the only way I can be certain you'll keep your appointments. Now, get your ass in the shower. Your first interview is in fifteen minutes."

Dagger rose from the bed and stretched, doing nothing to obscure his nakedness or his hard-on. "I already told you, I'm not doing the interviews today."

"It's too late to reschedule them," Tony said, watching Dagger cross the room toward the bathroom. "You can fuck your virgin bride later. We've got business to take care of first."

Two long strides and Dagger was in Tony's face. "Don't talk about Ryan like that," Dagger's voice roared. "Now, get the fuck out of my bedroom and shut the door behind you!"

Tony turned to leave. "You've got fifteen minutes," he said. "I'll be in the living room."

Dagger watched the door shut, then turned toward the bed.

Ryan slid his legs from the sheets and set them on the floor; putting his back to Dagger, elbows resting on his knees. Dagger walked to him and knelt down on the floor beside his feet.

"I'm sorry about that," Dagger said. "Tony had no right..."

"It doesn't matter," Ryan said, cutting him off mid-sentence. He found his clothing on the floor and started dressing in silence. He looked over his shoulder and noticed Dagger was watching him. "You better go jump in the shower," he said.

"You're pissed off," Dagger said.

Ryan zipped his pants and faced Dagger. "Not at you," he said. "It's just..."

"What? What is it?" Dagger asked.

"I think I should leave," Ryan said.

"You mean leave the suite while I do these stupid interviews?"

"No, leave Vegas and go home," Ryan said.

Dagger tugged Ryan against his chest. "I don't want you to do that."

"You're working, Dagger, and I'm getting in the way."

"No, you're not. You're keeping me sane."

Ryan shook his head. "You don't need me for that."

"Stay one more night," Dagger whispered beside Ryan's ear. The vibration of his voice made Ryan shiver.

Ryan set his head to Dagger's and sighed. "How long are the interviews?"

"Couple hours," Dagger said. "And then you and I can go do something... anything you want."

Ryan stepped back and nodded. "Okay. I'll find a place out of everyone's way and get some writing done," he said. "Go take a shower and I'll see you later."

Ryan went into the guest bedroom of the suite and began organizing his laptop bag in preparation to work. He pulled a notepad and pen out of the bag and set it on top of his laptop. He was about to leave the room to head to the rooftop patio when he heard Dagger's infuriated voice echoing in the kitchen and stopped just short of the doorway.

"Don't you *ever* talk about Ryan like that again or we're all done," Dagger said. "Is that clear?"

"You have a *job* to do here and that doesn't include fucking him," Tony said.

"My private life has nothing to do with my job – or you," Dagger shouted.

"Take a look at what you're doing, Dagger," Tony said. "Exactly how long do you think it's gonna take for Ryan to wake up and suddenly remember he's STRAIGHT? And then what? Do you think he'll be sticking around? Doubtful. In the end, you'll be dumped and I'll be stuck picking up the pieces of this mess you're creating."

"Fuck you!"

"You better think long and hard about this, Dagger," Tony yelled. "You have a LOT more to lose than he does. He'll slip back into his straight life with the memory of his first and *only* homo affair and you'll be lucky to escape this weekend still being in the closet. Is that what you want – to be outed by *him*?"

"Ryan wouldn't do that to me."

"You sure about that? You trust him enough to stake your whole career on it?"

"Shut the fuck up," Dagger said. "Let's get these interviews over with, and then I don't want to see your fucking face until tomorrow night's show. Got it?"

Ryan went back to the bed and sat down on the edge of it. He really wished he hadn't heard the heated exchange between Dagger and Tony. As much as he wanted to stay with Dagger in Vegas a while longer, he knew it was best he leave now – before Dagger fired Tony for no particular reason, except for interfering in Dagger's private life. There was no way Ryan wanted to become the bone of contention between them. If he had to, he could wait to spend time with Dagger until after the tour ended.

Ryan stood up and started loading his duffel bag with this belongings. A knock on the door of the suite announced the arrival of the first reporter, then Ryan heard their voices moving into the living room. He left the guest room and carried his duffel and computer bag down the hall toward Dagger's bedroom. He collected his shaving gear from the bathroom and the clothes he had scattered around the room on the floor and added it to the duffel. Then he went to the nightstand and took his cell phone and slipped it into his back pocket. He turned quickly and bumped into the bed. He looked at the rumpled sheets practically torn from the mattress and memories of him and Dagger rolling around on them flooded his brain.

Damn. I really don't want to leave Dagger right now.

He left the bedroom and walked down the hallway; following the voices in the living room, then stood in the opening of the doorway holding his bags. Dagger's head lifted and met Ryan's gaze from across the room and he stood up from the couch.

"Excuse me a minute," Dagger said to the interviewer and crossed the room to Ryan. Dagger looked down at the bags clutched in Ryan's hand. "What's going on, Ry? You leaving?"

"Yeah, I think it's best."

Dagger grabbed his arm and pulled Ryan back down the hall into his bedroom and shut the door. "Why now? I thought you decided you'd stay another night."

"That was before I heard the conversation between you and Tony in the kitchen."

"You heard that?" Dagger asked.

"Every word," Ryan said. He saw the anger pitching inside Dagger and held up his hand. "It's okay, Dagger. I don't agree with most of what Tony had to say, but he did have some valid points. You're working now and me being here is messing with that schedule. I can wait until your tour ends to see you."

"That's a few months from now," Dagger said, pressing his forehead to Ryan's.

"If you get lonely call me and we'll... talk over the phone," Ryan said.

Dagger chuckled. "And by talk, you mean jerk-off."

"There'll be talking, too."

Dagger thrust his hips forward and pinned Ryan to the wall with his groin and Ryan dropped the bags in his hand. "Dirty talk – at least on my part."

Ryan clamped his hands around the sides of Dagger's neck and pulled him to his mouth for an aggressive kiss that gave new meaning to the phrase 'tongue fucking'. When Dagger pulled away, they were both panting.

"Damn! You and I together are crazy good," Dagger said. "I'm gonna miss you like hell."

"Me, too."

"How you getting home?"

"I'll catch a commercial flight back to L.A."

"Fuck that," Dagger said, and pulled the cell phone from his shirt pocket. "At least let me do this much for you. Dagger made two calls and, in a matter of minutes, he'd arranged for limo service to and from both airports and had a private jet fueling and waiting on Ryan at the executive airport.

Dagger walked Ryan to the door of the suite and took his hand. "Will you call me when you get home?"

"Yeah, I can do that," Ryan said, awkwardly shifting by the door.

"I want to kiss you," Dagger whispered.

"I know, but don't. Your guests are watching us," Ryan said. "It's all good."

Dagger smiled and opened up the door. "I have a couple of back-to-back days off in two weeks," he said. "I'll either send a plane for you, or I'll fly back to L.A. to see you. One way or another, we'll be together."

"Two weeks it is," Ryan said and stepped into the hall. "Thanks for... everything."

"Oh, great. Now I'm getting hard," Dagger said.

"I'll call later and help you with that," Ryan said. He flashed an amazing smile at Dagger and waved good-bye. He walked down the hall toward the elevator and heard the door to Dagger's suite close. The noise was painful to hear; causing a clenching ache he felt in his heart.

Two weeks? It'd be a miracle if he didn't fly out to see Dagger long before that.

CHAPTER THIRTEEN

Ryan woke up the next morning in his own bed and had to think for a minute where he was. The memory of spending the night before in Dagger's hotel suite made his cock harden to the point of pain. He lifted the sheet and glanced down at his erection. This was beyond morning wood. It made him wish he were waking up beside Dagger again, so they could take care of each other. If there was a better way to start the day than that, he wasn't aware of it.

He rolled from the bed and headed toward the shower. He was grateful he had another day to himself before he had to go back to work on Monday. He needed that time to collect himself; maybe finish the article on Ivory Tower he'd left hanging in limbo for the last week and get it off his desk.

After breakfast he went to his office and turned on his computer. He opened a file containing his interview notes with Zander and the information on the page blurred.

Liam Whitmore. Dagger's real name flashed before his eyes. He wrote it down on a note pad and set it aside. Then, he typed the name into a search engine on his computer and waited to see if anything popped up that might be connected to Dagger. A few seconds later, several articles appeared for Ryan to read. He couldn't remember where Dagger said he'd grown up and had to sort through the articles one by one, eliminating the pieces he knew couldn't be connected to Dagger. Then something caught his eye. The title of this article read: Local Juvenile Sentenced to Two Years for Assault.

Ryan opened the page to read the full article and halfway through it he had to stop and walk away. It was too much to digest. The article was printed in the local newspaper shortly after Dagger graduated from high school from a small town in Ohio. A small black and white photograph showing Dagger being led into the police station in handcuffs confirmed to Ryan this article was indeed about Dagger.

Dagger couldn't have been more than eighteen at the time of the arrest, Ryan thought. Not quite a man, but certainly no longer a boy. In this old photograph Dagger was tall and lean. His physique hadn't yet filled out with the muscles Ryan intimately knew were threaded beneath the skin all over Dagger's beautiful body. His hair was about the same length as it was now, but unkempt – as were his clothes, making him look far more like a punk than a rock star. Ryan also noticed one other thing missing on Dagger's body: the Celtic cross inked on his right bicep. As many questions as the article had answered about Dagger, it also created more.

What the fuck?

Ryan scratched his head. He didn't know what to do with this new information. If Dagger had wanted him to know about this, he would have told him, and he hadn't said one word about it – so what did that tell him? This must be the dark period in his life Dagger had referred to while they were in Vegas.

Ryan cursed to himself. He shouldn't have researched the name and now he'd have to pretend he didn't know about this. Was it fair to Dagger – to have invaded his privacy like this? A knot twisted in Ryan's gut.

He shut down his computer and left the room.

Since Las Vegas, phone conversations with Dagger were a little tense for Ryan. Knowing what he now knew about Dagger was becoming more difficult to hide. Still, he wanted Dagger to be the one to tell him – not the other way around.

It had been nine days since they had been together. Nine emotionally challenging days for Ryan, and he was really wishing they could have some face-to-face time. Ryan was getting ready to leave work for the day when his cell phone rang.

"Can I see you tonight?" Dagger asked.

"Are you flying back?" Ryan asked.

"I'll be landing in LAX in a few hours," Dagger said. "Wanna meet me at my house?"

Ryan wrote down Dagger's address and finished packing his laptop bag.

"Oh, and Ryan? Bring an overnight bag," Dagger said. "It's doubtful you'll be making it into work tomorrow. You cool with that?"

Ryan's smile was wide. "Yeah, I'm cool with that."

"Good. I can't wait to see you," Dagger said. "I'll call you when I land."

Ryan drove home and tossed a few things into his backpack, then showered and forced down a dinner of leftovers. After that, there was nothing to do but pace a rut into his living room floor waiting to drive to Dagger's house.

Dagger's call finally came around midnight, saying he'd be at his house within the hour. Ryan could hardly contain his excitement, as he ran from his apartment building to his car. The ride to Dagger's house was a blur. He parked at the street curb outside Dagger's electronic security gate and shut off his car to wait. A minute later, his phone was ringing.

"Are you there yet?" Dagger asked.

"Just pulled up," Ryan said.

"I should be there in five," Dagger said. "Pull in behind the limo and follow us up the driveway."

"See you soon," Ryan said.

The limousine headlights came into view and Ryan pushed himself upright in his seat. His heart started thudding harder beneath his ribs at the sight of the long, sleek vehicle turning the corner into Dagger's estate. Ryan started his car and pulled in behind Dagger's limo. His hands were so sweaty they spun around the steering wheel with ease. It was amazing what this man did to Ryan; physically and emotionally.

Ryan parked in front of the detached four-car garage and grabbed his backpack. By the time he exited his car, Dagger was walking up to him; wearing black jeans, a periwinkle-colored button down shirt, and his trademark long tousled hair blowing about his head. Ryan's breath caught short.

"Fuck. You look good," Dagger said. "Come this way, I'm using the kitchen door."

"Afraid of setting off the alarm again?" Ryan asked.

Dagger laughed at the memory of Ryan's first visit to his house and waved good-bye to his limo driver. They walked side by side toward the back of the house. Soon as they moved around the corner and into privacy, Dagger pushed Ryan up against the clapboard siding of the house and took Ryan's mouth in a kiss that damn near melted his bones.

"You fucking taste good, too," Dagger said.

Ryan grabbed fistfuls of Dagger's shirt and tugged him back, claiming Dagger's mouth for a second kiss.

"Zero to a hundred," Ryan sighed.

"As in miles per hour?"

"Yeah, that's what it feels like whenever I'm with you."

Dagger smiled against Ryan's lips, grinding his erection into Ryan's. "I'm about ready to shoot right here, Ry. I think we better go inside."

Ryan let Dagger lead the way through the kitchen and out to the marble floored foyer. He rounded the corner to take the curved staircase to the second floor, running up the steps two at a time. Ryan was right behind him.

"The house tour will have to wait until tomorrow," Dagger said. "Right now, the only room I care that you see is my bedroom."

At the top of the stairs Dagger turned right. He walked down the carpeted hallway and opened up the wide wooden door at the end. His hand hit the wall, flipping a switch that basked the room in soft tones of filtered light.

Ryan moved into the room behind Dagger. An audible sign escaped his mouth as he scanned the room from left to right. It felt like he were stepping back in time and into a medieval bed chamber. The walls of the spacious room were painted in a deep merlot color; heavy tapestry drapes with valances covered two windows that reached nearly to the floor to the ceiling. Several enormous hand-carved mahogany pieces of furniture occupied the room. A double-door wardrobe cabinet stood with the doors opened; exposing a very high-tech entertainment center. Another large piece looked to be a dresser and several other matching accent pieces completed the set.

One spacious corner of the room was littered with handwritten sheet music and half a dozen guitars; a few stacked in cases, while others sat in stands waiting for use. An acoustic guitar exhibiting heavy wear and tear was resting over the arms of an antique chair that matched the rest of the furniture. This instrument seemed to be a favorite, Ryan thought, judging by the use it had received.

On one wall an enormous oil painting hung depicting Dagger in the throes of a stage performance; guitar slung low across his hips with purple and pink hued lighting basking him in a very moody light from above.

The bed was the focal piece. It beckoned at one end of the room; so large, it looked like the room had been built to fit around it. It was obviously antique, possibly from an old castle; maybe fourteenth or fifteenth century. Ryan found himself wishing he had paid more attention in history class to know for sure. The design of this bed was like nothing Ryan had ever seen. It had a solid, ornately-carved bed frame that rose from the floor to the top of the mattress, Two carved posts, rising ten feet at both foot corners supported a wooden canopy that fed into a masterpiece of a headboard that rose to meet the canopy. All the pieces were so hefty, it made Ryan wonder if extra support beams were needed in the floor to carry the weighty furniture.

Movement to his side pulled Ryan out of his trance. He turned and saw Dagger standing in a stone-tiled master bathroom; the room resembled more of a dungeon than a modern bathroom, with stone archways and cast iron accents. Dagger was pulling off his clothes, leaving them in a messy pile on the floor. Ryan walked to the doorway and stood watching Dagger moving naked around the room taking a clean towel from a linen closet and hanging it on a cast iron hook beside the shower door. Dagger must have realized Ryan was watching and stopped by the glass shower door. He glanced over his shoulder and smiled.

"Give me a few minutes to shower," Dagger said. "I went directly from stage to the airport and haven't had time to clean up yet."

Ryan leaned against the door frame and watched Dagger shower; his body captivated and aroused every one of Ryan's senses. Without much thought, Ryan began removing his clothing, then opened the glass shower door and stepped beneath the spray of water to stand behind Dagger. He slipped his arms around Dagger's wet waist.

Dagger bent into the embrace and moved Ryan's hands up onto his chest over his heart. "I really need this," Dagger said.

"The shower?"

"No, your touch," Dagger said, and spun around in the slippery hold to look at Ryan. "I heard something in your voice this week when we talked. It made me nervous and I wanted to make sure you were okay – that *we* were okay, and you weren't having second thoughts about us being together."

Ryan shook his head. "No second thoughts, Dagger." Between them Ryan's cock was hardening at an alarming rate.

"None at all?" Dagger asked.

Ryan turned them and pressed Dagger's back against the tiled wall. Dagger's hands gripped on to Ryan's ass, holding him in place. Then Ryan's hips began rhythmic rotations over Dagger's erection and his mouth swooped down to claim Dagger's. Ryan's tongue pushed into Dagger's open mouth, gently stroking, then plunging deeply, as his cock rubbed faster alongside Dagger's lubricated shaft. The wetness between their bodies created a perfect friction and quickly brought both of them right to the edge of orgasm.

Soon as Ryan felt Dagger release all over his stomach, he did, too, and he didn't break their kiss until his hips finally stilled. "Does it feel like I'm having doubts about being with you?" Ryan asked.

Dagger's head dropped back to rest against the wall. His breaths were still labored; his fingers fanned over Ryan's water slick chest. "You have no idea what you do to me," Dagger said. "I can't get enough."

"Pretty expensive booty call, don't you think?"

Dagger ran his fingers through the spray on Ryan's face. "You are more to me than a quick fuck," Dagger said.

"Likewise," Ryan said.

Dagger used the shower water to clean off his stomach, then squirted bath gel into the palm of his hand and began lathering Ryan's body. He started on Ryan's neck and shoulders then moved down to his muscled back, massaging each spot he touched. Dagger went lower reaching Ryan's hips and buttocks and the backs of his firm thighs and calves, then repeated the process to Ryan's front. By the time he finished and rinsed Ryan off, both of them were fully aroused again.

Ryan cupped Dagger's face and leaned in for a kiss; soft and full of emotion, making Ryan grateful for the water spraying his face to hide the tears pooling in his eyes. When Dagger pulled back, Ryan was certain he saw the same feelings reflected back in Dagger's gaze.

"Let's go to bed," Dagger said.

Dagger stepped out of the shower first and handed Ryan a towel before wrapping one around his hips, then walked into his bedroom. He stopped beside the bed and pealed back the thick comforter, finished drying himself; squeezing as much of the excess water out of his hair as he could, and tossed the wet towel onto the floor.

Ryan watched Dagger climb up onto the huge bed and smiled. "You call this a bed?" he asked, hoisting himself up beside Dagger at the center of the mattress. "It looks more like some sort of worshiping altar than a bed for sleeping."

Dagger rolled against Ryan and laughed. "I'll go with that, since we'll both be doing a little worshiping tonight."

And then arms and legs tangled; tongues teased, and fingers explored, until Ryan's lips lowered and circled Dagger's shaft, drawing him into the warmth of his mouth. He applied the perfect suction with his tongue and added a twisting motion with his fist that had Dagger begging to come in mere minutes.

Dagger sighed loudly as he released, throwing his head back into the pillows and arching off the bed. Ryan's finger inside Dagger's ass rubbing that sweet inner soft spot prolonged Dagger's orgasm, until he pulled Ryan off his cock and up onto this chest.

Ryan stared down at Dagger, gently rocking his hips in the cradle between Dagger's legs. Dagger looked so vulnerable beneath him, with emotion making his eyes sparkle. It made Ryan's breath catch at the purity of the moment. It felt like love. Was it possible he could be falling in love with Dagger? Was it possible Dagger could love him back?

Dagger's fingers skimmed over the bumps of Ryan's ribs and settled on his butt.

"Fuck me," Dagger said.

Ryan blinked, uncertain he had heard Dagger correctly.

"I want to feel you inside me," Dagger said.

Ryan lifted his weight onto his hands and shook his head. "I don't think I should," he said quietly.

"Why not?" Dagger asked.

"I'll hurt you."

"No, you won't," Dagger said.

Ryan turned onto his side beside Dagger and watched while Dagger stretched to reach the drawer in an antique table beside the bed. He tossed a condom packet and a tube of lubricant onto the sheets between them and looked at Ryan.

Ryan shook his head again. "I don't know what I'm doing and I'm too big," he said. "I'm certain I'll hurt you."

Dagger rolled his head closer to Ryan's on the pillow. "I want you to try," he whispered. "For me, Ry. Please. I really need to share this with you."

Ryan looked at Dagger, trying to read his eyes; almost holding his breath. Fear washed over him; fear because of his inexperience, and the fear of what this would mean for them. Dagger ripped open the condom packet with his teeth and rolled the condom over Ryan's cock and their eyes met again.

"Talk to me, Ry. Do you really *not* want to do this?"

Ryan nudged closer. "I've never done anal. Ever."

Dagger brushed lips with him. "It's really no different than what you've done in the past, except it's tighter." He took the tube of lube and squeezed a line out across the pads of his fingers, then smeared the gel in his crease. He reached for Ryan's hand and kissed the fingers, drawing the index and middle fingers into his mouth. "Use your fingers on me first," Dagger said.

Ryan lifted himself up on an elbow; his face so very close to Dagger's. "Are you absolutely sure?" he asked.

Dagger nodded and pulled Ryan's mouth down to his and kissed him. Ryan's fingers skimmed the length of Dagger's cock, then reached beneath his ball sac and into the slippery crack. He rubbed back and forth several times before dipping one finger inside. Dagger groaned into Ryan's mouth.

"Give me another finger," Dagger whispered.

Ryan complied, his heart pounding furiously in his chest. He kept seducing Dagger's mouth and added a third finger to Dagger's ass, slowly working them in and out; stretching the tight muscle. Dagger let out a humming sound that Ryan took as a positive sign. He had no idea what he was doing, just going through the motions that felt right to him and doing his best to read Dagger's body language for signals he was pleasuring instead of hurting.

"Lube the rubber on your cock," Dagger said.

Ryan did as he was instructed and looked at Dagger.

"You ready?" Dagger asked, his chest rising quickly.

Ryan nodded. "How do you want me to..."

Dagger held his arms out and invited Ryan on top of him, then waited until Ryan settled between his legs. "Just like this," Dagger said. "I want to be able see your face."

Ryan nudged Dagger's nose and brushed his lips, but his hips remained still.

"You okay?" Dagger asked.

"I'm nervous."

"Don't be," Dagger said. "Push forward; slow and steady."

Ryan lifted his hips and dropped his cock into the slippery crease. Watching Dagger's face, he felt for the indentation and pressed the head of his cock to it, without breaching the barrier.

"That's it," Dagger said. "Nice and slow."

Ryan started inching his hips forward and felt Dagger pushing back on him, then stopped moving.

"Don't stop," Dagger said. "Keep a steady pressure. Getting past the muscle is the hardest part."

Ryan's hips pushed forward again. Slow and steady. Slow and steady, he kept telling himself. Dagger's arms circled his shoulders and held him close. Ryan worked another inch inside and Dagger exhaled slowly, sounding much like a sigh. Then Ryan felt the ring of muscle inside Dagger release and another inch of his cock slipped inside.

"Am I hurting you?" Ryan asked, his voice low and husky.

"I'm fine now," Dagger said. "Kiss me."

Ryan lowered himself against Dagger's chest and took his mouth, sucking his tongue, then nipping it. Slowly he continued to ease his thickness inside Dagger. He closed his eyes and allowed himself to *feel* in that moment. The heat surrounding him nearly took his breath away and the snug hold of Dagger's body to him, it was enough to make him come without thrusting at all.

"Holy... shit," Ryan whispered.

Dagger opened his thighs wider and Ryan slid in completely. He stopped and looked at Dagger.

"I'm good, Ry, don't stop."

Ryan's hips started to withdraw and he heard himself groan. The pleasure circling and stroking his cock was blinding. He knew he wouldn't last long, not with this heat giving him the tightest stroke he'd ever experienced. He pulled halfway out and thrust in, holding Dagger's gaze.

"Fuck me harder," Dagger urged.

Ryan pulled back again and thrust, then again, and again.

"I'm not gonna last."

"I'm already there," Dagger said.

Ryan arched into the last stroke, throwing his head back and exploded inside Dagger. The sensations searing through him made him feel like he was floating. He collapsed onto Dagger's chest, his mouth curling into a lazy, satisfied smile.

As the euphoric haze began to clear from Ryan's head, he realized Dagger had stopped moving. He had vaguely acknowledged Dagger releasing between them; felt the sticky warmth shoot across his stomach, but his concentration had been elsewhere. Now, Dagger's quiet stillness seemed exceptionally loud to him.

Ryan lifted himself up onto his elbows and gazed down at Dagger. His eyes were closed and tears appeared to be seeping from the corners.

"Dagger?"

"Let me up," Dagger said, gently pushing at first on Ryan's chest, then using more force than was needed to get Ryan off of him.

Ryan pulled out of Dagger and rolled onto his side. He watched Dagger stalk across the floor toward the bathroom partially shutting the door and Ryan's heart shattered. He stood up from the bed and grabbed a handful of tissues to clean himself up and removed the used condom, tossing it into the trash. His eyes went back to the bathroom door. He didn't know what to do, what to say, or what had upset Dagger to make him shed tears.

He waited a few moments then walked to the door, lightly tapping on the wood.

"Dagger, can I come in?" Ryan asked.

"Yeah, go ahead."

Ryan tentatively opened the door and found Dagger sitting on the floor. His back resting against the vanity cabinet, his arms hugged his knees to his chest, and his forehead pressed to his arms. Dagger briefly raised his head to look at Ryan when he entered the room, then dropped his head back to his forearms.

"Did I hurt you?" Ryan asked.

Dagger shook his head. "No, Ry, you were fine."

"Then what is it?" Ryan asked, sitting on the floor adjacent to Dagger. "What did I do to upset you?"

Dagger sat back and wiped at his eyes. "I haven't bottomed for fifteen years," he said. "I hadn't anticipated the emotional impact that would have on me... until right now."

Ryan quickly did the math in his head and tried to calculate what Dagger's age would have been fifteen years back. His best guess put Dagger in the dark period in his life he'd referenced while they were in Vegas. He hoped maybe now Dagger would shed some light on what it all meant;

maybe answer his questions about the newspaper articles he'd read, too.

"I'm sorry," Dagger said.

"Don't apologize for feelings, Dagger. We all have them."

"I don't want you to think I'm reacting to anything you did," Dagger said. "That part was... *perfection*. It was the connection I felt with you at that moment; it brought back some memories for me. That's all."

"Do you want to tell me about it?" Ryan asked, cautious not to push Dagger too hard to talk if he still wasn't ready.

Dagger lifted his head again, pushed the hair off his face and looked across at Ryan. He nodded first, then cleared his throat. "Yeah, I would," Dagger said softly. "I think it's time I tell you about something."

Ryan stood up and offered Dagger his hand. "I'm happy to listen as long as you need me to," he said. "But, let's go back to bed where we can be comfortable."

Dagger looked at Ryan's outstretched hand. The hesitation Ryan saw flicker in Dagger's face killed him, but he kept his hand out and stepped closer. "I'm a really good listener, Dagger," he said. "And whatever you tell me, stays between us. You have my word."

Ryan sighed when Dagger clutched his hand. It was difficult to miss the relief washing over him. He tugged Dagger back to bed and laid behind him in a spooning position. His arms circled Dagger in a loose embrace. He wanted Dagger to feel held and safe, but not suffocated. He pressed his lips to the warmth of Dagger's shoulder.

"Trust me with your secrets," Ryan whispered beside Dagger's ear.

"I want to, Ry, really I do, but... it's been such a long time."

"Long time for what?"

Dagger reached for the Celtic cross on his bicep and covered it with his palm; almost hugging it with his hand.

"Does this have something to do with your tattoo?" Ryan asked.

Dagger nodded and Ryan rolled him onto his back so he could see his face.

"Tell me," Ryan said. "Please."

Dagger drew in a long breath. "In my senior year of high school, I met a kid in my class named Patrick Murphy."

"Are those his initials inside the cross?" Ryan asked.

Dagger covered his eyes and Ryan eased his hands away, then lowered his lips to kiss Dagger's lids. "Tell me about Patrick," Ryan sighed and rubbed his cheek to Dagger's.

"By then, I already knew I was gay," Dagger said. "But Patrick was... conflicted. I helped him figure it out. That's about it."

"Bullshit," Ryan said. "He must have played a significant role in your life if you willingly branded his initials into your skin."

Dagger held Ryan's gaze. Was it anger Ryan saw floating in Dagger's soft hazel eyes? Fear? He wasn't sure, but he wanted to keep Dagger talking, not allow him to shut down and put the lock back on the memories.

"I loved him," Dagger finally said. "I guess that makes him pretty fucking significant."

"First love?"

Dagger nodded and closed his eyes, squeezing out more tears; which Ryan gently wiped away with his fingers. "Patrick was the first and only guy I've let... top."

"Until me," Ryan said as he exhaled. The weight of Dagger's words almost too heavy for Ryan to handle.

"Feeling you in me like that... it brought it all back," Dagger said quietly. "I felt a connection with you – like I did with Patrick. It was as if we were all one in the same, and it scared me." Dagger pushed himself upright. "Christ! I'm fucked up. I'm sorry. Let's forget I said any of this."

"I'm not forgetting it and I don't think you're fucked up," Ryan said. "I think it's important we talk about this. It helps me to know *all* of you – not just the pieces you want me to see."

Ryan watched Dagger open his eyes and look at him. His eyes so watery and raw with emotion it broke Ryan's heart to see such a strong man struggling like this. Ryan held his breath wondering what Dagger would say next and bit his own tongue feeling the 'L' word ready to spill from his lips. It was too soon. He couldn't do it; couldn't risk losing this moment to an emotion he wasn't completely certain he was feeling - and didn't Dagger deserve at least that much?

"Patrick was special," Dagger said. "I could have loved him forever."

"What happened?" Ryan asked. "Why didn't it last?"

Dagger slid his feet closer to his body, resting his arms over his knees. "Patrick died."

"How?"

Dagger grimaced as if in pain. "It was an accident. He was chasing after someone and tripped; hit his head on a rock, and died right there in front of me." Dagger's head dropped forward to his knees. "There was so much blood. I didn't know what to do."

Ryan stroked Dagger's back, beautiful smooth skin soft as silk; his fingers could have touched him like this all night long. "Why was Patrick chasing someone?"

"There were a bunch of them – watching Patrick and I... having sex. I didn't care what they thought of me, but Patrick... no one knew about him. They started laughing and calling us names and Patrick freaked. He had a football scholarship to Boston College and was afraid he'd lose it if anything tarnished his reputation. We had everything planned. He'd go to school at B.C. while I attended my classes at Berklee and we'd get an apartment together in Boston. He wanted us to live like a real couple. Imagine that? Me and the star football player. I should have known that could never happen."

"Berklee School of Music?" Ryan asked.

"Yeah, I had a scholarship, but I never made it to Boston."

"Why the hell not?"

"The kid Patrick was chasing, I eventually caught, and I nearly beat him to death," Dagger said. "I did two years in jail for assault. My parent's disowned me for disgracing our family; which was a joke. There was no such thing as grace in my family. And Patrick's parents... they were disgusted their son would be involved with someone as disreputable as me – like I was the bad influence that turned their son gay. After I was released from jail, I left town and I've never been back."

"That's when you changed your name?"

"Yep. I wanted no connection to that town, or the people living in it – not even my parents."

"Are your parents alive?" Ryan asked.

"Last time I checked they were still living in the same fucking house I grew up in."

"Dagger," Ryan said, elongating his name. "They don't know about your success, do they?"

"Nope, and that's exactly the way I want it."

"Maybe if they knew..."

"Don't say it, Ry. Nothing I've managed to achieve with my music would mean a damn thing to them. I'd still be the son that brought shame to the family name – a name so worthless to me, I took legal means to have it amputated from my identity for good."

Ryan eased Dagger back against the pillows at the headboard and hugged him tightly. "Thank you for sharing Patrick with me," he said, kissing him at the temple. "What happened was unfair and I'm so sorry you lost him."

Dagger rolled to Ryan and ran his fingers across his scalp. "You continue to amaze me every day, Ryan Pierce."

"How so?"

"I tell you about an old love and you don't freak on me. You hold me while I cry about him and you don't run from the room screaming obscenities. What did I do to deserve someone as compassionate as you?"

Ryan snuggled closer to Dagger and smiled against his lips. "I think we're good for each other."

"I'd say perfect."

Dagger turned onto his back and pulled Ryan on top of him. He laughed when he felt Ryan's erection rubbing up against him.

"How many more condoms do you have in that drawer?" Ryan asked.

"It's full."

Ryan raised one eyebrow. "Think you'd be okay with me using another one?"

Dagger tipped his head back and laughed loudly. "Oh, now I see your plan. You're gonna send me back on tour walking funny, aren't you?"

"And, if anyone questions your weird swagger, be sure to tell them your boyfriend has a huge cock."

"Can I also tell them your name?" Dagger teased.

Ryan bristled at the thought.

"I'm joking, Ry. I'm not telling anyone a damn thing about you. You're all mine."

"Your dirty little secret?"

Dagger opened his mouth to Ryan and flamed the heat that had been sparking between them like fireflies.

"Zero to one hundred," Ryan sighed.

"Grab another condom, cowboy," Dagger said.

CHAPTER FOURTEEN

Ryan said good-bye to Dagger in his driveway and followed the limousine off his estate and out onto the main road. The pain he felt was very real, as he watched Dagger's limo accelerate onto the freeway heading toward the airport, and he turned in the direction of his apartment. A big part of him wanted to go with Dagger, but he knew that wasn't a realistic plan. He had a job to do and so did Dagger. The fact Dagger had taken time away from his tour to be with Ryan, was huge, and truly proved how much he cared.

He smiled to himself at Dagger's teasing comment about having to walk funny. Truth was, Dagger's swagger had changed a bit since the day before. Ryan was having trouble remembering all the different positions they'd had sex and in numerous locations, too. In the shower, on the bed – leaning against the bed, and even once on the floor, and each time it got better and better and he liked it. A lot.

Ryan cupped his groin, feeling his cock starting to swell beneath his palm. Thinking about Dagger made him hard so quickly, but more than that, it was the emotional aspect of being with Dagger that was surprising him. He was falling in deep, feeling things he'd never felt for another lover in his entire life. He stopped at a traffic light and pushed his fingers through his hair.

"Wow," Ryan said for his ears only. "Certainly didn't see this coming. Did you?"

Ryan's cell phone buzzed, announcing a text message. He lifted it to read and saw it was from Dagger.

"Miss you already."

He read the message and his chest tightened. Before the light turned green he typed a reply that read simply: *"Me too."*

What he wouldn't give to roll around in bed with Dagger for a few more days. Even then, he doubted it would be enough time. He hoped when Dagger's tour ended they could spend more uninterrupted time together, but maybe that wasn't something Dagger would want. As good as it felt when they were together, it would still have to remain a secret to everyone around them. Ryan wasn't sure if he'd be able to keep their relationship a secret or if he'd be willing to live such a monumental lie in front of his family and friends. No matter how he looked at this, it was not going to be easy and Dagger may not want to take on the challenge at all. Ryan couldn't blame him for that. Dagger knew all too well what exposed secrets could do to your life; how it altered your path.

He parked in the lot behind his apartment building and carried his backpack inside. After shutting the door, the quiet inside his apartment fell over him like a heavy blanket. How could silence be so fucking loud? He walked into the living room and stood at the wide window overlooking the main street, watching the cars speeding past.

The sudden turnaround in his life was profound. What he'd experienced in the last twenty-four hours was life changing. Yet, he was still standing upright. He hadn't burst into flames and died. The earth hadn't popped off its axis and people still managed to go about their lives without interruption. But, how could that be when he felt so different –

so changed? Surely others had to feel the shift in the atmosphere, right?

He sat down on his couch and pulled the cell phone from his pocket and dialed Beth's number. She answered on the second ring. Simply hearing the sound of her voice calmed him; much like Dagger's voice did to him.

"What's going on?" Beth asked.

"I don't even know where to start," Ryan said.

"Are things still good with your man?"

"Exceptional," Ryan said, the smile on his face pulling his cheeks tight.

"Wow! Dare I ask for details?" Beth asked.

Ryan laughed. "He flew back from his tour last night to see me."

"Hmmm, and it's mid-afternoon, Ry. Are you doing the walk of shame right now?"

"Don't make me sound cheap, Beth," he said with a chuckle. "It's good. Really good."

"I think you mentioned that already," Beth said. "This guy is special, isn't he?"

"Yeah, he is. I find myself wanting to be with him all the time and missing him when he's gone."

"Am I still talking to Ryan Pierce?" she teased. "You sound like a guy in love."

Dead silence. Ryan swallowed hard; his throat suddenly feeling clogged.

"Ryan, are you in love with this guy?" she asked.

"I don't know. Maybe." He sighed loudly and grabbed his head. "When I'm with him everything is easy. Comfortable. We can talk about anything and it's so relaxed. I feel... I feel connected. But, when he's gone I can see this for what it is: complicated. No one will understand this. He wants it to stay private; between him and I, but I'm not sure that's what I want – I'm not sure what the fuck I want."

"Jesus, Ryan! Take a damn breath! You're over-thinking this – as usual. Take it one step at a time. First off, does he know how you feel?"

"No, I haven't said anything," Ryan said.

"Do you think he's feeling the same way?" Beth asked.

Ryan's head dropped to the back of the couch. "Last night he trusted me with some pretty heavy shit from his past – stuff no one else knows about him. I don't think he'd share that with me if he wasn't feeling something."

"You're right, he wouldn't," Beth said. "So, what do you want to do with this? Where do you want it to go?"

"I want to be with him," Ryan said. "And, I'd like it to be like..."

"Like what – a real relationship?" Beth asked.

"Am I wrong to want something like that?" Ryan asked.

"No, not at all, but in order to make that happen," Beth said, "The relationship would have to be public knowledge and you said he doesn't want that. Right?"

"He thinks coming out could damage his career," Ryan said.

"And what about you?" Beth asked. "Aren't you afraid of the backlash of coming out?"

Coming out? Ryan felt a pain plink in his head. Is that what he was considering? But, what was he coming out from – the fog he'd apparently been in for the last fourteen years? He couldn't get his brain to comprehend this, no matter how hard he tried.

"I think it's a little premature to feel the need to tell anyone about this – especially the press," Ryan said. "At this point, I'm not even sure where this is going or if we both want the same thing."

"I've got a surprise for you, Ry," Dagger said over the phone.

"Did you send another triple X photo of yourself to my cell?" Ryan asked.

Dagger laughed. "Actually, no, but I'm happy to send you something if that's what you want."

Ryan smiled and adjusted the pillows behind his back at the headboard of his bed. "What's the surprise?"

"I got a tramp stamp inked onto my left ass cheek," Dagger said. "It says: Property of Ryan Pierce."

"Are you serious?"

Dagger chuckled again, using the dirty, throaty laugh he used when he was teasing. "No new tats, Ry. I haven't had time."

"Then, what's really going on?" Ryan asked.

"There was an electrical fire at the venue in Montreal," he said. "That means my two day break just turned into six."

"Sounds really nice."

"I was hoping you'd think so," Dagger said. "Tony signed us to appear at a charity event with a few other bands on Friday night in San Francisco, but after that, I have close to a week off."

"Hmmm, intriguing," Ryan said.

"Fly up for the show and we'll take it from there," Dagger said. "How's that sound?"

It had been three weeks since Ryan spent the night at Dagger's L.A. house. The idea of having several days back to back with Dagger sounded like bliss.

"What time do you want me in San Francisco?" Ryan asked.

"Did I just offer something you can't resist?" Dagger laughed.

"You're a hard man to refuse."

"How'd you know I was hard?" Dagger asked.

Ryan smiled, knowing all too well that Dagger wasn't lying, and his stomach did a flip-flop. The very clear visual in his mind of Dagger's aroused body did wonders for him. Knowing he was able to draw that kind of response from Dagger, worked the same magic.

"Oh, and Ryan," Dagger said. "Don't shave. You know how much I love you rough."

Four days later, Ryan flew up to San Francisco in a private jet chartered by Dagger. Soon as he cleared the arrivals terminal, Dagger was waiting for him with a tight hug.

"Wow! Someone's happy to see me," Ryan said, and smiled against the bend of Dagger's neck.

"I've been in a dangerous state of arousal since the day you confirmed your visit," Dagger said. "I only wish the limo ride to the hotel was longer so I could jump you in the car."

Ryan leaned back in the embrace and tipped his head. "We could always take the scenic route?"

"I like the way you think," Dagger said. "Come on, let's go for a ride."

Dagger waited for Ryan to settle into the leather seat in the back of the limousine, then gave the driver instructions, ending with a very firm directive not to bother him for the next thirty minutes. Ryan watched a smile spread across Dagger's handsome face and his cock started to thicken.

"You look good enough to eat," Dagger said. He slid over on the seat and wrapped his fingers around Ryan's neck, pulling his mouth to him. "Mind if I have a taste?" he whispered.

Ryan parted his lips and took the kiss Dagger was offering. He felt Dagger's hand skim down his chest, over his stomach, and stop on the hard mound already stretching his pants. When Dagger's fingers curled around the tent and tightened to squeeze his balls, Ryan moaned into his mouth.

"I can't wait to get you between my lips," Dagger said, using his tongue to tease the spot behind Ryan's front teeth. "You cool with that?"

"Fuccckk – yes," Ryan said, making a guttural sound in the back of his throat. His own fingers undid the button on the waistband of his jeans and pulled down the zipper, but it was Dagger's hand that reached inside to free the weight of Ryan's swollen cock.

"Is this all for me?" Dagger asked.

Ryan managed a nod and watched as Dagger's head dropped into his lap. Dagger dragged his cheek over Ryan's shaft, then kissed the broad head.

"Suck me. Please," Ryan said. He touched the back of Dagger's head, stroking the softness of his hair; letting the long strands slip between his fingers, then sifted deeper, massaging the warm flesh at the back of Dagger's neck.

"Slide down your pants," Dagger said.

Ryan lifted his hips and pushed his jeans down to his knees. His cock sprang free and continued to thicken under Dagger's heated gaze. Something strange and wonderful happened to his brain whenever he was in the backseat of a limo with Dagger. He turned into a brazen and crazed man;

bursting with sexual need and uninterested in stopping until satisfied – no matter the consequence or who might catch them. One kiss from Dagger and he lost all logic; thinking of nothing else but getting naked and wrapped up and lost in this man's touch.

Dagger slid the thick length of Ryan's cock inside his mouth; his tongue dancing over the crest, while his lips did amazing things to the shaft. Ryan hummed, then cursed. His head dropped to the back of the seat. His hands rubbed Dagger's shoulders and neck, holding him in place, not wanting him to ever stop delivering these exquisite sensations.

"Jesus, Dagger," Ryan sighed, elongating his words.

Dagger pulled off Ryan's cock and licked the tip. "You like that?"

"It's pure torture."

"Good," Dagger smiled up at him. "Hold on, I'm about to torture you some more."

Ryan arched in the seat, watching his cock disappear into the back of Dagger's throat. His head turned and looked out the window. The limo had stopped at a traffic light and there were about a dozen pedestrians standing beside their car waiting to cross the busy street. The car windows were tinted, but Ryan could see them looking at the passenger compartment with curiosity. The idea they could possibly see Dagger deep-throating his cock kicked up the thrill factor several notches.

"There's people beside the car," Ryan slurred.

"Maybe you should show them what they're missing," Dagger said.

Ryan thrust into Dagger's mouth and groaned. "I'm so close," he said.

"Shoot on my tongue," Dagger urged.

Ryan's eyes fell. He didn't notice Dagger stretch to press the button lowering the side window. They were now on full display to the pedestrians, as Dagger pushed Ryan over the edge. Ryan delivered several quick thrusts between Dagger's parted lips and ejaculated with a roar. A moment later the limousine accelerated in traffic passing directly by the people and Dagger chuckled around Ryan's still pulsing cock. He calmed him through the aftershocks, then sat up beside Ryan with an enormous smile displaying beautiful, straight white teeth.

Ryan lifted his head from the back of the seat and saw the open window, then glanced at Dagger. "Did you have that open when I got off?"

"Yep, I did." Dagger leaned into Ryan and lightly kissed his lips, then sat back.

"Did they see you, too?" Ryan asked, stroking the side of Dagger's face with the pads of his fingers.

"I doubt it," he said. "My face was busy bouncing in your lap."

A lazy grin lifted one side of Ryan's mouth. "For someone who wants to keep his sexual preferences in the closet, you sure take a lot of risks getting caught."

"You bring that out in me, you know," Dagger said, dragging his thumb across Ryan's lower lip. "You make me do crazy things – and want crazy things."

"What kind of crazy things do you want?" Ryan asked, rolling toward Dagger on the seat.

Dagger's lips were so close to Ryan's, they shared the same breath. "To live in the open with you and not have to hide behind tinted windows or locked doors."

"I'd like that, too," Ryan said. He closed the last inch separating them and took Dagger's mouth. They ended up reclined on the backseat, with Ryan making a one-handed attempt to undo Dagger's leather pants and wrestle with the zipper.

"You want what's in there?" Dagger asked.

"Get them undone for me. Quick."

Ryan followed Dagger into the meet and greet conference room before the San Francisco show. The room was already full of contest winners waiting to meet Dagger and his band, with many more people being escorted in as soon as the fans finished going through the greeting line and filed out the opposite door.

Ryan leaned against the wall across the room, happy to watch Dagger from a distance, as he played rock star; pressing-the-flesh with his adoring fans. Watching Dagger work the crowd always got Ryan's heart racing, and feeling the heat of his eyes land on him every now and then, was even better. Christ, what this man did to him was remarkable.

He moved off the wall and took a few steps to his right. His hands slid into the front pockets of his jeans. Again, Dagger caught his eye and winked. Ryan felt his face flush.

What was he – a school girl blushing at her first crush? He laughed at himself and moved deeper into the crowded room.

"Ryan? Is that you?"

Ryan spun around to face the voice and was shocked to see his ex-girlfriend standing there with her arms held open for a hug. "Beth, what are you doing here?" Ryan asked, pulling her against him in a tight embrace.

"I can't believe I bumped into you here; of all places," Beth said, squeezing him. "My friend won some silly contest to meet Black Ice and dragged me along for the fun and debauchery. What about you? Are you working this event?"

Ryan felt the color drain from his face. His mouth opened to speak and then closed. Fuck. Now what?

"Oh, my God! Ryan, is your mystery man here?" Beth asked. She stepped closer and pressed her face into Ryan's neck. "Is he a member of Black Ice?"

"Beth, I can't do this here," he said and grabbed her hand to pull her into the hallway. He walked several feet away from the open doorway and leaned up against the concrete wall, bending over to grab his thighs, feeling like he might pass-out. He took several deep breaths trying to calm himself but it didn't help.

"Ry, are you all right?" Beth asked. He stood up and Beth eased her arms around his waist. "Talk to me. What's going on with you? Is he here?" She said the last question in a whispered tone.

He wrapped her up in his arms and exhaled loudly. "Yeah, he's here."

"Is he in the band?" she asked.

Ryan leaned back. "Beth... I can't."

Ryan felt a presence beside him and stopped talking and separated himself from Beth. He turned to see Dagger step up, his eyes full of question and concern. For a brief moment they held each others gaze, as if silently speaking with their eyes, then Dagger set his hand on Ryan's shoulder and squeezed. He leaned forward and pressed his cheek to Ryan's. Their whiskered jaw lines scraped, making that delicious friction that always brought Ryan's cock to attention.

"Everything all right?" Dagger asked beside Ryan's ear.

Ryan nodded and Dagger pulled back; his eyes still holding Ryan's. "Would you like to introduce me to your beautiful friend?"

"Yes, of course," Ryan said. "This is Beth."

"Ah, the infamous ex-girlfriend," Dagger said, flashing Beth a thousand watt smile and extending his hand. "Ryan's told me a lot about you. I'm Dagger Drummond."

Beth took Dagger's hand and shook it. "I'm a huge fan, Dagger, but I can honestly say this is the first I'm learning of your friendship with Ryan."

"You know Ryan," Dagger laughed. "He likes to keep his personal life quiet."

Ryan watched the interplay between Beth and Dagger. Saying it was surreal would be downplaying the moment of seeing his old lover meeting his new. Ryan felt his face flush again. He felt lightheaded and wanted to go somewhere and sit down. Alone.

"Listen, Beth," Dagger said. "I have to get back to work in there, but could you do me a favor and keep my friend company – at least until the color returns to his face? I'm a little worried about him."

Dagger's fingers feathered across Ryan's back. He waited until Ryan's eyes shifted to him, then smiled. "Don't over-think it," he said in a hushed tone, then turned toward Beth. "It's nice to finally meet you."

Dagger glanced back at Ryan and smiled warmly. "Relax," he said, and made his way back into the room.

Beth waited until Dagger disappeared into the room and turned to Ryan. "Dagger Drummond? Are you kidding me?" She gave him a playful slap on the chest.

Ryan rubbed at his face. "Maybe now you can understand why I couldn't tell you."

Beth wanted to continue the conversation with Ryan but her girlfriend, Casey, joined them in the hallway; giddy from having just met Dagger.

"Look at this! He signed my boob," Casey announced, pulling at her tank top to display Dagger's signature just above her nipple. "That man is beyond gorgeous. I want to have his babies!"

Beth glanced at Ryan and laughed. "Well, I think it's safe to say that will never happen, but I'm thrilled you got his autograph."

Ryan tugged Beth up against him and kissed her temple. "Thanks," he said.

"For what?" she asked.

"For making something awkward not seem so bad."

Ryan clung to Beth until Dagger finally emerged from the meet and greet. Soon as he appeared, Ryan stepped away from Beth. A few straggling fans in the hallway rushed at Dagger, making security jump into action.

"I need a break from the chaos," Dagger said. "Follow me." He directed Ryan, Beth and her friend back to his dressing room. Along the way, Casey allowed herself to be abducted by Dagger's bass player and dragged into a rowdy party room.

"Is she safe with them?" Beth asked Dagger.

"Yeah, their bark is definitely worse than their bite," Dagger said. He opened up a door and stepped inside. The fragrant aromas of Italian food greeted them soon as they walked through the doorway.

Ryan looked at the buffet table against the wall and smiled at the array of baked pasta dishes spread out before them. Everything from lasagna to stuffed shells and an assortment of fresh baked breads and tossed salad greens to go with it.

"I see catering came through for me again," Dagger said, stepping beside the food table. "I'm starved. Hope you guys like Italian. I've been craving it since I left Canada."

Ryan moved beside Dagger and touched his wrist. "I'll be right back," Ryan said. "I need to use the bathroom."

Dagger watched Ryan cross the room and open the door to the private bathroom connected to the dressing room.

"You really like him, don't you?" Beth said, stepping closer to Dagger.

He looked down at her and drew in a long breath. "That would be putting it mildly," Dagger said. "Why? Are you going to tell me you still love him and want him back?"

Beth nodded her head. "I'll always love Ryan, but not in the way you're assuming," she said. "We're best friends. That's it. Ryan never looked at me the way he looks at you and seeing the way you look at him... takes my breath away."

"I've spent the last fifteen years searching for someone like Ryan," Dagger said.

"It's interesting you worded it like that," Beth said. "Because, I think Ryan's been searching for you his whole life, except I don't believe he knew *what* he was looking for – until he met you."

Dagger grabbed a plate. "Ryan mentioned he talked to you about us."

Beth nodded. "Early on, he came to me wanting to talk about an attraction he had for a man, but he wouldn't tell me who – even though I hounded him about it. He was scared. Nervous. Vulnerable. I urged him to explore these new feelings and I'm so glad he did. I've never seen him happier."

"Except for today," Dagger said. "He's a little rattled right now because you're here."

"Ryan over-thinks everything," Beth said.

Dagger smiled. "I know. It was one of the first things I learned about him. It's kind of cute sometimes to watch him sweat the details."

"You'll be good to him, right?" she asked.

Dagger set his hip to the food table. "I know I don't want to lose him, but I do worry my career and having to hide our relationship will ruin what we have."

"That's very honest," Beth said.

"Will you keep our secret?"

"You don't have to ask me that, Dagger. I'd do everything I can to keep that smile on Ryan's face."

"Come here," Dagger said. He set down the plate he was holding and opened his arms, pulling Beth against him for a hug. "Thank you for being so understanding."

Ryan stepped back into the room and stopped short. Seeing Dagger holding Beth stirred a lot of emotion in him. Then he saw the tears in Beth's eyes and felt fear rising up inside him.

"Did I miss something?" Ryan asked.

Dagger reached for Ryan's hand and tugged him against his side in a loose embrace. "Your girlfriend is an amazing woman, and smart, too," Dagger said. "You shouldn't have let her go."

Ryan grinned, feeling the calm Dagger's touch always lent him. "I didn't let her go – she dumped me."

Beth started laughing. "As it turns out, Ry, I don't have the necessary equipment for you."

Dagger tipped his head at Ryan; his lips slanting up in a sexy half smile. "Is that so?" Dagger asked, and leaned in to brush his mouth against the shell of Ryan's ear. "You don't like her equipment?"

"I think he prefers yours," Beth said.

"Hmmm, lucky me," Dagger said, his hand squeezing Ryan's shoulder, holding him firmly to his side.

Beth started shifting toward the door. "I think I better go check on Casey and make sure she isn't offering sexual favors to your entire band."

Ryan separated himself from Dagger and followed her to the door. "You don't have to leave," he said.

"I know, but you should enjoy some time alone with Dagger before he has to perform," Beth said. "We'll have lunch soon and catch up. How's that sound?"

"It sounds perfect," Ryan said.

Beth looked up at him. Her eyes shimmering with emotion. "You two look beautiful together."

Ryan's arms circled her and he kissed her forehead. "I love you," he said. "You know that, right?"

"Yes, I do, but the guy standing over there is pretty sweet on you, too. Go show him some love."

She stepped out into the hallway and gave Ryan a parting wave before disappearing into the crowd. Ryan watched for a moment then closed the door and faced Dagger.

"She's a wise woman," Dagger said. "Now, get over here and show me some love."

Ryan walked to him and Dagger stood up straight. Eye to eye, chest to chest; the warmth of their breath heating the other. Ryan swallowed hard. There were things he wanted to say, but lacked the nerve to do so. His chest felt tight, as he watched Dagger unconsciously lick his lips, then Dagger's hand slid around the back of Ryan's neck; fingers scraping across one of his newly discovered erogenous zones. A shiver of pleasure raced through Ryan and he closed his eyes. He felt Dagger lean forward and press his lips to Ryan, then open to sigh into Ryan's mouth. Ryan tipped his head, loving the feeling of Dagger's tongue slipping inside and how quickly he was ready for him.

"I thought you were starved?" Ryan asked, breathless from their kiss.

"I am – for you," Dagger said, and took another kiss from Ryan's willing mouth.

A knock at the door announced ten minutes until show time for Dagger. He drained half a bottle of water and looked at Ryan. "Ready?"

Ryan nodded and walked to the door with Dagger. He opened the door and turned to face Ryan, planting a soft kiss on his lips, in full view of anyone that might have been passing by them in the hallway. Ryan quickly pulled back, surprised at Dagger's brazen show of affection.

"You're risking a lot every time you do that," Ryan said.

"You make me so happy, Ry," Dagger said, leaning up against the door frame; his hand running from Ryan's shoulder down to his wrist.

Ryan's heart thudded harder in his chest. Dagger's words meant so much to him, made him want to return the sentiment, but here clearly wasn't the place.

"Ryan Pierce," a voice boomed behind him. Before Ryan could turn around, a hand slapped him on the back of the shoulder.

"Hey, Zander," Dagger said with a nod in Zander's direction. "How's the crowd out there tonight?"

Zander came up beside Ryan and smiled at Dagger. He was dripping sweat from their stage performance and doing his best to dry it with the towel wrapped around his neck. "I got the crowd all worked up for you, Dagger. They're all yours. Enjoy," Zander said, then he faced Ryan. "I wanted to thank you for the article you wrote. Great job. Our album sales spiked after it ran."

"No problem," Ryan said. "I didn't know Ivory Tower was performing tonight. I'm sorry I missed it."

"I thought I mentioned that to you," Dagger said. "Our bands are co-headlining, but Zander was kind enough to go on first."

There were dozens of people walking by in the hallway and not one was familiar, until the man behind Zander stepped fully into view. "Sebastian? Interesting I'd see you here," Ryan said.

Sebastian grinned at Ryan. The arrogance in the expression made Ryan want to punch it right off his perfect Ken Doll face.

"I'd say the same about you," Sebastian said, "But it seems wherever Dagger is these days, you *pop* up – just like magic."

Zander glanced at Sebastian and told him to go wait for him in his dressing room, then looked back at Dagger. "I'll let you go," he said. "Have a good show."

Ryan watched Zander walk down the hall, then felt Dagger's hand curl around his bicep.

"I gotta head down to the stage," Dagger said. "Care to join me?"

Ryan walked with Dagger to the holding area just to the side of the stage. He wished Dagger luck and found a safe spot to watch the show; out of the way and out of sight, but with a clear line of sight to the only guy in the band he cared to see. Dagger. Leather pants riding low on his narrow hips, white silk shirt unbuttoned halfway down to his navel, that one long silver chain with the G-clef charm dangling against his breast bone. Ryan smiled at himself, comfortably checking out a man – his man. Christ, he couldn't wait to get Dagger alone later, maybe watch that charm swinging over his face. He made a humming noise, visualizing the motion it would take to get that charm to swing back and forth.

Dagger's guitar tech handed him his vintage Gibson Les Paul guitar at the side of the stage and helped him sling the strap over his shoulder to attach the instrument. Then Dagger swaggered toward center stage, the crowd jumped to their feet in one giant tidal wave of emotion; the screams of adulation were deafening. Dagger lifted his arm above his head, pumping his fist at the audience. His smile was nearly ear to ear.

"San Franciscoooo," he screamed into the microphone. "How you all doing tonight?"

Another roar erupted from the audience and Dagger tossed his head back and laughed.

"You gonna let us play with you for a while?"

Whistles and a thundering applause reverberated through the back beat being set by the drummer. Dagger counted off the intro to their first song, a Black Ice classic, and the rhythm guitarist and bass player stepped out of the shadows to join Dagger at center stage. Before Ryan's eye's, Dagger morphed into the rock star he was known to be. Gone were the soft tones and textures of his personality he shared with Ryan when they were alone. Those traits were replaced with with a persona based on raw sexuality and swagger.

Dagger whipped the crowd into a frenzy that awed Ryan and it also turned him on. Was there anything sexier than a good looking man playing an electric guitar? And no one wore a guitar the way Dagger did: low enough for him to bump and grind his cock against the back of it with every thrust of his hips.

The faces Dagger made while performing were pure ecstasy, too, like he was about to come; riding the razors edge to hold off his orgasm for as long as possible, before allowing himself to free fall over that edge. Ryan had seen that look on Dagger's handsome face too many times to count. Each expression a little different, but all with the same desperate need for release masking his eyes. Ryan took a moment to visualize Dagger's face just before orgasm and smiled, feeling his own cock beginning to respond to the image in his head and the walking sex god performing before him at center stage.

Ninety minutes later, Dagger left the stage after one final encore and a wave to his appreciating audience, drenched in sweat and panting. He handed off his guitar to his tech and walked over to Ryan who was there to hand him a towel and a bottle of cold water. He stood beside Ryan and almost drained the entire bottle before speaking.

"That was fucking awesome," Dagger said.

Ryan opened his mouth to speak and several people swarmed Dagger; whisking him away. All Ryan could do was follow the sea of people moving Dagger from the stage and into the hallway. Halfway down the hall, Ryan saw Dagger stop and turn to look for him. Soon as Dagger spotted him, a wide smile lifted his lips.

"I thought I lost you," Dagger said, casually draping an arm over Ryan's shoulders.

They walked like that for a bit until two groupies pulled Dagger off Ryan and pressed him up against the concrete wall. Dagger engaged the women by pretending to be struggling in their embrace. Ryan watched a feminine hand reach between Dagger's legs and cup his groin and the expression on Dagger's face went from laughter to annoyance. He pushed himself off the wall and away from the girl's, coming up along side Ryan.

"Gotta go, ladies," Dagger said.

Dagger reached his dressing room and the same two women tried to run in behind Ryan. Dagger quickly redirected the women back out into the hall. "No party tonight, girls," Dagger said, and shut the door to his dressing room.

Ryan looked at him. "You don't party anymore?"

"Not with them," Dagger said. He started unbuttoning his sweat-dampened shirt and shrugged it off his shoulders.

"What if I wasn't here, would you party with them then?" Ryan asked, doing his best to ignore the perfect planes of muscle on Dagger's bare chest.

"Are you jealous, Ry, or are you questioning my loyalty to you?" Dagger asked.

"No, not really."

Ryan sat down on the end of the couch and Dagger walked to him. He knelt between Ryan's partially spread legs and rubbed his thighs. He looked deeply into Ryan's eyes; squeezing the firm muscles beneath his palms.

"I said in the beginning, if I'm with you, there won't be anyone else," Dagger said in a soft voice. "Don't you trust me?"

"Yeah, I do," Ryan said. "But it's difficult to see people touching you like that. You're surrounded by temptation every day. I couldn't blame you if you did go with one of them."

Dagger leaned forward and cupped Ryan's head in his hands; running his thumbs over the whiskered jaw line. "If I ever feel tempted, I'll call and talk to you. That's all I need, Ry. You – only you." Dagger licked at the center of Ryan's bottom lip, teased until Ryan's lips separated, then covered his mouth.

Ryan wrapped his arms around Dagger's back; losing himself to the touch and taste of him. Between them Dagger's fingers went to work opening the fly on Ryan's pants. Dagger pulled Ryan's cock free and gripped it, sliding off one tight stroke.

"Typically, it's the rock star getting the blow job, Ryan," Tony said, stepping into the dressing room and shutting the door. "I think you're confused with your role here."

Dagger stood up quickly and stepped into Tony's face. "Do you have a key to this room?"

Tony jingled the key pinched between his fingers in front of Dagger's face. Dagger ripped the key from Tony's hand, opened up the dressing room door, and tossed the key into the hallway.

"Get the fuck out," Dagger said. When Tony didn't move, Dagger grabbed him by the arm and physically tossed him into the hallway, then slammed the door. He looked over at Ryan and saw that he was zipping up his pants.

"What's the deal with you and Tony?" Ryan asked.

"There's no deal," Dagger said.

"Did there ever used to be a deal?" Ryan asked, redoing his belt buckle.

Dagger crossed the room and pulled a clean shirt off the clothing rack in the corner of the room. "Do you want me to be honest?" Dagger asked.

"Yeah, that was kind of the point in me asking," Ryan said.

"Okay, then, yeah, a long time ago," Dagger said, buttoning another silk shirt. "We fooled around a bit. It didn't go very far. It made more sense for me to keep the business relationship going with him versus a personal one."

"Did he want there to be more?" Ryan asked.

"Probably, but I wasn't feeling it," Dagger said. "After that, I occasionally let him watch me when I was with other guys. Turned out he liked that more."

"Are you serious?" Ryan asked.

Dagger laughed, as he tucked the clean shirt into his pants. "He's watched me a few times, but not because I invited him. He has an uncanny ability to know when I'm up to something and then suddenly he appears from out of no where."

"Like he did just now," Ryan said.

"Exactly."

Ryan leaned against the food table and crossed his arms over his chest. "So, no one in the band knows about you?"

Dagger shook his head. "Except for Dyson."

"Your drummer?" Ryan asked.

"We got drunk one night and things got a little too crazy for my straight friend to handle," Dagger said. "He's never mentioned it since and it's highly unlikely he'll ever admit to it, so I'm pretty sure my secret is safe with him."

"You've had a colorful past," Ryan said.

Dagger walked to Ryan and pulled him to his chest, then his hands slid into the back pockets of Ryan's jeans. "No one worth remembering," he said, and kissed Ryan. "Until you."

CHAPTER FIFTEEN

After spending majority of the last week at Dagger's house while he was on a break from his tour, Ryan realized things were serious enough between them that he felt it was time to explain his new life to his parents. Dagger agreed it'd be okay to do so, and gave Ryan his support, then he left L.A. to fly up to Montreal to resume his concert tour. A few hours after saying good-bye to Dagger, Ryan called his parents and set up a visit for the very next day.

A torrential rain storm made the drive twice as long to the little town outside of Anaheim his parents called home, and caused triple the amount of stress, too. By the time Ryan returned home, he was mentally exhausted from concentrating so intently on the road, in addition to the uncomfortable conversation he'd had with his parents about his new lifestyle.

Overall the visit had gone well. Their reaction to him being romantically involved with a man shocked them; the news made his mother cry. She seemed more concerned with Ryan not giving her grandchildren than anything else. His father didn't want to discuss it at first, then attempted to change the subject, but in the end he said he merely wanted his son to live his life as he felt was best for him.

They both wondered if this man made Ryan happy. Ryan smiled. Was he happy? That was an easy question. He could honestly say he'd never felt such a deep and complete happiness with anyone before Dagger.

Ryan did his best to explain why – seemingly so out of the blue, he'd fallen for Dagger and was careful not to give away Dagger's full identity. He wasn't sure they'd know who he was anyway, but he kept his word to Dagger by omitting his name to his parents. It made no difference at this point if they knew who he was with, just that he was with a man. That was the main objective in visiting his parents and it was a huge relief to have the subject out in the open and behind them.

He knew they didn't fully understand. How could they, when he didn't quite understand it himself? But, Ryan needed them to know the truth and wanted them to hear it from him: he had deep feelings; possibly love, for Dagger. The visit took all afternoon and, as Ryan drove away from their house, he knew they'd be unsettled about this new revelation about their son for a long time.

At least they hadn't turned their back on him, Ryan thought, and they asked to meet the 'man in his life' at some point, too. Not a bad outcome in his book. He had heard too many horror stories of parents disowning their children after hearing they were homosexual. His parents were hesitant to accept this truth about Ryan, but at least they were willing to attempt to embrace it, and that's the best he could ask for.

Now that his parents knew about Dagger, a huge load had been lifted from Ryan's shoulders. Someday down the road, he'd have to figure out a way to tell a few select friends and maybe a couple of co-workers, too. But for now, he was happy with his parents knowing and also Beth. Everyone else could go fuck themselves for the time being.

He found a parking spot in back of his apartment building and shut off his car. The rain was still pounding against the roof and windshield of his car creating a deafening sound. Ryan collected the few things he had with him off the seat and put them into his backpack, then prepared to make a mad dash for the entrance of his apartment building, doing his best not to get drenched in the process.

And then Ryan spotted him. Standing in the rain. Soaked to the skin. His face furrowed with anger and annoyance. Fists clenched at his sides.

Ryan stopped in his tracks. In seconds the water permeated through his clothing and chilled his skin.

"Dagger? What are you doing here?" Ryan asked. "Aren't you supposed to be in Montreal?"

"Never mind where I'm supposed to be," Dagger bit out. "Where the fuck have you been?"

The tone was cold and harsher than Ryan had ever heard coming from Dagger's mouth and he had no clue why.

"I was at my parents' house," Ryan said. "Remember? We talked about this."

Dagger shoved Ryan; making him stumble backward, his feet splashed in a deep puddle on the pavement. Something was horribly wrong with Dagger, Ryan thought, and it shook him to the bone.

"You fucking told them about us, didn't you?" Dagger shouted. "Your list keeps growing and growing, doesn't it?"

"What the hell are you talking about? I told my parents I was involved with a man, but I never told them it was you!" Ryan said, blinking the raindrops from his eyes. "We discussed this all last week."

"So, your parents know and let's not forget about Beth. You felt the need to tell her, too! How many others have you told, Ry? How many?"

"Just them – and only Beth knows it's you."

"Ah, yes, your precious Beth," Dagger snipped.

"She saw us together, Dagger. Don't twist that into me telling her about you."

Dagger quickly stepped into Ryan's space; eye to eye, his hot breath steaming in the cool, wet air and bouncing off Ryan's face. He glared at Ryan for several long seconds. Ryan's heart was pounding in his chest. The rain soaking even through his shoes and socks. He wanted to go inside, dry off, and get warm, but that didn't seem to be an option right now, with Dagger bearing down on him.

Dagger grabbed Ryan by the neck and claimed his mouth in a bruising kiss and Ryan dropped his backpack to the ground. Their teeth hit and lips mashed to the point of pain. There was nothing intimate or arousing about this kiss. It was meant to hurt and state a point; maybe of possession? Ryan wasn't sure.

Dagger broke the kiss but his hold was still too hard on Ryan's jaw line. Ryan raised his hands to get Dagger to loosen his grip, but Dagger was unrelenting and tightened his fingers instead, digging them into the flesh on Ryan's neck.

"Turns out your mouth is good for something other than sucking my dick," Dagger hissed, and pushed Ryan away from him, like discarding trash. Ryan nearly fell onto the ground.

"What the hell is wrong with you?" Ryan asked, his voice pitching higher.

"Fuck you, Ryan. Fuck. You." Dagger began stalking toward the limousine parked at the curb on the side street paralleling Ryan's apartment building.

Ryan watched him take a couple of steps. "So, that's it? You come here and shove me around, tell me to fuck off, then leave without an explanation?"

Dagger spun around and got into Ryan's face again. "You gave me your word, Ryan, and I trusted you. But, apparently advancing your career meant more to you than I did."

"You're not making any sense," Ryan said.

Dagger tipped his head. The rain had plastered his hair over his forehead and cheeks, even dripped off his clothing, but the anger and hate in his eyes burned bright. "You denying what you've done only pisses me off more, Ry."

"I have no fucking clue what you're talking about, Dagger! So, either spit it out or fucking leave. I don't care, but I'm not standing out here in the rain any longer."

Ryan turned and started to walk away. Dagger ran at him, tackled him from behind and sent them both crashing to the ground. Ryan landed hard on his side, with the muscled bulk of Dagger landing on top of him. He felt a painful crack in his rib cage and struggled to draw in a breath.

Dagger rolled Ryan onto his back, straddled his hips; pinning his shoulders to the wet pavement. Ryan still worked to take in shallow breaths.

"You lied to me," Dagger said, leaning over Ryan; the water from his face and hair dripping onto him. "You sold my story – *our* story, to the fucking media! I can't forgive that, nor will I forget."

"I did no such thing!" Ryan shouted. He tried pushing Dagger off his lap but Dagger didn't budge, he only pressed Ryan into the pavement with more force causing Ryan's head to hit the ground with a thud and that was it. Ryan used the strength in his legs to flip Dagger off him and rolled away, holding on to his side as he stood up.

"You sold me out!" Dagger roared.

"I did not, but go ahead and believe whatever the fuck you want. You've already made up your mind, so it makes no difference what I say."

"You'd be wise to go inside and read the headlines for the news outlets, Ry, and see what an overnight celebrity you've become – at my expense."

Ryan turned around to face Dagger. "Are you serious?"

Dagger picked up Ryan's backpack from the wet ground and threw at him. "Don't bother to call me later," he said. "I won't be taking your calls."

Ryan didn't stick around to watch Dagger get into the limo, instead he ran toward the entrance of the apartment building holding on to his ribs, and took the elevator up to his apartment. Once inside, he quickly booted-up his computer and then went through a series of links reporting the latest music news. What he saw made his stomach churn; various headlines all carried the same news bit: Dagger Drummond comes out as a gay man. Some articles even listed Dagger's lover as being Ryan Pierce, while others referred to Ryan as nothing more than an unidentified man. The bold, front page headline for Music Spin magazine screamed Dagger's sexual preference and included two blurry photographs of Dagger and Ryan kissing in the doorway of what looked like a backstage dressing room. Ryan's eyes lifted, then froze on the name of the reporter.

"Sebastian." Ryan sighed the name out loud and slumped in his chair. What the hell was he going to do now?

Ryan's cell phone started ringing. He glanced at the caller I.D. and saw that it was work calling him. He ignored the call, letting it go to voice mail, but half a dozen more calls followed in quick succession from various people. Another call was from Beth and Ryan answered it.

"Ryan, are you all right?" Beth asked.

No, he wasn't all right and wondered if he would be ever again. He felt like crying – screaming, anything to spin back the clock to yesterday and prevent this nightmare from happening. They were useless thoughts that made Ryan's head ache.

"I was at my parents house when this story broke," Ryan said to Beth. "Then when I got home, Dagger was waiting for me in the parking lot."

"Oh, no! What happened, Ry? What did he say?"

"He's understandably pissed off and believes I gave Sebastian the story."

"But, that's not true! Surely, Dagger would believe you, right?"

Ryan shook he head. "Nope, he's believing the worst," Ryan said, and his voice cracked. "And then he dumped me."

"He's mad right now. Give him a day to cool down and then he'll rethink losing you," Beth said. "Honestly, Ry, Dagger shouldn't have thought he could stay in the closet forever and he certainly shouldn't have put the burden of keeping his secret on you."

"I can't believe this is happening," Ryan said. He leaned forward, resting his elbows on the desk and held his head in his hand. "I told my parents I was in a relationship with a man; which wasn't easy, and they offered their support. I came home on such an emotional high, actually thinking good things would be ahead for me – and now this."

"Do you want me to come over and stay for a couple of days?

"That's not necessary, Beth. I'm a big boy. I'll figure out a way to face this and move forward."

"Fight for him, Ryan. Don't let him walk away."

Ryan scoffed. "I don't exactly have a lot of control over that, Beth."

"But, you love him," Beth said. "And, I've never seen you happier. That's worth fighting for."

"Dagger implied you might be partially to blame for our relationship leaking to the press," Ryan said.

"That's ridiculous and you know it."

"I know, Beth. I'm certain Sebastian is one hundred percent responsible for this story, and when I get my hands on him, he's a dead man."

"Don't do something so crazy you get yourself into trouble," she said. "Sebastian isn't worth it."

Ryan moved in his chair and winced in pain. "I think Dagger cracked one of my ribs," Ryan said softly.

"You two fought?"

"He shoved me a few times and then knocked me down," Ryan said. "I heard something crack when he landed on me."

"Are you kidding me? You should file assault charges!"

"And bring more attention to him in the press? I don't think so! The news outlets would love to add that story to their headlines tomorrow morning!"

"What are you going to do?" Beth asked.

Ryan rubbed at his head. "For the time being, I think I'll shut off my phone and take a shower. Tomorrow I'll go into work and do my best to hold my head high, maybe talk to my boss."

"You've done nothing to be ashamed of, Ryan. You remember that."

"Too bad Dagger doesn't believe that."

"He will. It may take a while though, but I am certain he will come around. I saw the way he was with you at the venue, Ryan. He's just as crazy about you as you are for him. The way he looked at you gave me goose bumps."

Tears began to pool in Ryan's eyes and he swallowed hard. The memories hurt too much to think about right now.

"Beth, I think I'll take that shower now and lie down."

"I'm so sorry you're going through this, Ryan, but you know I'm here if you need to talk about it. Please give me a call."

"Thanks," he said. "You've been a good friend."

"I'll call you later to see how you're doing."

Ryan ended the call and stared at the phone for a long moment. Every muscle in his body ached and that one rib throbbed, keeping a perfect beat to his heart. He slid his cell phone open and started a text message to Dagger.

"I'm sorry for what happened, but I DID NOT leak that story," Ryan typed. *"This is Sebastian's handiwork – not mine."*

A moment later, Ryan's cell phone buzzed announcing a new text message. Ryan looked at the screen and saw Dagger's message. *"Sebastian may have written it, but you fed him the story line,"* Dagger said.

"I did not do what you're suggesting," Ryan protested.

"He used my real name, Ry! How the fuck do you explain that, when you're the only other person that knew it?"

"I don't know how he got that information, but I swear to you, I did not betray your trust!" Ryan typed.

Several long minutes passed, while Ryan waited for Dagger's response. It was beginning to look like Dagger wouldn't respond at all and tears began to bite at Ryan's eyes. Then, finally his cell phone announced another text message.

Ryan grabbed his phone from the desk and looked at the screen.

"Lose my number and do not contact me again."

Fuck. So that was it for them, Ryan thought, and wiped at his eyes. He shut off his phone and threw it on top of his desk. This felt ten times worse than any of his past break-ups, including losing Beth. He walked into his bedroom, carefully holding on to his ribs, and started removing his clothing to take a shower. He walked by a wall-length mirror hanging on the back of the open closet door and saw the purple bruising already appearing on his side. It made no sense to go to the ER. There was nothing they would do for a cracked rib, and there was no way he'd risk more unwanted publicity coming to Dagger. He'd tough out the rib injury as best he could, but it wasn't his rib he was concerned about. It was his heart. The pain he felt there was indescribable and he wasn't sure he'd be able to survive it.

Ryan managed a shower and went directly to bed and slept straight through the night. When he woke in the morning he reached for the remote control for his television and turned on the news. Dagger's story flashed across the screen. Ryan switched the channel and found the same on that channel and the one after that, too. Every station was carrying it, slinging Dagger's name around like it was a household joke. A few stations also mentioned Ryan's name, too. Ryan struggled to sit up in bed, then remembered his rib. He eased himself from the bed and hobbled to a chair in the corner of the room and carefully slid on a pair of sweatpants.

How long would it take before the press approached him to comment on the story? For all he knew they were already camped outside his apartment building waiting to pounce. He thought of his parents and cringed. He wondered how supportive they'd be of his lifestyle now that their family name was smeared across every tabloid magazine in the country.

Damn it! This was not how he saw things playing out between him and Dagger. He left his bedroom and went to the desk in the spare bedroom to collect his phone. Soon as he turned it back on, it started ringing. He could also see he'd missed forty-two calls during the night. He skimmed through the unfamiliar numbers and cursed under his breath.

He called his parents first and his mother answered the phone.

"Hi Mom," Ryan said. His voice somber, like there had been a death in the family and in a way, there had been – his life, the life he knew no longer existed and that very much felt like a death.

"Ryan! Is it true what they're saying? You and this... musician... is he the man you were telling us about?"

Hearing his mother's frantic voice burned at every nerve ending in his body. He grabbed at his rib and sat down. "I'm sorry, Mom. I had no idea it would blow up like this."

"Are you okay, son?"

"Yeah, I'm fine," Ryan said. "How's Dad?"

"He's understandably upset, but I think he's more worried about you."

"Tell him I'm okay."

"And what about this Dagger character? How is he handling this?" Ryan's mother asked.

"Not well, Mom. He thinks I leaked the story on purpose, so he's no longer talking to me."

"Oh, Ryan, I'm so sorry."

"I'll figure something out, Mom. Don't worry about it. I'll be okay."

A knock at the door startled Ryan. He stood up quickly and regretted the movement soon as the searing pain sliced around his rib cage.

"Mom, I have to go, but I'll give you a call later. Okay?"

Ryan closed his cell phone and walked to the front door of his apartment. Using the tiny spy hole to see who was in the hallway, he saw a reporter for one of the local news channels standing there with a microphone in his hand and a cameraman ready to grab the next sound bite to put on the six o'clock news.

Quiet as he could, he walked back into the spare bedroom and dialed his boss's number.

"How could you let Sebastian run with a story like that?" Ryan asked, as soon as the man said hello.

"We report the news Ryan," Ed, his boss, stated. "Anything less would be neglectful of my job as editor of this publication. However, I didn't expect you to become a major piece to that story, Ryan. Why didn't you tell me about this before it became front page news?"

"I wasn't aware my private life was fair game for the media to exploit," Ryan said.

"Typically your sex life wouldn't be of interest, but when you're involved with Dagger Drummond, yeah, it's newsworthy!"

"Since when does Music Spin stoop to tabloid levels?"

"Listen to yourself, Ryan," Ed said. "We're talking about Dagger Drummond – King of the rock world, and notoriously *straight* – or so we thought. Him coming out is big news."

"He didn't come out – he was *forced* out! There's a huge difference, Ed, and the latter can destroy people's lives. Did any of you think about that before you ran the story?"

"Dagger Drummond will survive just fine, Ryan. This will probably boost his album sales and in a few weeks, this story will barely raise an eyebrow."

"And in the meantime, everyone connected to this story suffers."

"That's not the way I see it," Ed said.

"Yeah, and since I'm the one living the nightmare, that's exactly the way I see it," Ryan said. "I don't need this kind of attention."

"Listen, Ry, because of the attention this story is getting, I think it'd be best if you took a leave of absence for a while and lay low. You being here will be nothing but a distraction for everyone. There's already a few media outlets outside waiting for you."

"I have a couple of news trucks here, too," Ryan said.

"Take some time off," Ed said. "I can give any assignments you have coming up to Sebastian and we'll get everything covered."

"Are you fucking kidding me? Ed, you can't give my stories to Sebastian! He's the one that caused this mess."

"Ryan, I've respected your work for over a decade. If you could put aside your personal connection to the Dagger Drummond story, you'd agree Sebastian wrote a solid – and factual piece for the magazine. I want to try him on a few other big name interviews and see how he does. And when your private life becomes less public, we can talk about bringing you back."

"You know what, Ed, I think I'll have to take a pass on your very generous offer."

"Well, I'm sorry you feel that way, Ryan, but if you change your mind, please give me a call. In the meantime, I'll have security pack up the things in your office and we'll get it delivered to you."

Ryan hung up his phone without bothering to say good-bye. What was the point? Ed had made up his mind and there wasn't a chance in hell Ryan was willing to beg for his job nor was he interested in working in any capacity with Sebastian. So, it looked liked his career writing for Music Spin was over. Talk about going out with a bang, Ryan thought.

Wonderful. Now he was out of job, dumped by Dagger, and most likely had a cracked rib that would annoy him for the next few weeks. His day just kept getting better and better.

Ryan contemplated calling Sebastian and expressing his appreciation for his handiwork, but changed his mind. Instead he went to his bedroom and pulled on a pair of jeans and a t-shirt. If he was going to be stuck at home for a while, it made sense to stock his cabinets with food.

He grabbed a ball cap and sunglasses and opened up his apartment door; relieved no one was lurking in the hallway. He'd have to give the property manager a call later and put him on notice not to let the media in the building.

Ryan watched the numbers inside the elevator decrease with each floor they descended. When he reached the lobby he headed straight for the front door. Soon as he reached the sidewalk outside, the onslaught began. Ryan lowered his head and adjusted his hat and sunglasses to shield his face. Half a dozen reporters circled him and followed him all the way to the parking area behind the building.

"How long have you and Dagger Drummond been together?" one male reporter yelled.

"How'd you meet?" screamed another.

"Are you still together?"

Ryan ignored every question, keeping his eyes cast downward and his expression flat, but inside his heart was pounding. A cameraman got too close and unknowingly jabbed an elbow into Ryan's injured rib. The pain nearly buckled Ryan's legs and he saw stars. He wobbled on his feet, corrected his step, and continued to his car. The questions continued until Ryan was able to unlock his car and get inside; shutting the door to the noise. Even still, the camera flashes flared until he left the lot.

Never had he been so grateful to pull out into the traffic on his street. At the first traffic light he noticed one of the reporters following him in a news van and Ryan rolled his eyes. If the media was tailing him to this degree, what the hell were they doing to Dagger?

Ryan was sure Dagger was used to the constant attention from the press, but not in a negative light, as they were doing now. This felt like being stalked as prey, and he hated that his relationship with Dagger was being exploited for the entertainment of total strangers. This was more like cruel and unusual punishment, and for what crime – having the nerve to fall in love with a rock star?

Wow. Had he just admitted to himself he was in love? Too late to do anything about it now, he thought, since Dagger no longer wanted anything to do with him.

Ryan pulled into the first food market he found and noticed the news van took the turn, too. Damn it! There was no escaping this, was there? And, how long would this unwanted attention last before he could take back his life? Instead of parking, he turned his car around and exited the lot heading straight back to his apartment. This was bullshit, he thought, down-shifting his compact car, and grimacing when the movement strained his ribs.

Back inside the relative safety of his apartment, Ryan paced a grooved path into his rug. He'd have his food delivered, that was one problem solved. And he'd find work via the internet, maybe send out a few resumes, and do phone interviews instead of face-to-face meetings. Yeah, he could do this. It wouldn't be easy – or fun, but he could do this.

His phone rang in his pocket. He pulled it free and glanced at the caller I.D. Dagger? Why in the hell would he be calling; when he'd been very specific about Ryan never contacting him again. He thought about letting the call go to voice mail, but the truth was, he really wanted to hear the soothing timbre of Dagger's voice. He was desperate for the calm he always felt with him, needed it right now more than anything else, and because of that Ryan answered the call.

"What can I do for you?" Ryan asked.

"Your disguise sucks," Dagger said. "Is that the best you can do?"

Ryan blinked, not sure what Dagger meant by his comment, then realized his outing today must already be plastered all over the tabloid news stations. Perfect.

"I don't need your false concern, Dagger. I'll handle it."

"Ry, I've been dealing with this type of shit for the last decade," he said. "Let me help you."

"No need for that. I'm good."

The softness in Dagger's last sentence spread warmth through Ryan and for the brief cessation it offered to the enormous pain of loss he felt, he welcomed it. It was like a comforting hug, coming at a time he ached for it and would do just about anything to feel Dagger's arms wrapped around him. Then he began to let his mind ponder irrational thoughts, like the tone in Dagger's voice meaning something. That the care Dagger was offering was being done because he still had feelings for him. Did any of this mean a damn thing? Was there still a chance for them or was it really over? Ryan's head began to swirl and he sat down on the couch.

"You need a security detail," Dagger said. "I can arrange..."

"Don't trouble yourself. I'll lie low for a while," Ryan said. "They'll get bored soon enough."

"That's not how it works, Ry. I can't throw you to the wolves like that. Please. Let me help."

"This coming from the guy who told me to lose his number and never contact him again. How's that work, Dagger? How are you able to turn the charm on and off like that?"

"I'm not trying to *charm* you, Ryan. I'm simply trying to help you move beyond this in one piece."

And there it was; moving forward in one piece – without Dagger. Shit. Ryan slunk lower on the couch and closed his eyes. The change in position had him clutching at his ribs.

"I lost my job today," Ryan said quietly.

"Because of this?"

"My editor doesn't want the distraction of having me at the office," Ryan said.

"Fuck, Ry, I'm sorry."

"Whatever. I'll figure something out."

A heavy pause fell between them. Ryan could hear Dagger breathing and wished he were beside him listening to that same sound. The thought of that made his throat constrict.

"I'm also pretty sure you cracked one of my ribs when you tackled me in the parking lot."

"Are you serious?"

"Yeah, thanks for that," Ryan said. "Makes for a lovely parting gift."

"I didn't mean for that to happen."

"I'll survive," Ryan said. This seemed to be the catch phrase he kept repeating to anyone he talked to through-out the day, but this time his words had more than one meaning and he was certain Dagger understood exactly what he was saying. He heard him sigh and ached to hold him.

"I'm sorry it ended the way it did," Dagger said.

"I'm sorry it ended."

A moment later, their call ended and Dagger's soothing voice was gone. It was a better kiss-off than Dagger's last one in the parking lot, but this one hurt more, because Ryan knew it truly was over and Dagger was gone from his life.

CHAPTER SIXTEEN

The first few weeks without Dagger were nothing short of hell. The entertainment media were relentless in their pursuit of Ryan; making him a virtual prisoner in his own apartment. His rib was healing slowly and, after going through an entire rainbow of colors, the bruising was also beginning to disappear, too. As long as he didn't make quick movements, he was fine.

He had managed to line up zero jobs and had only one lead; a possible interview with Rolling Stone magazine for a job that didn't necessarily exist. Ryan had called in a few favors to get that meeting, but it likely wouldn't take place for at least another month or more – at best. And if he got that job, it would mean he'd be relocating to the east coast and away from his parents and everything he'd known for the majority of his life. Maybe that was for the best? Maybe moving was the only way he could truly move on with his life?

Being stuck around home did have one positive; he didn't have to give a shit about how he looked. No one cared if he was freshly showered and shaving was no longer necessary at all. Besides, Dagger preferred his whiskered chin over a baby smooth face.

Dagger.

It no longer mattered what Dagger preferred about him; which was a painful truth Ryan was still coming to grips with on a daily basis. Each day that passed without Dagger's enormous presence in his life, tore another piece from his heart. How long would this pain last? The phrase: the best way to get over someone was to get *under* someone else, rang in his head, but he had no interest in pursuing that option. In fact, he was losing interest in people altogether – male and female. The less he saw of people, the better he felt.

Was he bitter? Hell, yeah, but he'd been able to channel that anger and angst in starting the novel he'd challenged himself to write since his years in college. He'd managed to write several chapters in a few weeks. If his life continued on the current course it was on, he'd have the book written and published long before he got a fucking job.

There was one ass-wipe he was willing to leave his apartment to see; someone he'd gone out of his way to ignore until the media heat had died down a bit. But since that didn't seem to be happening anytime soon, he was going to have to face him under the glare of the cameras. Sebastian Keating; for him, he might even take a quick shower and shave.

Ryan left his apartment after showering and running a beard trimmer over his jaw line. He wasn't ready to grow a full-blown beard, but the effort involved doing a clean shave every day wasn't going to happen either – especially for Sebastian.

He took a chance and drove to the bar where Sebastian had taken him a few months back and parked around the corner on a side street, then went inside and sat at the bar. He ordered a beer and a burger; somewhat pleased that neither had anyone seemed to recognize him, nor had the media followed him inside. Maybe they were finally getting bored with him? He doubted he'd be that lucky.

He was almost finished eating, when Sebastian walked into the bar. He was by himself, but seemed to be looking for someone. Ryan watched Sebastian take a seat at a booth and the anger inside him began to pitch. He found himself pondering the various ways he wanted to hurt Sebastian as payback for the hell he'd been put through.

Ryan pushed his plate toward the bartender and asked for his tab. He paid the bill, then stood up to leave. He made sure he caught Sebastian's eye and diverted his path to walk by his booth.

"Holy shit, Ryan! How the hell are you?" Sebastian asked.

"Wonderful, Sebastian," Ryan said, and he sat down uninvited across the table from him. "I wanted to personally thank you for throwing me under the bus and totally fucking up my life. One day, I hope to repay you the same favor."

"Hey, listen, Ryan, I didn't mean for any of that to happen."

"You mean, you didn't deliberately plan the annihilation of my career or doing irreparable damage to my personal life?"

"I wrote a story to report the news," Sebastian said. "If you hadn't been a part of that story, you would have done the same thing."

Ryan leaned across the table in a predatory manner. It was all he could do not to slam Sebastian's perfect little face into the table and make him bleed. How pretty would he look with blood all over his face?

"You fucking piece of shit," Ryan said. "I *had* that story and chose NOT to run with it, because I knew doing so would hurt people that didn't deserve to have their private lives torn apart by the media jackals."

"Jackals like yourself?" Sebastian asked. "That's pretty self-serving, don't you think?"

"I'm self-serving?" Ryan asked. "What do you call helping yourself to notes in a private folder sitting on my desk?"

Sebastian slowly smiled. "You figured that out?" he asked.

"It didn't take me long, that's for sure," Ryan said, "And, you're the only asshole I know that would have used that information as you did."

"Maybe you shouldn't have left something that *private* sitting out in the open," Sebastian shrugged. "I wonder how Dagger would feel if he knew you left his real name sitting around like that for anyone to stumble upon."

"Fuck you!"

"Fuck me?" Sebastian laughed. "We both know who you're fucking."

Ryan nearly lunged across the table for him. Instead he slammed his fist onto the table making the silverware rattle. "Stay out of my life, Sebastian."

"Stop making yourself newsworthy and I'll consider your suggestion," Sebastian said. "But as long as you and your *boyfriend* continue to be the news... I will report it."

Ryan stood up from the table.

"It's a shame, you know," Sebastian said. "When such a fine piece of virgin ass, like yourself, is wasting himself on lowlife rocker like Dagger Drummond. You certainly didn't set your sights too high when you decided to jump into the gay pool, did you, Ryan?"

Ryan didn't spend so much as one second debating the right or wrong way to respond to a comment like that. His hand balled into a fist, recoiled, and throttled forward; landing full-force into Sebastian's smug face. He didn't even bother to stick around to help Sebastian off the floor. He merely stepped over him and walked outside to his car.

Driving home Ryan's hand throbbed, but the satisfaction of hitting Sebastian felt incredible and worth any possible bone fractures to his hand. Maybe punching Sebastian was the first step in taking back control of his life?

Ryan pulled into the parking lot of his apartment building and noticed the media had dwindled down to just one truck. That was exciting to see. He smiled thinking it was only a few months back when he was complaining about how boring and vanilla his life felt. Never had he imagined this would be his life now. He would surely use caution the next time he wished for something exciting to happen to him.

Dagger's cell phone rang in his pocket. It seemed to be a non-stop sound these days – ever since his life became front page news. People he hadn't heard from in years were crawling out of the woodwork to talk to him. Most expressed their support, but there were always a few that spewed hate, making Dagger want to use the time since his tour ended to hide out in his house. Dagger looked at his phone. He recognized this number and anger began to bubble through his veins.

"Zander," Dagger said. "Are you calling to kick me when I'm down, or to offer your condolences for the ruination of my life and career?"

"Neither," Zander said. "You know me better than that. If I had any idea what Sebastian was writing, I would have stopped him. You know that."

"Do I?" Dagger asked.

"We've been friends a long time, Dagger, and we've both been living for years with at least part of our lives in the closet. Am I right?"

"What of it?" Dagger asked. "I've always known you play for both teams, Zander. No secret there."

"You knew, but you respected my privacy and kept it secret," Zander said. "It's important you know I have always done the same for you."

"I appreciate that, Zander, but none of that matters now. Does it?" Dagger asked. "My private business is all out there for the world to judge – thanks to your boyfriend."

"I'm no longer hooking up with Sebastian," Zander said. "It's over and I am so sorry about what he's done to both you and Ryan. Looking back, I should have suspected he was up to something. He had such an odd interest in you two that I couldn't quite understand. When I finally confronted him about it, he admitted everything. He told me he took a private file from Ryan's desk and felt obligated to run with the story; felt the world had a right to know."

"You better hope he doesn't drag *your* name through the mud in his magazine," Dagger said.

"I threatened him with serious bodily harm if he did," Zander said with an uneasy laugh.

"He's lucky I didn't fuck him up," Dagger said.

"And, we should both be glad Ryan did," Zander said.

"What did Ryan do?" Dagger asked.

"You don't know?" Zander asked. "I thought by now Ryan would have told you."

"Ryan and I are no longer together," Dagger said. Admitting that out loud sent a sharp pain directly to his heart. "I haven't talked to him in several weeks."

Zander sighed loudly. "Dagger, I am truly sorry to hear that," he said. "Ryan is a great guy and I respect him even more for how he's handled this."

"What did he do to Sebastian?" Dagger asked.

"I heard he punched Sebastian in the face and broke his nose," Zander said.

A smile slid across Dagger's face. It shouldn't feel this good to hear news like this, but it did, it felt great. He should have also known Ryan wouldn't sit around on his hands while a scumbag like Sebastian trashed his name. He was proud Ryan had the balls to stand up for himself.

"I'm happy to hear that," Dagger said. "Sebastian deserved it. I only wish I'd been the one to do it."

"You and me both," Zander said.

A pause fell in their conversation and Dagger's thoughts drifted to Ryan; wondering how he was doing, and the idea of calling him crossed his mind, but he shrugged it off.

"Any chance of you and Ryan working things out?" Zander asked.

"I think I've managed to fuck up his life enough," Dagger said. "I'm doing him a favor by staying away."

"Ryan may not see it like that," Zander said.

"He's better off without me," Dagger said.

"You seemed really happy with him," Zander said.

"Happiest ever," Dagger said.

"That's difficult to come by, Dagger. Maybe there's still a chance."

Dagger rubbed at his forehead. "Doubtful."

"Well, I'm the last one you should be taking relationship advice from but, if there is anything I can do for you, please let me know – even if you just want to talk," Zander said. "I'm here for you."

"I thank you for that," Dagger said, "And, I appreciate the phone call."

Dagger ended the call and sat down in a chair beside his in-ground pool. He tossed his phone onto the table nearby, then pushed his fingers through his hair and sighed; gazing blankly at the sky above him. He'd never missed anyone the way he missed Ryan. The emptiness surrounding him was overwhelming; he was drowning in it. He turned his head on the back of the chair and glanced at his phone, wanting so much to dial Ryan's number. How much better he would feel just to hear the sound of Ryan's voice.

A moment later, the phone rang again. A part of him wished beyond reason it was Ryan calling. He reached for the phone and looked at the number displayed. It wasn't Ryan and he had no clue who it was on the other end. He wanted to let the call go to voice mail but something inside told him to answer it.

"Liam? Is that you?"

"Dad?" Dagger asked. "How the hell did you get this number?"

"Your mother and I have been trying to track you down since the news broke," he said. "We've made dozens of calls and finally got a number from your management company. We're so relieved you're okay."

"You're *relieved* I'm okay?" Dagger yelled. "Are you kidding me? Where was your concern fifteen years ago – when I watched my boyfriend die and went to jail? Instead of giving a shit, you turned your back on me for no other reason than because I was gay."

"Liam, please," his father said. "We didn't understand your lifestyle then. We thought it was nothing more than a passing teenage curiosity, something you'd get over."

"Patrick was not a *curiosity*, Dad! I was in love with him and I'm still not over him – I'll never be *over* him!"

"We realize that now," his father said. "And, we're so sorry, Liam. Please, if you'd let us, we'd like a chance to get to know you now, as a man."

"So, now I'm worthy of knowing, Dad?" Dagger asked. "Why's that, because I'm rich and famous and you think there might be something in it for you?"

"Liam... it's not like that at all."

"STOP calling me that!" Dagger screamed. "That is not my name."

"You'll always be Liam to your mother and I."

"I stopped caring what I was to you fifteen years ago," Dagger said. "I'm my own man now and what you think of me means nothing. I have no room in my life for a narrow minded, homophobic asshole, like you."

"You're right," Dagger's father said. "I acted like an idiot out of fear and misinformation, Liam. We've spent years trying to find you to make it right. Please. Come see us. We'll talk; get to know each other all over again."

"Fuck you," Dagger spit. "There isn't a chance in hell I'm ever going back to *that* town. If you want to see me, you'll have to get on a fucking plane to do so."

"We'd be happy and honored to do that, son. Maybe you could show us where you're living and perhaps introduce us to the man in your life, too?"

"You'd be willing to fly out to California to see me?" Dagger asked, his voice suddenly softening.

"We'd fly to the north pole if it meant having a chance to see you."

"I need time to think about this, Dad. I'm not sure I can handle seeing either of you."

"Liam, your mother would really love to see you, and I would, too. It would mean the world to both of us. Please. Let us come visit. Give us a chance to apologize to you in person."

Dagger closed his eyes. Emotion tightened his throat. How long had he waited to hear his father's voice – never mind his dad begging to see him, giving the impression his existence actually mattered to them. It was surreal.

"Maybe we can try and set something up after the Grammy show," Dagger said. "Between now and then, I'm pretty busy." He was lying about that, but he needed time to sort through the varied emotions this visit would dump on him. "I'll give you a call in a couple of weeks when I know what my schedule will be.

"We'll look forward to hearing from you, Liam."

What the fuck had Dagger just agreed to do? Could he really do this; sit in the same room as his parents and play nice? Could he do it alone? Shit! He needed Ryan with him for this; needed his strength and comfort to face his past. Oh, who was he kidding? He just needed Ryan – for no other reason than the fullness and warmth he always felt whenever Ryan was near. Thinking of him made his heart clench into a knot of pain.

Dagger purposefully waited two weeks before calling his father. They loosely set up the visit for the weekend after the Grammys. He agreed to send a plane for his parents and put them up in a hotel in downtown Los Angeles for the night, then fly them the hell home the next day. The actual visit would take place at Dagger's estate. It was the only way Dagger felt he could keep the press away and do this in relative privacy. Besides, there was a small part of him that really wanted his parents to see *how* he was living and what he'd accomplished since they turned their back on him.

Did they have any idea the pain he suffered heading off to jail without anyone to lean on for support? Leaving jail and having no one waiting for him; no one that cared enough to give a shit where he went or how he'd survive from that point on? And, what about having to grieve the enormous loss of losing Patrick alone; the bitter memory of holding his lifeless body while the blood pumped out of his head wound? Who was there to comfort him through all that and the nightmares that plagued him for years afterward?

Seeing his parents again would do nothing but pick off the scab that had formed fifteen years earlier to protect him from this hurt. Why was he subjecting himself to this all over again?

"It's been two months, Dagger," Tony said. "Call him."

Dagger rolled over on the leather couch in his recording studio; putting his back to Tony. "Leave me alone," he said.

"I'm not leaving," Tony said, and dropped down into a chair facing the couch. "You need to fix this with Ryan and make it right."

"Fuck off!" Dagger yelled, his voice echoing in the lofty space. "I don't need to do a damn thing! It's over. I've accepted it. Why can't you?"

"You're junk without him, Dagger. Nothing is getting recorded and your band is ready to dump your ass."

"Good luck to them finding a new lead singer," Dagger said. He turned onto his back and folded his arms behind his head. "We may not be recording, but I've been writing lyrics."

"I've seen five words, Dagger," Tony said. He lifted a page from Dagger's lyric notebook with one verse scribbled onto it and read the words aloud. "Losing you, I lost myself. You call that writing lyrics? Apologize to Ryan and get him back."

Dagger glared at Tony. "It's too late. I'm sure he's already moved on. He's probably back fucking pussy."

"You know that isn't true," Tony said. "Didn't the security detail you hired to stalk him for you say Ryan hasn't left his apartment in weeks?"

"Maybe he's no longer living there," Dagger said. "Maybe he's moved in with Beth? Who the fuck knows – or cares?"

Tony laughed, knowing how much Dagger did care. "Call him and apologize. I'm sure his cell phone number hasn't changed."

"Too much time has passed, dickhead," Dagger said, pushing himself off the couch. He knew he looked like shit and he sure as hell felt like shit. He hadn't showered or shaved in days, couldn't remember the last time he had a decent meal, and sleeping was a thing of the past. The last good night's sleep he could remember was in his bed... with Ryan – the same bed where he hadn't been able to sleep since. Damn it! Why must everything come back to Ryan?

"Zander told you Ryan had nothing to do with that article and that prick, Sebastian what's-his-name was one hundred percent responsible for the hell you've been through. Call Ryan. He deserves to know."

Dagger was standing in the small kitchenette with the refrigerator door wide open and staring blankly at the meager contents inside. He slammed the door in disgust and leaned against the appliance. "Ryan is well aware who's responsible for the article," Dagger said. "He punched the fucker in the face. That says it all."

"You're still in love with him," Tony said.

"Not your business, Tony."

"Why must you fight this?" Tony asked. "You're an asshole without him in your life. For the sake of the band and your own health – call him. I'm begging you."

"You really need to let this go," Dagger said. "I'll get over him... eventually. I just need time."

Tony stood up from the chair. "Time won't fix this, it's making it worse. I don't see you ever getting over Ryan. You're in too deep with him." Tony walked to the door of the studio. "Call him, Dagger. Please."

"I think I'll take a pass on your suggestion," Dagger said.

"Then, maybe I'll give him a call and tell him what a love-sick puppy you are without him."

"You fucking call him and you're fired! Stay the hell out of it!"

Tony smiled at Dagger. "I'll be by tomorrow," he said, and closed the door to the studio behind him.

Dagger walked to the front of the studio and looked out the wide expanse of window that faced his house and driveway. He watched Tony get into his sports car and leave the estate. Dagger ran his hands through his hair and closed his eyes. The pain in his chest was unrelenting and he wanted it to stop. He needed a break. He needed to take back his life.

He needed Ryan.

Dagger left the studio and locked the door behind him. He walked across the lawn to his house, entered through the kitchen, and went upstairs to the master bedroom. He stripped off his dirty clothes as he crossed the carpet and went into the bathroom. He turned on the water and while he waited for it to heat, he contemplated his reflection in the mirror above the sink. He should shave, he thought, and grabbed his razor as he stepped into the shower. It was time to clear his head of Ryan and get on with his life, maybe find someone new to occupy his time. Only problem with that: he didn't want anyone new.

He wanted Ryan.

Ryan shifted on to his side in bed, reaching for his cell phone on the nightstand. It was Beth calling again. He sighed loudly and picked up his phone.

"What, Beth?"

"Did I wake you?" Beth asked. "It's mid-afternoon, Ryan! You should be outside enjoying this beautiful day."

"Semantics," he said. "I should be doing a lot of things, but I lack a critical element to make that happen: interest."

"I hate seeing you like this," Beth said.

"The beauty in that statement is you don't have to see me," Ryan said.

Beth sighed loudly. "Did you hear the news?"

"You know I haven't been following the news ever since I *became* the news," Ryan said. "Funny how that works. Isn't it?"

"Okay, then I'll tell you," she said. "Dagger's band was nominated for best rock album of the year," Beth said. "Maybe you could call and congratulate him?"

"Yeah. That's not gonna happen," Ryan said.

"Ry, please."

"He made it clear he doesn't want to see or talk to me," Ryan said.

"That was two months ago," Beth said. "I'm sure he's hurting just as much as you are right now."

"That's doubtful," Ryan said. "By now, I'm certain he's found lots of new ways to occupy his free time."

"Do you still love him?" Beth asked in a soft tone.

Ryan squeezed his eyes shut and grimaced. "I don't want to talk about Dagger, Beth. It hurts too much."

"Why don't you just call and talk to him, then?"

"Stop it!" Ryan said. "Either we change the subject or I'm hanging up."

"How about I come for a visit?" Beth asked. "I could stay for a few days, we could talk, go do something? What do you say to that?"

"And how would your boyfriend feel about you sleeping at my place?" Ryan asked. "Or does he feel you'd be safe staying at your *gay* ex-boyfriend's house because I wouldn't want to fuck you?"

"Ryan, please don't talk like that."

"You don't like hearing the truth?" Ryan asked. "Is that it? You don't want to hear how the four years we lived together were a fucking lie?"

"Stop it!" Beth said. "Is hurting me going to make you feel better?"

Ryan rubbed at the fatigue in his face. He took a deep breath and slowly exhaled. "I'm sorry," he said. "You're the last person I want to hurt."

"Then, don't. Be the bigger man and call Dagger. Figure out a way to resolve this with him."

Silence fell between them and Ryan shifted in his bed.

"I didn't get the job with Rolling Stone," Ryan finally said.

"Oh, Ryan, I am so sorry," Beth said.

"I'm not sure I really wanted it," Ryan said. "It meant moving to New York and I don't think I can leave California. My parent's are here."

"And Dagger."

Ryan sighed. "Yeah, pretty fucked up, isn't it?"

"Call him," Beth said. "Please."

"I don't think I could handle rejection from him a second time," Ryan said. "I'm barely surviving the first."

A few minutes later, Ryan ended their call and stared at his phone. What would Dagger do if he called him out of the blue? Would he hang up? Tell him to fuck off? Ask him to lose his number again?

The pain of losing Dagger was consuming him. He lacked the interest to move forward with his life and he was certain there was no chance in going back. So, where did that leave him? He had a taste of what felt like perfection and he doubted he'd ever find that again with anyone else.

It was Dagger that made that connection special. Just Dagger.

Ryan swung his legs over the edge of the mattress and sat up. His head hurt and his stomach churned. The excessive amount of tequila he drank the previous night was bathing him in regret. He stood up and swayed on his feet. He waited a moment before he started walking, thinking it best to try and bring the room into focus first, then made his way into the shower.

Somehow, he needed to find a way to move beyond this, even though it didn't seem possible.

CHAPTER SEVENTEEN

Dagger fidgeted in his seat inside Nokia Theater in Los Angeles, uncomfortable in his tuxedo; uncomfortable in his own skin. He hated award ceremonies and this one was no different: boring as hell, and lasting far too long. Tony got his attention by jabbing an elbow into his ribs.

"The category for your award is up next," Tony said.

"This is ridiculous, you know," Dagger grumbled. "There's no way in hell my band is going to win 'Best Rock Album' of the fucking year."

"Have some faith, Dagger," Tony said. "You're better than any of the other bands nominated."

"Yeah, and in another five minutes you'll be telling me what an honor it was just to be nominated."

"It is an honor!" Tony said.

"Fuck you," Dagger said. "Considering what I've been through these last few months, I'm pissed I let you drag me here and sit for four fucking hours pretending to give a shit about any of these God damned awards."

"Are you through?" Tony asked.

"You're an asshole."

A moment later, Dagger heard his name announced along with his band mates, to accept the award for best rock album of the year. He felt the heat of the spot light slam into him and a cameraman appeared from out of nowhere; pointing a television camera at his face.

Shit. Shit. Shit.

Tony clapped loudly and stood, pulling Dagger up out of his seat. "Still think I'm an asshole?" he asked, leaning in to Dagger's ear.

"The biggest one ever," Dagger said.

Dagger took the stairs to the stage, repeatedly cursing under his breath, and found his way to the podium. His band members were right beside him, hugging him and each other tightly. Two women presented them with their golden trophies, then Dagger was nudged to the microphone.

He stood there frozen, sweating, and staring at the award sitting on the top of the podium as if it were mocking him; his mind devoid of any rational thought.

"Wow," he began, and cleared his throat. "I clearly did not see this coming, otherwise I would have prepared something to say." He scanned the audience for a moment, as if the words he needed might be listed somewhere out there on cue cards. "The timing of this Grammy is perfect for me and my band. Long time coming, or maybe it's my reward for having to go through the last several months of... well, you know. It was all very public." He laughed nervously. "I probably could have handled things better and because of that, I'd like to apologize to those that my words or actions may have hurt. Fear....*and* love, will make you do and say some crazy things and I'm guilty on both accounts." He rubbed his chin, his thoughts shifting to Ryan, wondering if what he was saying might give them some sort of closure; wondering if

Ryan might be nearby watching. "I was blinded by love. What can I say? But, it's out... *I'm out*, so I'll take this award home, savor it, and come back even stronger with the next album. Thank you. Thank you for all your support."

Dagger raised the trophy above his head and, to his surprise, the audience came to their feet offering him a thunderous applause along with their standing ovation. Dagger was nearly choked by emotion, disbelieving the support he was getting from those in the music industry and many that were total strangers. He thanked the audience again and left the stage with his band.

There was a sea of press waiting for him backstage. He answered a few questions; his eyes roaming in search of the one guy his apology was really meant for, but Ryan wasn't there. And why would he be? After all, it was Dagger's fault Ryan was unemployed and no longer held the necessary press credentials that would get him backstage at any venue.

Dagger left the award ceremony with his band and hit the first of three after-parties at the Chateau Marmont. Not a bad place to start, Dagger thought, stepping from the limousine in front of the old world European styled hotel. The place was dark and moody – just like him, Dagger thought.

By the time he and his band members entered the foyer and lobby, the place was crawling with music industry people, media, and a large assortment of wannabes. Dagger waded through the sea of people toward one of the bars and ordered drinks for his guys and an imported beer for himself. He turned around to hand the drinks off to his band mates and bumped into the wall of Zander's chest; spilling a portion of one drink onto the floor.

"Hey, Dagger!" Zander said in excitement. "Fuck, man, congratulations on the Grammy."

"This one means a lot," Dagger said.

"And, well deserved," Zander said. He freed Dagger's hands of two of the drinks and passed them along to the men waiting for them. When Dagger's hands were empty, Zander stepped in for hug. "How you doing?" Zander asked beside Dagger's ear. The smile left Dagger's face and Zander saw Dagger's hazel eyes turn dark. "Oh, crap. Still not back with Ryan?"

Dagger shook his head, then tipped the beer to his lips; drinking for a long moment.

Zander tugged him off to the side of the room, where he hoped they'd have more privacy to talk freely. "I'm sorry to hear that," Zander said. "Ever since we talked, I had hope you would find your way back together. Ryan's a great guy."

"One in a million," Dagger sighed.

"Did he tell you I hit on him during our interview?" Zander asked with a laugh.

The memory made Dagger smile, too. "Yeah, he mentioned it."

"Normally, I would've been more persistent, but the look he got on his face after I told him you and I were friends told me to back off."

"What'd you mean?" Dagger asked.

Zander pulled on his trimmed goatee. "It was sort of a 'stay-away-from-him-or-die' kind of a look," Zander said. "I knew then, you two were either already together or Ryan wanted to be with you, which meant I was out of luck. He's not the first guy I lost to you."

"You can't lose something you never had," Dagger grinned.

Zander tipped his head back in laughter. "Yeah, you're right about that," he said. "But, I know for a fact we've unwittingly shared a few guys. For instance, Chris."

Dagger nodded. "I knew about you and Chris."

"And, then there was Lincoln and Micky Sullivan."

"Definitely a big 'no' on Micky," Dagger said, and met Zander's gaze. "He wanted me to bottom. I don't bottom for anyone – except Ryan."

Zander's eyebrows lifted. "Wow – I really am surprised we never hooked up," he said. "I love a good top and it sounds like you and Ryan both got lucky in that department." Dagger got a faraway look in his eyes and Zander nudged him with his shoulder. "You really love him, don't you?"

"Big time – more than I thought possible," Dagger said.

Zander grabbed him by both shoulders. "Tomorrow, after you wake up from your award show hangover, you're going to call and talk to him. And, I don't want to hear how he's better off without you. Let him make that decision for himself!"

"What about you, Zander? What happens next?"

Zander stood up straight and pushed his long hair behind his ears. "We're on a short break from our tour," he said. "Then, we do another couple of months on the road down in South America. Once all that's done, I'm disappearing."

"What's that supposed to mean?" Dagger asked.

Zander drew in a long breath, expanding his broad chest. "I haven't signed the paperwork yet, but it looks like I'll be leasing a place on Martha's Vineyard – a whole compound to myself."

"For how long?"

"Maybe a full year," Zander said. "Maybe longer. I haven't decided."

"All because of Sebastian's bullshit article?" Dagger asked.

"Fuck, no – and fuck him!" Zander said, vigorously shaking his head. "I need a break, Dagger. This last year has been hell. My brain is fried. I'm not walking away for good, but I do need a rest."

"You're not going all celibate on us, are you?" Dagger teased.

"Why? Are you implying there's a chance I could bottom for you?" Zander asked.

Zander's throaty laugh told Dagger the question was a joke, but Dagger also knew it was best he didn't test Zander on it, either. Dagger watched the smile fade from Zander's handsome face.

"I want what you have with Ryan," Zander said softly.

"You mean, *had*, with Ryan," Dagger corrected.

"No, no, I believe it's still there waiting for you," Zander said. "You just need to find the balls to fight for it. Me? No more hook-ups. Been there, done that. I want something more; something substantial and hopefully lasting."

"Sounds like you're getting soft in your old age," Dagger said.

"Not soft. I'd call it realistic."

"Which side of the fence – dude or chick?" Dagger asked.

Zander was quiet for a moment. "Both. That would be perfection for me."

"Perfection? Maybe. But not realistic."

"Perhaps," Zander said. "I may end up dying alone, waiting for that perfect situation to fall into my lap, but I'm tired of wasting my time on relationships that do nothing but bleed me dry of emotion. Does that make sense?"

Dagger nodded. "Yeah, it makes a lot of sense."

"Once I get settled on the east coast, I'm going to call you," Zander said. "And, you and Ryan are gonna fly out for a visit."

"Me and Ryan?" Dagger asked. "I think you're being overly optimistic."

"I don't think so," Zander said, his mouth lifted on one side forming a devilish grin. "Take your balls out of your purse, strap them back on, and go win Ryan back." Zander laughed heartily and pulled Dagger in for a tight embrace.

Dagger hugged him back and an explosion of camera flashes lit up the crowded room.

"I see the media hasn't lost interest in us," Zander said beside Dagger's ear. He pulled back slightly, resting his cheek to Dagger's. "Watch this." Zander shifted again and pressed his lips to Dagger's and held the pose. Within seconds, half a dozen reporters surrounded them and all Zander did was laugh. "Call Ryan tomorrow – or I'll find your balls for you," he said, slipping into the dense crowd before Dagger could respond.

It was nearly four in the morning when the car service pulled up to the electronic security gate outside Dagger's estate, nestled high in the Hollywood Hills. As the limousine made the turn into his driveway, Dagger saw a man leaning up against the front of a car parked at the curb of the street. The form was strikingly familiar and Dagger's heart began to beat a little faster. He ordered his driver to stop the car and opened the back door of the limousine.

"Ryan? Is that you?" he asked.

"Yeah, it's me," Ryan said. He pushed off the hood of his car and stepped toward Dagger.

"What are you doing here?" Dagger asked.

Ryan pushed his hands deep into his front pockets. "Congratulations on your Grammy."

"You drove all the way out here to tell me that?" Dagger asked.

"I watched your acceptance speech."

"Yeah, and what'd you think?" Dagger asked.

"The apology was unnecessary, but it was nice to hear," Ryan said.

Dagger shifted in place. The expression on his face finally softened. "Doesn't seem like it'll ever be enough."

Ryan stepped closer. "The rest of it was quite a surprise."

"The rest of what?" Dagger asked. He watched Ryan turn and glance down the empty street. A long moment passed and neither man spoke.

"In all the time we were together you never said it," Ryan said softly.

Dagger looked at him and held his gaze. He wanted nothing more than to rush to Ryan, hold him tightly and kiss him hard, so very hard. That one beautiful thought had his body reacting, even as exhaustion was making it difficult for him to stand. He rubbed at his face and sighed.

"Would saying it have mattered?" Dagger asked. "Would it have changed one damn thing?"

"I don't know. Maybe," Ryan said solemnly.

"Look, Ry, it's almost four o'clock in the morning," he said. "If you want to talk about this, you'll have to come inside with me because I'm not doing this out here."

Ryan nodded and walked back to his car, started it up, and drove behind the limo up the long winding driveway to the portico in front of Dagger's mansion. He had been to this place numerous times to be with Dagger, often spending the night in his big, beautiful bed.

Ryan parked his car behind the parting limousine and stepped out of it. He followed Dagger up to the front door, watched him punch in the security code and push the front door open. They walked inside; side by side, across the glossy marble floored foyer and into the kitchen. Silent. The only noise coming from the central air conditioning unit cycling on and off above them in the ceiling.

Dagger set the finely polished trophy on top of the granite counter and removed his tuxedo coat, tossing it beside the Grammy, then pulled the bow tie from beneath his starched shirt collar and dropped it on top of his coat. After unbuttoning several buttons and rolling up the shirt sleeves, he looked at Ryan.

"That award is something else," Ryan said and smiled.

Dagger looked at the Grammy; his index finger outlined the edges. "When I got backstage after accepting this, the first person I thought of sharing the news with was you." Dagger lifted his head and met Ryan's gaze. "Now that you're here, it's difficult for me to look at you, never mind talk."

"Why's that?"

"Because when I look at you I feel guilt – piles of it, and a good deal of shame for the way I treated you. You deserved better and I could say I'm sorry every day and it still wouldn't be enough for the way I fucked up your life."

"You didn't fuck up my life, Dagger," Ryan said. "You fixed it." Ryan propped himself against the counter, his long fingers curling over the cool edge of the granite.

"I'm not sure I'd agree with that, Ry, but I thank you for trying to ease my guilt."

Damn, it felt good hearing Dagger say these things now, long after the dust of their relationship had settled. Losing Dagger had been huge for Ryan, but even at his lowest point, he never lost hope of them finding their way back to each other one day. Dagger's acceptance speech gave Ryan new reasons to believe that it might be possible.

Dagger rubbed at his temples, then glanced out the bow window above the sink. "I'm not sure we should revisit this now when I'm so tired, Ry. It'll be daylight soon and I've yet to get any sleep."

"These are normal hours for you," Ryan said. "You're implying you've never stayed up all night."

"Most recently those sleepless nights were spent with you," Dagger said.

Ryan took in a slow breath. Dagger's words and the memories they stirred had his heart racing and his forehead began to sweat. Christ, it wasn't so much what Dagger was saying, it was the deepening timbre of his voice that made his cock jump. Worked every time.

"Your speech at the theater," Ryan said, trying to keep his thoughts focused.

"What about it?"

Ryan crossed his legs at the ankle, doing his best to ignore the tingling sensations washing over his nerve endings and the knot forming in his gut.

"You mentioned love," Ryan said.

"Jesus, Ry," Dagger said, running his fingers across his scalp and pulling his long hair back with his hands. "You *really* want to go there?"

"I think we have to, I think we owe it to ourselves." Ryan said. "Don't you?"

Dagger walked to the refrigerator and pulled out two bottles of water and threw one at Ryan across the room. He pressed his hip into the stainless steel appliance and untwisted the bottle cap; taking a long swig of the liquid, and wiping his mouth off with the back of his hand.

"You want me to say it to your face, is that it?" Dagger asked.

"I want us to both throw it all out on the table, once and for all," Ryan said, "And clear the air."

Dagger nodded and started pacing the hardwood flooring. This was his chance – possibly his last chance, to try and make things right with this beautiful man. And if they were truly meant to be together, then Ryan would take him back. God, he hoped Ryan would take him back!

Dagger finally stopped pacing and faced Ryan.

"I was desperate for you to fall for me," Dagger said, then looked away. "And, somewhere in the middle of that... *obsession*, I realized how deeply *I* had fallen for you."

"Love," Ryan smiled slowly. "You called it love in your speech."

Dagger lifted his head, a nervous grin lifted one side of his mouth. "That wasn't part of my plan, you bastard."

Ryan crossed the room and cupped Dagger's face in his hands. Almost nose to nose, eyes locked, breaths coming hard and fast. "We fell in love," Ryan said. "Why are you pissed off at that?"

"We?" Dagger asked. "Are you saying..."

Ryan nodded and brushed his lips against Dagger's. Strong fingers gripped his hips. A second later their lips parted for a bruising, possessive kiss with tongues meeting in the middle wrestling for the upper hand.

Dagger pulled away, trying to catch his breath. "I won't do halfway again with you," he said.

"I know," Ryan said.

"Do you? Do you fully understand what that means?" Dagger asked, his hand circling Ryan's throat, caressing the solid column. "I won't hide or lie anymore about us and I want..."

Ryan's forearm came around the back of Dagger's neck and pulled him in for another steamy mating of their mouths. His other hand reached between them and latched onto the long length of Dagger's erection tenting the front of his tuxedo pants.

"What do you want?" Ryan asked, his voice a hiss of a whisper.

"I want... *all* of you," he said, his breath catching when Ryan lowered his zipper and slipped his hand inside; exploring fingers caressing his hot flesh. "Think you can give me everything, Ry?"

"Everything," Ryan sighed, laying teasing licks to Dagger's lips.

Dagger's hand gripped Ryan's ass cheek and squeezed hard making him moan.

"You'll let me top you; make you mine?" Dagger asked against Ryan's parted lips.

"I'm already yours; have been since the night we met."

Another kiss and Dagger nipped Ryan's bottom lip. Ryan returned the gesture and bit Dagger, spinning them around to press Dagger against a floor to ceiling cabinet. They crashed together with a thud on the cherry wood door; mouth to mouth, like they needed the others breath to survive.

Dagger's hand found its way into the front of Ryan's jeans and inside his boxer briefs. His palm cradled the thick heat of him and squeezed, then slowly started to pump. Ryan matched Dagger stroke for stroke, working the cock in his hand.

Even with the chilled air from the air conditioning swirling down on them, Ryan was sweating. It felt too fucking good. This intimate embrace with mouths fused, hard cocks rubbing side by side, hands grabbing to remove clothes. It reminded Ryan of the first time they were together in Dagger's kitchen; almost in the exact spot. They were just a few strokes away from repeating the very same scenario.

"You're gonna make me come all over your stomach," Ryan said. "Is that what you want?"

Dagger's hand stopped moving; his hips stilled, and he grinned. "I can think of better places for you to shoot." He pulled Ryan's hand out of his pants and tugged him toward the stairs to his bedroom.

As tired as Dagger was, he took the stairs two at a time, with Ryan right behind him. Dagger pushed his bedroom door open and grabbed Ryan by the shirt; pulling him against his chest. Together they began working on the buttons of each others shirts. Neither stopped until they were both naked, then Dagger's arms circled Ryan.

"I've missed you so much," Dagger said into the warm, familiar bend of Ryan's neck.

"Me, too," Ryan said. "I wanted to call you so many times, just to hear your voice."

Dagger ran his fingers across Ryan's back and down his spine. "I wish you had," he said, then leaned back to look into Ryan's eyes. "I treated you like shit, Ry. I pushed you away when you needed me the most, and I'm so sorry for that."

"We're together now," Ryan said. "That's all that matters."

Dagger smiled and stepped away; climbing up onto his big bed. Ryan joined him in the center, rolling together to share the same pillow as Dagger. Face-to-face, with fingers lightly touching and stroking; their eyes holding steady on the other.

"Just because I never said it, didn't mean I wasn't feeling it," Dagger said, swallowing around the lump in this throat. "It was always there simmering below the surface. I was so very close to telling you in Vegas, and then the night we spent here in my bed... it was there, Ryan. Always right there."

Ryan touched Dagger's face, ran his fingers over his lips. "Say it to me now," he whispered.

Dagger inched closer; his mouth almost against Ryan's. His chest was rising and falling quickly; his arms folded around Ryan holding him tight and his eyes closed. "I am crazy in love with you," he finally said, his words sounding like a sigh.

"I love you, too," Ryan said softly. "So much it hurts."

Dagger eased Ryan onto his back and slid up on top of him; straddling his hips. He bent forward resting his weight on his elbows and pressed his chest to Ryan's. "Being without you hurt," he said. "I don't want to feel that kind of pain again."

Ryan pushed the hair behind Dagger's ears and gently tugged on the hoop earrings in both his pierced lobes. "From now on, no pain – only pleasure."

A smile lifted Dagger's mouth on one side. "I can give you pleasure, Ry."

Dagger slid down onto Ryan's thighs and began laying a path of teasing licks and kisses on Ryan's torso. His tongue circled both nipples and pulled both tiny peaks into his mouth, then his cheeks rubbed through the soft chest hair between Ryan's breasts.

Dagger's fingers grazed the skin over Ryan's ribs. "Which one did I crack?" he asked Ryan.

"Left side," Ryan said. "Right about here."

The warmth of Dagger's mouth opened against the spot Ryan was touching and his lips lightly kissed.

"It kills me that I hurt you like that," Dagger said. "I'm so sorry, Ry; so, very sorry – for everything." Dagger stopped talking and went back to teasing Ryan's skin, his tongue dancing over each rib and across his stomach toward the indent of his belly button.

"God, I missed your touch," Ryan said.

"Is that all you missed?" Dagger asked, his tongue flicking around Ryan's navel.

"I missed everything about you; the sound of your voice, being near you, your scent," Ryan said. He softly ran his fingers through Dagger's long hair, stroking the scalp. "That makes me sound like a woman, doesn't it?"

"It sounds like the truth to me," Dagger said. "And, I could honestly say I missed the same things about you, so I guess we can be chicks together."

Dagger's mouth dropped lower; his tongue circled the broad head of Ryan's thick cock. "Nothing girly about this," he said, and pushed Ryan all the way into the back of his throat.

Ryan swore loudly and arched off the mattress. His thighs spread and Dagger's fingers drifted between them. He cupped Ryan's sac; rolled it in his gentle grip, then wet his middle finger before slowly sliding it inside Ryan. He added a second finger and Ryan began to sweat. Between Dagger's mouth and his probing fingers, Ryan was ready to explode.

"Dagger, you'll make me come," he warned.

Ryan felt Dagger moan against his cock. The vibration of his voice made Ryan's cock grow thicker, completely stretching Dagger's mouth, but Dagger never missed a stroke and the perfect suction he had on Ryan's shaft continued.

Dagger added a third finger to Ryan's ass and began a slow pumping rhythm. The pleasure made Ryan thrust deeper into Dagger's throat.

"I can't hold off," Ryan said.

"Go for it," Dagger said. He stretched his middle finger and rubbed the swollen gland inside Ryan and the first blast of come shot from Ryan's cock followed by several more.

"Oh, God! Oh, God! Don't stop," Ryan pleaded. "Don't stop!"

His orgasm seemed to last an eternity, then Ryan finally lay still. Euphoria made him grin like a teenager. Dagger crawled up beside him and shared the pillow with Ryan.

"How many fingers were you using?" Ryan asked.

"Three. Why? Was that too much for you?"

"No, it felt really good."

Ryan wasn't sure how much time had passed, as they lounged in Dagger's enormous bed. The sun was up and seeping in through the edges of the dense curtains hanging in the floor to ceiling windows. Neither of them had slept and neither seemed to care. They talked and endlessly touched, reacquainting themselves in a profound way that kept Ryan on the sharp edge of arousal.

"How long can you stay with me?" Dagger asked.

"As long as you want."

"Forever?" Dagger asked.

Ryan smiled. "Forever is a long time."

"Not long enough," Dagger said. He lifted up on one elbow and his fingers skimmed down Ryan's stomach and between Ryan's legs again. His mouth came over Ryan's and took a kiss, searing their lips together. "Will you let me top?" his asked, his breath hot against Ryan's lips.

Ryan's fingers curled around Dagger's thick cock. "You really think this is gonna fit inside me?"

"Yep, I do," Dagger said.

"Without killing me?"

"Your cock is bigger than mine and you fit in me," Dagger said.

"But you've done it before," Ryan said.

"I bottomed for one guy and that was fifteen years ago," Dagger said. "And for the record, Patrick was a lot smaller than you."

Dagger pressed his cheek to Ryan's chest. Ryan could feel Dagger's warm breath against his skin and rubbed the back of his head, threading his fingers through his hair.

"You've topped a lot of guys, haven't you?" Ryan asked.

The movement was subtle, but Ryan felt Dagger bristle beside him and he suddenly wished he hadn't asked the question.

"Yeah, I've fucked a lot of guys, Ryan, but in my mind none of them matter because I wasn't in love with them," Dagger said. "I love you. You're the only one occupying space in my head, my heart, and in my bed. Nothing else beyond that should concern you."

"You're right," Ryan said. "I'm sorry. I shouldn't have asked."

Dagger came up on his elbow and looked at Ryan. "I don't mind that you asked. I'll tell you anything you want to know," he said. "But I don't want to hurt you with the truth and I won't lie, so it's probably best you don't ask pointed questions like that."

Ryan rolled over and pinned Dagger beneath him; gently rocking against Dagger's erection. "How about we move forward from here; first day of forever, and no one from our past is relevant to what we have together."

"I like the sound of that," Dagger said. "Especially the part about forever." His hands slid around Ryan's hips and squeezed the firm muscles of his ass.

Ryan dropped down and kissed Dagger; slow and sensual, leaving them both breathless. "Top me," he said against Dagger's open mouth. "I want to have this with you."

Dagger's smile came easy; relaxed, then in one smooth motion, he flipped Ryan onto his back and came up over him. Anxiety and concern washed over Ryan and swirled in his eyes.

"Never fear my touch, Ry," he said. "I will love you with everything I am."

Ryan drew his fingers across Dagger's throat and touched his Adam's Apple; feeling it slide beneath the skin. "Those are lyrics from one of your songs."

Dagger smiled down at him and tipped his hips forward, then started to softly hum the melody to the Black Ice classic, Everything I Am. He dropped down to his elbows, pressed his chest to Ryan's, and left a gentle kiss on his lips. Then he started singing in a husky, whispered tone that made Ryan tremble.

Under me.

Over me.

You make me high.

Love me.

Take me.

Deep inside.

And I will love you.

With everything I am.

Emotion stung at Ryan's eyes. His chest felt tight and the lump in his throat was difficult to swallow around. No one had ever sung for him – and certainly not a solo performance like this, while naked in bed. If he doubted his feelings for Dagger before this serenade, none remained. Dagger was intricately woven around every cell fiber of his being, all the way to deepest recesses of his soul.

"I wrote that song thirteen or fourteen years ago," Dagger said. He moved a wisp of Ryan's hair off his brow with his index finger. "Patrick was gone and I was searching for someone I could love and be loved by – deeply. I was visualizing a man like you, but I never imagined I'd ever find you. It was a fantasy; one I never figured would be realized, and then you walked onto my tour bus."

"How different my life would be if I had found you back then," Ryan said.

Dagger slid the long length of his cock alongside Ryan's and stilled his hips when he reached the tip; both of them pulsing. "I don't think you were ready for me – until now," Dagger said. "And maybe I wasn't ready for you."

Ryan's arms circled Dagger's waist and dropped lower; his hands skimmed across his butt, then dipped into the warm crease. Dagger's head tipped back over his shoulders and he sighed. He stretched for the nightstand drawer and removed two foil packets and a tube of lubricant and set them beside the bedside lamp. He eased off Ryan and settled at his side. He set his hand on Ryan's lower belly; his fingers fanned through the soft hair, then ran the length of Ryan's shaft.

Ryan drew in a sharp breath, arching slightly on the bed, then turned toward Dagger. Their eyes met and held.

"You sure about this?" Dagger asked.

Ryan managed a nod and licked his lips.

Dagger took the tube of lubricant and squirted a thick line of it across his fingertips. He slid over on the pillow and took Ryan's mouth, nipping at his bottom lip, then sucking on it before slipping his tongue inside.

Dagger's hand moved between Ryan's thighs. He rubbed the back of his hand in a circular motion against Ryan's sac, then slipped behind toward the crease. His lubricated fingers ran back and forth, coating first, then pressing at the indent and easing inside. Another possessing kiss from Dagger and Ryan was bending into the touch, parting his legs and welcoming Dagger between them.

Dagger broke the seal he had on Ryan's mouth long enough to open the foil packet with his teeth and roll the condom over his cock.

"Do you want me to turn over on my stomach?" Ryan asked.

Dagger shook his head. "Not for the first time," he said, kneeling on the mattress between Ryan's legs. He crawled over him and pressed his lips to Ryan's forehead. "Trust me completely and I'll make sure you feel nothing but pleasure."

Ryan held onto Dagger's waist and watched him ease into the cradle between his legs. Dagger rocked gently; his cock rubbing against Ryan's, until Ryan started to relax.

"Pull your feet up toward your body," Dagger said. He bent down to tease Ryan's mouth again with his lips and tongue. His fingers caressed the back of Ryan's thigh; opening him wider, his tongue swirling around Ryan's tongue, then thrusting deeper.

Dagger's palm skimmed over the ultra sensitive head of Ryan's cock, then gripped the thick shaft. The lubrication coating his fingers made his hand slide easily over Ryan's cock. Dagger continued to pull off twisting strokes on Ryan, then his fingers moved lower and slipped inside. Ryan groaned into Dagger's mouth.

"Take me," Ryan said in a breathless whisper.

Dagger took hold of his own cock and worked the lubrication over the condom, then pointed the head down toward Ryan's puckered entrance. He applied a gentle pressure and eased down onto his elbows, his face hovering over Ryan's.

"You ready for me?" Dagger asked.

Ryan nodded and offered Dagger an uneasy smile, then he felt the head of Dagger's cock slip inside him and his muscles clamped tight.

"Breathe, Ry," Dagger said softly. "Bear down on me and breathe."

Another inch slid inside. Dagger turned slightly, resting his weight on one elbow. His hand moved over Ryan's chest, then down lower, until his fingers were able to circle Ryan's cock. Dagger's teeth nipped at Ryan's full bottom lip; his cheek rubbed against Ryan's whiskered jaw.

"That spot inside you I can rub with my finger, and give you what feels like a ten minute orgasm," Dagger said. "I'm gonna rub that spot with the tip of my cock, Ry. It will feel so good you'll swear your head is gonna blow to pieces."

One more inch of Dagger breached Ryan's muscled entrance and he gasped. His forehead was starting to sweat.

"Baby, relax for me," Dagger said. "Push out and relax the muscle."

"I'm not sure I can do this," Ryan said. "It hurts – a lot."

Dagger stilled his hips, but his fingers kept working on Ryan's hard cock; twisting, stroking. He collected the precome seeping from the tip and used it to coat Ryan's shaft.

"Do you want me to stop?" Dagger asked.

"What you're doing with your hand feels really good."

"Then, concentrate on that," Dagger said. "Feel this with me, Ry. Feel me loving you."

Ryan slowly exhaled. His arms wrapped around Dagger and pulled him closer. His hand gripped the back of Dagger's neck and eased him to his mouth.

"Kiss me," Ryan said.

Dagger's lips rubbed against Ryan's, then his mouth opened and he took the kiss Ryan was offering. A quick thrust of his tongue had Ryan moaning and clinging to him tighter, the rough scrape of Dagger's chin against Ryan's electrified his nerve endings. Dagger's tongue dipped again, going deeper, and Ryan's hips opened, allowing Dagger's cock to slide further inside. Dagger groaned at the additional penetration he had with Ryan.

Another tip of his hips and Dagger was snug; deep as he could go. He adjusted the angle of his cock and started to pull back, then slid back in, and out, and in again; using quick and precise movements all concentrated on the same spot. It took only a few seconds for Ryan to feel the effects of Dagger's subtle thrusts.

"Oh, my god!" Ryan said, arching into Dagger.

"Does my cock feel good inside?" Dagger asked.

Ryan tugged him down by the neck again and kissed him hard. Hot panting breaths bathed each of their faces. "Deeper. Go deeper."

Dagger withdrew and thrust all the way, then rocked against Ryan; pulled partway out and thrust again.

"Right there – right there." Ryan said. "Feels so good. I could come."

Dagger ground against Ryan; pivoting his hips, and then thrusting. "I am going to make you come so hard, Ry," he said. "When you let go, I'll be so deep, I'll feel your release from the inside out."

Ryan tipped his head back into the pillows and exposed his throat. Dagger's tongue licked a line under his jaw and sucked hard on the skin. Ryan knew there would be a mark left from Dagger's mouth but he didn't care. He wanted Dagger's brand on him – ached for it.

One more pitch of Dagger's hips and Ryan felt himself crashing over the edge. He cried out and gave himself over to the sensations sweeping over him and allowed Dagger to carry him through the most glorious release he'd ever experienced – or imagined, and shot an endless stream of come between their stomachs. It went on and on; Dagger's subtle inner caress beautifully prolonging his bliss. Lights flashed behind his closed eyelids, his heart pounding nearly out of his chest; he didn't want it to end.

Ryan opened his eyes and watched the same bliss creasing Dagger's handsome face; eyes closed, his head slightly tipped back over his broad shoulders, mouth partially open. Dagger lifted and arched into his last thrust and exploded, a loud exhale crossing his lips. In that moment, Ryan wished there wasn't a condom barrier preventing Dagger from spilling inside him because he wanted to feel it. He wanted to feel that connection with Dagger, same as when he took Dagger in his mouth.

A lazy smile curled Dagger's lips, then his eyes slowly opened to gaze down at Ryan. He leaned forward, trying to catch his breath, and pressed a soft kiss to Ryan's mouth.

"You okay?" Dagger asked.

"Never better."

Dagger nuzzled Ryan's lips and chuckled, then dropped down onto Ryan's chest; his face cradled in the bend of Ryan's neck. Ryan sifted his fingers through Dagger's long hair. Emotion was choking his throat. In all his years of being sexually active, this was the first time he felt like he'd just made love. He knew no matter what the future had in store for them, he'd remember this one moment the rest of his life.

Ryan took shallow breaths, listening to the sounds of contentment coming from Dagger. He could feel Dagger's heart beating between them, smell the scent of his hair; his skin, the soft aftershock pulses bringing attention to the spot they were still connected with Dagger deep inside. The closeness Ryan felt with Dagger was overwhelming.

"I love you, Ryan – so much."

Ryan hugged Dagger tighter and kissed the top of his head. "I love you, too."

Dagger slowly pulled out of Ryan, then rolled to his side and sat upright. "Let me get something to clean you," he said. He left the bed and walked to the bathroom.

Ryan heard water running, the toilet flushing, then Dagger reappeared carrying a washcloth and a towel. He climbed back up on the bed and started washing Ryan, running the warm, wet cloth across his stomach, then lower to clean the lubricant out of Ryan's crease. Ryan winced when Dagger brushed the cloth against his puckered flesh and Dagger met his gaze.

"Are you sore?"

Ryan nodded. "A little bit."

"But, you liked bottoming for me?"

Ryan laughed. "Yeah, I did – once I got over the initial shock of you being in there. I'm not surprised you like to top," Ryan said. "You obviously know what you're doing."

Dagger used the second towel to dry Ryan, then fell down beside him and Ryan turned to face him. "I hope there was more pleasure than pain," Dagger said.

"It was better than anything I've ever felt," Ryan said. "But, what are the odds the one guy I sleep with is hung like a horse?"

Dagger rolled onto his back in laughter, then his expression turned serious. "I'm so happy you're here with me, that you reached out and drove to my house like you did, not knowing what kind of reception I'd give you."

"It was your speech," Ryan said. "You mentioned love and I thought that might be your way of opening up the door again for us. All I had to do was find the balls to walk through it."

"I love your balls," Dagger said, cupping them in his palm.

"To be totally honest, I was nervous as hell you might be talking about a new boyfriend when you mentioned love in that speech," Ryan said. "Driving here, I knew I was taking a risk, but I had to do it. I had to know if there was a chance for us."

Dagger's fingers spread over Ryan's chest. "I haven't been with anyone since you, Ry," he said. "There were plenty of opportunities, but I had zero interest. I wanted you and no one else was going to do." Dagger set his forehead to Ryan's on the pillow they were sharing. "I hate to ask, Ry, but what about you? Did you switch back to girls?"

Ryan smiled against Dagger's lips. "Not a chance of that happening."

"Then, you're mine?" Dagger asked. He opened his mouth to Ryan and sighed.

"I'm *all* yours."

Dagger moved in for a loving kiss that turned hot in a matter of seconds. He pulled back breathless and panting. "I knew you'd fall for me," he said.

"You fell for me first," Ryan teased. He pushed Dagger onto his back and crawled up on top, holding Dagger's arms above his head in a tight grip against the mattress.

"I fell so hard for you, Ry," Dagger said, looking up at him. "Almost from the moment we met, I knew I wanted to be with you. Forever."

"And, that makes me the luckiest guy in the world," Ryan said.

CHAPTER EIGHTEEN

Ryan woke to an empty bed. He had no idea what time it was or where Dagger had disappeared. He sat up and reached for his phone on the nightstand and looked at the time displayed. It was almost three in the afternoon. How had he managed to sleep that long? He glanced across the room to the open bathroom door and saw no movement, then slid from the bed. Every muscle in his body was sore. Sex with Dagger was always like an Olympic sporting event, but last night was over the top and he was definitely feeling the after effects today.

He walked into the bathroom and saw a clean, folded towel sitting on the vanity counter top beside the double sinks and a brand new toothbrush sitting on top of it. He smiled at Dagger's thoughtfulness and opened the glass door to the over-sized shower stall and started the water. In his haste to meet Dagger at his house, Ryan hadn't taken the time to pack an overnight bag, but at that time he also hadn't thought staying overnight was going to be an option. At most, he hoped they'd spend some time talking and that would be the extent of it. He never imaged he'd be waking up in Dagger's bed.

Ryan finished cleaning up and left Dagger's bedroom. He took the wide curved front stairs down to the foyer and walked into the kitchen. Barefoot and shirtless, he wore the same pair of jeans from the day before. He found the kitchen empty, just like the bedroom, but the scent of fresh brewed coffee hung heavy in the air. He stepped past the granite-topped island in the center of the kitchen and saw an empty coffee mug with a handwritten note propped up against it and a plate of fresh baked muffins sitting beside it. Ryan picked up the note and read it.

I'm in the studio above the garage. Coffee is fresh. Help yourself and come find me when you finish eating. Love you, D ~

Ryan's heart did a flip-flop. Could this man give him any more reason to love him? Ryan filled the mug with coffee from the pot and took a paper towel and set a blueberry muffin on top of it. He broke the treat apart with his fingers and ate it in three bites, then grabbed a banana from the fruit bowl on the counter, slid it into his back pocket, and headed toward the kitchen door with his coffee in hand.

He heard the first guitar riff before he opened the kitchen door, then a series of ambling notes vibrated around him, ending with one loud strum across the strings of the instrument. It was a good thing Dagger didn't have neighbors that lived close by, Ryan thought. He smiled as he stepped out into the sunshine, sipping his hot coffee and walked toward the garage. He followed the music and walked up the stairs attached to the side of the four-car garage to the recording studio. Dagger had talked about this studio many times, but Ryan had never seen it before now.

Ryan turned the knob on the door and pushed it open. Across the expanse of room, he saw Dagger sitting on a stool, bent over his guitar and looking like he was jotting down notes onto a piece of paper on the table in front of his knees; his back facing Ryan.

Ryan approached slowly, glancing around the lofty space as he walked. Dozens of instruments sat in stands, hung on the walls, or were stacked in cases. One large upright crate was opened and revealed a dozen or more guitars stored inside.

To the left there was a glassed off room within a room that appeared to be where the recording took place. Behind that was the sound engineer's room. Ryan could see a long row of mixing boards lining one side of that room. The space Dagger was sitting in looked more like a lounge area, with couches and chairs, a bar, and a wide-screen television mounted on the wall. The wall overlooking the driveway and Dagger's house was all window and offered a nice view of the property.

Ryan stepped closer and Dagger lifted his head from the sheet music he was working on. "Good morning," Dagger said. "Although, technically I believe it's afternoon. Did my guitar playing wake you?"

Ryan shook his head. "I didn't hear the music until I came down to the kitchen," he said, smiling ear to ear. "I can't believe I slept that long."

"I guess you were tired," Dagger said, returning a smile just as goofy to Ryan.

"You wore me out," Ryan said. "How long have you been working?"

"Five hours – give or take," Dagger said. "As much as I wanted to be with you when you woke up, I had this melody swirling around in my head that I wanted to get down on paper before I lost it."

Ryan crossed the room. He set his coffee mug down on a small table and stood in front of the wide window looking at the view. "Can you play it for me?" he asked. He turned around to face Dagger and leaned against the window frame.

"Dagger pointed to Ryan's throat. "Is that my handiwork?"

Ryan touched the red circle with his fingers and grinned. "Yeah, you marked me."

"I like the idea of marking what's mine," he said.

"I like being yours."

"I'm glad, Ry, so very glad."

"Play for me," Ryan said in a soft voice.

Dagger nodded and bent over his guitar again. He was shirtless and Ryan watched how the muscles in his shoulders and arms flexed with each chord he strummed. Ryan's eyes drifted lower. Dagger was wearing athletic pants and was bare foot. The sensuality rolled off of him with each new note he struck and Ryan swallowed hard.

Dagger played the first couple of phrases, then stopped. "This is the first time I've felt inspired to write in months," he said. "I have you to thank for that."

"You're welcome," Ryan said. "Although, I feel like I should be thanking you."

"For what?"

"Being you," Ryan shrugged. "Taking me back. Loving me. All of it."

"I was an idiot to let you go," Dagger said. One side of his mouth lifted in a lop-sided grin. "And you don't need to thank me for loving you, Ry. That part was easy."

Dagger ran through a few more chords, then began rolling into the new song he'd been composing while Ryan slept. The talent flowing through Dagger's fingers was magical. Ryan stood in awe of this man's creative genius. It made him feel lucky to be witness to this song-in-the-rough in its infancy and it excited him to think he'd be around to hear it again in its polished form, too. The idea he may have had a part in inspiring this song, made his chest feel tight.

Ryan pulled the banana from his back pocket and peeled it, just as Dagger finished up a short series of riffs. Dagger looked up at Ryan and did a double take, and then burst out laughing.

"You're eating a banana?" Dagger asked. "You couldn't have grabbed an apple or an orange? How am I supposed to concentrate with that in your mouth?"

Ryan grinned and shrugged his shoulders. "I didn't plan that, but yeah, I'm eating a banana."

Dagger lifted the guitar from his lap and set it on one of the couches as he walked to Ryan. He stopped directly in front of him; his eyes canvassing Ryan's bare chest. Dagger's hungry gaze had Ryan's cock coming to attention.

"A banana makes you lose concentration?" Ryan teased.

Dagger's hands spread over Ryan's chest, covering both his breasts. "Seeing it in your mouth makes me want to stick something else in there."

"Is that so?" Ryan asked. He reached for the elastic waistband of Dagger's athletic pants, stretched it open, then eased his hand inside. He was greeted with a hot piece of hardened flesh pulsing against his palm. "No underwear today?"

Dagger shook his head. "I was afraid if I hung around the bedroom too long, pulling out drawers to dig for stuff to wear, I might wake you." His hand reached behind Ryan's neck and pulled him in to claim his mouth. His tongue probed and stroked Ryan's, then pulled out to lick the arch of Ryan's upper lip.

Ryan's fingers circled Dagger's cock. He tightened his grip and started to stroke.

"I can't get enough of you," Dagger said. "We fucked around for hours last night and all I can think about is getting you naked and on your back again."

"I feel the same way – about getting you on *your* back," Ryan said. His hand pulled off another stroke on Dagger's organ, then his fingers dropped lower and gripped Dagger's balls.

Dagger moaned. "I see we're in for a cock fight, to see which man tops. Is that it?"

Ryan leaned forward and licked at Dagger's lips. "What can I say? I like fucking you."

"Suck me first," Dagger said. "Then you can fuck me."

"Right here?" Ryan asked, glancing around the room.

"Sure. Why not?"

"This is your work studio and you're working," Ryan said.

Dagger reached for the button on Ryan's jeans and released it, then eased down the zipper. "I've been at this for hours. I can take a break," Dagger said. "Besides, I've got other things on my mind now and it's doubtful I'd able to concentrate on music."

"Other things, like me eating a banana?"

"Other things, like you eating *my* banana."

Ryan came back into the lounge area of the studio using a towel from the bathroom to carefully wipe at his eye.

"I flushed my eye," Ryan said. "And, I think I got most of it out, but it will likely be red for a while."

"That's why it's always a good idea to swallow," Tony said.

Ryan quickly pulled the towel away from his face at the sound of the familiar voice and looked up. Tony was standing beside Dagger; a smug smile tilting his lips at a funny angle.

"Typically he does swallow," Dagger said. He stepped toward Ryan and stood in front of him; his arms circled Ryan's waist. "But, this time he wanted to watch me shoot." Dagger pressed his lips to Ryan's temple, then kissed the lid of his irritated right eye. "I should have done a better job aiming – especially at close range when you're on your knees like that."

"Good to see you again, Ryan," Tony said. "I'm glad to see Dagger finally decided to take my advice and give you a call."

Ryan gripped Dagger's hips. "I saw his Grammy speech and decided to come see him," Ryan said, then his eyes bounced back to Dagger and they smiled knowingly at each other.

Dagger brushed his lips against Ryan's. "I expect to be busy for the next several days, Tony, so if you don't mind... could you leave us alone?"

"I came by to let you know I confirmed everything with your parents," Tony said. "Here's their travel itinerary." Tony tossed a piece of paper onto the table beside the couch and started walking to the door. "They arrive Saturday morning."

"Fuck! I forgot about that," Dagger said. He stepped away from Ryan's embrace and picked up the paper Tony left.

"Your parents?" Ryan asked.

Dagger sat down on the couch. "Yeah, they tracked me down a couple of weeks after my fucking birth name was splashed all over the news," he said, his eyes lifting from the paper to meet Ryan's inquisitive look. "They want to come visit."

"After all this time, they want to see you?" Ryan asked.

Dagger nodded. "My father said they'd been trying to find me for years, but they didn't know I changed my name."

Ryan sat down beside Dagger on the couch. "Jesus," he sighed. "Are you okay with this?"

Dagger tipped his head back against the couch and ran his hands through his hair. "I don't know," he said quietly. "They wanted me to fly out and see them, but you know how I feel about that town, so I refused, and suggested they come to California instead. Now I'm regretting I suggested that. I'm not sure I can handle seeing them."

Ryan watched Dagger's eyes close. He reached over and touched Dagger's thigh and squeezed. "What can I do to make this easier for you?" he asked.

Dagger rolled his head and met Ryan's gaze. A long moment passed and Dagger simply stared at Ryan; a faint smile curling his lips. "I love you," Dagger finally said. "And, I don't think you'll ever understand how much."

Ryan swallowed hard. He could feel the emotion building in his eyes and his heart swelling to a painful degree. He set his head on the back of the couch beside Dagger. He tried to speak, then stopped when he saw tears teetering on tips of Dagger's bottom lashes. Ryan used the pads of his fingers to wipe Dagger's eyes, then moved in to kiss him.

"I love you, too, Dagger. Completely."

Dagger smiled warmly. "They'd like to meet you," Dagger said.

"How do they know about me?"

"Some of the news reports mentioned your name," Dagger said. "At the time my dad asked, I'm sure he assumed we were still together. I couldn't tell him we'd broken up. It hurt too much to admit I threw away the best thing that ever happened to me." Dagger took Ryan's hand on the couch and laced their fingers. "Ry, I want to ask you something," he said, obviously struggling with the words.

"Anything. Whatever you need, I'll do it."

"Move in with me," he said in a breathy whisper.

"While your parents visit?"

"No, I mean permanently," Dagger said. "Like we talked about last night – beginning of forever."

Ryan sat up on the couch; his eyes widened in surprise. "Live here... with you?"

Dagger leaned forward and claimed Ryan's mouth. "Same house. Same bed. Every night," he sighed. "You and me, living like a real couple. Think you could commit to something like that – with me?"

"Wow, that's a lot to process," Ryan said, and rubbed at his face.

"My house is huge, Ry. You can take over one of the spare bedrooms and use it as your office to finish writing that book you told me about."

"What about when you go on tour?" Ryan asked.

"You can come with me – if you want," he said. "You can write on my tour bus. Work on your own stuff or maybe you could maintain my website and do a blog report of 'life on the road' for fun, in addition to your articles and books. Whatever you want to do, it's fine with me as long as we're together."

When he didn't respond, Dagger slid closer to Ryan on the couch. "What's going through your head, Ry? Am I asking too much? Is it too soon? What?"

"I want to be with you, Dagger, that much I know for sure, but living together? That's a lot."

"I told you, I don't want to hide this relationship anymore. If we're together, I want to live this out in the open. Don't you want that, too?"

Ryan nodded. "Yes, I do," he said, looking at Dagger. "But, aren't you a little nervous about that, what it will mean, and how everyone will react to it?"

"Fuck, yeah! But being without you scares me more."

"I didn't like that, either," Ryan said.

The smile on Dagger's face began to grow. "Okay, then how about we take a ride to your place and pick up some of your clothes?" Dagger asked. "We'll get a moving company to haul the rest of the stuff over here later."

"I'll pay rent," Ryan said.

Dagger's brow furrowed and his hazel eyes turned dark. "Please tell me you didn't just say that."

"I don't want to feel like..."

"Feel like what, Ry?" Dagger asked, cutting him off. "I'm not asking you to live here for financial reasons. I'm asking for *personal* reasons – because I love you and want you here with me. Are you uncomfortable with that?"

Ryan's gaze dropped to his lap. Suddenly feeling self-conscious, he needed to wipe his hands off on his thighs. "I've done a couple of feature articles since leaving Music Spin, but nothing of great magnitude, and money has been... tight. Truth is, I've barely been making my rent. I don't want you to think I'm in this for whatever monetary help you can provide."

Dagger took his hand. "I'd never think that, Ry. I know you're in this for the same reason I am: love."

Ryan squeezed Dagger's hand. "That's true."

"Then, live with me," Dagger said, and leaned forward, skimming his lips across Ryan's cheek, then pressed them to his mouth. "I know you're nervous about this, and I am, too. I've never lived with anyone – male or female, and you have; which means you have more experience with sharing space. It will be an adjustment for both of us, Ry. I say we take this step and work through it together, one day at a time."

"Living with you will be nothing like it was with Beth," Ryan said.

"I'm hoping you'll think it's better," Dagger said.

"I'm certain it will be," Ryan said. "My feelings for you are much deeper than they ever were for Beth."

"And, a part of you can't help feeling bad about that, right?" Dagger asked.

"Is it that obvious?"

"I can see the sadness in your eyes every time you talk about her," Dagger said. His fingers ran through Ryan's thick hair, pushing it off his forehead. "Don't feel bad about that, Ry. You were meant to be with a man, and I will be eternally grateful you chose me."

"If we don't change the subject, I'm going to start crying like a chick."

"So, you'll move in?" Dagger asked.

Ryan moved closer to Dagger on the couch, gently eased him onto his back, them climbed up over him. "I love the idea of waking up beside you every day."

"Just think of all that morning wood, Ry."

"At the moment I'm thinking of afternoon wood, then maybe a little dinnertime wood after that."

Dagger's hand slipped between them and gripped onto Ryan's growing erection through his pants. "Are you going to fuck me now?" he asked.

Ryan shook his head, then lowered to kiss Dagger. "I'm not going to fuck you, Dagger. I'm going to love you."

Ryan slid into the passenger seat of Dagger's black Porsche and latched the safety belt. "You do realize there's a chance one or two reporters could be hanging out in front of my apartment building, in the hopes of catching a glimpse of you, right?"

"Then, I guess today will be their lucky day," Dagger said. He smiled at Ryan, then shifted the powerful sport's car, and accelerated from his driveway like a rocket.

Dagger could have pulled into the parking lot behind Ryan's apartment building, but instead he choose to make a statement and parked at the curb directly out in front. One small media crew was waiting with their camera rolling to catch Dagger step from his car.

Ryan exhaled loudly, annoyed at what he saw, and stepped onto the sidewalk; shutting the car door behind him. How quickly he had adapted to this lifestyle, slipping into protective mode by dropping his head like he'd been doing this his whole life, focused on nothing but getting to the front door as fast as possible without saying a word. Halfway to the door he realized Dagger wasn't following him. He turned around and saw Dagger happily engaging the reporter and answering questions; even smiling for the camera, his intense eyes hidden behind dark, rock star glasses. Even still, Ryan could feel the power of them, as Dagger waved for him to come back to the reporter.

"Where are you running off to?" Dagger asked Ryan, his arm slid around Ryan's waist and tugged him closer, then he pressed a soft kiss to Ryan's lips.

Ryan bristled in Dagger's embrace. "What are you doing?" he whispered, keeping his face turned away from the camera.

Dagger smiled proudly. "I'm living life out in the open, Ry." Dagger's hand skimmed down the length of Ryan's arm, then he laced their fingers together and squeezed. "If you'll excuse us," Dagger said. "Ryan and I have some moving boxes to pack."

"Is Ryan moving in with you, Dagger?" the reporter asked.

"Yes, he is."

"Things must be getting serious between you, then?"

"Very much, so," Dagger said. "Thanks for asking."

They didn't stop walking until they were safely on the elevator alone. Ryan leaned against the back wall and bent over holding on to his thighs.

"I don't know how you deal with that," Ryan said.

"It takes time, but you get used to living inside the fish bowl," Dagger said with a shrug. "You're not pissed I told them you're moving in with me, are you?"

Ryan straightened on the wall. A part of him was terrified about what all these admissions would mean for him, his family, and career. He wasn't sure how much of his life he wanted to share with the world. After all, he was still coming to terms with the fact he was in love with a man. Was it really necessary they expose the extent of their relationship and living arrangements with the media? Ryan did his best to tamp down the feeling of panic threatening to rain down over him – as it always did when he spent too much time over-thinking things.

The elevator door opened and Ryan stepped out into the hallway with Dagger following close behind. He used his key in the door and pushed it open, then made his way into his bedroom. He stood in front of his closet and surveyed the contents for a minute and reached for a large duffel bag. He didn't look for Dagger, but he could feel him standing close behind him.

"Are you thirsty?" Ryan asked. "I think there's beer in the fridge. Help yourself."

Dagger stepped around and stood in front of Ryan; almost nose to nose. He had removed his sunglasses and the full power of his gaze bore into Ryan.

"No grand tour?" Dagger asked.

"What's the point?" Ryan asked. "I'm no longer staying here."

Ryan stepped away from Dagger and walked to a bureau, pulling out the top drawer. He began tossing socks and boxer briefs into the duffel and shut the drawer. Behind him, Dagger took a seat on Ryan's unmade bed; silently watching Ryan move around the room, throwing things into the duffel.

"Ryan."

Too focused on what he was doing, Ryan didn't hear Dagger say his name until he reached for him as he passed by the bed and physically stopped him from moving.

"Sit with me," Dagger said.

"I need to get this stuff packed," Ryan said. He didn't look at Dagger, instead his eyes drifted around the room, mentally assessing what he wanted to bring with him on this first trip and what could wait until later. He remembered his shaving gear in the bathroom and started to move, but Dagger held him in place by the hips. Finally, Ryan looked down at Dagger.

"What's going on with you, Ry?" he asked. "Are you rethinking your decision to move in with me? Or maybe you're over-thinking in general."

Ryan plunked himself down on the bed beside Dagger and rubbed his temples with his thumbs. "I'm not doubting my move, Dagger," he said, staring at his hands in his lap.

"Then, what is it?"

"I'm not sure I can articulate it."

"You have to try," Dagger said. "The only way this is going to work is if we communicate to each other."

"I know. I know," Ryan said. "I'm nervous about everyone knowing our business."

"The story of us being a couple is old news, Ry."

Ryan met Dagger's gaze. "It doesn't bother you that everyone knows you're gay?"

Dagger drew in a long breath. "It did at first," he said. "It made me feel a little over-exposed and I would have preferred to have come out on my own, but now that it's public knowledge, I'm relieved." Dagger set his hand on Ryan's thigh. "Are you upset you were 'outed'?"

"See, that's the thing," Ryan said. "I'm not sure I have anything to come out for and that makes me a little resentful for what the press has done with my private life."

Dagger glanced away and sighed. "Gay for me," he said softly.

"What'd you say?"

"You think you're gay just for me, and sleeping with only me doesn't make you *full-blown* gay because you've never had an attraction toward men or slept with any other guys – except for me. How close is that to what you're feeling?"

Ryan smiled uneasily. "Pretty fucking close."

"You're not comfortable with people labeling you gay or even classifying yourself as being gay, are you?"

"I'm still processing it," Ryan said.

"I wish I could help you with that, but I can't," Dagger said, regret hung from every word. "It's up to you to find a way to accept it. Love who you are, Ry. I do."

Ryan looked at him, saw the lines creasing his forehead, and hated that his words may have hurt Dagger. "I know what

I feel for you is real," Ryan said. "Beyond that, does it really matter what label I slap on myself?"

"I'm not going to push you on this, Ry, because I think it's important you figure it out on your own. All I can do is be a supportive factor in your self-discovery."

"Fair enough," Ryan said. "Still want me to move in with you?"

Dagger pressed on Ryan's chest and laid him flat on the bed, then rolled against him. "Do you still want to be gay for me?" he asked, his face hovering over Ryan's.

"I'm comfortable being any kind of gay you want," Ryan said. He slipped his hand behind Dagger's neck and pulled him down for a gentle kiss. "When it's just you and me, I'm okay with what *this* is. It's when we take *this* outside I get nervous."

"A few months ago, you didn't want to be gay with me in private – couldn't even bring yourself to use the word gay. So, I think we're making progress," Dagger said with a chuckle. He rubbed Ryan's stomach, then his hand slipped lower to cup his bulge. "We'll work on the rest of it, Ry. I don't mind keeping our relationship quiet for a while, but I live a very public life, and eventually *this* will be out there for everyone to dissect however they see fit."

"Considering who you are, I guess it's selfish of me to want to keep you all to myself," Ryan said. He sat up on the bed and stood up, then lifted the duffel bag from the floor and walked toward the closet again.

Dagger watched him move around the room from the bed. "This won't be easy, Ry, and there will always be those who want to hate us for loving each other." Dagger stood up and walked up behind Ryan. His arms slid around Ryan's waist and crossed over his lower stomach. He set his chin on Ryan's shoulder and tipped his face toward the warmth of his neck; inhaling his scent. "You'll need to dig deep for the strength to push beyond those moments you feel animosity or hostility from total strangers and hold what we have – and the feelings we have for one another, close to your heart."

Ryan hugged Dagger's strong arms tighter to him. He closed his eyes, feeling the heat of Dagger's mouth pressing to the bare skin of his neck, then his tongue licking a trail up to his ear lobe. "All of this scares the shit out of me," Ryan said. "But the rush I get from you is like no other. I can't get enough and I can't walk away."

Dagger turned Ryan to him; rubbed their noses together, then opened his mouth against Ryan's, giving him a kiss that damn near buckled Ryan's knees.

"You're making me horny again," Ryan said. "Keep sucking my tongue like that and I'm gonna have to throw you on my bed and this packing will never get done."

Dagger unbuckled Ryan's belt. "I'm in no hurry to leave," he said. "Besides, it might be fun christening your apartment. Don't you think?"

CHAPTER NINETEEN

Friday arrived quicker than Dagger wanted. They had spent a large portion of the week getting Ryan settled into his house and enjoying being a couple – in the privacy of Dagger's house. Although Dagger had suggested they go out at night to a club or to sample a few new restaurants, Ryan deferred to staying at Dagger's. A few of the dinners they ate completely naked, either in bed or in the kitchen. Ryan demonstrated his limited culinary talents to Dagger with Italian food; which Dagger enthusiastically gobbled down, and one night Dagger grilled steaks for them out by the pool.

In between preparing meals together, there were the long hours they spent in bed loving each other nearly senseless; discovering new ways to pleasure, and simply talking. Ryan had never revealed so much of himself to anyone before Dagger. It was freeing for Ryan and Dagger made him feel safe to let go. In return, Dagger fully opened up about his youth, Patrick, and the dysfunctional relationship he had with his mother and father.

"Are you sure you want to see your parents here in your home?" Ryan asked. He tugged Dagger closer to his bare chest and Dagger slid a leg over Ryan's thigh.

"Doing it anywhere outside of this house means the press with show up," Dagger said. "If this visit is going to happen, it needs to be done in private."

"Is seeing them going to be emotionally too much for you to handle?" Ryan asked. "I won't let them hurt you again."

Dagger lifted himself up on one elbow; his fingers fanned through the soft hair on Ryan's chest. "I love that you'd stand up for me, Ry," he said on a long exhale. "But, I really think I need to face them. Last time they saw me I was a punk-ass kid. I'm a man now and I don't give a shit what they think about me being gay. Empowerment comes with an attitude like that." Dagger kissed Ryan, dipping his tongue inside the warmth of Ryan's mouth, then teasing his lips. "They can't hurt me anymore, Ry. There is nothing left they can say or do that will cause me pain."

"I hope you're right," Ryan said. "Because I *will* stand up for you – no matter what it takes."

"Duly noted, my chivalrous boyfriend," Dagger said with a laugh.

Ryan rolled over and pinned Dagger's shoulders to the mattress. "Do you think me sticking up for you is funny?" Ryan asked, doing his best to create an angry face, but his unrelenting smile gave him away.

Dagger shifted beneath Ryan and their cocks touched. Dagger was already very hard and Ryan was well on his way. Dagger slowly tipped his hips and ran his cock along the full length of Ryan's and both of them moaned.

"Again?" Ryan asked, with a gentle rock of his hips.

Dagger nodded. "Yeah, why not?"

Ryan lowered himself down onto Dagger's chest. He brushed his lips to Dagger. "Because I worry I'm hurting you with all this... sex."

"Ryan, you are not hurting me. I love taking you inside me and I know you love being there, so it's a win-win."

Ryan rolled his eyes and smiled. It was difficult to argue with logic like that. "Hand me another condom."

"No condom," Dagger said. "I want to feel you bare."

Ryan sat back on his knees, looking down at Dagger in disbelief. "Are you sure?"

"I'm clean, I know you're clean, and we're in a committed relationship. No more barriers between us, Ry, and that should go both ways. Agreed?"

Ryan swallowed hard and nodded. Going bare is something he'd wanted since their first time together. Feeling the release without a condom would bind them in a way he knew Dagger hadn't shared with with anyone else and Ryan really wanted to have that with Dagger. He wanted to have this level of trust and intimacy with him to solidify what they had together. It seemed like the natural next step for them to take, but it was still scary.

He came down on Dagger again and claimed his mouth in a hard kiss. "You have no idea how much I want you right now." Ryan whispered his words into the bend of Dagger's neck. He kissed Dagger's skin, then nipped at it, and heard his appreciative moans in return.

Dagger's arms draped around Ryan's back; his hand gripped Ryan's head and held him in place. "Then, take what's yours," he said.

Ryan slid off to Dagger's side and ran his fingers over Dagger's ribs, squeezed his hip, then moved his hand down onto the back of Dagger's thigh. He lifted Dagger's leg and held it in his palm; caressing the firm muscle, and moved in behind him. His lips found soft skin behind Dagger's ear. He licked first, then lightly kissed. His teeth nipped at the gold hoops piercing Dagger's lobe and tugged.

Dagger's head turned and caught Ryan's mouth. "You're driving me crazy, Ry," he whispered.

Ryan cradled the length of his cock in Dagger's crack; enjoying the snug warmth there, then drew his hips back and dropped the broad head between Dagger's legs. He found the puckered entrance and gently pushed forward. The lubrication remained from earlier and Ryan had no trouble easing into Dagger's heat in one slow thrust.

Still holding Dagger's leg up, he pulled almost completely out, then thrust inside, pulled back and plunged in again. Dagger sighed Ryan's name and pressed his butt into him, his hand gripped onto Ryan's thigh. Ryan buried his face into Dagger's neck. He closed his eyes and inhaled the scent of him; his hair and skin, completely lost in him.

Loving him.

"Dagger, you feel so good," Ryan said. "Every sensation is..."

"Magnified, by ten," Dagger said, finishing Ryan's thought.

Ryan gripped Dagger's leg tighter; lifted it higher, and thrust into him deeper.

"Oh my, God! Ryan, right there – right there!"

Ryan opened his mouth against Dagger's neck and sucked the skin. "I'm really close," he said. He could feel himself slipping over the edge, wanted to hold it off, but the orgasm was right there in front of him. Close enough to touch. Taste. He grit his back teeth, feeling the release buzzing the length of his spine, roiling around his groin, pulled his balls up tight to his body, then shot from the tip of his cock bathing Dagger with him and binding them forever. Dagger followed Ryan in orgasm, screaming out and rocking through Ryan's aftershocks, until they both stilled on the bed.

Dagger tipped his head back and locked eyes with Ryan. Their gaze held, while Ryan stroked the hair off Dagger's face, their breathing slowly coming back to normal.

Dagger's smile was easy; relaxed, sated. "Forever," Dagger whispered. "Can you give me that?"

Ryan leaned forward and caught Dagger's mouth, deeply tasting him. "Forever and then some," Ryan said. "Just like this."

The caterers were arriving when Dagger and Ryan descended the front stairs after showering. Lena was showing the crew into the kitchen and going over the set-up for the luncheon.

"Dagger," Lena called to him. "Would you prefer the table be set-up inside or out?" she asked.

Dagger glanced at Ryan. "What do you think?" he asked.

Ryan saw the panic rising in Dagger's eyes and set a hand on his shoulder to calm him. "Out by the pool. It's a gorgeous day," he said, and winked at Dagger. "We might as well take advantage of that."

Dagger's face relaxed into an amazing smile and nodded. "Then, outside it is."

A florist came into the kitchen delivering two very fragrant floral arrangements in a rainbow of colors displayed in sapphire blue vases. Lena took one glass vase and centered it on the kitchen table, then instructed the woman to carry the second vase out to the table under the canopy beside the pool garden.

Dagger glanced at the clock hanging on a wall in the kitchen. Everything was on schedule, he thought, then he looked across the room at Ryan, who was directing the caterer on plates and silverware placement. In minutes, his normally quiet and very private home had been transformed into a beehive of activity, with a dozen people he didn't know, working to create a welcoming lunch for his parents visit.

His parents visit? What the hell was he thinking? On what parallel universe did he think this would work; him sitting at a table breaking bread with his parents? Dagger turned and left the kitchen. He walked through the foyer and into the room in the front corner of the house: his office, and shut the door.

This room was less like an office for business and more like a room solely for his awards, gold and platinum records covered most of the wall space and a specially lit glass shelved cabinet displayed his statue awards of every category imaginable. All of it acknowledged his decade-plus success in the music business, but with the impending arrival of his parents, Dagger felt none of the achievement associated with each and every item in this room. Instead he felt insecurity and self-doubt. It overwhelmed him and made this large room suddenly feel very small, and him even smaller standing in it.

Dagger pressed his fingers into his eyes, trying to tamp down the emotion building there. He couldn't let them do this to him. Not now. Not after fifteen years of him busting his ass to prove he was worth something; that he mattered. And wasn't there enough proof of that plastered all around this room?

He was standing in front of the glass cabinet, when Ryan came into the room.

"Here you are," Ryan said and crossed the room. "I've been looking all over for you."

Dagger's shoulders were slouched, his gaze cast down to his feet. He didn't respond to Ryan's entrance and dread washed over Ryan. He walked up and stood behind Dagger.

"The caterers are done. Everything is all set-up," Ryan said. "The pool garden looks amazing. And Tony called. He said your parents were just picked up at the hotel by the limo service. They should be here shortly."

Dagger remained silent and still. Ryan touched his shoulders and lightly squeezed the tight muscles; wanting Dagger to feel his presence without pushing it on him. He knew how close to losing it Dagger had been since the day before, and he needed to be his rock through this.

"I'm not sure I can do this," Dagger finally said in a soft voice. "I'm not sure I want them here."

Ryan slowly turned Dagger by the shoulders to face him. He saw the tears marking Dagger's handsome face and his heart shattered. "You don't have to do this," Ryan said. "If you want, I'll have Tony call the limousine driver and have them turn around right now."

Dagger slid his arms around Ryan's waist and pressed his face into the warmth of his neck. "If I cancel this meeting, doesn't that give them the satisfaction of knowing they got to me once more?"

Ryan cradled Dagger's face in his hands. "Canceling gives them nothing, Dagger. They go home without the satisfaction of seeing how amazing their son is or the man he became. Is that what you want?"

"I want to rub their faces in who I've become," Dagger said, in a soft but firm voice.

A smile slowly grew on Ryan's face. "Then, together we'll do just that," he said.

Over his shoulder, Ryan saw the glint of sun reflecting off a car window and glanced toward the front windows. He saw the limousine slowly pulling beneath the stone portico.

"Looks like our guests have arrived," Ryan said. His hands slid down the length of Dagger's arms and gripped his hands. "It's still not too late to cancel this," Ryan said. "I have no problem going out there and telling them to their faces you don't want to see them. I won't let them hurt you. I promised you that."

Dagger nodded and closed his eyes; drawing in a deep breath, and attempted a smile that looked more like a grimace.

Ryan pulled him against his chest and kissed him. "I'll be right beside you every step of the way. Okay?"

Dagger's fingers skimmed down Ryan's backside. "I love you," he said. Behind Ryan, he watched his parents exit the rear passenger door of the limousine and approach the front door. The passing years hadn't changed much about them. His father was still a strapping man, of close to sixty years Dagger imagined, and his mother was still the slender beauty he remembered from his youth.

A tight knot was squeezing Dagger's stomach. The thought of his parents stepping through that front door made him want to vomit hateful obscenities from his mouth at them. If he could somehow make them suffer a fraction of what he had fifteen years ago, then this meeting would be worth all the stress it was giving him.

He heard Lena invite them into the foyer, heard the oohs and ahhs of their first impressions of his home, then heard the click of their feet crossing the expensive marble flooring as Lena led them out to the pool garden. In minutes, the bliss and tranquility in his life would be ripped open like an old wound and he would bleed self-loathing – all over again.

"Are you ready to do this?" Ryan asked.

"No, but I will," Dagger said.

A moment later, Lena knocked on the office door. "Dagger, your parent's are here," she said.

"We'll be out in a minute," Ryan said, then he turned his attention back to Dagger. "Say the word, Dagger, and I'll ask them to leave."

Dagger grinned, knowing with certainty Ryan would do exactly as he said and he loved that about him. "Nope, no need to do that," he said. "Let's do this – before I do change my mind."

Ryan held his hand and walked toward the door. Dagger stopped in the foyer and glanced at Ryan.

"How do I look?" Dagger asked, smoothing down his dark blue jeans and crisp white dress shirt.

"Good enough to eat," Ryan said, knowing it would give Dagger the boost he'd need to get his feet moving in the right direction and it worked.

Dagger burst out laughing and together, they walked through the kitchen and out the double French doors that opened up to the pool patio and garden.

The sun hit their faces and Dagger froze in place. Ryan stopped, too, saw the anguish take hold of Dagger's face and reached for his hand, lightly squeezing it. The soft touch of confirmation was all Dagger needed; knowing Ryan was right there beside him, and again he moved forward toward the table where his guests were already seated.

His father was the first to jump to his feet. "Liam, my God, look at you!" he said.

Ryan watched as the man embraced Dagger, who stood as stiffly as a flag pole. Dagger's mother joined her husband and they did their best to wrap their arms around their son. Both were shedding tears, but not Dagger. He remained as emotionless as Ryan had ever seen him. The subtle flex of Dagger's jaw muscle told Ryan how much restraint Dagger was using to accomplish that feat. Even still, Ryan was proud Dagger was holding it together.

Ryan stepped closer and placed his hand against Dagger's back and pressed the pads of his fingers into the skin, as if passing along his strength to him. He soon felt some of the tension leave Dagger's body and his muscles began to relax. Dagger found him with his eyes and Ryan nodded as confidently as he could manage, and Dagger's arms lifted to touch both his parents.

"Liam! Let us get a good look at you," his father said. "My Lord! You turned out to be a fine looking man!"

"Call me Dagger," he said softly.

His mother fused over Dagger's broad shoulders, checking every square inch of her son, and Dagger took it all in stride; his gaze rarely leaving Ryan. Dagger's father finally glanced in Ryan's direction.

"You must be Liam's friend," he said, extending his hand to Ryan.

Dagger almost pushed his mother's fawning hands off of him and stepped beside Ryan. "This is Ryan Pierce, Dad, and he's much more to me than a friend."

The man nodded at Dagger, seeming to understand but Ryan wondered about that.

"The name's Sean Whitmore, Ryan, and it is a pleasure to meet you." He gave Ryan a firm handshake, then directed Ryan's attention to Dagger's mother. "And, this is my wife, Mary."

"It is so nice to meet you, Ryan," Mary said, also shaking his hand.

Ryan's eyes danced between them. Mary's dark brown hair brushed her shoulders and matched her son's in color; as did her eyes, the same warm hazel. There was no mistake she was Dagger's mother. The resemblance was uncanny. Sean had harsher features, more pale in comparison to Dagger and his mother's complexion, too, but his frame was solid like a brick shit house. Ryan could easily see why Dagger was intimidated by this man. He found himself wanting to pull away from Sean, too, but knew if Dagger sensed that, he'd crumble and he needed to be strong and level headed for Dagger.

"Liam, your home is amazing," his dad gushed. "How long have you lived here?"

"Please, call me Dagger," he said again. "I've been here about six years."

"It's so big," Mary said. "You must get lost inside of it."

Dagger smiled at that comment and motioned for them to sit down at the table. He and Ryan sat across the table from Sean and Mary. The low rise of the floral arrangement was their only barrier, making Ryan wish they had gone with a much larger vase of flowers.

"It's not *that* big, Mom, and I don't live here alone. Ryan lives here with me and Lena, my housekeeper, has a small suite off the kitchen."

Soon as they settled in their seats, two waiters wearing black slacks and white shirts and aprons approached the table carrying trays of food and set them onto the table. They filled the glasses with ice water and left a pitcher of iced tea with sliced lemon, along with two bottles of Napa Valley white wine before retreating again to the kitchen.

Ryan surveyed the array of food on display. He had helped Dagger select the menu and was pleased to see their final choices spread out before them in such a beautiful presentation. As nervous as he was, he couldn't help but feel his mouth water.

Grilled salmon with a lemon dill sauce was spread in a circle on one platter, a bowl of chilled cucumber salad was nestled in the center. Several pieces of roasted chicken; sliced, and fanned in a decorative pattern rested on a second tray, with cherry tomatoes adding a splash of color. A ceramic bowl contained a fresh garden salad with an assortment of dressings sitting nearby, and there were baskets of warm baked bread, too.

Ryan glanced at Dagger; leaning back in his seat, almost glaring at his father. No one made a move toward the food and Ryan decided to break the ice and began serving. He reached for a basket of bread and passed it over to Mary, then used the serving fork to select a piece of chicken and offered it to Mary. Slowly, Mary and Sean filled their plates with food, making idle chit-chat with Dagger; who hadn't taken any food at all and almost seemed to have checked out of the meeting altogether.

"Ryan, what do you do for work?" Sean asked, and cut into his piece of chicken.

"I'm an entertainment writer," Ryan said.

"He also writes novels," Dagger offered.

"That's impressive, Ryan," Mary said.

"It is," Dagger said.

"You are both so creative in what you do," Mary said.

"We compliment each other well," Dagger said. He glanced at Ryan and smiled warmly.

"Have you been together long?" Sean asked.

Ryan met Dagger's gaze. The questions were getting more personal and he wasn't sure how Dagger would react to them. He knew Dagger's body language too well, and could see the icy transformation building around him like a protective shell.

"We met around seven months ago," Ryan finally said. "I interviewed Dagger and then wrote an article about him for the magazine where I was working at the time."

"I never thought our son would turn out to be so famous," Sean said.

"You never thought I'd turn into anything at all," Dagger said.

"Liam, that's not true."

"God damn it!" Dagger seethed; hitting his fist on the glass table top making a loud clattering sound, as the dishes rattled. "My name is Dagger."

The table fell silent and Ryan held his breath.

"Your father means no disrespect," Mary said. "But, we only know you as Liam."

"Liam is dead, Mom," Dagger said. "I buried him fifteen years ago when you both threw him away like trash."

Every word that left Dagger's mouth became louder until Ryan set his hand on Dagger's thigh.

"Take a breath," Ryan said quietly to Dagger. "And let it go."

Dagger pushed away from the table and stood up from his chair. Ryan came to his feet beside him. "It's okay," Ryan said.

"No, it's not," Dagger said. "Their failure to acknowledge my name tells me nothing has changed." He started to leave and Ryan touched his forearm. "Ry, please. I need a minute. I'll be right back.

"Promise?" Ryan asked with a hint of a smile.

"Yeah, I'll be back."

Ryan watched Dagger walk toward the house. He wanted to go with him, hold him, and reassure him that his feelings were okay and they'd get through this together. When Dagger disappeared inside the open kitchen doors, Ryan sat back down in his seat. He felt lost, his heart aching to be with Dagger, but knowing he somehow had to address the questioning eyes staring at him from the other side of the table.

"I won't apologize for Dagger. He wouldn't want me to," Ryan said, which he guessed wasn't what either Mary or Sean expected him to say, but he didn't much care about their feelings at this particular moment. Truth was, Dagger had made many attempts to politely correct them on his current name and they had ignored every one of them. "He prefers to be called Dagger now. It is his legal name and it may seem insignificant to you, but it sure would be a nice gesture if you could respect him enough to start calling him that."

"Ryan, Mary was right," Sean said. "We weren't trying to disrespect Li... I mean, Dagger."

Ryan smiled tightly. He wondered how long Dagger would be gone; wondered if he really was going to come back.

He reached for his water glass and took a long gulp of the cool liquid.

"Are you in love with my son?" Mary asked.

Ryan set his glass down on the table and looked directly at the woman, who's son bore such a striking resemblance to her. He blinked and drew in a breath. That moment brought clarity for Ryan. He felt no hesitation in answering; knew the answer before Mary had finished asking the question. It was simple and Ryan had no problem being honest. "Very much," he said. "He's an amazing man and has accomplished so much with his career; his life. I don't know what I'd do without him."

"Despite what you may think, we're very proud of our son," Sean said.

"Then, tell him that," Ryan said. "He needs to hear it from you."

"Regardless of what he's obviously told you about us, we did not toss him aside," Sean said. "He was released from... prison early and we weren't made aware of that until after the fact. By the time we came for him, he was gone."

"He said you never visited during the two years he was there," Ryan said. "Had you showed up even once during those two years, he would have notified you of his early release."

"We made mistakes," Sean said. "I won't deny that."

Ryan rolled his eyes. "Mistakes? Is that what you call it?"

"Maybe we shouldn't have made this trip," Mary said softly.

"No, I think this visit was necessary for a lot of reasons," Ryan said. "It's not too late for you to fix some of the mistakes you referenced. I know deep down Dagger would like a relationship with you, but you're not making it easy for him to want that connection."

"He's all we have left," Mary said. "We feared he might have died, until we saw the news reports on television. You can't imagine our relief. It was the best news we could have ever heard."

"Please, you have to tell him these things," Ryan said. "He needs to know he matters to you. This is common sense. I shouldn't have to explain this to you."

"Ever since we found out about him and Patrick, we felt like we didn't know our own son," Sean said. "He had this secretive life that we didn't learn about until someone died because of it."

"Patrick didn't die because Dagger loved him," Ryan said. "He died because of ignorance on the parts of the idiots spying on them. Dagger was left to live with the unjustified shame of having loved Patrick. Carrying around that burden was a lot for Dagger to overcome, but he did it and I'm very proud of him."

Fuck! Ryan wasn't sure how much longer he could play nice with these people. This was their son they were talking about and they simply didn't seem to get it. Ryan rubbed at his forehead. The strain was starting to make him unravel. He glanced over his shoulder and didn't see Dagger anywhere in sight. He felt desperate to know how Dagger was doing.

"Dagger is lucky to have a nice man like you in his life," Mary finally said. "I think you're good for him."

Ryan looked across the table at Mary; surprised she had used the proper name when referring to her son. Her eyes were filled with tears but Ryan could see something else, too. Acknowledgment. Ryan nodded, her acceptance didn't require words to justify. It just was and Ryan was grateful for it.

"It doesn't matter to me who my son loves," Mary said. "I still want to know him; have him be a part of our lives."

"What about you, Sean?" Ryan asked. "Do you feel the same?"

Sean dropped his head. "I'm ashamed of my past behavior," he said. "I want to try and fix this with... Dagger; make it right." The name obviously felt uncomfortable rolling from his mouth, but at least he had said it.

"Do you think you could help us, Ryan?" Mary asked.

Ryan smiled with relief. "Yeah, I'd like to help you reconnect."

Ryan heard the scuff of shoes on the stone patio bricks behind him and turned to see Dagger approaching. He stood up to greet him and Dagger pulled him against his chest in a tight embrace, uncaring his parents were right there watching.

"I'm sorry," Dagger whispered, kissing a spot below Ryan's earlobe. "I shouldn't have left you out here to deal with them alone."

Ryan pulled back and held his gaze. "I don't care about that. I was worried about you."

Dagger lifted Ryan's hand to his mouth and kissed the knuckles. "I'm okay," he said, then he turned to face his parents. "I'll come out of this – like everything else, a stronger man for it."

Dagger sat back down in his chair. He took his cloth napkin and spread it across his lap and glared at his father. "Just so we're clear, I didn't suggest you visit because I was looking for acceptance," he said. "I don't give a shit what you think of how I live my life, but on some twisted level I did want you to see the success I had achieved. I realize now that that was stupid on my part because all of this is superficial and in the end it means nothing. The stuff that truly matters is what's inside ourselves and that can't be seen."

"Dagger..." Ryan said, leaning closer.

"No, Ryan, I need to say this," Dagger said. "And, you two need to listen. I loved Patrick, no doubt about that, but I realize now it was a boyhood love because what I feel for this man sitting beside me is... beyond words. It's limitless."

Dagger looked at Ryan, his eyes clear, focused, and filled with warmth. "I am completely in love with him. Nothing else compares. He is my everything; there is no other way to say it. I wouldn't be sitting here with you if it weren't for him." Dagger took a sip from his water glass. "I spent the last fifteen years acquiring things I thought would give me what was missing in my life: acceptance, and the feeling of worthiness. I won awards, built up a net worth that stuns even me, had this house designed and built, but putting that aside I was walking through life feeling horribly alone; drifting, and emotionally starved. Each new goal I achieved gave me more of the same; which was next to nothing." Dagger reached for Ryan's hand on the table. "And, then the most amazing man walked into my life and now I have everything I ever wanted, right here beside me." Dagger's gaze turned on his parents. "I guess you could say I had an epiphany just now when I was inside fuming over your behavior. I realized it doesn't matter what you think or what you fucking call me," he said. "You can call me faggot if you want, because I simply don't care. I'm happy, I'm in love, and the rest is irrelevant bullshit. So, I suggest we enjoy our lunch, we'll catch up, and then we'll say good-bye."

"Dagger," Sean said the name and all eyes at the table turned to him. "Our behavior should be blamed on ignorance not hate. We don't care who you love. It doesn't make us love you any less or make us less proud to have you as our son. Please. Help us to know who you are on the inside. We never had the opportunity when you were young and then you were gone. Can we at least give this a try?"

Dagger was stunned into silence. Ryan watched Dagger blink and saw the emotion building in his beautiful hazel eyes. He touched Dagger's thigh and leaned in close to his ear.

"It's okay to let it go," Ryan whispered. "I'm right here."

Dagger's gaze dropped to Ryan's hand resting on his thigh. He blinked again and sent a single tear to splash against the back of Ryan's hand.

"You've never said you were proud," Dagger said. "Not once. Ever."

"We always were,... Dagger. We were proud of the way you handled your sister's death and Patrick's. Proud you held your head higher then we ever could as they led you off to jail, all of it. You're a far better man than I am, that's for sure."

"Meghan would be proud of you, too," Mary said.

Hearing his sister's name mentioned snapped the last thread of control Dagger had on his emotions and his hands covered his eyes. Ryan turned in his seat and embraced Dagger; kissing his temple. Dagger wrapped his arms around Ryan's shoulders and held on tightly. A moment later, Sean and Mary were beside Dagger. Sean rubbed Dagger's back, while Mary stroked her son's long hair, and then Dagger came to his feet and warmly wrapped his arms around both of them.

Seeing this show of genuine affection had tears stinging at Ryan's eyes. He wiped at them and moved in behind Dagger. He touched the back of Dagger's head, then slid down to grip his neck.

"You are my son," Mary said. "And, we are so sorry, so very sorry. Can you find a way to forgive our past mistakes and give us another chance?"

Dagger stepped back and into the wall of Ryan's chest and Ryan was there to hold him upright. Ryan pressed his lips beside Dagger's ear.

"Acceptance runs both ways, Dagger," Ryan said softly into his hair. "Take what they're offering and see where it goes."

Dagger reached back and squeezed Ryan's thigh. "Can we sit back down and talk some more?" Dagger asked his parents.

"Yes, of course," Sean said. He patted Dagger on the shoulder and walked back to his seat.

Dagger rolled into Ryan and hugged him so tight, Ryan struggled to draw in a breath.

"What would I ever do without you?" Dagger whispered.

"You're doing fine all on your own," Ryan said. He leaned back and held Dagger's gaze for a moment, then smiled. "I'm proud of how well you're doing."

"Me, too," Dagger said.

"Good, let's eat," Ryan said.

It was late afternoon when Dagger led his parents back through the kitchen and into the foyer. It was Ryan's gentle nudging that had Dagger escorting his parent's into the office. He stood in the center of the room self-conscious to be standing in front of all his awards.

"I like to refer to this space as Dagger's trophy room," Ryan said. He took Dagger's hand and tugged him against his side. "Wasn't that gold record for your first album?" Ryan asked, pointing to the framed disc hanging on the wall. He already knew the answer to his question, he was merely encouraging Dagger to elaborate on his achievements for his parent's benefit. It worked. Dagger began talking about himself, answering everything they asked. Ryan stood nearby, leaning up against Dagger's oak desk, and smiling ear to ear.

When they got to the end of the awards, Mary cupped the side of her son's face. "You have no idea how much it means to your father and I to be here, in your home. This has been an amazing experience."

"Yes, Dagger, thank you so much," his father said. "I hope we can do this again, maybe get you to come east?"

"Thanksgiving isn't too far off," Mary said. "Perhaps you and Ryan could come for the holiday? It would mean so much to have you both with us."

Dagger glanced at Ryan. "I'm not sure about that, Mom. I'll have to talk to Ryan first, and then check with my manager before I commit to anything."

They made their way out into the foyer again and Sean shook Ryan's hand. "Thank you," he said. "I have a feeling you played a major role in making today happen and Mary and I thank you for that."

"I'm glad it worked out," Ryan said.

The hugging started again and Ryan sensed another round of tears wasn't too far off. Dagger promised to call them the following week and they agreed to stay in touch, too. Before Ryan knew it, Mary was sliding into the back seat of the limousine.

"Take care of my son," Sean said to Ryan, before he joined Mary in the backseat.

"I will," Ryan said. "With everything I am." He said it softly, almost for himself, but Dagger clearly heard it and recognized the phrase, too.

Dagger's gaze shifted to Ryan. He reached for Ryan's hand and laced their fingers together, then watched Ryan's eyes follow the limousine as it pulled out from under the portico at the front of the house.

"You really mean that, don't you?" Dagger asked.

"Mean what?" Ryan asked. He waved one last time at the car as it departed through the cast iron gates of the estate and turned onto the street, then he looked at Dagger. The emotion building in Dagger's eyes made them sparkle in the dimming afternoon light.

"You're in this for the long haul," Dagger said.

"Were you doubting that?" Ryan asked.

Dagger swallowed hard. "I guess a small part of me was – until today, and this very moment."

Ryan faced Dagger and stepped closer. "I'm not going anywhere," he said. His hands slid along Dagger's whisker-rough jaw line and cupped his face. "This is exactly where I want to be – where I'm *meant* to be. I'm certain of it."

"And, that makes me the luckiest guy in the world," Dagger said.

"That makes two of us," Ryan said. He smiled broadly, having said the same words to Dagger a week earlier, but now the words held an even deeper meaning. After spending the last several days sifting through the minefields of their personal histories, Ryan knew he was where he wanted to be – with Dagger. He would face whatever Dagger put before him; whether it be meeting his band members as Dagger's boyfriend, or socializing in public as a couple, Ryan would do it with pride and love.

"Come on," Dagger said, lightly tugging on Ryan's hand. "Let's go inside, so I can properly thank you for getting me through the last four hours of my life."

"Hmmm, I like the sound of that," Ryan said.

Ryan stepped over the threshold behind Dagger and shut the large wooden door behind them, then he punched in the security code to activate the alarm system. When he turned around, Dagger was already on his way up the stairs to the bedroom – *their* bedroom.

Ryan smiled to himself, thinking for a moment how far they had come together; how much they had grown, and how happy he was with his life. He truly was where he wanted to be.

He was home.

Author's Note

Fall for Me is a love story involving two beautifully creative men: one a famous rock star, and the other is an entertainment journalist. This story literally exploded inside my head. The visual qualities and layers to it were so vivid, and the character's voices so loud, I simply had to write it. The first draft took three months to write; a short amount of time for me when writing a book, but the resulting love story left on the pages was very powerful and emotional for me. I truly hope you, too, will feel the love and devotion that grows between Dagger and Ryan as their story unfolds; how it changes both men, and makes them stronger individuals for loving the other.

Fall for Me is **Book One** of my new **Rock Gods** series. All the books in this series are stand-alone stories, but tied together with rock stars that are friends, as well as colleagues. Each of my rock stars are flawed and emotionally damaged men at the height of their musical careers and in search of the one thing that still eludes them: love.

I hope you'll take this musical journey alongside me with each of the **Rock Gods** novels and discover what it truly means to love; love unconditionally, love without restrictions or labels – just simply love.

Scheduled Books in the Rock Gods Series:
Fall for Me ~ Spring 2013
Take What You Want ~ Fall 2013
Make You Mine ~ Spring 2014

Other Titles by Ann Lister:
Sheet Music: A Rock 'n' Roll Love Story ~ 2009
For All The Right Reasons ~ 2010
Without A Doubt ~ 2011
An Early Spring ~ 2012
Covered In Lace: The Lacey Sheridan Story ~ 2012